"Little-know[n] [...] [...] Lovecraft once stole a [...] [...] eades into the future, [...] [...] [...] ne and Steven Spiel[...] [...] [...] est horror-adventure-Western mash-up imaginable to human minds. Or so I'm assuming, because I just read *Fury From the Tomb*. Obviously, 'S A Sidor' is the pseudonym they all agreed upon so no meddlers would come after the time machine. But I'm not fooled."

Steve Hockensmith, *New York Times bestselling author of*
Pride & Prejudice & Zombies: Dawn of the Dreadfuls

"Unforgettable, spellbinding, and darkly suspenseful. Sidor must have sold his soul to the devil to write this well."

Steve Hamilton, *award-winning author of the Alex*
McKnight series

"S A Sidor is a master of the unsettling, and each twist is more grisly and unexpected than the last."

Publisher's Weekly starred review

"Sidor keeps the pacing piano-wire taut and selects his words with a vivisectionist's diabolical care."

Stewart O'Nan, *author of* West of Sunset

"Dark, harrowing, and unpredictable as a run of danger-ous river. Sidor plunges you into chilling waters on page one and barely lets you up for air."

Gregg Hurwitz, *author of the Orphan X series*

BY THE SAME AUTHOR

Skin River
Bone Factory
The Mirror's Edge
Pitch Dark

S A SIDOR

THE INSTITUTE *for* SINGULAR ANTIQUITIES

Fury from the Tomb

ANGRY
ROBOT

ANGRY ROBOT
An imprint of Watkins Media Ltd

20 Fletcher Gate,
Nottingham,
NG1 2FZ
UK

angryrobotbooks.com
twitter.com/angryrobotbooks
Bring on los mummies

An Angry Robot paperback original 2018

Cover by Daniel Strange
Set in Meridien by Argh! Nottingham

Distributed in the United States by Penguin Random House, Inc., New York.

ISBN 978 0 85766 761 8
Ebook ISBN 978 0 85766 762 5

Printed in the United States of America

9 8 7 6 5 4 3 2 1

For Ann Collette
Agent & Amiga

1

DEAR ROM

New Year's Eve, 1919
Manhattan, New York City

Sand.

For someone who has spent the better part of the last four decades digging, burrowing like a scarab, day and night it seemed, into mountains of dry, golden trickling, windswept tombs, I have never gotten comfortable with the stuff. Indeed, the sight of dunes often causes me a great explosion of nervous trembling. I must force my mind elsewhere. An excess of thought, my wife would say, as she often does. *You think too much, Rom.*

I am certain she is correct.

After an unfortunate childhood incident with a top-heavy traveling trunk, I will admit to more than a touch of claustrophobia, but the idea of being buried alive – in sand particularly – has haunted my dreams these last few weeks. Strangely, I wake some mornings, gasping, and taste crystalline grit on my lips. Haunted my dreams *once more* would be closer to the facts. I have suffered nightmares of smothering sands in the past, triggered by the actual experience of nearly drowning and witnessing others drown in waterless seas, the whirlpools and crushing waves of granular yellow death all around. I cannot help but think those long-ago events in the Sonoran Desert are at the core.

I received a letter at the beginning of last week.

The envelope.

Fine, creamy paper. Signs of travel evident on the creased packet. Rain had fallen upon it, but my hazy name and address remained readable. It could have been from anyone, anywhere. But somehow, I knew who wrote it. And with equal certitude I apprehended what news the pages inside would convey. I put off reading the letter as long as I could – two nights (*You think too much…*) – and then I swept it from the nightstand.

Dear Rom,
    I regret to be the one who must tell you…

I stopped reading.

To my students, colleagues, and acquaintances I am Dr Romulus Hugo Hardy, Egyptologist, employed by the Montague P Waterston Institute for Singular Antiquities of New York City. The institute is a private research library and ancient history museum. Finest of its kind in the world, despite the unsavory rumors of its origins… all true by the way and then some, oh, the stories I could add…

Only my oldest friends call me Rom.

Dear Rom,
    I regret to be the one who must tell you the great man is among us no more. He has gone to the stars.

That was his wish, he confided, as I sat him up on his horse only two evenings ago, and we walked around the corral. Our world is more desolate for his having left it. I remind myself the bottomless grief I feel at this moment too shall pass. At least he did not suffer. I happily took away his pain during these final twilit days. My medical training proved worthy of the years I spent in study if only to accomplish this task. The opium tinctures made him sleepy yet inclined to conversation. We talked about old times! About Mexico, and the "bandaged bastards" as he still called them. To the end he slept with loaded pistols hanging from the bedpost, saying he saw the raggedy, gauze-bound corpses lurching forward in his dreams. Going through his night chest, I discovered a newspaper cutting of Miss Evangeline I had never seen before. Does an art song recital in San Francisco ring any bells? It was sweet of him to keep it for so long. Would you not agree? I hope this subject is not too tender to broach. I am aware your last parting was not on the best of terms, and in recent years no communication passed between you, the great rift only widening. Yet history – beginning with our dangerous ride south and the ill-fated Mexico expedition! – will always bind you together. So, I was wondering if…

I could not read another word.

The onrush of emotions was too strong. They trampled me, left me dazed. With them came memories like a parade of spirits marching before my eyes. I decided to go for a walk. The street life of Manhattan wields the power to distract even my most troubled state of mind. Not so this day. Through a flurry of snow, I gazed vacantly into shop windows. I saw every person on the street, including myself, doubled in ghostly reflections.

We are all transient.

This life is but a dream we dream together.

Some dreams are better left undreamt. I speak of living terrors that most people would never believe. But I believe. Though I am a scholar, a man of science, and a skeptic by nature, I cannot entertain doubts on this subject.

For I have witnessed them with my own eyes.

When I looked up I saw I was at the Institute. Bodies follow habits. My legs took me where they did six mornings a week. Dark hallways greeted me on this holiday afternoon. I locked the front door behind me and climbed three flights of stairs to my office and its adjoining state-of-the-art laboratory. I have come to prefer the lab over the field, choosing to toil in the stuffiness of classrooms rather than the dank and ruinous graveyard of ancient civilizations.

But this predilection was not always the case.

In my youth, I yearned for exotic travel.

One place called to me above all others: Egypt. Land of the pharaohs. The Great Sphinx of Giza. Khufu's Pyramid. And the *Book of the Dead*.

If I had been a farmer like my father, and loved the land the way he did, then I would have missed out on many wondrous adventures, and the curses that have accompanied them, and were, some might speculate, their price.

I have no regrets.

A clot of shadows inhabited the lab, and I did nothing to banish them. Work was far from my intention during this unplanned visit. I opened the shutters beside my desk; in dull steel daylight, I crouched and built a small fire in the fireplace. I felt old and cold and I wanted a whisky. These Prohibition advocates hope to make Methodists of us all. Soon they will have their law. Thank heavens I live in New York City. I keep a bottle hidden in the cabinet behind my personal collection of ushabti. Mummiform figurines – my favorites are those made from chiseled stone or faience whose aquamarine glazes are splendid to contemplate while sipping Kentucky bourbon. I set four of the funerary statuettes on my desk top. They were the size of tin soldiers I played with as a child. I uncorked the bottle and filled a cut-crystal glass.

My desk remains barren when I am not working at it.

I balanced the glass in my lap.

The four figures stood alone on a mahogany plateau. I could almost imagine they were the four of us lost in the Sonoran – or the Gila Desert, if you prefer. Death advanced from every direction.

Four seekers in deep over our heads...

We knew nothing. The tip of the tip of the iceberg was all we saw. (Mixing talk of deserts and icebergs – I could blame the snow. Or the cursed sand still in my blood.)

I drained the glass. Then went to the cabinet and poured another, bringing the bottle along. I set it beside the leg of the chair.

The electric winds of memory lifted the hairs off my collar. These stirrings of the past were strong enough to make me feel physical sensations. The blazing Mexican heat slapped my face red (*though it might have been the whisky*). I breathed alkaline dust. My eyes squinted at the forge of a molten sun. I could swear I was traveling back in time, merging with my younger self. How did we get there? How did I survive? What catalyst, what driver, took hold and propelled me as if I had no free will, not then, and not now?

Egypt.

Egypt was how I got to Mexico.

2

THE WATERSTON EXPEDITION

Summer, 1886
University Hall Library, Northwestern University, Chicago

The word is like magic itself. *Egypt*. The letters look scrambled, a puzzle waiting to be solved. Who doesn't like a puzzle? What young man isn't convinced he's the one to crack it? I was no different. Ripe for an adventure, I wanted life to start. Nothing had ever happened to me and I was slowly becoming convinced that nothing ever would.

"Hardy, your mail."

A letter came flying over the top of my study carrel, landing in my lap.

"Thank you, Carlson. You deliver with speed if not precision."

"Speed's better." And Carlson was gone around the corner.

An Egyptologist without a wealthy sponsor is a lonely man indeed. I had been such a man until that day. I tore into the letter. I didn't know it yet, but I had received my first correspondence from Montague Pythagoras

Waterston of Los Angeles, California.

He wrote that he had heard "promising things" about me from one of my old University of Chicago professors (he did not mention any names) and had read a scholarly paper I penned entitled *Magic and Mummified Kings*. He quite liked it. I liked it too, and the praise made me glow. He offered to pay for my very first expedition – near the Valley of Kings, no less – for the purpose of unearthing yet undiscovered tombs. I could not believe it. The man had never even met me and here he was opening his bag of gold for my expenses. I found later that he had much gold at his disposal (he owned several copper, silver, and gold mines in California and the western territories); also, unknown to me, he had made such offers to other young Egyptologists, and their excursions had ended in catastrophic failure and even death. All I knew at the time was he would pay my way. He only required that I keep him informed about every step of my project, and that any antiquities I might recover would become his sole property, to which I must surrender any claim, legal or otherwise. I also had to promise extreme discretion.

I had big dreams for my future, but my future had lagged in its arrival. Who can fault a person for chasing their dreams, even recklessly, when at first they seem to appear?

Without a second thought I wrote back and accepted the terms of his offer.

A shadow flickered above me.

"Carlson? Is that you?"

"Who else passes through the dullest aisle of the known universe?"

"Not me, not any more. I'm going to Egypt on an

expedition. I leave this dreary little cubbyhole to you and the library mice. I am on my way to becoming a legend. Make a note of it in your journal. Someday you'll tell your children you delivered Rom Hardy's mail."

"Crack a window, man. You're delirious."

"If I am, then that's fine with me. See you in a year or so. I have to start packing."

"Beware the hyenas and malaria," Carlson said. I saw a hand waving.

Again, I was alone.

Summer, 1886
Cairo, Egypt (and environs)

Shall I say how I felt?

Like a boy transported to the land of his fantasies.

From the moment of my arrival I had to keep reminding myself I was really in Egypt and not dreaming. To see for the first time with my own eyes the silt shores of the Nile lined with spiky-leafed palm trees and dhows, sailing up and down the river, their lateens spread like the pectoral fins of giant flying fish. Over the water, I smelled fresh animal dung and smoldering cook fires. The low mud walls and squat buildings huddled under a sky of powder blue enormity dusted gold at the horizon. The sun above the delta blazed unlike the sun in my homeland; its piercing whiteness seared like the eye of eternity. Ashore, I sought shade among the sycamores. For a while that was how I moved, tree to tree, in my dark suit and derby. The streets of Cairo boiled with a cacophony of alien noise. Coffeehouses crowded with shisha-smoking men and their smoking stares. Everything appeared to me too big, too loud. Too much. My senses overloaded. I could not take it all in. Yet more and more came at me. Like a sleepwalker, I floated between worlds. But I was too excited to sleep. Too excited even to think! I wandered, outwardly blank and numbed but feeling very, very alive. I loved it so dearly, in fact, that I feared if I closed my eyes it might all disappear. The jet black night offered a bit of relief from my mania. I retired to my lodging and waited, prone but awake, restless for first light. The next days were going to be no less stimulating.

How much more did I love the sights from the Pyramid road!

And to know I was not there as a mere traveler. My life's work was truly beginning. I absorbed more in a week than I had in years of study. Though I might yearn to, I could not indulge my leisure like a tourist. I was a scientist on a timetable.

Inside Egypt, I sailed south to visit the megaliths at Karnak and ultimately to Luxor, where I set to work. I attempted to make contact with local guides, unfortunately with little success for my efforts and much discouragement. Yes, I found men willing to guide me into the burying desert, but none struck me as capable and trustworthy.

It was while I rested my feet at an outdoor café table that I met my future foreman, Hakim. I was bent over at the task of loosening my shoelaces, and when I sat up, there he was standing across from me and smiling warmly, a steaming pot of mint tea and two cups in his hands.

"May I join you, sir?"

"Certainly, you may. What I mean is, *please do*."

I glanced around and noticed several empty tables.

He filled the cups, sat down, and pushed one cup toward me. His brow furrowed for a moment as I hesitated. "Do men not drink tea in America?"

"No, we do."

"Enjoy then, sir. This café makes the second best tea in Luxor."

"Who makes the best?"

"I do, sir, and my wife agrees it is the finest she has ever tasted."

I sipped the tea. Indeed, it was delicious as he claimed, and it struck me that drinking a hot beverage in the heat did not make one hotter but rather equalized with the environment.

"How did you know I am American? Is it my accent?"

"No, sir, and although we have only just met I must confess that it is not by accident. I have heard that an American in a derby hat has been asking for guides in the cafés. So, I came here to drink tea and wait. My name is Hakim, and I am the finest guide in Luxor."

Clearly a man of admirable bearing, he proceeded to tell me a long list of desert excavations which he had taken a part in or led. I did not doubt him, nor could I check his references, given my lack of contacts. We talked more over a second pot of tea. I was going to have to make a leap of faith based on what my father the farmer called "gut feelings." I wasn't exactly buying pigs here. But I hoped I had inherited my father's good intuition. My life was going to depend on it.

Hakim possessed a round jovial face and unusually large eyes, almond-hued, sympathetic and feminine in their cast: a gift from his mother, he said.

"Have you led many expeditions?" Hakim asked me.

"This will be my first in Egypt," I said, beaming.

"Ah, so where else have you dirtied your hands in the sands of time?"

I looked squarely into his almond eyes as I drained the dregs of my cup.

"Nowhere," I said.

Hakim was nodding and smiling as if I had told him a joke. Then the smile faded.

"I have read a great deal about your country and its history," I added quickly. "I know it as well as if I had been born on the shores of the Nile. My scholarly background is impeccable."

"Reading is good," he said.

He picked up the teapot to refill our cups but found it empty.

"I only need a chance to prove myself." My fists clenched under the table. I leaned forward as the words raced out of my mouth. "I know what to do. My sponsor, Mr Waterston, has confidence in my potential to achieve astounding things."

"A wise fellow, no doubt. His name circulates among certain men of my acquaintance. He has a lot of cash to spread around. I hope that is not impolite to say. You know him well?"

"Reasonably well, I'd say." In the heat of the café, I stretched the truth and found it to be awfully elastic. "The two of us have grown closer recently… much closer than ever before."

Hakim considered my exaggerations. His infectious smile returned.

"You will hire me then?" he asked.

"Absolutely," I said. "I believe you have the job. You earned it. We both did!"

Hakim drummed the table with his big calloused hands and let out a hearty laugh to accompany the racket. Men in the café looked over in alarm.

"Bless you, sir. My wife blesses you. My children, all of them, they bless you."

That was how I made my first Egyptian friend.

3
BLACK STAR

We had the finest equipment Waterston's money could buy and, with Hakim's help, the best pick of laborers: experienced diggers with strong backs and keen eyes for reading the Saharan sands. I had left New York in a hurry, at my benefactor's urging, and the planning of the entire dig was a product of our two minds. I consulted with none of my colleagues. There was no time. And, once we struck our pact, Waterston fostered in me a habit of secrecy that, though foreign at first, came to be my second nature. With each other we discussed matters freely, exhaustively. I have never had, before or since, such a thorough and voluminous exchange of letters.

I soon realized that Waterston's knowledge of Egyptology rivaled my own, although his study proved to have significant historical gaps. His scholarship was less impressive in its breadth than it was in certain focused depths: precisely speaking, he only researched what interested him, and what interested him were the practices related to death, burial, and the afterlife. To my embarrassment he knew vastly more concerning the occult beliefs and religious rituals of the ancient

Egyptians than I did. It is fair to say he was obsessed with them. So burning was his passion for hunting and excavating mummies that I grew curious to ask why he did not make the journey with me. Finally, I did ask. He wrote back saying he was in grave health and had been declining quickly. He did not expect to live more than a year or two longer. But he hoped his battered body would hold out until I made a thrilling discovery and returned with it to New York. I took his looming meeting with death to be the driving force behind his relentless curiosity.

I was closer to the truth than I might have guessed.

Money paves roads where none before existed. I learned this fact firsthand. The Waterston dollar bought our expedition a path near the Deir el-Bahri cliffs, location of the First Royal Cache, and the gorgeously linen-wrapped Amenhotep I. I could hardly believe I was within walking distance of that famous tomb shaft, let alone leading my own dig. These days the Egyptians paid a lot more attention to *who* was exhuming *what* from their land. I did not blame them. Europeans had been looting treasures as fast as the desert could reshape itself, which is to say, constantly.

Mummies became exotic party favors rich people unraveled for their own titillation and gruesome delights, only then to be discarded like so much used gift ribbon and leftover bones. Disgraceful and unscientific plundering was commonplace. The locals rightly took offense at the treatment of their ancestors and cultural history. Now permits were required and inspectors visited sites, overseeing every stage of excavation.

Most importantly, no mummies left Egypt without

written permission. Inviolate tombs were owned by the government. That was a problem in Mr Waterston's view. He was paying for this exploration, by God, and he demanded possession of whatever our labors and the timeless, shifting sands turned up.

In plain English, he wanted his mummy.

His requests were so calculated he almost seemed to have the retrieval of a specific mummy in mind. That was absurd, I thought. When I jokingly prodded him about the subject, he apologized, saying he had for so long daydreamed of unearthing a mummy, he must have created a romantic ideal.

He is like an old friend I long to see again, Waterston wrote. *Thoughts of the mummy are my only escape from the bodily insults I must suffer daily.*

I felt pity that his infirmities kept him a prisoner.

Though I suspected there was more than romance to his obsession.

The first digging season I failed to find anything more noteworthy than the carcass of an ass that had stumbled into a rubble-filled pit, and which proved by its smell to be of recent, rather than antique, vintage. I scoured my maps. The deepest appeal of the nearby Valley was how very promising it all seemed to the beholding eye. One could imagine plunging one's hand anywhere into the hot crumbling grains and yanking up untold riches. And that too was its curse.

Each crest, every dip in the landscape screamed out "Dig here! Dig here!"

I took the early missteps hard. Waterston took them harder. His health had worsened. I could see the evidence in his penmanship. Smooth elegant letters degraded into a cramped, blotchy, almost unreadable, scrawl. His patience eroded in equal measure. He wrote several letters stating his funds were not unlimited. He threatened cuts if I did not show results. He told me outright that if he died, the expedition would come to an immediate halt. I would pack and head home – empty-handed.

Halfway during my second fruitless digging season, the handwriting and tone of the communications changed dramatically again. In the leading paragraph, Waterston informed me he was too ill to write and would henceforth be dictating his letters. The transcriber was his young daughter, Evangeline.

A bold, yet graceful, voluptuous calligraphy painted the pages. My initial impression was that if she were a third as beautiful as the ink she spilled, Evangeline Waterston would justify the proudest father. I would later see how far she transcended expectations when encountered in the flesh.

At the time, I appreciated reading without using my magnifying lens.

It was in Evangeline's fine, clear prose that I first read about the horrible dream. Calling it a dream fails to do it justice. *Dark vision* would be more suitable.

In the days prior to the beginning of our second digging season (a mere forty-eight hours before the letter I was holding in my hands had been dictated), Monty Waterston suffered a sudden high fever. He lay confined to his bed, delirious. His heartbeat galloped. Doctors could find no source of infection. Nor could they bring down his temperature a single degree. They had all but admitted defeat. In a final attempt to prevent his brain from cooking inside the pot of his skull, and in keeping with the Waterston tradition of actions writ large, senior mansion staff ordered a wagon to be filled at the nearest icehouse and emptied into the indoor swimming pool. Servants plunged their naked febrile master under frigid waters while a bevy of medical experts – with stern warnings the shock might trigger immediate death – skeptically looked on.

Waterston's screams echoed throughout the estate.

Slowly, his fever diminished.

When he was able to speak again, Waterston told Evangeline of his fever dream. Though cautioned about his weakened condition, he insisted on recounting every detail before it slipped from his memory. His nightmarish chronicle is too lengthy and disjointed to pass along in full. The transcription ran some thirty pages and made my head pound with confusion. But the last revelation surpassed confusion with sheer terror.

A phantasm visited Hugo Waterston.

It spirited him to Egypt – to my very tent.

And together they observed my sleeping body. Waterston attempted to shake me by the shoulder, but his corporeal structure had no substance. His hand passed through me and appeared again on the other side. He said I shivered and tossed yet did not wake. The phantasm laughed at both of us. Then it directed Waterston to my collection of maps. With a swing of its smoky arm, the shadow creature flung my scrolls and binders to the floor. It was true. How else could Waterston know? Pure coincidence would not suffice. Because I had indeed awakened one morning to find my maps thrown about the tent and until this moment could not explain it. Waterston said he paid close attention to every move the phantasm made because it never spoke. Gestures were the only clues. What Waterston deduced was that my charts, and the expedition, were doomed to failure.

"Can you draw us a map?" he asked the visitant.

It could and it did.

I turned the last page of the letter to find a sketch of the map and a crude illustration of what could only be described as a highly unusual and morbidly eroded rock. Unnerved by the drawing, and intrigued by the map, in a dry-mouthed whisper, I read aloud Waterston's note (scribbled in his own hand) at the bottom of the page.

"Cease your explorations at once! I am certain we have found the KEY! Dig at this exact location. When you uncover the tomb, bribe the inspectors and bring me the contents, and by that I mean the MUMMIES. Whatever your interpretation of my dream may be, I remind you that I am the employer and you are my employee. I command you to follow these instructions TO THE LETTER!"

Command me?

I bristled at his choice of words. When did I enlist in the army? I could not recall doing so. What twisted logic commanded me to follow a dream – a byproduct of an overheated brain rather than scholarly reason? Wasn't I the expert here?

Yet, this point I had to surrender: I had retrieved nothing of value from the baked Egyptian soil. Principle rather than evidence supported me. I allowed my anger to cool. Afterward, I found myself lured to the map, lingering over it, and, yes, tempted to try my luck with it. The truth was, like many a man, I virtually had signed on as a soldier in a rich man's private army. I did not wear a uniform *per se*, yet Waterston's power over me was absolute. If I confronted him, I would soon be returned to the dimly lit stacks of a lonesome library where I might read about another Egyptologist glorying over the latest additions to the Waterston Institute. I could not stomach such lost opportunity.

No, I would do my job – as specified.

I folded the map and put it in my shirt.

Later I took it out again and studied the coordinates for our relocation.

My heart raced, though I knew not why. We would go north, back toward Cairo, in the direction of Dahshur and Saqqara, locations of the most ancient necropolises, the first known pyramids, and the even older, pre-dynastic, mastaba tombs. After an arduous journey on camelback, we would – according to the prophetic diagram of the ghostly creature – spy a hillside with an outcrop shaped like an emerging, bulbous, and generously horned skull. A Cyclopean cave gaped at the base – there, we would dig.

Waterston had conveniently marked our target with a five-pointed black star.

I immediately summoned my foreman, the honorable Hakim. He moved nimbly in his robes and never seemed to break a sweat. A true marvel he was. He greeted me this evening with his usual smile.

"You have news?" he asked, eagerly.

I told him of our change in strategy. We would travel

light. Take a minimum of men. If the map proved worthy, we would shift operations to the virgin site. I was suffering from doubts again. A compulsion to look at the map grew in me, each subsequent glance fed my confidence, like sips from strong and foreign liquors, but liking the peculiar taste, my thirst doubled, and I soon required more to sate me.

I shared the Waterston plans with Hakim.

His tanned face turned the color of a Nile perch's belly.

"That is forbidden," he said, pulling back from the paper, examining his fingers as if he feared the ink had stained them permanently.

I nodded, thinking I understood. "We will file for the permits afterward. The area is remote from other active digs. No one will even know we are there. Have confidence, man."

Hakim stared hard at the map but refused to touch it.

"Where did you get this?"

"You would not believe me if I told you. Never ignore a lucky break. Now, be quick. Assemble the men and supplies. I want to begin digging the day after tomorrow."

"I do not know if I can find volunteers."

"Tell them I am doubling wages. They will come."

"But, sir…"

"Pay triples if we leave tonight. What do you say to that, my friend?"

I thought this last news would bring a smile to his face. He only bowed his head and backed out of my tent, never taking his eyes off the pages in my hand. Egyptians are a superstitious lot. Hakim needed time to adjust to our surprising new mission.

I told myself that as I packed my bag.

We left at nightfall. I did not recognize the men Hakim had mustered. Perhaps he was correct in assuming volunteers would be difficult to find. These diggers seemed to be a cut below our regulars, not in their size and skills, but their character. They looked more like the graverobbers Hakim had pointed out to me in the days when we were first hiring. Nonetheless, they were game. I could feel a palpable energy in the group. And a giddiness that bordered on hysteria. As we rode, they barked out harsh words, unintelligible to my ears, and swiped at each other like a pack of jackals.

Hakim and I led the way across the moonlit landscape.

"There's something I need to tell you," I said.

"I am listening."

"When we find the tomb…"

Hakim raised his eyebrows.

I stopped to correct my bold presumption.

"*If* we find the tomb… Mr Waterston wants me to bring the mummies back to America. I have enough resources to bribe the inspectors. We can make it appear the tomb has already been raided. Your reputation will remain unblemished. Our interest is in the mummies only. Montague Waterston will take the greatest care preserving and studying these antiquities. Other artifacts discovered in the tomb can be cataloged and turned over to the inspectors… or you may sell them on the black market and keep the profits. I will not raise any objections."

Hakim was silent.

"I mean no insult," I added. "These are extraordinary duties we are asking you to perform. You should know we are willing to compensate you for doing them."

"I fear the price we all might pay for this excursion."

"If there were no price, anyone might do it. And the world wouldn't care a whit." I reached out and seized Hakim's arm. "My friend, we can all be winners here. You will get rich, Waterston shall have his mummy, and I will be famous. Imagine how life might change."

The moonlight inserted shadows between us. I could not read his face.

"Our dreams wait for us underground," he said. His voice was joyless.

"Soon we will unearth those dreams," I said.

I did not let him see it, but Hakim had summarized my own rising dread. I had no name for the cause of my anxiety. It was indefinable. My physical body reacted rather than my reason. Dizziness, chest quakes, and a bath of cold sweats – I had attributed these symptoms to my lack of experience riding in the nocturnal desert. It was fear. But what did I fear? Failure?

No, my terror sprang from the premonition we would succeed.

4
THE TOMB

We found it right where the phantasm had indicated.

The horned skull rock.

I used my telescope to make a quick survey. The surrounding desert supported no life. Not a bird, reptile, or the lowliest dung beetle left any visible mark on the landscape.

The exhausted camels grumbled and spit in our faces.

We encamped.

It was good to not be riding any more. My backside had grown calloused, but I had yet to acclimate to the seasick pitch and yaw of an ambling camel.

I rubbed the dirt between my fingers. It felt decidedly unclean. There was oiliness to it, as if it had absorbed a viscid liquid that would not drain off. The men were tired and no good for any work that day. Yet an unusual cheerfulness had arisen in them, almost mania. They poked at each other like boys, smirking, and a few began to dance, stomping their feet with spirited vitality. This buoyancy I attributed to our arrival.

We lit fires, ate our meager rations, and all quieted.

A moonless night – so impenetrable I could not discern

the skull rock, though I knew it hunkered in the sands a few yards away from camp. Once inside the tent, my prone body fell quickly to sleep and – quite unusual for me – I did not dream.

On the morrow – after merely a day's worth of digging – we uncovered a wide, partially collapsed ledge carved in the existing stone, followed by another, cleaner, unbroken *step*, going down.

The evening sky purpled. We lit our torches and continued to excavate.

Soon a stairway materialized.

I do not know who was more surprised – me, Hakim, or our crew. The diggers' dirty snouts had grown foxier as they scraped and hauled baskets of sand away from the limestone treads buried in the mouth of that hideous cranial outcrop, descending, yard by yard, until at the bottom, their shovel blades struck the slabs of a subterranean doorway.

"Stop!" Hakim shouted.

He ordered the men up.

They were reluctant to climb out of the ground but, after some growling and whispers, they complied.

Scrabbling to the surface the way they did, on all fours, further attested to their beastly alterations. I sensed another shift in their mood too. Greedy, black-toothed, canine smiles were exchanged all around, and for the first time I feared the prospect of mutiny.

As a pack, they slunk away from the steps and fell to the sand, lying atop each other, panting, and following us with their torchlit, yellowy eyes.

I drew Hakim close.

"Who are these men?"

"Outcasts. Their father stole from the dead. His arm was chopped off. He became a magician and had many children, but no one knew his wives. Foul rumors spread they were not women. He used his spells to seduce stray animals. The family lived apart, on cursed land."

Hakim pointed emphatically at the ground.

"Here?"

He nodded. "Other men will not dig in this place. But, see? They are not afraid. Come, let us inspect the seals."

Which was worse, watching the men stare at us or leaving them unobserved?

I grabbed a torch and followed Hakim into the pit beneath the skull rock.

The seals were intact.

I broke them myself. They bore no names or hieroglyphs; neither did the slab blocking our entrance. With my pickaxe I cut a peephole in the door. I held a candle to the aperture. The flame trembled under streams of ancient air. The exhalation brushed my cheeks. Its silky coolness shocked me, as if I had stuck my head into a wishing well.

Did I smell incense? Impossible, but... myrrh, cedar, dead flowers, honey, and wine – the symphony of perfume dissolved around me. I inhaled deeply, hoping to extend the sensual delights I had sampled, only to be choked by the musk of my fellow diggers, who, reinvigorated, crowded around me like children at the hole of a circus tent.

"Back away," Hakim said. "I hear something."

I heard it too. We all did. From inside the sepulcher

echoed the clop of sliding rubble and a slow persistent hiss of falling sand.

Abruptly, as if they knew we were listening, the sounds ceased.

"Get your tools," I told everyone. "Here lies our destiny."

If I had stopped to think about what we were doing, I might have walked away. But something seized me, an absolute need to enter the crypt. It did not feel like my own desire but as if a greater force swept over, possessed, and utterly controlled me. I was an instrument: no different than the pickaxe in my hand. Whatever power gripped me I could not name. I did not resist, nor could I. My mind whirled as if intoxicated by a hypnotic drug. Time splintered.

Hakim and the brothers displayed heavy-lidded, glazed looks I would have sworn to be drunk with lust. Instinct warned me: Leave this evil place alone. Yet the hidden dominator bid me harshly, *"Dig!"* We were merciless in our frenzied attack upon the stone. Tearing and slashing at the blockage, ripping away chunks, and disgorging them up into the desert. We did not take care or employ caution.

It was most unscientific.

When we finished, my shredded palms bled. I wiped them on my legs. With the pain, my logic returned. I stared at the passage we had hacked into the chamber – a stone throat yawned, beckoning us to feed ourselves into the crypt.

One of the younger brothers rushed into the dark channel.

"Wait!" I yelled.

A second brother followed. Dropping to his knees –
for the passage was low and cramped – he scurried into
the unknown. The bottoms of his sandals, like two pale
signals, faded quickly in the murk.

The next brother lunged.

I threw my body across the entrance.

"We must let it breathe," I said.

"Later," he said. "I only want to see what is in the
tomb."

I waved a torch and the flames whipped like a flag.

"What will you see? Your brothers didn't take any
light."

He stumbled back. Rubbing his hands, he paused to
reconsider.

"It isn't safe," I said.

The horror finally sank into his brain. His brothers
were running around like rats in a potential maze of
tunnels, and without as much as a candle to guide them.
Madness.

He called past me, screaming into the hole, for them
to turn around.

Silence.

The rest of the diggers gathered at the opening. They
bit their lips and tore their clothes. Their enthusiasm at
uncovering the vault had swiftly changed to confusion,
then, in the bat of an eye, anger. Who did they blame?

I was the one stopping them from rescuing their kin.

That I might be saving their lives in the process did
not matter.

Hakim came forward.

"We will go in after them. Bring shovels and lanterns.
We can tie ourselves together with this rope." He tossed

the coils on the steps. "If we encounter danger, we turn around immediately. It does no good for all of us to die chasing a foolish pair."

The brothers agreed.

I felt I had little choice in the matter.

"Hakim, may I have a word?"

"Certainly."

Our diggers began lashing themselves together. Each had his shovel. There was no room to swing a pickaxe in the tunnel. They lit paraffin lamps and distributed them to every third man in line. The eldest, who had taken the lead spot, extinguished one torch, strapping it to the handle of a second. He held the extension, set ablaze, at arm's length. This way he could probe ahead inside the tunnel without flames licking back at him. I nodded at the forethought. Under his belt a curved dagger gleamed like a fresh wound.

I kept my voice low.

"Since I was a boy," I said, "I have had a fear of tight spaces."

"Most unfortunate given the present circumstances," Hakim said. "You have chosen a curious profession for yourself."

"I thought that my imaginings were actually worse than what the reality would be."

"And what are you finding now?"

"Reality is worse." Acknowledging it only made my breathing accelerate. I sunk to my haunches. "Forgive me. I tend to panic under these types of circumstances. Being buried alive, you know? Walls closing in on me and no air..." I shook my arms, as they had begun to tingle.

"That is, indeed, worse for all of us."

Hakim folded his hands as if he were about to pray to a Christian God. It was his habit whenever solving problems. He touched the finger steeple to his lips.

"Stay here and wait for us."

I shook my head.

"I am the leader of this expedition, and I will be there when we penetrate this tomb."

"You can go last. That way you have no one between you and the exit."

"Last man in, first man out – doesn't exactly ring heroic." I dug my fingers in the dirt.

"Tombs are filled with heroes already," he said, smiling.

The brothers were waiting.

I stood and motioned for them to join us.

Hakim secured himself to the group. One by one each digger advanced Indian file into the underground gap, squatting before the entrance then crawling forward – eyes seeking wonder, glittery, cheeks flushed – like children at play in a huge snow fort. I half expected them to breathe out frosty plumes. The limestone muffled all evidence of chatter. In the snug darkness, the diggers grew reverent.

Hakim passed me the end of the rope.

"We don't need a hero," he said.

I looped the cord around my waist and tied a bowline knot. I lifted my oil lantern from the gravel. "Right, let's get on with it," I said. "The tomb likely won't pick today to collapse."

Hakim clapped me on the back.

"Good man, Mr Hardy."

"How far do you think the tunnel goes?"

"Not far," he lied.

He bent at the hole and stuck his head in – then withdrew abruptly.

I hoped he would express second thoughts. What a fleeting relief. He only twisted around to say, "Hold my ankle. If you are in trouble, pull on my leg."

"Lucky I don't tear it off," I muttered. I tossed my shovel onto the steps.

Hakim wriggled ahead.

I crouched and squinted. Lamplight smeared the hollow. *Here goes.* I squeezed my shoulders together until I was narrow enough to fit. But a damned tight fit it was! Immovable weight pressed on me from every angle. I inched up to my midsection. My legs were still kicking outside; I could already taste the air turning stale and thin. I puffed open-mouthed, feeling lightheaded, and wedged my body farther into the cavity.

Like a cork crammed in a bottle. The lamp creaked rustily as my arm shook. The dangling light wobbled shadows cast against the rough-cut walls. My head spun.

I cannot do this, I thought.

I tried backing out. I absolutely needed the sight of stars overhead, vastness, and night-cooled desert air in my lungs. The rope grew taut, pulled. Against all instinct, I closed my eyes and plunged deeper, groping for Hakim's ankle. I patted the stone floor. Nothing. The rope jerked me again. I opened my eyes to a spray of fine dust. Blinded, I forced myself to advance until the rope slackened and I collided with my venerable foreman. I seized his leg. As I dabbed at my gritty eyes with a shirtsleeve, I realized Hakim was whispering to me.

"Do you hear it?"

"Hear what?"

"Shhhhh…" he said, "listen."

·5·

The Tomb (Part II)

A low moan reverberated up through the passage. The timbre fell somewhere between an oboe and an owl. Hearing it quickened my pulse. I could recall stillness in the desert that night: no wind was blowing through the rock above us.

"Do you think someone's been hurt?"

"Too deep," Hakim said. "I feel it coming up from underneath."

Vibrations trembled, almost musical, certainly rhythmic.

"Is that a drum?"

The moaning stopped.

After a few beats, the thumping faded as well.

I listened to myself and Hakim panting like two mice in a cobra hole.

A murmur transferred down the line of diggers. Hakim talked to the man ahead of him. The line began to move.

"They think they saw one of their brothers," Hakim said.

"Good," I said, although I wasn't so sure.

We were crawling quickly now. The passage, I noticed

happily, had widened a few inches and appeared to continue relatively uniformly, which was a comfort of sorts, though I had an irrational fear it might taper again, funneling down to nothingness. As it was, the confines were too small for me to turn myself around. If we reached a dead end, I would have no choice but to negotiate crawling out in reverse, and blindly. I had no torch, no shovel for probing. My body was a clog, trapping the lantern light ahead of me and allowing few rays to pass. I shot backward glances into the dimness at regular intervals. In the event of a cave-in behind me, I did not worry I would be killed immediately, rather that I would not... I tried to think of the burial vault instead, how it might be tall enough to stand, how it might be filled with treasure and mummies.

I had Hakim within my sight. I released his ankle and began tapping my fist against the right wall every yard or so as a means of marking our progress. Ten taps. In this dreamy world of ancient wonders, I was touching something absolutely solid, solid, solid. Twenty taps. I hoped we were getting close. The line slowed. Thirty taps. We had reached a ninety-degree left turn in the tunnel. Thirty-five. Hakim rounded the corner. The rope connecting us tautened. I scooted forward until I saw past the doglegged bend. The tunnel sloped at a forty-five degree angle: a ramp.

At the fortieth tap, directly opposite the turn, I saw a rough diagram etched into the limestone – a circle filled with spirals. I hit it dead center with my clenched hand and thought I heard hollowness, in fact, I felt the rock face ever-so-slightly yield.

A secret chamber?

Or a mere deviation in the thickness of the limestone? Perhaps a dangerous fault?

No time to investigate. The rope pulled me downward. I went with it. Here I found myself never having been inside a tomb before, and all the others, even Hakim, had passed the strange drawing without so much as a second glance. Was it no more than a signpost? An indication we were closing on our target?

I was about to ask Hakim this very question, when the gurgling started.

Upon my life, I would have sworn it was water coursing through pipes. Below us, above us – the noise of flowing liquid surrounded our position. And a second disturbance, equally odd, and more troubling to me because of its proximity, stirred in the tunnel to the rear: a dry scuffling and the clatter of loosened falling rocks.

I stared through my legs.

Only shadows – then something dropped into the passage with an unmistakable thud; a small eruption of pale dust bloomed. Before I could judge its cause, the turbid cloud prickled my eyes, and I heard a weight being dragged, not away, but *toward* me. The liquid noises had all but receded, so it surprised me when Hakim started backing up, forcing me in the direction of the yet unidentified activity.

"Stop pushing," I said.

Hakim did not respond. But he did stop pushing. Against my wishes I was nearer to the source of the scuffling, and it sounded very much to me like a schoolboy kicking his way along a gravel path. Also, I detected a soft pip-pip-pip that was at once moist in origin and air-influenced; *blowing kisses* was the first thought to enter my head, although the laugh building in my chest had more to do with abject terror than humor.

The gurgling returned.

With it came a horrible vapor which stunk like a dog's mouth as it tears apart rotten meat. Hakim rammed his backside into me and I shouldered him in return.

"What are you doing?" I shouted.

Again, he gave no reply.

I would have insisted he answer, except at that instant I spied movement in the space behind me: a side-to-side bobbing which coincided with the pips and suggested in its pantomime a quality of searching. I rolled onto my back to get a better view.

Holding the lantern between my knees, I buttressed my elbows and peered hard into the illuminated burrow.

The maggot-thing squirmed into view.

Fat as a wild boar, it nuzzled the walls. Eyeless, dumb, glistening with its own vile excretions – its skin shimmered transparently, and inside the body tube sloshed a white jelly, melting and congealing with every undulation of the great boneless menace.

I felt my gorge rise.

The conical head of the maggot-thing twitched, wet and eager, a slit at the tip dilated, then clamped shut again, and finally I knew where the pipping had come from. Wormlike segmented rings bristled with hooked blond hairs. The maggot-thing edged closer. I drew my legs as far from its mouth as I could. Because it did, indeed, possess a mouth. Tasting the air, the tip blossomed obscenely. Flesh petals splayed to reveal thousands of spiky teeth carpeting the underside of each flap. Enough to denude any man's skeleton.

"Hakim, go!"

"I can't," he said.

"For the love of God, why not? Do you see this?"

"I do but…"

Hakim stuck a wet red hand in front of my lantern.

"The tunnel is bleeding."

Normally I would have said that was impossible. In the presence of the maggot-thing I found myself less able to pass critical judgment. I was speechless.

"The diggers won't go any farther!" Hakim shouted.

Steadily the maggot-thing progressed. Its supremely oral visage – hideously lacking in structure, like a deboned face – gaped at me. I kicked it hard under the flaps, hoping to stun it or even cause its retreat. Rather the head, alarmingly swifter than any previous motion had suggested, darted downward.

Teeth raked my shoe.

I tucked my knees to my ribs and realized that my backside was soaked. The blood sloshed around me. Quickly its level rose to my waist. It was warm.

Horridly warm.

I mopped my hand across my sweating face and knew by the stickiness that I'd succeeded in smearing myself with more blood. A gush of crimson washed over the lantern, not extinguishing my light, but dimming it and dyeing the glass ruddy. I curled my body tighter to avoid the encroaching maggot. My lungs were squeezed flat, I could not draw a breath, and when I tried to stretch out again I had even less room than before. The meager air grew salty and humid as the sea, and nearly as unbreathable.

"Where is the blood coming from?" I gasped.

"Everywhere," Hakim said. The word gurgled, as if his lips were being dunked.

Hissing, shouts, and the acrid smell of smoke: the bloody gobbets raining from the ceiling were snuffing out the men's torches and lamps. The line of diggers reversed in a raw panic. Only Hakim's strength and his barked commands calling for order kept them from driving me straight into the maggot-thing's maw. Red gore surged like a flash flood in a gully. My body lifted, buoyant. I had to brace to keep from being swept away. I held my lantern high. Losing my handhold in the slippery incoming tide, I banged my forehead against a wall. Stars danced in the lamplight.

Undiscouraged, the maggot-thing lapped up the scarlet fluid.

Nothing, I thought, could have made the pale worm look worse, yet crimson splashes did the trick. Its red-dipped slurping head quivered with joy (if such a creature might know joy). Behind me, the diggers floundered and screamed. The gurgling in the walls amplified into a roar of rushing liquid – I knew it now to be blood, somehow, uncannily, circulating in the dead rock. I clamped the lantern handle with sticky fingers. Blood gagged the diggers' mouths, quieting their cries. What choice did I have? To drown in blood or be worm-eaten? Hakim could no longer hold back the kicking men and unstaunchable sanguine river – he slid into me. I sunk neck-deep in red.

The maggot-thing lifted its mouth, splitting wider to welcome me.

I smashed my lantern against the ceiling.

Glass shattered. Burning oil sprayed worm flesh. The

maggot-thing knuckled sourly into itself. Its sickly white meat charred and bubbled, and the creature emitted a high-pitched shriek as it skidded snappily down the tunnel from where it had come.

A wave of blood crashed into me, shot me through the channel and into the blunt body of the retreating worm. Luckily the underground dweller was more interested in escape than a meal, though I felt it thump into my gut like a medicine ball. Feet first we rode the ruby stream up the ramp where the maggot-thing, blistered and smoking from its wounds, squirmed back into its hole in the wall (at the place where the spiral-filled drawing had broken apart); past the turn I tumbled, the rope tangled in my legs but it did not matter because I glimpsed a square of gray light – the entrance – and the bloody force vomited me and my companions onto the steps of the tomb.

6

SECOND ENTRY

Two from our group – the first pair who scrambled headlong into the tunnel – were dead, drowned in blood. I stared at their grisly faces: bulging eyes, jaws locked in silent screams, and tongues like chewed rags hanging down their chins. The terror of their final moment was all too apparent.

What had they encountered in the bowels of the tomb?

I could not fathom it.

The surviving brothers coughed, spit, and gulped fresh air until discovery of the harrowing condition of the bodies started them swaying. Sorrowful wails rose above the pre-dawn desert. I slunk over to Hakim who was on his hands and knees retching.

"Are you all right?"

He nodded. His eyes bugged out like sheep's, and his clothes appeared as if he had rolled around on a butcher shop floor. His limbs trembled uncontrollably.

"What the hell happened in there?" I asked.

"Nothing… I have ever seen before." He shook his head to clear the vision. He tried to spit but could draw no saliva. His skin had turned as rough-looking as the sand.

"You're the one who lives here, damn it! I was almost consumed by a worm!"

"It is most strange." He tugged at his peeling lips. Like an opium eater, he stared into some hazy middle distance only he could see. Sighing, he sat back heavily on a step.

"Here, drink." I handed him a jar of water. "Worms! I didn't sign on to this expedition to get drowned in a bloody tunnel no bigger than a sewer pipe." I shook my gore-matted head. "I'm a man of science. I don't believe in, in… any of this! Why can't there be a decent amount of dirt to remove and then you get your relics? Remove dirt. Receive relics. Wouldn't that be nice?"

"Maybe we are dreaming."

I stared hard at my foreman. "That was no dream, man." I paced, glad to be in the open air. "There must be an explanation. We don't have all the facts to draw a reasonable conclusion."

"Curses don't care about reason. This is sorcery, not science."

Sorcery, not science. How was I to argue with that? I had seen what I had seen and it was not reasonable or scientific. *A worm and a tunnel of blood. Moans and drumbeats from an underground passage that hadn't been opened in several thousand years.* The stuff of legends. Weren't legends what I wished for? Instead, I had an abundance of evidence but no way of explaining any of it. I needed to see more. To know more. There would be answers, later. My panic slowly subsided. Despite the lives lost and my own brush with the crawling hideousness, I felt energized, even thrilled. This new headiness was strange to me. I did not recognize myself, but my surprise did not restrain my drive – nay, obsession – to get back into the tunnel.

"Hakim, we will send a rider to Cairo at once, to gather a second full crew of diggers and additional equipment. This time we proceed in an orderly manner. No rushing blindly into tunnels. Proper excavation will take months. But I know something is down there."

Hakim looked at me as if I had lost my mind.

"You want to go back inside?"

"Yes, of course."

"But it is cursed. You said yourself this is unbelievable," Hakim said.

"I've never done anything like this before. I'm learning as I go."

"Foolhardy or stubborn, I don't know which is worse." He muttered something more and raised his hands to object. "Return to that insanity? All the blood... I have a beautiful wife whom I love, six happy children, and another on the way. We are poor but not stupid... no, sir, I am sorry, but I will not be going with you."

I trod along the partially exposed step. Already the drying blood had stiffened my clothes. On five sticky fingers, I counted the reasons for returning underground. "An unmarked seal, a secret panel covered in spiral glyphs, mysterious music accompanying cries of unknown origin, a sandworm, and a river of blood... I'd say this tomb is beyond extraordinary. Don't you see? You call it cursed. I don't disagree. Say we're right. Then it's cursed for a reason, my friend. That reason is whatever lies in the bottom of the crypt."

"Better to bury the doorway–"

"Treasure," I said.

Hakim's eyes shined like wet gold nuggets. His mouth hung open.

"You really think there's treasure to be found?"

"Of one kind or another… Look, all I know is I can't turn my back on this mystery and wonder for the rest of my life what's down there. Those two brothers died for a chance to see it."

Thunder rumbled from the tomb.

"Cave-in?" I asked.

Hakim braced his arms out as the stone steps vibrated. Pebbles danced wildly along the slabs and dropped into cracks. "No, effendi… the ground is moving."

A great seizure began to rattle everything in sight with a crescendo of agitation. Our tethered, and now wildly upset, camels rolled their eyes and uttered watery burbles of distress from the backs of their throats, baring their teeth as they tried to break free from the minders who scooped up their reins. The shaking nearly tumbled me headfirst down the steps. I watched, stunned, holding my arms out for balance, while the entire arid plain undulated atop a mound of jelly. Dust clouds puffed around us, and a strange, sand-choked, ocher wind swirled out from the tomb.

Hakim crabbed his way up the stairs, crying, "Earthquake!"

We ran away from the skull rock. As my feet trampled the unsteady ground, I heard an enormous rending of earth ahead of us. I sensed the land cracking, splitting apart. I say *sensed* because I could not see anything – away from our torches, the desert lay black as cast iron. I was convinced that to continue onward meant driving ourselves like lemmings off a cliff. Someone, or some entity, was sending us a clear message.

I threw out an arm and grabbed Hakim.

Our diggers ran past us.

"Halt!" I yelled, breathless. "Tell them, Hakim! Order them to stop running!"

Hakim shouted, and the men froze. All but one unfortunate soul whose scream – a piteous frantic howl – faded as the unseen chasm swallowed him whole. The desert floor roared from within, and then fell silent.

We stood like panting statues.

"Don't move. Hold completely still," I said.

Hakim repeated my command.

Sand sifted softly into the open fissures.

After counting to a hundred, I turned around to view the skull rock. Kicked-over lamps and hastily dropped torches littered the steps, but the light they shed was sufficient for me to see the rock had grown, not horizontally, but vertically – it stood taller now, more shadows plugged the vacant eye sockets, its bulbous forehead tilted back in mute laughter, and inside of its yawning jaws the stone throat had widened.

Here was where we belonged. Here – in this horned skull – was where I belonged.

"We must return to the steps."

"Sir–"

"Tell the brothers to pick up their torches and tools. We've breached the door, and any attempt to leave here spells our certain doom. We have opened the puzzle, and so it is ours to solve or die trying. Turning back is not permitted. The desert will drop beneath us like a trapdoor. The pieces are falling even as I speak. We cannot stop them. I see no other way but forward. The tomb waits. So we go to it. Or we are already as good as dead."

Was I afraid? Yes.

Did I feel the heady confidence of a man who might achieve something meaningful for the first time in his life? Absolutely. I wanted to make my name, to discover the hidden and bring it back into the light of the world. I was ready to risk my life and the lives of others to make it happen. But did I have any choice in the matter? Or was my Fate determined for me?

That is a question for future scholars and philosophers to ponder. I felt I had no choice but to search the tomb and claim its contents.

Hakim stared at the terra firma beneath his sandals. He had translated what I said, and the brothers obeyed, taking up their tools. Fear, I thought, made them compliant. Now I know the truth. Some among this digging tribe desired even more than I to see the crypt exhumed. We all think we are masters of our futures. But who can resist the voice that calls to him inside his own head? Or the invisible whip that bites into his flesh at every pause and drives him on and on, well past all reason?

7

THE SIXTH BOX

We thrust our torches into the gaping rocky mouth.

The quake had lowered the floor by several feet and the walls were drawn apart. No crawling this time, we walked in upright. Our progress continued unimpeded. The tunnel sloped, snaked around on itself, and repeated this pattern, so that we retraced the same ground, each pass taking us one level deeper. We zigzagged down and down.

I led the way. Curiosity propelled me. I did not pause to contemplate the tons of sand piled above us or the pressure of the walls on either side. I forced myself not to think. No evidence of the mysterious blood geyser, which had flushed us out the first time, remained. The maggoty beast had squirmed back into its lightless lair to heal or to die. As I marched ahead – the angle of the tunnel hurrying me along – I breathed in cool damp air with a liquid heaviness reminiscent of a dense fog. Despite years of scientific study, I swore I was about to discover a mineral spring in one of the driest regions on the planet.

Everywhere, my flesh felt skimmed with cold grease.

"We've reached the bottom," Hakim said over my shoulder.

I waved my torch. Flatness stretched out in all directions. Scores of shadows poised to leap from the well of darkness. Our silhouettes danced on the rock face. But I swore I saw others lilting forward to join us. What were these half-formed profiles swimming on the periphery of our light? No one else paid them attention. Was I their sole witness? Did my overactive mind create them?

Look away, I told myself. *Or you will be sorry.*

Yet each glimpse brought the desire to gaze more.

I feigned that the torch smoke was vexing my eyes – blinking, wiping away tears – while I stared at my shoes until the fascination passed. The success of this expedition was my charge, and I had the responsibility for safeguarding the lives of my men. So, with duty as my guidepost, I attended to solid matters at hand.

I stepped forward.

"A room with no doors – it is unsealed," I said, failing to hide my disappointment. Robbers, I conjectured, must have dug their way in from another direction and ransacked the chamber centuries ago. Alas, we would find nothing but empty wreckage for our troubles.

"Begging your pardon, Mr Hardy, but I believe the quake unsealed the tomb." Hakim ran his fingers into a pair of strange linear grooves along the floor, at the very threshold to the room. "See? No dust. They are clean."

I lowered my fire.

Crouching, I brushed my fingertips over the top of a stone slab which, judging by its dimensions, weighed several tons. "The door's right here. That's why there isn't any rubble. The whole door has dropped into this slot, as

snugly as a woodworker's joint." If Hakim had not spied
the outline of the slab on the floor, I would have stepped
right over it. The engineering was phenomenal.

"What mechanism lowered the door?" Hakim
wondered aloud.

"I have a better question. Why build a door only an
earthquake can open?"

We entered the chamber. The brothers pressed close
at our backs, rubbing themselves against the wall,
crowding one another but hesitant to go farther than
my flame. The ceiling hung low above our heads.
Hakim flipped his torch into the gloom. It landed with
a burst of sparks.

Astonishing – the room was perfectly round!

How did the architects of this mausoleum carve a
circular room from bedrock? With hammers and copper
chisels? I think not. For as I ran my fingers over the walls,
I felt the faint ovoid traces of a large, dare I venture to
say, *mechanical* cutting tool. Our entrance would also
be our exit. No other passages penetrated – or, to put it
another way, escaped from – the depths of the vault. All
at once my chest tightened. I struggled to draw a breath.
An overwhelming urge to run back up the tunnel, and
keep running, seized me. But I stood my ground.

This was no royal tomb. Earthly treasures – the
customary gold, jewels, and exquisite artifacts amassed
to reflect social preeminence, and most importantly, in
keeping with the Egyptians' religious beliefs, to provide
for the journey to the afterlife – were completely absent.
The unpainted room before us was sparse as a jail cell.
Anyone interred here would be sent to the next world to
wander eternally – starved, bankrupt, and unprotected.

Yet it *was* a burial place, and its contents in time would prove most rare.

Six coffins.

Without a second thought, I rushed ahead to inspect our discovery. Wood splinters crunched underfoot. The ancient funereal display occupied the center of the room – five caskets, each roughly man-sized and badly damaged.

The sixth box loomed much larger.

"Sarcophagus!" Hakim clapped his hands in joy at the sight.

It was made of stone, not wooden like the others. And by our smoky torchlight, it appeared to be fully – one might even call it pristinely – intact.

I surveyed the arrangement of the five cedar coffins, noting the gaps between the planks of their half-shattered lids and deep splits running along the sides. Had some grave robber attempted to pry them apart? And in frustration had he turned to smashing them? Why did he stop? And why did the boards appear not to have sustained an attack from above so much as one from–? No. I shook my head. That was impossible. And robbers could not be the answer either. Since the burial, no one had been down here. This bleakest of tombs had never been violated.

Until now.

I passed my torch to one of the diggers and knelt, withdrawing a lucifer from a box I always carried in my pocket, and using my thumbnail to strike it.

I hunched over the nearest coffin.

Through the ages, and in perfect darkness, a length of tattered, soiled binding had unraveled and snaked its way to where it poked a few inches out through the largest of the cracks. The dangling linen looked as delicate and black as Chantilly lace. I put my nose next to it and sniffed. It smelled *burned*. When I touched the edge, the mummy cloth disintegrated on my fingertips.

I wiped the ashes off my hand.

After careful investigation, I determined all five of the damaged coffins contained mummified bodies. I could not judge their states of decomposition by peeking through holes while hot matches scorched my fingertips, but I looked long enough to know they were present and accounted for. My throat was so dry it crackled when I swallowed. I had no spit and wished I had brought my canteen with me. "Look at the pattern they make," I said. My voice rasped. "Like spokes of a giant wheel…"

"Or the radiant beams of the sun," Hakim said.

"A blackened sun," I whispered.

Was I afraid I might be overheard?

The illogical answer is yes. Yes, I was. I had the impression that someone hidden from view was eavesdropping on our conversation.

Who was listening?

That very question hovered foremost in my thoughts.

The largest coffin, the sarcophagus, was like no other I have witnessed before or since. Nine feet of cigar-shaped black quartzite, fashioned without corners or sharp edges. I had not spotted any seams either. Only by scratching with my fingers in the grit did I detect the hint of a lid tucked underneath the hulking encasement. The stone was unadorned, faceless. I stood and pondered the width of the casket – twice as thick across the chest as I was, tapered at both head and foot. If the occupant's size resembled this box, he was a giant. The question popped into my brain: Why were this giant and his five lesser companions inhumed with such harsh unforgiving methods?

Using my sleeve, I rubbed away a scrim of dust. Along the side here... what was this? A diagonal row of hastily carved hieroglyphs – a name enclosed by an oval: a cartouche. But cartouches were for the names of royalty and gods. How puzzling. These carvings, shallow scratches really, appeared to be an older, cruder variation of the glyphs I had learned back home at the library. I trailed my finger underneath the symbols, doing my best to parse them.

The great hidden one, born wicked in the darkness, priest of chaos–

That was all.

The rest of the message had been gouged away, and in a flash I envisioned the long-ago writer, surprised during his secret act, being dragged off, watching his unfinished work mutilated with a chisel.

The quartzite held alluring depths. I buffed a porthole. I peered into a silica sea and glimpsed – what, exactly?

Surely not the suggestion of anything *moving* – but when I looked closer, I saw it again. It was like viewing a fish swimming under a layer of fractured black ice. Down at the bottom – an alert human form shifted restlessly, straining to break free from its imprisonment. How could anything in there be alive? I blinked and stared harder.

And saw only rock.

Behind me I heard rapid footsteps.

8
AMUN ODJI-KEK

Inside the tenebrous tomb, I never saw the dagger descending toward me, only the grotesque contorted face of the man who gripped it. He filled my vision. My reaction was to flick the lit match I was pinching between my fingers squarely into his right eye. He grunted – a lucky shot. The pain was not enough to stop him, though it succeeded in making him miss his target. We crashed into the sarcophagus. The point of his dagger scraped along the lid. His other hand grabbed my shirt. All my buttons popped, scattering like beetles, as he pulled me roughly around. I shoved him back as hard as I could while regaining my balance. Quickly I turned my shoulder at him, figuring if he slashed me that would be about the choicest place to take the damage. He paused, steadied himself, and did his best to find me, one-eyed, in the semi-dark.

I put up my fists.

A lot of good they would do in a knife fight. Though I never had a chance to discover how poorly I might have fared. For as the devilish digger raised his weapon to kill me, a sound like an axe splitting a wet log exploded from the back of his head, and his eyes, even the blinded one, grew big and round.

My would-be assassin fell at my feet.

Hakim hoisted his bloody spade and hit him again.

"Stop! He isn't going to... he's dead."

Dead he was, indeed. Even in the dimness, I could see exposed bone glistening like the white of an eye in the red gash across the back of his neck. My thoughts turned to survival, for Hakim and I were below ground with a dozen of this murdered man's brothers.

Their silence chilled me.

Hakim addressed the men with authority, but I heard desperation edging into his voice. If he lost control of them, we would never see the desert sky again.

He exchanged words with the dirtiest of the diggers, a sun-leathered veteran whose beard was striped like a skunk's tail. The longer the gaunt digger talked with him, the more confused Hakim looked. The digger pointed emphatically at the dead man, then at the sarcophagus. He stepped into the spreading pool of blood and kicked the corpse viciously in the head. Then he pointed his gnarled finger at me.

"Amun Odji-Kek," he said, smiling. And he bowed in thanks.

"No," Hakim said.

But the digger just nodded, his skunk-tail chin whiskers bobbing in the shadows, as he grinned at me with snaggletoothed glee. Perhaps the sun had boiled his brain while it cured his skin.

Hakim approached the sarcophagus and read the cartouche.

He staggered backward.

"What's going on?" I asked.

"Very bad... I cannot believe..."

"Can't believe what? That man tried to kill me! How can they blame us?"

Hakim shook his head, never taking his eyes off the glyph.

"They don't care about him."

"What?"

"They're happy he's dead."

"Why on earth would they be *happy*?"

"He was a religious man, a reciter of the Qur'an. He betrayed them by trying to stop you."

"Stop me from what?"

"If that cartouche is correct, then this coffin houses the mummy of Amun Odji-Kek, Sorcerer of Set. I never believed the stories, but... this is real." Hakim thumped the sarcophagus and drew his hand back, alarmed. He stared in disbelief. "Amun Odji-Kek is a tribal legend according to the priests, someone to scare the women and children. The pharaohs denied his existence. He is known by many names, but they all mean the same: He Who Disturbs the Balance, Plague Bringer, Corruptor of the Land, Slayer from the South, Lord of Demons. Mr Hardy, he is the embodiment of evil."

The brothers fell to their knees and began chanting as they bowed in unison. Inside our tight little hollow beneath the skull rock, the noise was quite alarming. I felt the smallness of our presence, the pressing of the earth above, and my heart fluttered.

"Why don't they fear him?"

"They are the only living survivors of his cult. For generations, they have been making offerings, carrying out necromantic rituals in his memory. When a traveler disappears, a child from the village cannot be found... there are rumors... of human sacrifices. You see, sir, Amun Odji-Kek feasts on the flesh of innocents."

Somehow the act of supplication made this gang more threatening. More mindless, yes, and at the same time more formidable – as if they were not a group of individuals but one entity knitted together by invisible threads and under the control of a single intelligence. Their previous fears had vanished, and in their place a wild exuberance was born. The chants grew faster. They rose and straightened their backs and commenced pounding the floor with their feet, turning in circles with horrible coordination as if they had rehearsed this dance their whole lives. Spittle flew from their mouths. I wondered if we would have total frenzy at the climax, a blood orgy staining the floor of this grim hole that spouted red as if it were a fountain.

"I expect they'll kill us after their prayers."

"Not necessarily," Hakim said. "They have searched for the body of Amun Odji-Kek for thousands of years. They are in the mood for celebrating."

"For at last they have found him," I said.

"You found him," Hakim corrected me.

I nodded. "Yes, absolutely I did. Excellent point! So they must be feeling grateful to me to a certain degree. Do they appear grateful to you?"

The brother diggers twirled and the torches bent with the wind their movements made.

"It is difficult to say. I do not know what language they are speaking, or if it is language."

The tiny vault vibrated with shouts and the brothers'

rhythmic stomping.

"Any idea what their plan is?"

"Why, only one – to bring the sorcerer back to life."

Montague P. Waterston's phantom had drawn us an uncanny map. Waterston's money had paid for the digging. I was Monty's man, but I felt more in the dark than any of my native workmen. Did the feverish California gold baron have any clue where he was sending me? Or what I would find? Or in time would he discover, like me, that he had sunk himself deep in the soil of an ancient land he could only pretend to know?

9

OUT OF EGYPT

Waterston-Hardy Expedition, 2nd digging season, 1888
Approx. location: Saqqara, Egypt

The task of bringing to the surface the entombed sorcerer Odji-Kek and his five lesser companions was foremost in the minds of our crew. Regarding this matter, we had no quarrel. What to do with the bodies afterward was something I decided to deal with, well... afterward... making a timely gambit to stay any blade from cutting Hakim's throat and my own. I tried in earnest to persuade the skunk-bearded digger – whose name I discovered was Chigaru – that we needed more men and supplies if we hoped to empty the tomb safely. Chigaru insisted I was wrong. The smart devil feared another earthquake would steal their "god" just as fickly as the one which had unveiled him.

"Sink, sink," he repeated, pointing down. Then shaking his head, he added, "The land is not happy. We must rescue the Lord of the Demons. He is a prisoner no more."

"I don't know if we can do it with so little help," I said.

Sitting between us, Hakim translated.

"He says he will show you how."

Chigaru clapped and shouted a name. One of the youngest workmen, a skin-and-bones high-cheeked lad whose perpetual smile unnerved me, came forward. Chigaru whispered instructions in his ear. The young man nodded, snatched a torch, and took something from one of the gear packs before he disappeared, grinning, up the tunnel.

A few minutes later he returned.

He had taken a clay pot and trowel. The trowel he had tucked away under his belt, as diggers will do, but in the crook of his arm he carried the pot, now heavily filled. He handed the pot to Chigaru, who petted him on the head as if he were a hurdy-gurdy man's monkey.

Chigaru removed the lid and bid me to look inside.

My nose reacted before my eyes did. A stew of slime threatened to overspill the rim – indeed, several thick trickles already had. Here was the pungent smoked-gray exudation of the maggot-thing, left behind as its bulk heaved along the passages; the boy had, bravely or dumbly, scraped residue from the entrance of its wormy burrow.

To what end?

Chigaru pantomimed painting the contents of the pot onto the floor.

Worm slime as lubricant? I dared not laugh. I thought it better at this point to indulge the devout cultist, and in the inevitable event of his plan's failure, I would volunteer myself to procure additional workers and new equipment for our team. Better to take my chances in the cursed desert than to remain here. If I made it to

Cairo, I would round up men, but also rifles, to regain control of the excavation.

I feigned enthusiasm for Chigaru's methods.

I ordered six men to retrieve our sturdiest ropes, and our block and tackle. I measured and told them the specifics to build a sled for transporting the sarcophagus. "Bring down more lamps," I said. "And fetch the long iron pikes so we can lever and guide the stone box onto the sled." In the meanwhile, I supervised careful removal of the mummies in the five damaged cedar coffins. Despite this activity in and out of the tomb, Hakim and I were unable to leave at any time. To keep my spirits up, I thought, *I shall go free when this immense sarcophagus refuses to budge a damned inch.*

Now I swear to you, dear Reader, we should not have been able to move that stone sarcophagus out of that tomb with hardly enough men to play a baseball game. How could we maneuver and drag tons of rock with only ropes, a simple pulley, and a great deal of sweat? Consider the slope of the ramps. The hairpin-angled turns. No, no.

But move it we did.

Chigaru slathered the runners of the sled with the maggoty juice.

The coffin almost seemed to lift itself at the very moment the men strained to raise it. They quickly pushed the sled underneath.

I could not believe what I was seeing. The men divided into two teams, each dedicated to one of the pair of ropes securing the sled. Chigaru positioned himself at the front and took no cords in his hands but led the men with his barking voice. Hakim and I went behind the coffin to watch for any slippage or signs the sled might collapse under the weight of its load.

The men began to pull.

The effort seemed to take them to the brink of death, so unchecked was their exertion, the total physical dedication, yes, stressed to the brink but not over.

I could not stand by and watch these men, whatever their occult beliefs, without lending my own effort to the cause. I planted my hands on the stone and pushed for all I was worth. Hakim did likewise. I do not want to give the impression the sarcophagus moved with a sudden ease. Quite the contrary. It did not. But its slow journey up the ramp felt queerly frictionless, like a steel ball rolled in an oily track. And at each turn – where I feared the ropes would snap or the men might lose their footing and the sled come crashing back on Hakim and me, grinding us into bloody paste – the coffin pivoted neatly, swiveling at a precise center point so the sides did not jam into or even bump the tunnel walls, and without reason, the giant box held itself, as if it were braked, until the men found enough breath and muscle to continue.

At the last turn, the air freshened. The tomb-space grew brighter, overcoming the shadows and the monochromatic flickering of the torches. A makeshift ramp led up the steps. We leveled the sarcophagus and exited the death chamber.

"I've done it. I've excavated my first sarcophagus."

Sweat darkened my shirt. I was elated. I had never felt more alive than I did in that moment, leaning back, resting my elbows on Odji-Kek's funereal stone box.

"We will never forget this day," Hakim said.

"You are right, friend." I patted the warm granite. "This is a piece of living history."

Pale, lavender dawn greeted us. Relief, liberation, joy – all these emotions bubbled in me. I rounded the massive encasement and congratulated Chigaru on his technique. He bowed. We rested from our labors and sat in one big jovial circle, drinking tea and admiring the sunrise.

Hakim turned his cup in his hands and stared at the horizon.

I squatted beside him, complimenting the diggers in earshot, before I leaned close to whisper. "We need to get these mummies on a barge for Alexandria. Waterston will buy a ship to convey me to New York if he needs to. So, friend, the question is how do we convince Chigaru to take our prize to the Nile?"

"We may not have to," Hakim said. He pointed off in the distance.

I shielded my eyes. I saw it then – a dark line like ants crawling on an anthill.

"Who are they?"

Hakim shrugged. He pulled a brass monocular from his belt pouch and aimed it at the ants that were growing larger and turning into men as we watched.

"No one comes here," he said, handing me the monocular.

To this comment I had little to add other than the obvious: *Are we no one?*

But I held my tongue.

They traveled on horseback – thirty well-armed riders at my count, and still more driving two large covered wagons on sturdy axles in their caravan. The soldiers – if they were soldiers – were dressed in uniforms I did not recognize by their cut or lack of insignia.

Government men from Cairo?

Through the gauzy heat, they aimed their weapons at us, leaving no doubt any rash movement would be answered with bullets. At twenty-five yards, they halted. From the rear of the caravan one man rode forward, attired unlike the others, his burly chest being overstuffed in a tweed suit. As he advanced farther, I noticed a waxed red handlebar moustache and a general lack of chin; everything higher was wedged under his pith helmet. The moustache quivered. "Do you own rights to this concession?"

An Englishman – judging by his accent.

"Who is in charge here? Speak up one of you!"

"This is my dig," I answered, on my feet. "I am Dr Romulus Hardy."

I approached him at an easy pace.

Gunsights followed me.

The Englishman dismounted.

"Where are your permits?"

"Who did you say *you* were?" I asked. "And by what authority–"

The Englishman drew his Enfield revolver and stuck its barrel in my face.

Offering my best smile, "Our papers are still in Luxor. Left behind by accident. But if you allow us to return with you to Cairo, we can clear up this simple clerical issue."

He lowered his sidearm. "Your name is…?"

"I am Dr Romulus Hardy, as I already said. You might not have heard me."

"Hardy?"

"Yes… H-A-R-D–"

I did not have a chance to say 'Y' before the Enfield sped upward again, butt forward this time, and the handle cracked against my left temple.

I went down into swift blackness.

And into blackness I emerged. I feared for a moment I had gone blind from the blow. But, no. I could see something before the tip of my nose. Texture, folds, little creases of light. I smelled my own sweat and hair tonic. I had a sack pulled over my head. My wrists were tied to the horn of a saddle. Someone was sitting pressed up tight against me from behind. Rough hands covered mine. Arms clasped under my ribs, keeping me balanced on the horse.

I thought to hide the fact I had regained my senses, but already I felt the rider behind me alertly register my change of state. He loosened his arm hold, slightly. He was waiting to see what I would do next. I wanted off with this blindfold, to be freed, to understand what was happening to my expedition – all at once preferably. I turned my head left, snapped back right, how comical it must have looked, and to no purpose. I was still hooded. I saw nothing, said nothing. If they wanted to unmask me they would pick the time.

I concentrated on breathing and listening.

What was I hearing?

Commotion. Thudding hooves. Horses snorting clouds of bitter dust. The swift movement of a goodly number of tense, armed men. Someone kicked the fire pit where we had boiled our tea – the embers hissed and a wave of smoke penetrated the bag over my face.

Shouting.

A rapid succession of orders.

The horse I was on walked away from the direction of the clamor.

We did not go far.

An unsettling quietness sprung like a trap. Disoriented, I realized this hush was worse, much worse, than the noise. Cut off – the silence fooled my jarred mind into thinking I might be suffocating inside the airless pocket snugged around my head. I lifted my hands to tear the sack off, but found they were were tied. I wanted to call out. For what, I could not say, and so I held my tongue. But I knew some new misery approached.

Under me the horse's flesh quivered. The rider abruptly turned the animal around. *Is he looking at something?* I was dizzied with vertigo, feeling the blackness tugging at me. *Why turn? What does he desire to see?* I found my voice and yelled.

"Hakim! Run! They're killers!"

But it was too late.

Judging by the screams, the first volley of rifle shots murdered most of my crew.

Afterward: a dreadful scuttling, heavy pawing about; limbs thrashed in the dirt. The wounded tried to crawl away from their fate. The dying groaned. No mercy came.

The second fusillade finished them off.

All but a man, or maybe two – for I heard the sharp reports of bullets ricocheting minutes later… one here… another farther away… there – echoing off the skull rock, a man's scream. Whoever got away tried running down the tunnel. That was my best guess. Where else would they go? Does one escape a summary execution? Usually not.

I felt sick and responsible. Certainly, the diggers were a threat to my objectives, perhaps even to my life, a significant obstacle, to be sure, yet by no account did I wish them murdered. So why did guilt's rat teeth gnaw at me as if I were an accomplice to this slaughter? What did my heart intuit that my brain missed? How was I to blame?

The sack came away then, and I saw how.

Sunlight like a bucket of shiny water splashed my eyes. I blinked repeatedly until bits and pieces of the tweed-bound Englishman came into focus. Cheery, all smiles, he tossed my hood to the sands. "Sorry about the tap on the head, poor fellow. I had to do something." He inspected the plummy cranial knot. "You'll patch up good as new. Let's get you off that horse and onto one of the carts. You look positively squeamish."

He gestured to the man over my shoulder, to my riding partner.

"Cut his hands free, Ali."

Today was not my day to die. No bullet to the brainpan for me. I climbed down from the saddle, with the aid of Ali, and landed on wobbly legs, nearly falling sideways. The day had not been so fortunate for Hakim. He lay on his stomach, not twenty yards from me, a half-dozen red poppies pinned to his broad back. Of course, they weren't poppies at all but bullet holes.

I turned away. "Who are you people?"

"Care for brandy?" the Englishman on horseback asked, ignoring my query. He offered me his uncapped canteen. I sniffed the fumes before gulping a torrent of biting hot liquor.

I coughed into my sleeve. Lifted my head groggily.

"You killed my foreman," I said. "He had a pregnant wife, six children…"

The Englishman shuddered. "They litter like vermin. Heathens, filthy hordes of them. But you're in the company of a civilized man now. I worked with one of your, ah, predecessors in Mr Waterston's employment. Egyptologist from Philadelphia. Tall chap went by the name of Krazwell? Norby or Norton was it? Norman, I believe. Ned! Ned Krazwell. Were you two acquainted? No. Well, he's been dead for years now. It doesn't matter one whit, trust me. Ned had the air of doom about him. Dead Ned. Doomed from the start. They found his decapitated torso in the Sweetwater Canal, at Crocodile Lake. An open latrine is more like it. The crabs had a real feast that night."

Black splotches inked my vision. I bent over to get the blood flowing.

"Are you all right? Heat will kill a man quicker than the cold. That is fact. Nothing to worry about, my American friend. Ali, get the man a hat."

Ali found me a pith helmet. I put it on and took another swig from the canteen.

"What is your name?" I asked the Englishman for what seemed to me the umpteenth time. Instead of answering he passed me a slip of paper and in exchange took back the remainder of his brandy.

"I have a telegram here for you from Mr Waterston. Sent two days ago to Cairo. Read it when you're ready. The desert sun plays havoc with a man's eyes. The sands will scratch them out if you live here long enough." He pointed to the paper. "That explains everything. He had a presentiment you'd run into trouble and commissioned me to form a rescue party. We're to accompany you all the way to Alexandria… you and the mummies. You're going home, lucky bastard!"

10
PRIME MERIDIAN

March 21st, 1888
Transatlantic crossing

DEAR BRAVE HARDY – (STOP) – DREAMING OF
YOUR DANGER – (STOP) – ARMED ESCORT WILL
TAKE MUMS TO SAFE HARBOR – (STOP) – SHIP
WAITING – (STOP) – EMISSARY WILL MEET YOU
AT NY DOCK – (STOP) – GODSSPEED
  M P WATERSTON

I reread the telegram at least a hundred times. During
my first reading, while standing next to the Englishman
on horseback who was upending the last drops of his
canteen, I had made it as far as the second stop, when
the skull rock exploded. Chips of limestone hailed
down from the heavens. The unnatural monument
where Odji-Kek and his minions had been interred for
millennia crumbled into a pile of rubble. A plume of
smoke escaped a gaping hole in what had been the top
of the skull and fled skyward.

The Englishman remained unperturbed.

My ears were ringing after the nearly deafening boom.
"Gelignite," he shouted. "The boys put your dead
diggers inside, wheeled a box of jelly sticks into the
mouth of the tomb, and blasted the thing. Not to worry,
all's well."

But I did worry, and with good reason, my concerns
continued to mount for days, and later aboard ship in
Alexandria my fears were confirmed. The telegram did
not sit well with me. That extra "S" in Godspeed, a poor
speller in the telegraph office, no doubt... but how on earth
did Waterston know we had found anything? Well, his
dream phantom told him, I supposed, the same one who
showed him the location of the tomb. Was it necessary
to slaughter my crew of workmen, to kill the loyal and
honorable Hakim, simply to cover up our discovery and
subsequent illegal removal of antiquities? I was disgusted,
utterly baffled by the brutality. If this was how we treated
the Egyptians, I could well understand their wariness at
allowing us to rummage in their sacred sites.

I could not grasp why on earth Waterston had ordered
such drastic measures. Had he gone mad? Was it the
money? Surely, he had enough already, although rich
men seldom feel they do. These mummies, even the
sarcophagus, were hardly priceless. Once the identity of
the man in the sarcophagus became known, the news
would draw the interest of certain specialized collectors
and occultists. This odd crowd had always struck me as
rather silly, though my exposure to them was limited
and mostly through reading their outlandish and often
amateurish papers. Now I was not so sure.

In for a penny of occult supernaturalism, in for
a pound – it is one thing to ponder occult matters in

distant ancient times and quite another to admit them to your own. I had no rational explanation for what was happening around me. Until Egypt I had been skeptical of anything I could not observe, catalogue, and analyze. I had lived without benefit of faith in the unseen. Yet I could not reject Waterston's fever dream, nor could I disprove the eerie powers at work in Odji-Kek's tomb. In plain English, I was stumped. If I were going to curate this sorcerer's exhibit, I thought it might be best to subdue my own prejudices and open my mind to outré possibilities. What choice did I have?

Regarding this matter I was resolved.

However, I was not happy.

Here I had come to Egypt with such a thrill of excitement, and presently I was leaving like a thief in the night, an actual thief if the Egyptian authorities ever looked inside our six crates. But they did not. They had been bribed by my English rescuer, who also bought my passage, using Waterston dollars, on board the tramp steamer *Derceto*, with its curly-haired, tawny, Greek captain and a crew who spoke not a word of English.

We had set sail on the twentieth, the Vernal Equinox, and I grew appropriately green about the gills. After a day's journey, I had yet to establish my sea legs. I tried to console myself with the prospect of only a nine- or ten-day voyage ahead of me. Plenty of time for acclimation – ha! With any luck, we would arrive back in America before Easter. Not that I have ever been a strict Christian. I had given up churchgoing for the library and the laboratory, and I liked to work on Sundays. But I did, and still do, enjoy the holidays, especially the pagan aspects. Spring-time rites on parade. Rabbits and eggs –

fertility symbols ushering in the season of birth or, more accurately, re-birth.

All along we carried him like an egg in a basket, did we not?

Amun Odji-Kek, the golden yolk inside the shell of his sarcophagus. Now he nestled down inside the hull of the ship and waited for me to deliver him to America. I knew precisely where in the cargo hold the sarcophagus rested, the starboard bow. I felt a kind of vibration in my legs when I walked over the foredeck. This feeling of connection at one spot came despite the fact I had not witnessed the crates being loaded. Yet, I knew. Without logic, I began to sense his awareness of my exact whereabouts, too.

Did his spirit loom over me?

Nonsense, I told myself. This tethered-ness to the mummy was purely mental. I was willing to concede as much. The mummy was under my guardianship. He occupied my mind. My intellect alone might have created our bond. Yes, that could be true.

But it felt like this: *a PUSHING, originating outside my physical body, a telepathic assault. Multisensory points of attack. A cold, scaly hand touched my neck. I brushed it away. There was nothing there. My ears filled with pressure until I became stone deaf. The pressure subsided. Quick, erratic drumming in the blood – a pulse overtook my pulse. It made me nauseated (though I supposed one might chalk that up to seasickness). I noticed deep smells of waste that came and went with no hint of any source… and the queerest sensation of something which crawled inside my mouth and squirmed beneath my tongue.*

Everything lessened if I walked away from the foredeck. I felt normal again.

Aft, I found two sailors shoveling an alarming number of dead seabirds over the side of the steamer. I watched this dumb show with amazement. Scrape, scrape. Another shovelful of birds tossed over the rail. Where did the birds come from? How did they perish? Out of the sky flew answers. A dozen gulls crashed into the ship's boards; with furious thumps they snapped their necks, the little heads twisted awkwardly to one side, or tucked straight down, and their wings remained open on impact. Then the shovels scraped. The reaction of the sailors told me they had not witnessed this behavior before today.

They looked as if *I* spooked them.

I saw grayish white arcs gliding in the wind. More birds were following our wake, swooping low and drawing closer.

I could not watch.

The interior of the steamer was a narrow warren of darkly paneled, ill-lit passageways. A wordless sailor showed me my living quarters for the next week and a half, a man-sized shelf essentially, with a little cubby for personal belongings and a moth-eaten privacy curtain. I wanted to spend as little time closed in there as possible, and hopefully all of it asleep. When he left me, I went about inspecting the rest of the ship. It took no time to discover its finiteness.

I had no access to the cargo compartments.

The galley effused an aroma of garlic and cuttlefish, which I might have sampled had we not hit rough seas coincidental to our intersection with the prime meridian. A persistent Levanter wind battered us through the Strait of Gibraltar; rain, mists, fog – these three overlapped interchangeably. I poked my head above deck for fresh air, and returned soaked through to the skin, feeling no hunger or encouragement, as we pushed into the long North Atlantic deep.

Chilled, I retired to my musty berth, where the heat of the boilers soon had me shucking out of my clothes. We sailed with less than a full crew. The bunks around mine were unoccupied. The crewmen slept in a different section of the ship, on the opposite side of the engine room. Coal-fed machinery turned the great screw propeller underwater, and if it did not falter, neither did its hellish noise. I hung one leg out of my bunk to mitigate the sense of interment. Our mummies enjoyed more spaciousness.

I read the tattered telegram again.

Dreaming of your danger… an emissary… Godsspeed…

Exhaustion overcame discomfort, and I slept.

Nightmares of premature burial. I woke with a start in utter darkness, and, forgetting where I was, in a state of half-awake panic, shot my arms upward, encountering the sealed lid of my coffin, which I soon realized was only the empty bunk above me. My wrists shivered with pain. I rolled out of bed and hit the floor, elbows and knees landing hard.

"Damn it!"

From that vantage point, with my senses sharpening into focus, I spotted a sliver of moonlight at the end of the passage. Curious, I drew on my trousers and coat, stuffed my sockless feet into my unlaced and still sand-filled shoes, and thrust my hand searchingly into my bag to rummage for my pipe and tobacco pouch. I had all but given up the nighttime habit of smoking while at work in Egypt – so dry was my mouth, so constantly racing my brain.

Life at sea had rekindled my taste for a good pipeful.

Besides, I was wide awake and needed to chase away the demons.

The ship seemed steadier. Perhaps I had gained my sea legs while asleep. Trailing four fingertips along the wall of empty bunks, I made it to the stairway. The handrail under the moonlight appeared dipped in mercury.

Grabbing hold, I ascended the steps.

Night had transformed the wooden deck into an assortment of metallic grays. Iron, lead, cobalt, zinc – I counted them all among the boards, the mast, the ladders, and the shed-like wheelhouse. Our steamship seemed to be constructed of heavy elements afloat on a rippling ebon ocean. The air was cold but not unpleasant. I gladly traded the oily steam bath below for the seaweed salty tang. The winds had quieted, and I could see the puffs of my breath in front of my face. Our forward progress produced a breeze. I turned up my collar and fastened a few buttons as I walked to the foredeck. Peering up, I saw the first quarter moon, and a cloudless sky hoarding stars.

What a spectacle the constellations were.

Stargazing, I went to the rail and began to pack my pipe bowl. It was only as I stepped back from the breeze to shield my match that I realized I had crossed the deck without feeling the odd vibration I had registered each time before, and which I was convinced synchronized with the location of the sarcophagus in the cargo hold.

Now I paced back and forth and felt nothing.

"Hmph," I muttered, "all in my mind apparently." I turned to smoke at the rail.

And saw I was not alone on deck.

My midnight companion stood in the shadow of one of the lifeboats. That was why I had missed seeing him before. The prow of the little raft obscured him.

"Hello," I said. "The weather's much improved. Chilly, but it feels good compared to the stuffiness down below. Not raining at least. We can be thankful for that."

He said nothing.

Under most circumstances I am not one to pursue conversation with strangers, especially those who signal their hesitancy to talk. Unmarried and with no prospects for marriage on the horizon, I was quite used to being alone. At home I had few friends, and most of them were not known for their repartee. My only real friend in recent months, Hakim, had just been murdered, and I felt partially responsible for that. What did I have to think about but my alleged career? What was my career but servitude to the whims of Montague P. Waterston? A man I had never even met!

Then I must confess, more than anything else on that March night at sea, I was feeling lonely. How I wished for a traveling partner, someone to distract me, to help pass the time, and keep me from feeding upon my thoughts, if only for a few minutes while I smoked my pipe.

"HELLO," I said again louder, much louder, and I was immediately embarrassed.

Still the other did not reply.

Ha ha! I laughed to myself. I had the solution.

He was a foreigner. A sailor, no doubt, as I saw no passengers on this voyage who were not sailors, other than me, and come to think of it, since I had awakened, I saw no sailors either. Perhaps he was on night watch. Was he not allowed to talk, or was he unable to understand? Either case would account for his silence.

What was I doing trying to chit chat with a man who spoke another tongue?

I say, *man*, but looking back, I could not see enough to judge who, or what, it was.

He was a shape.

A shape that did not talk and had not yet moved.

Judging by his bulkiness, I took him to be wearing a great-coat, tight and evidently poorly patched. Even in the shadows I could see holes. A long gray scarf wrapped several times around his head and face. The loose, frazzled end dangled off the boat side as he leaned forward, staring out over the glittering waves.

I stepped closer to the shape, determined to get a better look at him. As I said, the night was cold but not so cold to be bundled like an Esquimau.

Now the shape did move. Not to retreat, spider-like, into the dark crevice under the lifeboat, as I expected at this point, rather it pulled away from the rail, unbent, and stood tall. Quite tall he was. He continued to show me his back and not speak.

"Sir, I do not mean to disturb you in your duties..."

Foolishness – I started again.

"I mean, sir, firstly do you speak English?"

He did not turn his shrouded head.

But he answered my question with a low, wheezing chuckle.

Hearing this sound broke the tension between us, until I noticed that no cloud of exhalation formed around his face.

I was, on the other hand, making quite a fog.

Iciness zipped along my spine. I glanced toward the pilot house, thinking I would run there if I had to, and wondering how fast I could traverse the distance.

I risked one look back at the shape.

He – *It* – was gone.

I heard no splash.

There were two men behind the glossy black windows of the pilot house. I told them what I had seen. A man, maybe a man, who was there one moment, then not.

"Did you see him?" I asked. "Did you see the man who went overboard?"

They did not completely comprehend my words, but they did understand the meaning of overboard. We looked past the stern. We circled round. The sailors conducted a quick head count. All hands accounted for. No sailor on board matched my description. *A huge man, tattered coat, a very long scarf.* The captain, disturbed from his sleep, regarded me with annoyance and later, pity. I believe he thought me mad.

"Very well, then," I said. "I am mistaken. Good night to you all."

Blankness in their stares, and as I walked off, I could not mistake their snickering.

On my way back to my bunk, I passed by the lifeboat and saw something I had not noticed earlier. I crouched and rubbed it between my fingers. A trail sparkled on the deck, leading from the lifeboat to the cargo hatch. My legs were vibrating.

A trail of sand.

11
NEW YORK, NEW ORLEANS

New Year's Day, 1920
Manhattan, New York City

Let me pause here in my tale, dear Reader, to wish you a Happy New Year. It is quiet in the offices of the Waterston Institute as the calendar turns to welcome a new decade. I am alone and adding another log to the fire. Likely as not, those who might worry about me will assume I decided to sleep at the lab, which I often do when I work late. I have drunk a fair bit of whisky, but I am an accomplished imbiber and feel none the worse for wear. I feel quite good, relaxed finally, though I think the telling of my tale – letting the weight of it go – may have had as much to do with my state of mind as this fine bourbon. Time is a funny thing, funnier the older I get. And by funny I do not mean whimsical. I mean strange.

Where was I?

On the *Derceto*, yes, in the briny Atlantic, sand on my fingertips...

Perhaps it is not so odd to find sand on a boat. Yet

this sand did not feel like it had been scuffed up from a sunny Mediterranean beach. I know that makes no sense. I even had gritty remnants of the desert stuck inside my own shoes. But somehow this sand, this glittery track on the deck boards, felt *wrong*, out of its proper time and place. Time again. It changes us, and it changes on us. It moves differently for different people. It passes not at all the same in foreign lands either, and if you have traveled much you know what I mean. Time changes over time, too. Time in the Manhattan of 1920 is not what it was in 1888. I should know, I was there then, and I am here now. Today everyone rushes around like they have escaped the Bellevue insane pavilion. I suppose a seasoned man will always feel the current of time speeding around him as he struggles not to sink in the flow. I'm beginning to sound morbid.

Now then, where am I?

I am here in the comfort of my office, dusting bits of log off my trousers and refilling my glass. I am looking out at a nighttime Central Park where the falling, mounding snow fills up the park like ice cream scoops.

Also, I am at sea soon before I saw the cliff-like skyline of New York, before I met my fate, before death and love and the deathless one converged and forever altered–

But I am getting ahead of myself. Let's go back then, you and me...

New York.

The port... less than a month after a blizzard ravaged the city... the Great White Hurricane of 1888...

I am about to see the clipper ships in the crowded harbor, the New York and Brooklyn Bridge connecting the boroughs, spanning the East River, a density of buildings, of milling immigrants, business and crime, new life created in a New World.

New York harbor, 1888

A pilot boat met us.

We could not yet see land. A week had elapsed since my nighttime encounter with the apparition – what I believed to be Amun Odji-Kek's spirit manifestation. (*Or was it a stubborn remnant of the suffocating burial nightmare that had earlier awoken me? A waking dream perhaps, a hallucination inspired by over-breathing the engine fumes? Did I create as well as witness it?*) Skepticism engaged, nagged at me. I tried to dismiss the incident but the best I could manage was to ignore it. The sea at night plays upon the nervous mind I told myself. Men see things around big water. Let it be.

The rest of my voyage was notable because nothing unusual happened. I was bored and eager to see my homeland again. I wanted to meet Waterston's emissary at the dock and talk to someone in English, to walk on solid American ground, and be done with oceans for a while. I wanted a mug of beer.

Mostly, I wanted to open the sarcophagus and examine the mummy.

When we came into sight of land, the city coastline appeared much as I remembered it when I left for my expedition many months ago. Clipper ships crowded the harbor and the marvelous East River Bridge loomed above. Evidence of the historic snowstorm that had killed several hundred people weeks earlier, paralyzing the Eastern seaboard and creating general havoc, was disappearing fast. Most of the snow had melted away into slush and fog. Though I was ignorant of the storm's passage at the time – no newspaper delivery at sea – I could not miss the terrible damage to the piers. Windy water is a great ram. The tide bullied many chaotic shipwrecks even as it filled them with its inescapable opaque weight. Damp salty wood, wet bricks, streets gray and glistening – whatever did not slurp against pilings flooded down the gutters to the bay.

The sun was out. The air smelled of rotting fish.

We docked but could not go ashore until we had been cleared. The authorities needed to make certain we were not trafficking in contraband or smallpox. I smoked my pipe, enjoying the hustle and bustle of so much life. Comfort there, undeniable reality. My heart swelled while in sympathy with my countrymen. Here was civilization at work, Western civilization, making order from chaos. The idea pleased me to no end at the time. My love of Egypt was no less strong but far more complicated than it had been before going there. Returning to the West was coming home. Here was a world I could trust – or so I believed after landing ashore in New York on that crisp, clear, and sunny day.

Two men broke from the dockside crowd and headed for the *Derceto*'s gangplank.

Minutes later they were aboard. Serious men, beefy in their somber jackets, their eyes took in everything and their faces gave up nothing. The taller one had rounded stooping shoulders, but otherwise they might have been cousins, so alike were they in both bearing and physical attitude. The shorter man passed an envelope to the captain, which the seafarer pried apart, thumbing the contents, before he stuffed it in his pocket.

Then the captain pointed at me.

I had the awful impression I was about to be arrested.

The duo cornered me against the rail. I looked deeply into the frigid water. No jumping.

"My name is Kittle," the shorter man said, "and this is Detective Staves."

"Good morning. How are New York's Finest today?"

The men exchanged glances. Kittle said, "We're not policemen, Mr Hardy. We're private detectives from the Pinkerton Agency. We were hired to protect you."

I frowned. "Are you Waterston's emissaries?"

Another unspoken communication passed between them.

"Not sure what you mean, sir."

"My benefactor, Montague Waterston, sent a telegram before I absconded from Egypt. In it he said his emissary would meet me at the New York dock. Therefore, I ask, are you his emissaries?"

"Uhh… no, sir. I mean, yes and no."

"Yes and no? Were you sent to meet me when I disembarked or not?"

"You aren't disembarking, sir."

My feet suddenly lacked a certain degree of stability and I spread my legs to counteract the disequilibrium. I saw the dock moving away. Rather, we were moving from the dock. The water widened. The *Derceto* had set sail again.

Kittle said, "Your benefactor sends his sincerest apologies. Unfortunately, this change in plans could not be avoided. I can't tell you more, only that it was not safe to bring the cargo ashore here today. Staves and I will guard the shipment until it reaches its destination. We'll watch over you too, of course."

Good-bye, Manhattan. Good-bye, bridge. Good-bye, dry land and wet beer.

Both men were wearing Colt .45 revolvers on their hips under the flaps of their jackets. Staves carried a leather rifle case. It was their only baggage.

"Might I ask where the hell we're going?"

"We're catching a train."

"Are there no trains in New York, Mr Kittle?"

"The train we're taking waits in New Orleans."

New Orleans harbor

Kittle and Staves proved to be companionable if unimaginative. Like me, they had never met Waterston face to face. To us he was a name, a signature at the bottom of a letter, and a source of funds. Kittle informed me it was a woman – Waterston's secretary, in the flesh – who appeared at their offices and paid for the guard services. Perhaps it says something about my anxious state of mind that steaming off the coastal islands of South Carolina, I wondered if Kittle and Staves worked for Waterston at all, or if they had kidnapped me and re-routed the mummies to the bayous as part of a clever ransom plot, and if my odyssey might end in the swollen belly of an alligator. But it was obvious they were not clever men. Stalwart, plainspoken if called upon, reticent if not. I do not think Staves said more to me than good mornings and goodnights, except when he was practicing his marksmanship off the stern by shooting those suicidal seabirds haunting the *Derceto*'s wake. He would call out which target he was aiming for prior to each shot, pull the trigger, and invariably the chosen bird exploded. It was a quick drop among the bull sharks who submerged with the carcasses post-haste. They never seemed nefarious, not these two honest gents.

"Do you enjoy shooting birds?" I asked Staves one afternoon on the poop deck.

"No more or less than shooting anything else," he said.

I nodded and puffed at my pipe. "Is there any sport to it?"

"Sport? I reckon they could fly above or below my shot. A bird on the wing is no easy target, and from a moving boat…?" He shrugged.

"But they can't dodge a bullet. The bullet is too fast."

"I don't know any animal speedier than hot lead."

"Then the sport is not whether or not they can outfly or outwit you. It's only a matter of your aim. If you choose a certain bird and your aim is true, then the bird dies." I removed my pipestem from my mouth and pointed it at Staves. "You are the decider. The responsibility of their deaths lies solely on your shoulders. And no one else's."

Staves cradled the rifle in the hinge of his elbow and turned to frown at me.

"They're birds," he said.

"Nonetheless, their lives must mean something to them."

"They're flying into the stern to bash their brains in."

I nodded solemnly. "Yes, these were – are – particularly strange birds."

Returning from his latest patrol around the perimeter of the steamer, Kittle cheerfully joined us. "Is everything well with you two gentlemen?"

"Mr Hardy wants to talk about dead birds," Staves said.

"Not at all," I said. "We were discussing philosophy, I thought."

Kittle, curious if he should be alarmed, asked, "What is a philosophy of dead birds?"

The gulls that Staves had paused in assassinating began to arrive at the stern with neck-snapping speed. Soft thumps, most of them followed by a fluttery spasm of feathers. We three observed the flock's disturbing behavior. Broken gulls lay scattered whitely at our feet.

"Have either of you ever killed a man?" I said.

"Yessir" and "yes" were their answers.

I'm certain the causes were justified. I didn't ask for more information.

"You live with it, then?"

"No other choice," Staves said. Kittle agreed.

"What about you, sir?" he asked.

"I, myself, have merely gotten other men killed."

Kittle absently pushed the dead birds into a pile with his boot while Staves reloaded.

I retreated to the bow alone to finish my smoke.

Cruising into the port of New Orleans, I could almost smell the malaria. The miasmatic air weighed upon us with its velvety green decay. I feared the mummies would turn to soap and dissolve. I supervised the transfer of the crates from the *Derceto*'s hold to our train.

One of Waterston's poker-playing cohorts owned the

Southern Pacific railroad. He had added a special car to the end of a line of standard coaches: a glossy black mammoth, dreary in design, but spacious enough to transport us and the six mummies to Los Angeles in seclusion. We need not worry about mixing with other passengers. We had no bother with changing trains either. Ours was to be a long, private ride out West.

We had an hour until departure.

Kittle and Staves stood sentinel over the midnight carriage to California.

"She's a black beauty," I said, indicating the train car. "We'll be like a permanent shadow following the rest of the train."

"I've never ridden in a private car," Kittle said. "Is she up to your usual standards?"

I had never ridden in a private car either, but the detectives didn't need to know that.

"She'll do," I said. "Care for a little ramble? We'll be cooped up on that train for a long time, I'm afraid."

"No, sir, but thank you. We are on duty and need to watch the mummies," Kittle said.

"If they get up and start walking, make sure you fetch me."

Neither man answered. I wasn't sure if they understood I was joking. Their seriousness gave me a chuckle, but at the same time I felt a peculiar tickle at the nape of my neck. I wondered if I had carried a fever home with me from my foreign travels. But the sensation soon passed. I decided to stretch my legs in the city and do a little shopping. I bought a bottle of absinthe, a few cigars, and a tin of perique blended tobacco.

It is unfair to judge a city in so brief a visit, and even

more suspect to make statements about its culture by exclusively studying the wharf and those local amenities known to cater to men's vices, but New Orleans did not feel like the United States to me. The languor, the smooth sensuality, the wild scents of the place, and the half-dreamy, half-violent gazes of its citizens – I think the French missionaries and Spaniards of old must have lost themselves in a fit of tropical delirium. Smoky-eyed Indians and Africans nursed them back to life. That explains the city. Or nothing does.

On my stroll back to the train depot I had the unsettling sensation I was being followed, so I changed my course – one too many turns and I found myself disoriented. As I tried to get my bearings, a figure emerged out of a doorway. I could not judge its sex or age. It was only when she spoke I knew her to be a woman. Skinny as sugarcane she was, but her dusky face glowed, and she wore drilled coins tied in the whorls of her hair. Her nostrils dilated. She tilted her face into a slant of coppery sunset. I saw her eyes were like oyster meat. A blind woman. She rolled her head on her stalk-like neck.

A necklace of cowry shells clicked.

"Ain't you dead, chile?"

I kept silent. Her question froze me in place. So did her gluey stare.

"Somebody bring you back for no good?" She laughed deep in her throat and stepped into the street, a terrifying smile creasing in my direction, as she swayed to and fro. I thought she might offer herself to me for money. Nothing about her appearance told me so. But it was that kind of street I had ventured down. Such an offer did not happen. She leaned on a stick of intricately carved wood.

Her hands were as large as a man's. Fingers stuffed into gold rings.

"What you doin' out before dark?" she asked. "The sun don't like you, no?"

I heard melodious amusement in her words, as if we shared a secret. When I did not respond, she frowned and closed the distance separating us. Her nose crinkled. She ducked her head, lifted it slowly.

She was *sniffing* me.

"I smell the grave on you, *cher*. Did they cut out your tongue, or are you shy?"

I wanted to run, but her movement was so odd I stood transfixed.

She tucked her face into the crook of my neck and inhaled deeply. I heard the air suck inside her like wind down a chimney. Then she stopped and her mouth fell open.

The witchy woman leapt backward as if she had been scalded.

"Stay away, jackal!" Her walking stick broke in two pieces. The joint hid a sword that tapered to a thin, nasty point. She jabbed the blade in my general direction.

"You mistake me for someone else," I said, doing my best to remain calm.

"Bokor!" she shouted. "Sorcerer, get back!"

She slashed, retreating farther. She reached back with her free hand and found the gap she was searching for. Backing into her doorway, she hissed and slammed the door in my face. I put my ear to the center of it, and felt the hot, peeling paint against my flushed skin.

Inside, her sobs grew frantic. "Please, leave me alone! I did not know it was you!"

I did not want to distress her further, so I obeyed.

I had never visited New Orleans before, and surely had never met this disturbed woman. Shaken, I departed. Around the next corner I glimpsed a column of train smoke. Fiery red sparks lit it from within. I followed that sign in the sky to the station and soon observed the now familiar forms of Kittle and Staves staying near the train like a couple of well-trained, loyal mastiffs. It might have been the frightened voodoo woman setting me on edge, or maybe the heat put my mind onto strange and worrying paths. Regardless, upon returning to the station, I purchased a pair of tickets from the stationmaster.

I sauntered over to our private car.

Kittle was pacing along the platform. Through the open carriage door, I saw Staves had already climbed on board, sitting beside the row of crates, his uncased rifle resting on his knees. The heat inside the black car was stifling. Sweat popped from his hairline.

"Tell me, Kittle, did I mention the mummy's curse?" I asked.

"No, you didn't."

"Perhaps I did and you forgot."

"I wouldn't forget a thing like that."

"Oh, they are awful stories… superstitions, I assume. They say a man who sleeps in the same room with the mummy will never sire children. His future dies."

Kittle raised his eyebrows. "Really?"

"I'm afraid so. His seed is somehow curdled. Well, to be blunter, he can't sow the seed at all. Cursed with perpetual softness, some say rot. Dreadfully gruesome stuff."

"Rot?" Staves asked. He was standing in the carriage doorway now. His rifle, firmly gripped in one hand, pointed at the platform.

I nodded, bit the end of my cigar, and spit it on the boards.

"Is there a cure?" Kittle had stopped his pacing.

"None whatsoever. Prevention is the key. It's a question of keeping one's distance from the dead man's magic. In Egypt, the workmen never sleep in the tombs."

"I don't think I could either," Staves said, stepping onto the platform to join us. He wiped his brow with his sleeve.

"The origin of the curse probably stems from disease. The dead carry every kind of blight and pestilence. Who knows what lingers inside those glorified pine boxes, eh?"

Kittle and Staves turned, staring into the carriage.

I lit up and blew my smoke at their backs.

Staves coughed. He stepped away from the open door.

"Gentlemen, I have a proposition for you. I haven't had a good night's rest since I left home months ago. Privacy's the thing. I can't bear sleeping near other people. Every toss and turn, each breath and sigh wakes me. Would you fellows mind letting me ride alone with the mummies? I have taken the liberty of purchasing two tickets and–"

"That's no problem at all," Staves said.

He snatched the tickets as soon as I slid them from my pocket.

Kittle hesitated, and I thought Staves might use the rifle butt on him right there.

"You could ride one car up and sit at the windows," I

said. "Of course, whenever the train stops, I'd expect you to come back here and stand guard."

"We could do that," Kittle said.

"I caution you to remain generally alert. That is your mission."

"You can count on us," Staves said.

"It's settled then. I accept all responsibility for this decision. But I expect no trouble either." The train whistle blew out a piercing shriek. "Stay sharp. Here you go now." I gave each man a cigar to mitigate any second thoughts.

It worked.

"What about you, sir? Aren't you worried about your… future?" Kittle asked.

"I am an Egyptologist. My concern is solely with the past."

Both men knit their brows as they trotted forward one coach, the speediness in their strides told me they were relieved not to be spending four days entombed in a rolling mausoleum with six dead Egyptians and a mad scholar. Myself, I had no choice.

I finished my cigar waving at the curtains of mosquitoes that descended during the twilight hour. If I were going to die I was determined not to take anyone else with me. Flicking away the well-sucked stub of tobacco, I watched its spark redden, and then fizzle in a ditch. I climbed aboard and secured the door behind me.

The train lurched.

A uniformed Negro entered the car from the train.

"I'm Thomas, sir. I'll be your porter. If there's anything you need, if you have any questions, just ask me." He appeared as tidy as I felt disheveled. I stared absently counting his polished jacket buttons until I blinked.

"At the moment I am quite content," I said, adding, "tired, but content."

"I'll bring you a drink if you'd like. Or I can make down your berth if you're ready to get to sleep." He had a pleasant voice and a soothing, yet confident manner.

"Sleep is the farthest thing from my mind. A drink of water now and something stronger later would do nicely."

"Very good," he said.

We were on our way. Swampland fled past the windows. Soon the whistle screamed like a banshee over the marshes. Saltwater lay black between thatches of grass and pods of humpbacked islands. Out of the wet sprung skeletal trees, at trackside some waved as if hoping for a ride. Moon and stars pricked the bayou with silver needles.

The city lights of New Orleans faded.

I had made up the story of the curse. But was I afraid to sleep with the mummy?

Partly... curious mostly, foolhardy...

Something I could not explain – the witchy woman had mumbled a word through the door, the same word Hakim used when naming the sleeper inside the sarcophagus.

"Kek," she said, repeating it over and over. "Kek, Kek, Kek..."

12
THE TRAIN

April 3rd, 1888
Southern Pacific RR's Sunset Route, east of El Paso, Texas

I lay in my bunk, awake for the second straight night. The clack-clack-clack of the train and the West Texas heat were not to blame. Not entirely. A cotton sheet wound taut around my legs. I kicked loose from it. Though I had removed my shoes, I wore my clothes. They were sour with sweat, but so was every one of the suits I had packed. I rolled over to my side. My shirt collar pinched and my trousers twisted. Sleep refused to come. I thought I knew why. I sat up and fiddled with the lamp at my bedside until a smoking bud of light bloomed. I was alone in the cavernous private railcar. The Texas night slid by on the windows like oil.

I was experiencing an attack of guilt (*my friend, Hakim, my workers – all dead*).

I gazed into the shadows at the other end of the car but saw only a void.

Before too long I looked away.

The daytime heat had bled the varnish smell out from

the carved wood of the decorated car and its furnishings. The air felt close and my chest grew tight.

Here I was in the lap of luxury.

Yet I felt like a man trapped in a box for days.

And I was, of course, if you considered the boxcar surrounding me a *box*, which I did. It only took one trip in another box – a child's-coffin-sized steamer trunk I dragged around my grandmother's attic, screaming my head off at the age of four, unable to escape, my cries muffled, knees bloodied – to bring about a lifelong hatred of enclosure.

Since then I had been enclosed in other, less obvious ways.

The comforts I, for the moment, enjoyed came at the behest of Montague Pythagoras Waterston of Los Angeles, a gold magnate turned sickly, bedridden, amateur occultist. My expedition was his doing. He was the mover, I was the one moved. I disliked being played like a game piece. No one forced me to sign onto this journey. True enough. It was my choice. But at what cost? I was a rich man's surrogate, and had been for going on three years (how time flies!), on two continents, and across the wide blue expanse of an ocean. I had never met my benefactor, though I expected to in less than three days. Thoughts of meeting him gave me much excitement, and more than an equal portion of anxiety.

Who was he?

Who was I since I had become his instrument?

The train jolted me out of my revelry. I glanced at my pocket watch: one minute past midnight. We were taking a curve at good speed. The floor tilted and righted itself with a wiggle. On my feet, bracing my arms against the window frame for balance, I pressed my nose to the glass and saw – much closer than I would have liked – high sandstone cliffs, taller than the train. Moonbeams chiseled down the mountain chute.

Another bump, another sideways shove.

The wheels shrieked to make my molars ache. Outside, a shower of brassy sparks lit the rock walls, revealing a blood-red stain running parallel to the tracks. Natural geologic phenomenon, I guessed. But it did not feel natural. I snapped my head toward the darkness at the other end of the railcar.

I saw instead the opened tomb. The dead we left behind, and the dead we stole. I was restless, feeling vaguely criminal, although I had done nothing wrong; or nothing purposefully, intentionally wrong. However, I could not shake off the impression that I was somehow being used in ways I, myself, would not choose if only I knew a little more than I did.

Kittle and Staves were sleeping better in their seats in the public car. At least I hoped so, for their sakes. I wondered if I would stay awake for the whole trip west. I found my way to the bunk and lowered the lamplight.

From the soft bed of a rich man I watched the abyss.

April 4th, 1888
The Rio Grande Rift

I heard a knocking on the door connected to the train. I looked at my pocket watch. One minute past midnight. The exact time I had read from those hands hours ago, or so it seemed to me. I wound the stem and pressed the dial to my ear, the watch chain tickling my jaw. The damned thing had stopped. Outside, the night was pitchy. I bent my head and discovered the moon stuck up like a horn between the Juarez Mountains.

More knocking. I put the watch away.

"Enter," I said.

I observed the door open and close. But I saw no one come through. The crated mummies who shared the car with me – in fact, they dominated it – also blocked most of the doorway from my sight. Soon a rattling of plates and silverware traveled around the left end of the cargo, and along with it came a Chinese boy, no older than ten, dressed in a blue denim jacket that fell past his knees, and silky black pajamas. He was carrying a tray and upon it a carafe of freshly boiled coffee, a single porcelain cup and saucer, a teaspoon, and a bowl of sugar cubes. He wore a skullcap. His braided pigtails rested on his shoulders. The coffee smelled wonderful. I saw his eyes dart to the crates. His hands were trembling. He stopped at my table and waited with his chin tucked down at his chest.

"What do we have here?"

"Mr Thomas saw your light on and thought you might want some coffee."

"I do, I do." I relieved him of his tray. He filled my cup, his eyes straying back to the other end of the car.

"No sugar, thank you. And what is your name, son?"

"Yong Wu, sir."

I picked up the cup. "You are definitely the youngest steward I've ever met."

My weak attempt at a pun on his name went unnoticed.

"Oh, I'm not a steward. I only help Mr Thomas."

"You're doing a fine job." I sipped the coffee. "Don't be nervous. Do your parents work on the train?"

"My parents are not alive," he said in a quiet voice.

I felt terrible pity for the poor child, and I thought I knew now why he was so upset by the crates. Someone must have told him there were coffins inside.

"They can't hurt you," I said.

His eyes shot up at me in a panic I found perplexing.

"My parents would never hurt me."

I frowned. "I'm quite certain they would not. But I wasn't talking about your parents. I was talking about the bodies inside those crates."

"Mr Thomas says they're from Egypt. The Egyptians have a powerful mojo. Their witches can make the dead walk."

So, the porter had spooked him with stories of living mummies. He had also likely filled his head with hoodoo, hexes, haints, and tricksters. I wanted to tell the boy there was nothing to be bothered about in those legends, but he seemed awfully agitated as it was, and I worried he would see clearly through my half-truth. I elected to change the subject.

"Your English is excellent for an immigrant."

"I was born in San Francisco. My father was a schoolteacher before he went to work for the railroads. He taught me to read and write. Mr Thomas gives me books passengers sometimes leave on the train."

"Your father was a railroad man?"

The boy nodded.

"He worked on the tracks. My mother cooked for the laborers. They were… attacked one night in the desert. I help out Mr Thomas now. He treats me very well."

I had heard stories about Chinese workers getting killed by Anglos or Mexicans who resented the cheap labor competition, and, of course, the railroad companies did not care if a few Chinamen died, as long as the tracks got laid. It was an ugly business. Here I was rehashing the tragedy of this little boy's orphaning, and he was just bringing me coffee to help me through the night. He looked tired, like he never slept, in fact.

"You go back to bed now, Yong Wu. Don't let Mr Thomas shock you with his tales. The Egyptians had a special talent for preserving the dead. Naturally, you can understand how rumors of bringing the dead back to life might get started." I waited to see if he believed me, or if he could detect my own doubts lurking behind my words.

"The dead back to life… yes… that would be bad."

The train shifted and the crates creaked.

The boy stepped closer to me, but his attention stayed on those boxes. The shipping containers were hulking in the smoky light. Dozens of nails hammered into the pine stared out unblinking. Each crate had been bound with chains and secured with a padlock as wide as my hand. I patted Yong Wu on the back and felt him shiver.

"Go on. It's all right. Tell Mr Thomas I appreciate your service. The sun will be up before we know it. Leave the coffee. I don't think I'll be sleeping much myself."

Yong Wu left the way he came, his head swiveling to keep watch over the crates as he passed them. He shut me in again with my desert memories and the dark cargo I had brought up out of the sands. I realized he and I were no different, really. I had been watching those crates with eagle eyes ever since I sailed away from the shores of Alexandria.

Watching and waiting…
Here finally, despite my prediction, I slept.

13

TRAIN ROBBERS

Approx. 3 miles east of Yuma, Arizona Territory
April 5th, 1888

Morning. Dawn broke a hot runny egg across the horizon behind us. Red membrane webbed the cloudless bulge of light. In a few minutes it would be impossible to look straight at it without going blind.

To the south: a dust devil rose.

I sponged my dripping brow and opened the carriage windows as far as they would allow. Smoky wind at the back of the train burned my eyes. Swallowing the last cool dregs of the coffee Yong Wu had brought me during the night, my throat was crackling, and my face puckered like paper about to ignite as I poked my head outside.

How many days on a train before a man will consider suicide?

I was there, friend.

Egypt. New York. New Orleans. All were as distant to me now as planets, as dreams. For I knew I had been on this damned train forever. While the heat turned from humid to desert dry to hellish, I roasted with the already dead. Much more of this sweat-boxing and I swore I would pry a coffin and join the corpses if only for the shade.

The door at the other end of the carriage opened. I expected to see the porter or Yong Wu with my breakfast. But it was Kittle, looking haggard and unshaven. The car rocked and he brushed his hip against the crates, jumping back as if he had been clawed.

"Don't worry," I said, doing what I could to hide my smile. "I'm told the curse is less potent in the morning hours." Kittle nodded. I perceived in him an apprehension more acute than superstition or travel weariness. "Is something the matter?"

"Suspicious events, Mr Hardy, I don't know if they signal danger or not."

"Speak then. At the very least they will take my mind off this demonic heat. What's got you so worried, my good Detective?"

"Do you recall Mr Waterston's secretary?"

"I remember your mentioning she came to the Pinkerton office and hired you."

"Well, I've seen her."

"I would hope so. Otherwise your prospect of being paid is awfully slim."

"No, sir… I mean I've seen her here… this morning, on the train."

"What? You're certain it's the same woman who visited your office?"

"There's no doubt, and Mr Staves agrees. She's not the sort of lady a man easily forgets. We first spotted her last night in the dining car. She saw us too – and quickly retreated down the aisle in the opposite direction, leaving her meal untouched, and without as much as a backward glance. We found her in a seat two cars forward, though the lights were dim and she pretended to be asleep. Sunrise confirms it. She is the same woman. Staves is watching her now. Why would she be on board and keep it a secret?"

"I don't know. But we will solve the mystery by asking her. I'll follow you immediately." But I didn't follow. I lingered, my eyes fixated on the rear window and what lay moving beyond. "Tell me, Kittle, is that dust whirlwind getting closer?"

Kittle shielded his eyes and pressed nearer to the vibrating glass.

The sand cloud billowed, gliding quickly along the flat ground. Its funnel shape collapsed into a tarnished golden fog that rolled and boiled like poison. Why did I fear its progress would soon overtake ours? It was only sand after all.

The grainy curtain parted.

Riders.

Spectral humanoid blurs, and every inch snuff-colored. Gaining fast on the backs of gaunt horses. I counted six. No... more than six. The number doubled – an even dozen.

Was the train slowing down?

Kittle stepped away from the window. "Banditos. We're being robbed. They've come for the mummy's treasure."

"But there is no treasure," I said, dumbfounded.

"Tell them that." Kittle bolted past the crates. The train was slowing. Why was the train slowing? Already the riders were close enough I could see their weirdly slack, frozen faces. "I must get Staves and the rifle. Stay down, Mr Hardy, low on the floor."

At that instant: the crack of a gunshot. The rear window shattered. A tiny glass spear brushed my cheek. Blood dripped off my jaw. I sank to my knees and crawled until I wedged my body between the crates, trying to become as small a target as possible.

Kittle was gone from the carriage. The door banged loose between the cars. The sound of clacking train wheels, the wind, and the robbers' rising whoops entered freely.

I carried no weapon.

And I could no longer keep still in the cramped spot I chose for cover. As I backed out from the mummy boxes, my hand dragged over a crowbar leaning coldly where it must have fallen during the loading, behind the cargo against the back wall. I took it. Now I had something heavy to lay out thugs who invaded my compartment.

Next, my attention turned to the banging door–

I reached but failed to shut it.

Too short an arm, too far a stretch. I attempted hooking it with the bar.

A dark hand closed tightly onto the crooked iron and, by instinct more than strategy, I pulled hard and brought the bar toward me along with the off-balanced porter, Mr Thomas. Momentum carried him right into my chest and sprawling backward I went. I do not know which of us was more startled, though I am willing to bet it was me because I could not talk for several seconds but Thomas spoke on impact.

"Excuse me, Mr Har– why, you're bleeding! Are you shot?" His alarm made me question whether or not I had been shot. I checked myself all over.

"Not shot… just a scrape. Give me a hand, will you?"

The porter helped me to my feet. "The conductor's trying to stop the train and the brakeman's having a hell of a time. Not good. I hope we don't jump the track." He looked past me, worry evident on his brow. "Is the Chinese boy in here with you?"

I shook my head. "Why stop? Shouldn't we go faster?"

"But there aren't any tracks ahead. Blown up. Just a big ugly hole left in the ground." He leaned and spied out the broken window. "If that's not the necrófagos, they'll sure pass for 'em. Change my train into a butcher shop is what they aim to do, and here they come." He banged his fist in frustration above the window and several shards of glass flew away.

"Who are they? Mexicans?"

"Don't know, and don't want to find out. They show up and the blood flows. Except they can't bleed, or whatever they got inside isn't red. I've heard stories tell it both ways. They're worse than Apaches. Not least of all because you can't kill 'em."

"Say that again?"

"They don't die because death is what they love." He seemed very determined to convince me of this principle. I was baffled and frankly more unsettled by his degree of dread.

I recalled Yong Wu's telling me how the porter filled his head with spirit talk.

"So they're ghosts? Is that what you reckon?"

The porter looked at me as if I were crazy. Then he pointed to the riders.

"They aren't dead, mister. They *eat* the dead. Love them, too, like any natural man loves a woman who's alive. There's a big difference, if you don't mind me sayin'."

"Yes, of course. Not ghosts, then."

"Ghost riders would be bad, no doubt. But I'd gladly trade that cursed lot for these here. Necrófagos are too nasty. They make a man's skin crawl. Can't you feel it?"

I did not want to dwell on unpleasant specification. Thomas was telling me the robbers were cannibals and corpse defilers of the lowest grade. Indeed, that sufficed.

The train rattled and stuttered and slowed to a walking pace.

One of the necrófagos passed close enough I could see a hatchet strapped to his thigh. His deadened face, which I initially took to be as void as the faces of all the riders, was in fact hidden beneath a mask tied behind his head. I stared out again and, yes, they all wore masks. Each mask differed slightly from the others in hue or shape or decoration, but they were made alike, and fashioned from the same grisly material.

Skin.

Peeled, tanned, human skin. Thomas was more right than he knew.

They wore faces over their faces.

The same holes were there – though more like slits – to see, smell, hear and shout. That closest one, with the red-handled hatchet, saw me looking at him and he smiled through two pairs of lips. He slid the hand axe from his leg and rode on ahead.

"Where is Yong Wu?" I asked.

"I couldn't find him anywhere. I was hoping he was here with you. Last I saw him he was in the dining car, preparing the breakfast trolley. Then he was up and gone."

I did not like that news one bit. Meeting horrors directly is one thing, but contemplating a child being forced to do it is another. I had no idea how many women and children journeyed together with us that morning, but if what Thomas said about the necrófagos were true, then any number was too high to surrender without a fight.

"Are there armed guards on board this train?" I asked.

"Old Man Toleson in the mail car. He has a pistol. But he's a drunkard and will do nothing unless they try to steal his bottle of rye."

"I have two good men, Pinkerton guards – ah, here they are now."

Kittle rushed into the car with his Colt drawn. Sharp-eyed Staves marched behind him, Winchester rifle in hand, looking grim and determined. My heart lifted seeing these two ready for action. I would have felt supremely confident had it not been for the woman sandwiched between them who appeared more flushed with indignant anger than worried for her safety. Golden-haired, pink of cheek, and fashionably attired for long-distance travel – she was resisting the detectives. Kittle had a petite handprint glowing on his face. Staves' attitude mirrored that of a man ordered to seize a live bobcat.

"What's she doing here?" I asked.

"This is Waterston's secretary," Kittle said, his forehead knit in consternation. "We brought her along."

"What the devil for?"

"Good question," she said. Staves grabbed her elbow and she pulled free.

"I thought she might… *we* should ask her–"

Kittle stumbled for an answer, and then the trio literally stumbled forward as the train jerked to a final, unsettling halt.

"They'll come for us now," Thomas said to no one in particular. He stared at the floor, his shoulders slumping as if his strength were draining from him. While drawing a deep breath, he looked heavenward and mumbled a silent prayer, presumably asking for our holy deliverance.

"Can we lock this door?" I asked.

"No, the doors don't have locks."

The secretary squirmed around the crates to stand beside the largest. "Odji-Kek's sarcophagus?" she asked, rapping her knuckles against the side and putting her ear to the box to listen, oblivious to the impending danger of the robbers.

"Well, at least close the damned door," I said. Staves did just that.

"Have you seen him?" the secretary asked.

"Seen who?" I grew alarmed once I noticed the small hammer in her grip. She began to pry at the lid. It screeched. She flicked her wrist and a nail fell to the floor.

"Does he visit you in your dreams?" Her eyes flashed at me.

"What? Stop doing that!"

She kept up her assault on the sarcophagus crate, working loose the next nail.

"Get away from there!"

The secretary backed off sulkily and returned the hammer to her handbag.

Reports of gunshots and a piercing scream traveled from the direction of the engine. Then silence, except for the ticking of the wind. Kittle stuck his head out a side window. Sand scoured the length of the train. He pulled back. Grit peppered his hair.

"I can't make out a damn thing! It's worse than a blizzard."

"If they start robbing passengers from the front of the train, we will have some time to fortify our position." I tried to sound hopeful.

"Necrófagos don't rob anyone till they've killed everyone," Thomas said.

"Thank you, Thomas," I said.

"Then they can take all they want from a man and even more from a woman–"

"Enough! We are fully aware of the direness of our situation."

"What does he mean '*even more from a woman*'?" Kittle asked, rubbing his eyes.

"They lay with their corpses," the secretary answered. "But I wouldn't grant they are as choosy for partners as the good porter thinks. And tastes among men do vary."

Her comment did more to silence Kittle and Thomas than mine had.

14
ANOTHER AXE IN THE DOOR

"Exactly who are you, Miss?"

"I told you, she's Waterston's secretary. Staves and I are both absolutely–"

I interrupted Kittle, "I'm asking the lady."

She had collapsed sullenly, dramatically into one of the leather armchairs. She did not look at any of the men. Her gaze aimed outside, into the blowing sands, but she did not look there either. It was something internal she dwelled on, and whatever it was, I pitied it. Disappointment, frustration, anger – judging by her frowns, these feelings mingled and vexed her, and she would demand a toll for enduring them.

Exactly who am I?

My question was obviously turning around in her mind as she considered various answers, but what she said finally, with a mocking formality, was: "I am Montague Waterston's assistant in matters of occult interest. I manage his extensive library of rare books, papers, and illustrations. When necessary I act as his business secretary concerning affairs related to his... unique collections. Mr Waterston is quite ill, near death

I'm afraid." Here I detected genuine concern. "Of late, I handle all his correspondence."

My skin prickled.

"But you aren't–"

"Yes, that too. I am... also his daughter."

"Evangeline," as I said her name, she looked at me.

She has very green eyes, I thought. *Cat's eyes.*

"Did your father send you to spy on us?"

"No one sends me anywhere. Not even my father. That's more than can be said for you, Mr Hardy. Coming was my choice. If I had asked, Father would have forbid me to go. He doesn't know I'm here. In fact he thinks I'm still in New York shopping." She sighed. "I suppose he'll find out everything now that we've had this disaster."

"It isn't a disaster yet," I insisted. "The banditos don't know about the mummies. If they open the crates, what will they see? Coffins. That sarcophagus is too heavy for them to steal on horseback. We've only hit a bump in the road, if we can survive it."

There came a solid bump then, not in any road, but above us.

Somebody had landed on top of the carriage.

Footsteps began a slow walk toward the back. They paused over our heads.

Staves aimed his rifle, but before I could caution him to hold fire, he pulled the trigger. The noise was huge. My spine tried its best to jump out the back of my suit. Staves' bullet punched through the roof and a weight above us collapsed heavily, but no evidence of a body rolled past the windows. Burnt gunpowder hazed the room.

A sunbeam shined down through the hole.

"Storm's blowin' itself out," Thomas said, as the windows lightened.

All eyes stayed fastened to the ceiling. Ten ears hearkened for any sound.

"I think you got him," Kittle said, at last. He clapped his partner on the shoulder.

Staves smiled.

We all exhaled our relief, nodding in agreement at his marksmanship.

Then Thomas shouted, "Up there!"

The bullet hole went dark, and a long, gummy gray finger twisted through.

It wiggled, intelligently if you could call it that, and it made me wonder if the exposed flesh could somehow sense we were watching. Or, in fact, if it somehow watched us back.

"Son of a–!" Kittle fired his Colt .45. Once, twice – the finger snapped off and, hitting a wall, tumbled into Evangeline's lap.

Kittle squeezed another shot into the upper boards.

"Easy," Staves said. He put up his hand. "Don't waste ammunition."

Evangeline had not moved. She slipped on a pair of lace gloves – they opened into white ruffles at her wrists – and picked up the finger. Pinching it by its overgrown and mossy nail, more of a talon actually, she inspected the severed digit.

"It smells bad."

"Of course it does," I said. "It's been blown off."

"No, it smells *old*. Rotten." She prodded, stroked, and gave a not too gentle pinch. "It feels wrong as well – all cool and waxy, like a candle."

Inquiry ended, she tossed the finger out the window.

Thomas said, "Look at that! Not a drop of blood. I told you they don't bleed like us." The porter stepped under the hole in the ceiling. "Where's the damn blood at?" he shouted.

The bullet hole closed up a second time, but now it was a gun barrel doing the plugging. The gun barked downward, close enough to scorch the porter's uniform. An angry red fountain lifted his cap. The blast unhinged his jawbone, which tried to work in disbelief until his eyes rolled like two ivory balls and he slumped to the floor, dead.

Kittle emptied his revolver over our heads.

Staves followed the retreating footsteps with a line of hot flying lead that perforated the roof but had little or no effect on the rooftop walker, for the next sound we heard was someone dropping outside the door and decoupling our car from the train.

Evangeline and I dragged poor Thomas into a corner. She covered his face with his blood-soaked cap, opened his jacket, and unbuttoned his shirt. I watched as she retrieved a small vial from her handbag; in it amber liquid wobbled with the consistency of oil – a quick shake released bits of herb from the sediment. She dabbed the vial's stopper along the dead man's neck and chest, leaving behind a weedy aromatic scent.

"What are you doing?"

"What little I can to keep them off him," she said.

Kittle shakily reloaded from his pocket. Staves shouldered his rifle, taking aim at the door, beyond which the slithering clink and clank of metal had long since ceased.

Minutes – though they seemed like hours – later, the train began to reverse, and then with a bump and a rough jolt it pulled forward again, but without us attached.

I dared not stick my head outside for a curious look.

Horses… I heard horses.

The four of us raced to join Thomas on the floor, below the window level.

"I don't like this," Kittle said. "What're they waiting for?"

My thoughts turned to ingress and egress. Where could the necrófagos come in, and where could we go out? I waited for the horrid sham faces to press at the windows. I wondered if they could smell Thomas' fresh corpse or the oil Evangeline used on him.

The carriage had four doors. The two large center sliding doors for loading baggage – how we got the crates aboard – were padlocked from outside. The conductor had the only key. The rear access led to a balcony, a hip-high iron railing, and gated steps going down to the left or right. The third doorway had connected formerly with the train. Kittle chose to open that one just a crack. The train had moved but not far.

"If the tracks are missing, where do they expect to go?"

I had no answer for Kittle, nor as it proved did I need one.

A voice called, "Hello? Won't you come out, gentlemen? Please, please join us."

I was surprised to hear a necrófago speaking at all, let alone words I understood, and doubly surprised at the calm civility of the request.

Kittle nudged the door with his boot, his .45 pistol

upraised for any trouble.

The door slammed shut.

Chuuunk! An axe blade burst the wood above Kittle's head. He threw himself down and curled on his side. Inches of steel, a gleaming edge – pull, squeak, pull – and the blade jerked free. Wood splinters framed the crack. Shadow blurred it. Then an eye and a circle of rouged cheek filled the gap, looking left looking right. The eye vanished.

"I'm fine," Kittle said through crossed arms. The pistol lay under him.

The voice, again.

"Amigos? Use the back door, no? And come out please so very, very slow and one at a time. Your hands are holding up to the sky, yes? You do this now. We wait."

The English was imperfect, the diction languorous and slurred, as if it came from farther away than a Mexican train robber's mouth. The speaker was not our axe man. He sat on a horse out there somewhere behind the train. I looked for him. The sun's white fireball floated up from the desert and stole the vapor from my breath.

"I can't see anything… just awful, terrible brightness," I said.

"Stay here and all they have to do is to keep shooting until we're dead. I don't need another axe in the door to tell me when it's time to leave." Evangeline stood and brushed out the lines of her dress. "We have no other choice but to talk to them."

I reached for her, but she had already swung the door wide and stepped out onto the balcony. Though there was a canopy above, she shielded her gaze, her eyes picking at pebbles in the dirt. Her silhouette moved, replaced by a bright white shaft that cut across the coffins inside the black carriage.

"And a lady, too. Ahh, miss, forgive me for not realizing. Come. Push your hands up... hi-higher... mmmm... women kill same as men, you know? Gooooood."

If I said I felt cold that would sound strange, but those sunrays burned like ice pressing on bare skin, not hot or cold but only burning, and the voice burned the same way. I did not know Evangeline then, but how could I let her walk out alone to meet the owner of that voice?

I went after her.

15

El Gusano

We stood side-by-side blinking in the desert glare.

Five riders were fanned out behind the train car. One sat upon a huge black Paint Horse between the tracks. Two pairs of armed banditos flanked him, spaced a few feet apart on either side of the rails, these four were dead-faced and slumped in their saddles as scarecrows would be if they took to riding. Even with the wind dying down, the stink of carrion was overpowering. First, I heard the buzzing. Then I saw them everywhere, the source of the noise: flies, a cloud of hundreds, maybe thousands, searching, landing, crawling. I felt a tickle on my cheek, tiny legs moving – testing. I flicked it away.

They're waiting for something, I thought. *Something they know is coming.*

The necrófagos were waiting too.

"They're wearing masks," I said to Evangeline.

"I see that. Faces of their favorite victims, I imagine."

"You take the news rather well."

"There's nothing to be done about it. They're ghouls, as the local legend states."

"So you know something about ghouls?"

"Only what I've read. This is the first time I've met any personally." Evangeline inclined her head closer to me – those large green eyes changed depth with the light. She lowered her voice. "But there's something really bothering me about the middle one."

My sight had adjusted somewhat. Squinting, I tried not to stare too hard.

The middle one. He seemed even uglier and quite a bit bulkier than his cohorts, but no worse. And he wore no mask, I noticed with surprise. Perhaps, if they were all this repulsive, that was the reason for the masks. A yellow-gray tuft grew out of the bloated place where he should have had a chin. His face shimmered with dots of sweat.

I said to Evangeline, "What's the problem? Other than our obvious predicament…"

"He's too fat. Ghouls aren't supposed to be fat."

"Ssssss… no talking. You listen now to me. Get your friends to come out here or I'm going to burn the train and cook them." It was the fat one who spoke. The big black-and-white horse shifted under his weight. "Bring out the dead man too."

How does he know about Thomas? I wondered.

"Because I can smell him, amigo."

Keeping my voice to a whisper I said, "Can ghouls read minds?"

Evangeline shook her head.

From behind us, still hidden in the dark recesses of the private car, Kittle called to the bandito ghouls. "All right, we're bringing out the body like you asked. Nobody shoot us."

Kittle exchanged a few hurried, indecipherable words with Staves.

Then he shouted, "We're coming out!"

The Pinkertons emerged carrying Thomas. Staves, gripping Thomas' ankles, backed slowly down the carriage steps. Kittle had his hands under the dead man's slack arms, and the detective's chest forced the head of the corpse forward, baring its ghastly red wound.

Evangeline and I moved aside to allow the men to pass.

"Where do you want him?" Kittle asked the train robbers.

"Lay him here in front of us. Very good." The fat one licked his lips. His tongue looked like a toad. It went back to hiding in the shadows.

I had some idea what Kittle and Staves were planning to do. I thought a distraction might help them to succeed. I stepped forward. "What is your name, sir?"

The fat one's eyelids folded back in amusement.

"I am called El Gusano."

He smiled. He had no teeth, but his gums were not smooth either. A bumpy purple cavern lurked in there. The flesh on my arms tingled with horripilation.

"Are you a Mexican?"

"I do not come from Mexico, though I have lived in her desert hills for many years." His words clapped out dry as bricks. It made me thirsty listening to him talk.

"In this country," I said, "we believe in the law. I hope you understand the grave seriousness of your crimes." Ignoring my accidental pun, I continued, "Justice will come for you in one form or another. If not today, then one day soon. Remember that."

"Worry about what's coming for you, amigo. In one form or another, as you say."

Kittle and Staves advanced with Thomas' body.

Gravity pulled at the porter's trouser leg and I saw the outline of the rifle. As the detectives squatted to lay the man's body down, Staves clasped the Winchester and hauled it forth – or attempted to – while anchoring himself for some serious rapid shooting. The front sight snagged on the porter's shoelace. Such trivial things decide men's futures. Not long did it stay snagged, however. Staves quickly twisted it free.

Only not quickly enough.

A ghoul rode up and, drawing a cavalry saber from the wings of his long coat, he skewered Staves between the scapulas. The angle of impalement cut through his torso nearly perpendicular to the ground. Dropping his rifle, Staves stood tall and turned in a full circle. The red tip of the saber jutted through the fly of his pants.

"Sweet Lord," he said, looking down. His thumb tested the naked point as if to judge its sharpness. A few stuttering paces carried him south of the train. He pivoted east, his face whitened and nodding a bit, he adjusted his course again, his mouth pursed with an unasked question and his gaze settled on nothing. Like a sleepwalker alone in dreams, a quizzical look affixed to his brow. After a paroxysm of body shaking – *Awake, sleeper!* – he fell down.

The Mexican ghoul whose saber it was led his horse over and coaxed the animal into stepping on the Pinkerton's back until all nervous movement subsided. He dismounted, extracted the sword – a terrible, moist grating sound – and sleeved it, still red, in his scabbard.

We all watched, frozen at the spectacle.

Kittle, who had drawn his Colt from inside the porter's jacket sleeve, regarded the revolver as if it had appeared by magic in his shaking hand.

He snapped to–

"*Arrrrgghhh!*"

–and charged.

One of the banditos had a scattergun hidden under his serape. We did not know this, of course, until he pulled both triggers, shredding wool in a sparking smoky flap of colors and fringes. Kittle's head broke into flying pieces. Pink and gray mush kicked out behind him. He rolled into a silent heap before the living dead horsemen.

"Throw them in the pit," El Gusano said.

"My God, Hardy–" Evangeline said. She pressed against me and dropped her hands to grab at my sleeve with tight fists. Her chin quivered, though she held it high.

"I know," I said. "Don't look if you can help it."

But I forced myself to witness the removal of my recent companions. What desecrations were to come I did not wish to contemplate, yet my mind drew me those pictures too.

A pair of necrófagos dismounted and tossed the murdered detectives over their horses. But when they came close to Thomas they backed off, turning their heads away.

"Ghouls hate mugwort. See? They won't eat him."

Eat him.

"How much of that do you have in your bag?"

"Not nearly enough," she said.

The ghoul with the torn serape pointed his filthy clawed finger at us. He was asking a question of his boss.

El Gusano said, "Stake them while we deal with the train."

The buzzing black flies lifted en masse into the sky and moved up the line.

16

Seeketh Whom They May Devour

Did I mention their eyes? The ghouls' eyes?

Probably not and I know why, because I try to forget them. They were moist and swollen like poisoned bubbles about to pop in my face, and they lacked the tiniest hint of humanity. They did not show any pupil, no white sclera either, but were thoroughly black hemispheres. I looked into those rotten-eggy eyes as the ghouls wrestled me to the dirt and pinned my limbs down. *Are these the eyes of people-eaters?* I asked myself. *Would they be the last I would see in this life, which as I might have mentioned was the only life I ever expected to have?* The unfortunate answers were *Yes!* and *Yes!* I did not believe in Heaven, but how could I discount Hell?

The necrófagos rifled through my pockets and stole all my coins.

Now a naked foot has never struck me as a particularly vulnerable specimen, Achilles' heel notwithstanding, yet when my legs were wish-boned apart and my ankles ligatured to wooden stakes in the sand, I felt nothing short of alarm, and the stripping of my shoes followed by the brisk unpeeling of my socks led me into such a state of panic as if the entirety of my clothing had vanished and I lay publicly nude. The sun broiled my soles. The ghouls, once I was immobilized, scrapped with each other to see who would be the first to try my shoe leather on their horny gargoyle pads. How much worse it must have been for poor Evangeline. They snatched her petite soft pink slippers with glee and attempted to work them on their own deformed feet, tearing the seams and poking their dactyls out of the new holes for airing. Her silk stockings – sage green, I noted – they bunched over their noses and mouths, and with exaggeration sucked gouts of air off the wrinkled bouquets, uttering appreciations as one might if one sat ravenous for supper and smelled the savory fumes of a soon-arriving hot meal. I credited her for not crying.

"Can you move?" she asked.

"Not much. They've done this before, I'd say."

Our arms were extended and pulled taut at the wrists, cuttingly bound, a loop and another loop for good measure, hard little knots at the ends like marbles – the binding material being, as best I could judge, dried animal (human?) tendons. Our bodies spread into two Xs before the troupe of demonic corpse-lovers. Dazzling light forced our eyes closed. No comfort was there for us on that cracked desert floor. None whatsoever.

Through my shuttered eyes I saw the red inside my skin and wondered how long it would be until that redness spilled. A shadow floated over me, and I peered up into the face of El Gusano. I could not see his eyes, just black sparkles in the fat multiple folds of his skin, cheeks studded with moles like cloves in a Sunday ham and sprouting coarse pale hairs all the way up to his lower eyelids, the lush almost feminine lashes batting as he gazed down at me with curiosity if not pity. He had no neck to speak of. Rolls of belly and rolls of chest defined a superabundant shape that did not fit entirely inside his clothes.

A shirt button popped under the strain, landing on my chest.

El Gusano shuffled to Evangeline and I was back under the sun and blinded.

I felt two thumps in my back – earth tremors – and realized El Gusano had kneeled on the ground between us. I turned my head and opened one eye – a slit. He removed his sombrero and held it out, blocking the sun, so Evangeline could see him.

"Eh, are you thirsty?"

Evangeline lay in the dust cloud he had stirred.

"Yes," she said.

"Me too." He leaned over and licked the dewy sweat from her skin.

The necrófagos snickered.

"You I'm going to save for last." He pushed his boneless hand into her ribs and she struggled. "I leave a little room for dessert."

"Don't touch her," I said.

"You mean like this?" He balled his hand into an enormous fist and hammered it down into her stomach. Evangeline cried out.

I jerked at my bonds.

El Gusano scooped a handful of sand and trickled it onto my face.

I twisted my head. His hand followed until I was spitting the warm grains.

"Hey, no more entertainment. I got work to do." He slapped my cheek the way you would a child's, eased his bulk up off the ground, and walked over to his horse. He came back with something in his hands: a long, lacquered tube, stoppered on one end with a cork. He pulled the cork and peered down into the tube. "You know bark scorpions, señor?"

I said nothing, thinking it wiser to keep my mouth shut this time.

He shook the tube. "It no matter if you do."

"Why torture us?" I asked, unable to stay silent. "Do you enjoy it? You're depraved."

"I hear you battled a nephew of mine in the Tomb of the Living Skull – a gusanito, one from my dearest sister's fiftieth hatching – I am told you threw fire on him."

"What? I don't–"

Tomb of the Living Skull? His dearest sister's fiftieth hatching?

"The bark scorpion is slender and delicate like a preeety lady. But her sting is most venomous." He laughed. "My ladies don't like being out in the daytime under the hot sun. So they will look for places to hide."

He dumped the contents of the tube on Evangeline and me. I heard Evangeline catch her breath. I felt the crawling almost immediately. Little bodies searching...

"You better not move too much, amigos. At night the ladies will come out to dance." He snapped his fingers in the air. Looking into the tube, he scowled and tapped out one last scorpion on my forehead. Then he placed his sombrero over my face.

"You take a siesta while we fill our bellies. Tonight we see how you're doing."

"I hope you choke, you devil," Evangeline said.

"If your face was not so small I make a mask – I like you that much."

"And if my mouth were not so dry I would spit in yours."

I enjoyed her comment, but the scorpion crossing the bridge of my nose prevented me from saying so.

The necrófagos left us to attend to the train and its doomed passengers. Despite the direness of our circumstances the train riders had it worse. We could not see their fates unfold, but we could hear, and the sounds were as harrowing as they were gruesome. The ghouls commandeered the engine and drove the train straight into the open pit. Because they themselves did not fear death and in fact courted death, it was no act of daring, but still it has to be admitted, derailing the train into a hole in the ground was unexpected. I am certain the people on board felt shock. They worried about robbery, not slaughter. The luckiest ones died first. Such destruction! The tumble and crash of the train cars seemed never to end. Screams carried above the ripping metal and cannonade of exploded wood. In the aftermath, when the quiet settled, there came an almost rain-like sizzle of sand and clapping rocks signifying a small landslide. We listened as one by one the necrófagos dropped into the pit and began to feed on the dead. A renewed chorus of cries (the dying, and the living who found themselves trapped and forced to bear witness) joined with wretched moans – sexless, ageless, equalized in their misery – echoing from the hollow. The cavity had to be deep – deep enough to swallow the whole train and hamper any survivor from climbing out.

Evangeline and I did not speak. I tried to distract my thoughts from the carnage but found little success. The scorpion had wandered from my face. Where it went, I knew not, though I felt a tickle in my collar that soon enlarged itself in my imagination so that the sensation might have been a stream of acid pouring along my neck.

"Hardy? Have you been stung?"

Evangeline's voice was a great comfort.

"No. How about you?"

"I'm fine. I can't feel them moving any more, which may be the only good thing about all the layers of clothing I'm wearing."

I risked a smile under the sombrero. "I've been thinking about something El Gusano said. He's definitely not a ghoul."

"Do you speak Spanish?"

"No."

She paused for a long while and I guessed that she felt them crawling again.

Then in a soft voice she said, "*El Gusano*. I wonder, what does that mean?"

"I think it means *worm*."

After that we were both quiet until the sun slipped low, then out of the sky, and in the sudden coolness another, even softer, voice decided it was time to say something.

17

HOPPING INTO CAVES

"Excuse me, Mr Hardy. I think I can save you and the elegant lady, but we must act quickly before the ghouls finish eating in the pit."

I turned and lifted my head as high as I could under the sombrero. "Yong Wu! It is awfully good to hear your voice if not to see your face. I thought you were dead."

"Sir, I am also glad you have not... gone to the west."

I frowned inside the hat.

"Will you uncover my head? It's airless under here and I'm having the damnedest trouble with it. Take it off slowly, though. I am temporarily infested with scorpions."

"I cannot do that."

"What did he say, Hardy?" Evangeline whispered.

"He said he 'cannot do that.'"

"I thought that's what he said. Ask him *why*."

"Tell us, Yong Wu, *why* you cannot save us from certain death."

"I wish to rescue you and the lady. But I have to insist upon one thing. You must not look no matter what happens. It is necessary. If you look, then I will go from here."

134

"Is this some Oriental superstition? Because now is not the time for old legends."

"Old legends are the only way I can help you. So please agree."

"All right then, I'll keep this filthy thing over my head," I replied. "Let's move!"

"And Miss must shut her eyes until I can blindfold her."

Evangeline called back, "I promise. No peeking… please hurry."

I took the boy's silence as tacit approval.

"Can you spot him, Evangeline?" I muttered beneath the lid of the smelly felt sombrero. "He's dressed in black silks. The young Chinese server who helped the porter – you'd have seen him before, in the dining car – he must be terrified."

"The sun's almost down. Everything is in shadows. Wait… I see him climbing from under the train – here he comes. I'm closing my eyes. I don't want to spook him."

"He just might be braver than both of us–"

"*Shuush…*"

It was seconds until I felt the lightest pressure of Yong Wu's hand on my arm.

"Don't move," he said.

"I couldn't if I tried."

A tugging began on my bound left wrist. The ligature hummed like a plucked guitar string. Braided hairs tickled across the palm of my hand. "Yong Wu, you will never bite through those cords."

"Be still."

How could he talk and bite at the same time? At my right ankle vibrations struck courtesy of a persistent gnawing. *Left wrist, right ankle, and all while talking!* I caught my breath. The boy had not come alone. I heard a *plunk!* and my left hand was freed.

"I am blindfolding you, Miss," Yong Wu said, having shifted off to my far right.

"Yes, of course. Thank you. That will be easier."

As Evangeline and Yong Wu conversed, someone chewed through the tendon securing my ankle, and *another* someone snapped at the binding on my right wrist. I heard teeth clicking together. The sound made me clench my own. Who were these rescuers? Passengers who had escaped the train? Where else could they have come from? Did they not have a pocketknife among them? The temptation to tip my sombrero for a look-see set in hard. But I had made a promise, one that my life as well as Evangeline's depended on, or so I had been told. I curbed my curiosity for the moment.

Yet I could make do with my other, non-ocular, senses and wonder.

How remarkably quiet it grew in the night-infused desert. By all evidence, the necrófagos had satiated themselves in the pit. They would be up soon. I could not detect the breathing of my liberators though they plied unwaveringly to their cord biting. There were two of them, if I guessed right: Yong Wu's quiet assistants. All my bonds were soon severed. I wanted to rub my hands but dared not stir for fear of being stung to death.

"Stand him up," Yong Wu said. "We will take them to the hills. Go quickly!"

"Remember the scorpions," I said. "That is very key I do believe."

"The scorpions have fled. Now we must too."

Someone, but it felt vaguely more like a some*thing*, hooked my shirtfront and pulled me upright as if I were a sack of dirty linens. I waited for a rash of barbs to jab me with hellfire pain, but none came. Yong Wu had been correct. Reader, do you understand that scorpions are armored arachnids? One cannot reason with armored arachnids, though admittedly I never tried. Yet by necessity more often than not it is instinct, and not logic, that rules in the arena of desert survival. Get going or get dead. So I asked myself, what scared off those deadly little buggers? I detected the smell of coal dust. And coldness moved around me. Two stiff arms, strong as whisky barrel hoops, fastened tight across my chest from behind. Coal dust and a bleachy fragrance like, like... *mushrooms* – that's what I smelled. Not exactly foul, but loamy and organic, with more than a hint of dark subterranean growth.

"To the caves in the hills," Yong Wu said. "We will hide there."

The thing that held me fast forced me down into a crouch. Together we leaped skyward, higher than any man can jump, and landed with a crunch on the rocky ground, only to spring up again, even higher on our second try. So we propelled onward. I felt a speedy wind whipping past as we hopped like crazed man-sized jackrabbits to the hills.

To the caves that Yong Wu somehow knew were there.

The particular cave we occupied for the remainder of the night turned out to be more of a crevice, like two prayerful stone hands steepled together cupping us in the hollow of their palms. A slice of night filled the entryway. Stars glinted at the top. Purple moonlit desert carpeted below. Evangeline and I sat flush against a wall with a stubby red candle burning between us. Yong Wu stood watch outside the crevice, speaking in what Evangeline said was Cantonese to his two silent, and as yet unseen, partners. We assessed our conditions with similar results: sore wrists, bare blistered feet, and thirst.

"I'm sorry you're here. That all this has happened to you. I feel responsible."

"Better here than in that hole with the train wreck," she said.

"Of course. What I mean is I'm sorry you're not somewhere safe."

"Why would I want to be safe?"

"Because… well, because you're a, a…"

"A woman?"

I nodded. "A woman of means… accustomed to polite society."

"There's more wreckage and horror in polite society than in that ghoul's pit."

"I seriously don't know about that."

"Well, I do."

I said no more on the subject. "I wish we weren't at such a disadvantage." I gestured at our surroundings, including a pile of scavenged objects, a real magpie's collection, dim though it was, and apparently property of our mystery helpers, and from where Yong Wu had produced the candle. "But our options are unfortunately limited."

"Options change, often in the daylight. I think we should rest. We can figure out a strategy in the morning. Together we will come up with a plan of attack."

"My only plan is to get you back to Los Angeles, to your father."

She looked at me. Candlelight did nothing to soften her stare.

"Hardy, those ghouls are going to steal the mummies. Are you really prepared to allow that? After all the searching you did, and digging about in faraway Egyptland? Not to mention all the money you spent. How will you explain *that* to my father?"

"I think he'll take the return of his daughter over a half dozen crated mummies."

"You think incorrectly. He will make certain you never work in this field again."

I paused at that prospect. The possibility of my fledgling career ending before it really began was unsettling. But Waterston could no doubt do it. Powerful men often assign blame to those who are unlucky enough to be around them when fortunes change. They can be notoriously vindictive where money is concerned. I resorted to wishful thinking to quell my anxieties.

"Ghouls, mummies… maybe they'll just leave them alone. Ride off."

"They won't."

"And we have to get them back? Is that it? Simply retrieve them?"

"See, now you're thinking. Together we will bring the mummies home to Daddy."

"We can't do it alone. Impossible." I dusted myself off.

"No, you and I will need help."

"And we have no money. I spent it all, as you said. When I discovered the mummies the first time, *on my own*, I might add."

She was nodding. "I recall a foreman and diggers helping."

"You are correct. I will never forget them. But every Egyptologist has his diggers. I orchestrated things. The entire operation was under me."

Her eyes twinkled with mischief. "You had a map as well."

"I must remember to thank the phantom when I see him. Maybe I can ask him to draw me a map to find some money too." I pantomimed the action of map drawing and nearly knocked the candle over with my gesticulations. My clumsiness charmed Evangeline more than my words had.

"I can get money, silly," she said. "We have lots of money. If it's wisely put to use–"

"The two of us together? That's the concept, is it?"

"And Yong Wu. I think it's appropriate that we invite him to join us."

I was pacing, though given the confines, it was not easy.

"Oh, splendid. We'll have a little partnership. A consortium."

(Evangeline smiling in the darkness – fetching, frightening, maddening–)

I said, "My partners of late – the foreman and diggers you mentioned, as well as the Pinkertons – have had a tendency to die. Not too peacefully either, as you might have noticed."

I told her everything that had happened to me from the time I accepted her father's offer to lead an Egyptian expedition until the moment she entered my train car. Much of this information was not included in my letters to Waterston. I presumed it would deter her.

It did not.

"I'll take care of myself. I'm not your responsibility any more than you are mine."

I considered this arrangement.

"I am uncertain whether that makes me feel any better about things."

"It's a deal then?" She reached out and actually shook my hand.

A deal it was.

18
THE PIT DISCOVERY

Evangeline was right. In the morning, the mummies were gone. Crates and all. Our private car was empty. How the necrófagos took them, I cannot explain. I saw no wagon wheel tracks, only hoof prints stamped in the sand. The trail headed south through the desert and beyond to the borderland and Mexico. It was like the diggers in the tomb moving a sarcophagus they never should have been able to budge. Physics did not apply. Ever since I entered the skull rock, impossible things suddenly seemed possible. It made my head throb. I cinched the cord of my newly acquired, thoroughly stinking, yet functional sombrero under my chin and soldiered on. In the refreshments cabinet of the railcar I found a pitcher filled with water and a cut crystal glass. I poured, swallowed a few sips, emptied the remainder into my canteen, and slung it over my shoulder. Warm as bathwater, but no drink has ever tasted sweeter on my tongue – its weight gave me some comfort. The necrófagos left my pipe and tobacco unmolested which added to the mood of positivity. So too the bottle of absinthe, a flash of gemmy green as I held it up to the sun for inspection, before stowing it in my satchel along with my field notes from Egypt. I turned, searching for anything else salvageable. The floor looked awfully damned big without the coffin boxes sitting there. Even though I was starting to entertain evil feelings toward the mummies, it made my heart ache to see them stolen by those good-for-nothing dead-eaters. The mummies might be cursed, I was willing to admit, but they were *our* cursed mummies.

Finished, I stepped out into the Arizona blaze.

Evangeline and Yong Wu were not pleased with me and I was eager to make amends.

I had started the day being stubbornly insistent regarding the identity of Yong Wu's companions. They were gone now, vanished before dawn. Evangeline and I had not seen so much as their shadows playing on the cave wall. And, despite the mystery, we were told nothing more about them. That did not satisfy me one bit. I wanted answers.

I began friendly enough.

"Yong Wu, I'd like to know to whom we owe our gratitude for freeing us, besides you, of course." Here I smiled at him.

The boy glanced up at me as we walked together, but he quickly looked away.

"Are they friends of yours?" I tried to lead him. "Maybe fellow employees of the railroad?"

No look this time. His pace quickened. Mine did too.

"They are Chinese. We deduced that much from hearing you talk…"

He stopped and turned his face sharply away from me. I looked in the same direction. His eyes pointed back to hills, to the caves where we had hidden from the robbers. Dry, rough country: cacti standing like so many frozen sentinels in this place where nothing worthy of any protection grew; a black putty of shadows spread between the rocks. He started walking again.

"They had to come from the train. I mean, I suppose they were on the train before we were hijacked. They certainly weren't living out here in this wasteland. Let's see now. Chinese and on the train, and I recall their clothes smelled like coal dust. So my guess is they worked in the coal car stoking the engine. You get muscles shoveling coal all day, and the one who grabbed me was strong as an ox, but I cannot understand the absurd hopping. It was… inhuman."

The boy sped up, but my legs were longer. I stepped into his path and seized him by the shoulders. Bending, I leaned my face down into his, eyeball to eyeball.

"Who are they?"

Pale streaks cleared the dirt smudged on his cheeks. He was crying.

I released him.

"Hardy."

Evangeline had caught up with us.

Lips pursed, and her stern brow was fixed as a bayonet. She aimed herself at me.

"Why can't he tell us who they are?" I had hoped she would take my side and help to convince the boy to explain what had happened. She was not cooperating.

My examination grew more heated.

"Maybe the reason Yong Wu escaped was that he knew the necrófagos. Even knew of their plans to overtake us. Maybe his two friends *are* necrófagos. Maybe this is all some ghastly game they're playing and we're going to end up just as dead and eaten by scavengers as those poor souls who remained on the train. Maybe he stays quiet because he's guilty of spying for the enemy. I know one thing about your hopping Chinese friends, my unforthcoming Wu. I know they smelled like a pair of moldy old corpses."

"Enough, Hardy! Stop!"

The boy was shaking. His body jerked with terrible little spasms as he cried harder – his nose ran and he wiped it with the tattered edge of his shirt. He opened his mouth to gasp air and let out a loud, shuddering, wet sob. His face contorted into a distressing woeful grimace.

Feeling pity I reached out to him, and he lurched to get away.

"They're not necrófagos! They're not!" he shouted.

Evangeline went straight to him. I was surprised to see how easily he welcomed her embrace. Just folded into her arms as if he were falling forward, all his tension dissolved against her softness. That gentle collision seemed to soothe his pain.

"Hush. Mr Hardy does not know what he said. If he knew, he would not have said it."

She looked at me and raised a prompting eyebrow.

Well, I did not mean it. I did not even know what I did not mean. So there was no lie. Awful stirrings of regret for my harsh behavior toward the child suddenly arose. The trauma of our predicament had begun to turn me into someone I did not recognize, or very much like.

"She's right. I don't know what I'm saying." The truth – I spoke the truth.

Twin silences answered me.

I followed my solitary shadow to the railcar to search for supplies.

It was then in a spirit of repair that I returned from the confinement of the railcar with my full sloshing canteen, hoping to return to the good graces of my companions. I did not locate them straightaway in the heat-wavering tan-on-beige horizon. A cold jolt of fear passed through me. But there they were tucked around behind the car: Evangeline squatting near the prone body of Detective Kittle and Yong Wu chasing several turkey vultures away from Thomas the porter's corpse.

"I have good news," I said, and shook the canteen. "Water, the elixir of life. Come join me in the shade under the train's rear awning."

Evangeline accepted the drink wordlessly. Her throat being parched, I did not blame her. She had been attempting to remove Kittle's shoes; his feet had swollen grossly in the heat, stretching the leather past its limits. Picking at the tight laces, she'd broken two fingernails and they were oozing blood. Her face colored a deep unwholesome pink from exposure to the sun.

She tilted her head back swallowing and swallowing water.

"Easy there. We've got to make this last."

She handed back the canteen and sucked on her injured fingertips. Sliding her fingers out momentarily, she said, "We need footwear or we're as good as dead."

I nodded. I had been trying not to think about my blistered feet or how the necrófagos had ridden off with my stolen shoes. The injury doubled with the indignity.

"Wu," I called out. "Stop chasing and have a drink with us."

But the boy did not come. He kept after the hunched, black birds, which would flap a few feet over his head, just out of reach, and drop down behind him to grab some more of Thomas.

"Calm down, boy. I know you cared for your old friend, and he for you. I think wherever he may be in the spirit world he wouldn't want you running yourself to death for those feathered fiends. I'll take his body and close it in the railcar. They will harass him no more."

So, he *had* been hearing me, because the aerial battle ended. The birds advanced. The boy came over to us.

"Evangeline has water. But watch she doesn't drink it all. The same goes for you."

Yong Wu went to his spot in the shade, and I dragged the murdered porter away.

I couldn't leave my bodyguards, Kittle and Staves, rotting in the elements, could I? So I laid them all three, side-by-side, in a row on the floor of the private car where yesterday the coffins had been stacked. "If there is a God, may he take better care of your souls than the world has done with your bodies," I said before shutting the doors. I was not sure if any of the men believed in God, but I assumed at least one or two of them did, nor did I know how to bless them on their journey – I drew an invisible cross in the air, bowed my head and hoped for the best.

Before my prayer, but after a sweaty bit of tugging, I had succeeded in separating Staves from his boots and Kittle from his shoes. Staves' boots were a decent fit, if longish in the toe and a bit pointy-ended for my taste.

Kittle, having a surprisingly dainty foot for a policeman, made a nearly perfect match for Evangeline. Testing my boots, and pondering how the Apache went about his errands in this wilderness without a cobbler, I strode over to the pit where so many had died yesterday.

Here the rocks below told me of another surprise.

"Evangeline, have a look." I walked to the rim of the hole. "This catastrophe is the result of a collapse and was not caused by any dynamiting. We were wrong to assume so."

"How does one decipher that, Hardy?"

"The ends of the rails are neither twisted nor blown apart. Rather they were bent downward until they snapped from their own weight. Clearly, this was a cave-in, and a deliberate one, to be sure. Look at the walls of the pit. The earth has been hollowed out from underneath."

Evangeline kneeled, craning her neck for a better, if skeptical, view.

I was too excited to stay in place and jogged around the bowl of sunken ground.

An excavated passage extended in two directions away from the pit. I pointed at the matched openings. "North and... slight angle turning... due south. Someone dug in this way and went out that way, or vice versa. But I'd bet on south for the destination. I would be willing to wager this is how they took the mummies. Underground, by way of that tunnel. No wagon tracks because... no wagon. Ha-ha! No mystery after all."

At the pit's bottom lay the mangled train on its side.

Windows dripped broken glass. A pall of dust, mixed with gray smoke, hung over the entirety of the disaster. Most eerie was the stillness. No bodies showed amid the debris, but death's putrid breath fumed in our faces. The vultures whirled and began dropping onto the wreckage. I watched as bird after red bald-headed bird disappeared inside the silent carriages.

"What do you say to my theory, Evangeline? Pretty observant on my part..."

But when I looked over to where she had been kneeling, she was gone.

"Evangeline?"

A shifting of sand, tumbling of loose stones...

"Here, Hardy! Down here!"

I peered intently through the mantle of haze, and with dismay I spotted Evangeline – a splash of pastel skirts – moving along the length of tipped railcars as if on a garden path.

Her hand was flapping at either me or the vultures.

"What in God's name are you doing?"

"I want to get closer. To see if you're right. Does the hole go on like you say, or not?"

"Climb out now!"

"No, I'm fine. Wait for me up there if you're worried. I won't be but a minute or two."

As soon as she spoke the locomotive let out a bovine moan. A shrieking teakettle whistle followed this sour bass note, so that they sang together. Billowy, raw steam ejected out of the front-most car. What little I could spy of Evangeline cottoned over with fouled whiteness.

"I fear she's unstable and could explode any moment!" I shouted.

Yong Wu, who had crawled up beside me at the mouth of the pit, cocked his head, wondering whether my observation described the train or the woman.

"Come up, come up, come up…" I mumbled as I tried willing her back.

Evangeline remained unseen and unheard from.

But it must be loud in the pit, I told myself. She can't hear anything. *Or she might have taken a wrong step and hit her head, or toppled into a vise-like jumble of wood and sharp hot metal within the crushed hulk, or maybe there was a clever necrófago crouching in the dark, grinning, half-sated and freshly awakened…* I said these things to myself too, although it did not sound like me saying them but someone more imaginative than I was, and more anxious.

"I suppose one of us should go after her, Yong Wu."

He lay on his belly trying to catch sight of her.

He's a boy, only a boy, this is your task, Rom, the worried voice said.

"I will go. You stay here, at the very edge, in case I need your assistance."

Wu's vigorous nodding met my offer. "The birds will fly away if the boiler's going to blow," he said. "They are most sensitive to little changes."

"I sincerely hope you are correct."

With that I lowered myself, boots first, into the hellish crater.

Unbreathable. I almost went up before I had even climbed low enough to consider myself down in the wreckage proper. My eyes watered, shut of their own accord, so I was a blind man stumbling inside a puzzle box of what was formerly a train, now a deathtrap. Below the steamy fog, I could see and breathe, but I did not see Evangeline. I had been right about the noise. The shrieking deafened me. What a meal it must have been for the vultures to stay inside those cars. I did not want to encounter any of the dead. Though I had not killed them, in a way my mummies did. I was now convinced that we were the target of the necrófagos and the train might have passed safely to California if we were not aboard. Also, though the ancient dead are my obsession, the freshly dead cannot help but haunt the mind. I had had enough attending to my three executed friends in their train car. My stomach roared at the thought of coming upon more.

I walked alone, gladly.

I did not call out for Evangeline – she would not have heard me in the din.

What I did was look, look, look.

I found her in the southern tunnel. She'd fashioned a torch from a sun parasol (I know not how she did this, but it was crimson bright and dangerous seeming), and she was waving it about, bits of flaming fabric falling here and floating there, in her attempt to learn the secrets of the recess.

I approached her from behind. She spun on me with her fiery stick.

"So you did follow me," she said, sounding pleased. By some acoustic mystery, the tunnel was less noisy than the pit. We could hear each other without shouting.

"I would not venture here for any other reason."

"Then you would have missed this." She took her flambeau off me and raised it to illuminate the passage, which was large enough and profound enough to consume all the light she offered and give back pitch darkness in abundance. It was cooler underground despite the steam. A gentle breeze was blowing at us, tilting the sputtering parasol flame backward like a flag. What could've dug this manner of hole? But I knew. Didn't I? I had kicked such a creature in the face the last time I saw one, but one not nearly capable of these proportions. The smell was the same, the oiliness hanging in the air like a foul miasma.

"Have you ever seen anything like it?" she asked.

"Yes, actually, I have. Though the retreat I explored was a hundredth of this size."

"What is it then?"

"Worm lair."

"*Worm lair,*" she said. The chill running through her was contagious, for I felt it.

"El Gusano is," I began, "a worm who can take on semi-human form as we observed him. But, naturally, or perhaps better stated, supernaturally, he's this other thing too... this monster." The bandit leader had admitted as much to me, mentioning his nephew at the skull rock. *Gusanito.* Little worm. Well, what did that make him? I finished my tidy summary, "The occult is at play here. I don't expect you to understand."

"Oh, but I do." She twirled the smoking parasol and tossed its blackened bones away.

"You do?"

I was astonished at her readiness to believe. It was not naiveté, quite the contrary. I had the distinct feeling that Evangeline had seen much strangeness in her short life, and although she was not yet jaded, she was prepared to admit that anything, anything at all under the sun was... and is... possible.

"You accept what've I've suggested?"

Evangeline nodded. "The man-worm leading the necrófagos is not a necrófago himself. He has stolen

Daddy's mummies – I suspect it is Odji-Kek he is helping. Odji-Kek has called to him across the mists of time. No doubt promising him unholy rewards of the most savage, obscene kind."

At first, I couldn't tell if she were joking with me. Her eyes grew wide, glinting. I suspected then she was not prodding me for sport. This woman would never shy away from obscenity or perversity. Rather, she might choose to study her findings.

"Yes, let's go then," I said.

She began to walk farther into the tunnel.

"Let's go *up*," I said, and took hold of her sleeve.

"But–"

I didn't want to argue.

I especially didn't want to argue and then die in a steam explosion.

"Yong Wu is waiting for us. We cannot leave him alone," I said.

With this she could agree. "And we need reinforcements as well."

"I suppose we do."

We climbed together out of the swirling vapor, and I moved faster when I noted the vultures fleeing before us, exiting the train, their black wings slowly pumping. Vile birds – always on the lookout for the badges of death – one cocked a drowsy, wizened eye at me, his belly stuffed, and a sample of carrion swaying tick-tock, tick-tock from his beak.

He seemed to be sizing me up for his midnight snack.

"Not if I can help it," I said.

I chucked a small stone in his general direction, and fled.

19

A Bad Man Who Might Help Us

"Yuma is about two miles, that way." Yong Wu pointed to the whip black rails running west. "There's a man who works sometimes for the railroad company. He hunts down train robbers for money. Like the wanted posters say, dead or alive."

"A bounty hunter?" I asked.

Yong Wu nodded. "I saw him once on the train. He has very bad eyes."

"I would think poor vision is a hazard in his field," I said.

The boy gawked at me, astonished. "He can shoot a man so far away you can't tell there's any man there."

"But you just said…"

"One look into his shining eyes and I wanted to jump off the train."

"Sounds exactly like the man we need." Evangeline flushed at the news.

"Or he might make matters worse. Do we really want more violence?" I asked.

"If it brings the mummies back, then yes. I don't think we're going to get what we want by asking nicely. Do

154

you?" Her voice climbed higher, flimsy, "Please, sirs, can we have our antiquities back?"

Yong Wu giggled at her caricature, and soon he and Evangeline were laughing out loud.

No, simply asking would not suffice. I was not suggesting that. I wanted to evaluate this hunter before we handed over our cash and rode into Mexico with him. Measure up the man.

"I only want to get a good long look at him before I decide anything."

"Me too," Evangeline said.

This time when she laughed she covered it with her hand.

"So this shining eyes bounty hunter, do you know his name?" I said.

"McTroy," the boy said.

"McTroy something, or something McTroy?"

"I only know they call him McTroy. 'McTroy will catch the sons of bitches and then they will wish they never were born. They will cry for their mothers when McTroy tracks them down. If any man knows how to flush vermin, it's that god-damned McTroy!' That's what the bosses said. And then McTroy would come around."

The boy appeared positively in awe of this gunman.

"And…"

"A few days later he brings the bad men to Yuma. With their hands tied, all walking behind his horse. Or over the backs of their horses with flies crawling on them."

"I do hope he's available," Evangeline said.

I stumbled and blamed Staves' pointy boots.

"For hire, Hardy. I hope he's available for us to hire."

"I know what you meant."

"Where do we find him, Wu? Does he have an office?" she said.

"The people in Yuma will know him."

The people in Yuma did know him. We were parched, sunburned, and covered in dust from ankles to eyebrows – just like everyone else in Yuma, or so it seemed from those we encountered in the street. We turned no heads. Well, Evangeline did. But not because she'd walked in from the desert. A pretty woman is always noted by the males of the species. Evangeline ignored their tipped hats, dingy grins, and words of self-introduction. She did take advantage of the attention to inquire into the whereabouts of McTroy.

At the saloon they said to check at the jail.

At the jail they said, did you check at the saloon?

When we said we had, they said, "Out. Might be he's gone on a manhunt. Or ask Sheriff Mike Nugent." And where is the sheriff? Did you check at the saloon?

So back to the saloon went our little three-car train of Hardy, Miss Evangeline, and Yong Wu. We found Sheriff Mike Nugent sitting at a table of drunken silver miners. He didn't look drunk at all, and they didn't look happy to have him there.

"McTroy? What do you want him for?"

"Business, sheriff. We aim to hire him to trail a gang of robbers," I said. I kept the news of the train wreck, robbery, and murders private for the time being.

"That's what he does best," Nugent said. "You ask at the jailhouse?"

"We've just come from there."

"Look for him at the country club on the river, did ya?" asked a miner. His head rested on the tabletop. His eyes were closed. The puddle he laid his cheek in might have been beer. He held a five-card poker hand (a pair of deuces) out for all to inspect. If I hadn't seen his lips move I would have guessed him beyond speech in his present state.

"Frank, you gab in your sleep too? Well, there's a rowdy Bisbee mucker for you." Nugent swatted at his back. "He's talking about up on the hill, at the territorial prison."

I had heard stories of the Yuma Territorial Prison and I had no wish to visit the place for myself. I could not imagine bringing Evangeline up there, or Yong Wu.

Frank's comment and Nugent's response seemed to rouse the seedy, red-eyed miners from their evening stupor. They tipped their hats back and rubbed their benumbed faces as the lamplight turned them to gold. In doing so, they noticed that a woman was standing behind me, and this manifestation piqued their curiosity if not their vocabulary. Chairs scraped. Backs straightened. Smiles appeared, if not teeth.

"You folks appear a mite foot-weary and out of your element. You sure about what you're doing? McTroy isn't a man to trifle with. He might be at Sam's Hotel. But it's no place for a lady or a child to walk into." Nugent directed this last comment at me.

"We will go wherever it is necessary to get what we want," Evangeline said, "or in this particular case, who."

The miners elbowed each other and quaffed their drinks in amazement.

Nugent nodded.

"McTroy keeps his horse in Black Shirley's barn. She'll tell you if he's in town. Moonlight. That's his horse's name. A white mustang mare. Pretty horse. Good luck to you." He leaned forward to get a fuller view of Evangeline. "Good evening, ma'am."

He touched his hat. Raised a glass of beer and pressed it to his brushy mustache.

"Where is Black Shirley's barn?" I said.

Foam in the whiskers – he wiped the bubbles with his sleeve.

"Down the street. Red shutters. Shirley's a big, black-haired gal. Can't miss her."

"Thank you, sheriff."

"Welcome to Yuma," he said.

The miners laughed as the doors swung shut behind us.

20

BLACK SHIRL'S BLACK BARN

Yuma, Arizona Territory
Evening and night, April 6th, 1888

Black Shirley was indeed hard to miss. She stood a head taller than I did and she smoked the biggest calabash pipe I'd ever seen. She wore buckskin britches and a white, collared shirt with floral embroidery. Her namesake hair hung below her waist. A pair of bloodhounds lounged on her porch along with a smaller dog that looked like a thatch of curly pondweed caked together with mud. The only parts of the bloodhounds that were moving were their sad eyes, but the pondweed skipped and barked and watered the tips of my boots after I climbed the steps. Shirley's shoulders were broad as a man's, and when she shook my hand I feared she might grind the bones to dust before she released me.

"Black Shirl is who I am. You say Sheriff Nugent sent you?"

I confirmed that he did and told her why.

"Is Mr McTroy presently in town?" I asked, trying to sound hopeful.

Shirl puffed her pipe and squinted past me at my companions who waited at the bottom of the steps. "That your wife?"

"Ah – no, she is not my wife. We are business associates."

Evangeline smiled and waved to Black Shirl.

"The boy don't look like either of you two," Shirl said, not waving back.

"Yong Wu works for us. Are we in luck with Mr McTroy? We have walked several miles in the desert heat today. Yesterday our train crashed and we were robbed. Many people died. We are, in fact, the only survivors. And we have not slept or eaten and we really would like to find McTroy so we can settle this contractual matter and then rest."

"He's back there with Moonlight."

"McTroy? He's here?"

Shirl nodded. "I've got beans and cornbread. Two sleeping rooms in the back. Rates aren't as cheap as some places in town, but there's no lice. I keep a clean house."

"Is McTroy staying here at your place?"

"Sleeps in the barn. You want the rooms?"

"Yes, yes we do," Evangeline called from the street.

This time Black Shirl waved to her.

"The lady who isn't your wife says you want them. She can have the room on the left. You and the china boy can take the other. I run a respectable Christian house."

"Of course we will take the rooms. Thank you."

"You pay first." She told me how much and waited for me to change my mind.

"I will, yes." I fumbled in my satchel bottom for loose

coins. "What is McTroy doing now?"

"Sleeping, I imagine. Or not sleeping, hell if I know. I don't go in the barn to bother him after sundown. You shouldn't either, if you're asking me my opinion. But you're not. So go. See what happens. I'll only caution you. McTroy don't like surprises. He's what you might call intolerant to strangers. You all are about as strange as I seen around here in a good while."

I handed over the money for the rooms.

"You got bags?" Shirl asked.

"No, only what we carry."

She jingled my coins in her large hand.

"Go back then. Get it over with. You can't turn around now. Come all this way to turn around? I don't think so. I ain't responsible for what he says to you. I am especially not responsible for what he does to you. You remember that. I said, 'Don't go.' Now go. You are frying my nerves. I'll heat the beans. Rooms are through the kitchen. Barn's right back there."

The pondweed nipped at my trousers as I descended from the porch.

"Is she saying to go or not to go?" Evangeline said.

"Both and neither – as far as I can detect."

Black Shirl nodded. "Both and neither. Fella's right about that."

She went into the house. Pondweed followed her. The bloodhounds watched us.

"What are we going to do?" Evangeline said.

"I will proceed to the barn and talk to McTroy. You will join Shirley for beans."

"Maybe we should go together."

"No, I think not."

"But I want to be sure he says 'yes.' We desperately need his help."

"I will get him to say 'yes'."

"It's my father's money. I should go too."

"If he shoots me, then you can go next. Does that sound fair?"

The purple dusk – her eyes changed to seawater gray in the dimness. "Hardy, you are a funny man, I think. Would you like us to save you some beans?"

"Beans and bread. That would be very nice. If I die, you're welcome to eat my portion."

"Thank you. I am famished actually. Yong Wu must be as well."

"It's nothing. Black Shirl seems like quite the conversationalist once you break the ice. Perhaps she can give you valuable background about McTroy and Moonlight."

She loosened a ribbon from her chignon and tied it around my wrist.

"For luck," she said, and smiling, patted my hand.

The moon rose crooked in the sky like a wizard's finger. Black Shirley's barn was black, or looked black in the failing light. The barn door stood partly open, and that crevice was the blackest part of the whole tableau. I was slow going down the path. I shuffled my feet. I whistled a tuneless melody to disguise my fear and to inform McTroy a visitor, just a harmless, bookish visitor, was approaching. Second thoughts crowded out any firsts I had.

Here was the barn door.

"Hello in there?" I said.

No answer. My heart knocked. My hand refused to touch knuckles to the wood.

I tried calling louder. "Hellooo in the barn…"

Now he had to have heard me that time.

Still I got no reply. Not even a whinny from the horses, and I could smell them – a good farmy horse smell. It reminded me of my boyhood, of animals I knew like family, of mornings rising up in the gloom to take care of our stock: the first living things I saw each day before breakfast. Maybe it was that homey memory that gave me a dose of courage, I don't know, but I laid my hand on the door and pushed.

"Say there, you're a pretty girl. Aren't you?"

The horse – his horse, Moonlight, and she did look like a piece of cool nocturnal magic – gazed nobly upon me from her stall. She was smallish, as horses go, and well-muscled. Later I would learn of her otherworldly endurance and an intelligence that surpassed many men. She was the only being McTroy would show his love to plainly. Rubbing her nose. Laying his face against her broad neck. I didn't know this sentimental side of him yet. I only saw the beautiful animal he loved staring at me, quiet as marble.

Maybe the infamous man wasn't here…

I pushed the door wider to see more.

Other stalls, other horses.

A lantern hung on a hook to my left. My fingers dug into my pockets and out came a match, quickly fumbled, dropped, lost, then a second match and my thumbnail scratched at it till it found its spark, flaming tall as I passed it under the lantern's smudgy globe. Smoking, aflutter, enough light to walk behind, but casting shadows.

Indigo blanket folded on a bed of clean straw: McTroy's nest. Empty. A Mexican charro saddle – well-traveled, the leather tooled and red as a drop of blood – was pegged on the wall.

So where was this mercenary man?

The cold muzzle of a gun touched my cheekbone.

"I'm looking for the bounty hunter, McTroy," I said. "Are you he?"

"*You he*? Am I dealing with a fancy man or an idjit?"

I didn't wait long to answer.

"My name is Romulus Hardy. I am a scholar and an archivist of ancient Egypt."

"Fancy man it is then." With his free hand he flicked the ribbon on my wrist. "Tell me, do they teach fancy men to sneak up on people?"

"I didn't sneak. I called to you."

"Huh. Maybe you did."

Reader, this book is about how I – how we three from the train – became intimate with the supernatural world. You might think we introduced McTroy to it, too. But you'd be wrong. He was acquainted with the nightside of things. He may not have talked about it, but he was touched with something southern folks call the gift. I don't mean he could see far into the future. Obviously he couldn't, or he would have turned me away. But he could peek a little bit. More than that, he knew what lurked beneath the surface life. He felt that clammy stone feeling in his stomach. It often arrived with no warning, because it was a warning: a slippery promise. Death signs. Evil juju. Corner-of-the-eye creatures that lurked, mocked, and hated every soul that lives in the light – McTroy knew them. In dreams… on mud streets after a driving rain... inside jail cells and lonesome, tilted, windblown shacks... fallen backward into lakes of blood... he had seen... things. He wasn't one to share his uncanny experiences. But now and again he talked to me. That's how I know.

There in Black Shirley's barn we were still strangers to one another.

He greeted all strangers with suspicion.

We might have stayed strangers if it weren't for my good luck and his bad. That's how he would tell it if he were around. He would be joking, of course. He never told a story without a joke inside. But he would mean it too. Some parts. About the bad luck, about how it was coming for him that night as it had been coming all his life. His lifetime's due.

The barrel of the gun stayed where it was.

"I really did call to you. If you were sleeping soundly perhaps–"

"Quiet."

"What? I can explain."

He poked the gun into my jaw where my teeth were.

"You got partners? Outside? Coming up the walk after you?"

"No, I'm alone... I..."

"Step right there and hold that lantern up."

He shoved me in front of the doorway.

"You let 'em come," he said.

He withdrew behind a wall post.

I felt like a fool standing there, teeth chattering, watching the same space I had been contemplating from outside the barn a minute earlier. I saw not a thing, heard nary a soul approaching either by coincidence or in stealth. It crossed my mind that though I may sometimes play the fool, here again I was dealing with a madman. I ask this: *Why would a learned and habitually logical person get himself into such positions on a semi-regular basis?* I will leave that question for people other than myself to debate.

So, I waited with the lantern, which grew heavier by the second, as if the escaping smoke were somehow replaced with lead deposits. My arm trembled. My eyes watered sufficiently enough to give the impression I was crying. I was not crying.

McTroy did not emerge from his hiding spot.

"Nothing is happening," I said.

I was prepared to repeat myself, even if it meant being shot, when McTroy sprung from behind another wall post, reached into the door void, and dragged in Evangeline.

She entered with her wings open and quite colorful like a flushed pheasant.

"Ohhh..."

As soon as he saw she was a woman he let her go.

While Miss Waterston was a sight to behold, this was my first chance to get a full view of McTroy. He stepped away as she regained her balance and then her composure.

People always remember Rex McTroy as a big man, but he stood average height and went underweight his whole life. He belted his pistols high and butt forward. When he drew them he habitually did so in the Cavalry twist style, quick as a rattler strike. He had unholstered a Colt single-action army revolver, and its twin remained sedate on his hip. His suit was unremarkably somber, his hat black as the barn we sheltered in. He wore a mustache and his hair reached his shoulders. Both were ashy.

"Ma'am," he said. To add to his politeness, he shifted his weapon back to me.

"Pleased to meet you, Mister... McTroy, is it? *He* is the man I seek."

"You found him. Is this joker with you?"

"I'm afraid I've never seen him before in my life," she said.

Here I nearly dropped the lantern and started a fire.

"What on earth? Evangeline, tell him who I am. This is no laughing matter."

She shaded her eyes from the lantern. "Dr Hardy, is it you? I almost did not recognize your face. You have a red mark on your cheek, yet you appear rather pale."

"You know who I am. Stop playing games."

"For a refined gentleman I don't like your tone," McTroy said.

"That is Dr Hardy, my associate. He is right to be upset with me. Now is not a good time for diversions. We need your help. And the doctor is no threat to anyone, so please put away your weapon. I think we all need to sit some place well-lit and talk."

I wanted to argue that I was a threat, but I saw no winning.

McTroy sheathed his iron.

We followed the lady up the path to Black Shirl's kitchen.

21
RAGDOLLS

We all ate beans. I was a little angry at the way McTroy
had been talking to and about me – not to mention
digging the gun into my face. But I remembered the
warnings Black Shirley and Sheriff Mike Nugent had
given us about McTroy's prickly disposition. I was a
good deal hungry as well. So, I kept my mouth filled
with beans and empty of words. I don't think I could've
slipped more than a phrase into the proceedings
edgewise, as Evangeline had taken control of the
conversation and would not have let go without a
quarrel. It was more monologue than anything else.
She told him our story, from my expedition through
the murderous robbery on the rails and right up to our
parley in the barn. Only she left out any reference to
the supernatural elements – which I don't need to tell
you is an omission of major dimensions. It was her
show. I let her run it.

Once she had gotten to the part about the necrófagos
– and notably left out the fact that they were necrófagos!
And definitely not your ordinary cutthroat Mexican
banditos! – Yong Wu started giving me pointed looks

across the table. They were on the order of, *"Hey, that's not what happened!"* and *"Whoa, there! Are you going to just sit quietly while she lies through her teeth?"* and even *"What about the giant worm!!?"*

The answer was in my silence.

Wu either realized my position on the subject, or perhaps it was his status in our traveling group. But he said nothing. Maybe he was really hungry too. The boy ate like a farmhand.

"There you have it, Mr McTroy. That is our story beginning to end. Only I must admit I have skipped over a most important part." Evangeline tucked her chin coyly.

I stopped chewing.

McTroy had already wiped his plate clean with his bread. He leaned back on the creaky legs of his chair. In the kitchen light, I could see what Wu meant about his eyes. They were unnaturally light-colored in the irises. Cold and sparkly like the edge of a stropped razor.

"What part is that, Miss Waterston?"

She had paused long enough to force him to ask.

"Why, the money, sir. We don't expect your expertise to come for free."

I held out my plate to Shirl. "More beans, please, if you would."

Shirl scraped out a last mound from the bottom of the pot.

"Thank you kindly," I said.

"I do not typically work for hire unless you are a railroad. Miss Waterston, you are not a railroad."

"But you hunt men for bounty?"

"I do at my discretion."

"I guarantee there will be a generous bounty offered for these... evil men."

"If your tale is true, then I don't doubt it."

"Then we can count on you to join us?"

"No." McTroy started up from his chair.

Evangeline sighed. "The railroad's owner," here she mentioned him by his nickname and that impressed McTroy though he tried to hide it, "he and my father play cards whenever they are in town together. They do frequent business, but they are also friends. He will be greatly outraged at the misfortune we encountered on his train."

"How does your padre come by his money?"

"Mining... mostly gold," she said.

McTroy sat back down. He motioned to Shirley and she fetched him a bottle of whisky from the cupboard. She pumped water into the sink and filled a tin cup. He received the bottle, uncorked it, and drank directly from it. She passed him the cup and he wet his lips.

"Gold will do it," he said, letting out a long, fragrant breath. "Your daddy paid spiffy boy here to mine up those dead Egyptians for him?"

I laid down my spoon and dabbed the corners of my mouth with a handkerchief.

"Father's interests are diverse," Evangeline said.

"Diverse and underground it seems."

I cleared my throat to disguise my chuckling.

"The railroad will offer a substantial reward. My father will quadruple it – that is to say, double the amount twice. I do not know how you are accustomed to living. But it's safe to assume you would never need to work again. Be sure of this: there will be a posse of bounty hunters in pursuit of the creatures who perpetrated this horrendous crime. If you help us, I promise you the whole prize. Dr Hardy and I want none of it. We know the ones who did this. No one can find them as fast as we can. Working together."

"These creatures are already in Mexico. If what you say is true, they stole nothing from the train but a load of ragdolls."

"It is true," she said. She winced at her slippage of the word "creatures."

"See, that makes less sense to me than digging up dead bodies for your art collection. A Mexican outlaw has enough corpses at hand, he don't need yours. And he wouldn't know what to do with them once he got them. So, either this scum didn't know what they were stealing or they are loco. Either way, your ragdolls got dumped in the desert for crowbait or they sit in a cantina catching bullets for a bunch of tequila-soaked cholos."

"May I say something?" I said.

"No," McTroy said.

"Please do, Hardy. Tell him he simply must help us."

I said, "McTroy, you do not need to help us."

Evangeline made a quick move to slap my hand, but I was quicker in pulling away, and she hit the table hard enough to make the silverware jump. Yong Wu startled in his seat.

I went on. "Though we were assured by all who we asked that you were the hardest man in the territory, I, for one, completely understand if you feel you are not up to the challenge of capturing these hostile foreign gunmen. They are numerous and fierce. Not to mention ugly as sin. You are but a man. Miss Waterston and I thank you for listening to our plea. In the morning, we will announce a call for the formation of a posse. They will guide us in collecting our ragdolls from over the border. The more I think about this plan of Miss Waterston's, the more I think it is beneath a man of your caliber – despite the ludicrous financial compensation."

I pushed myself from the table. "Come, Yong Wu, we must get to bed. Tomorrow there are contracts waiting to be drawn and crowds of fresh men to be hired."

We had dusted the crumbs from our clothes and were about to cross the threshold into our humble bedroom before McTroy stopped us.

"Wait," he said.

"Goodnight, sir. I hope you can return to your slumber in the barn."

"I said, 'Wait.' Now tell me again what you all want from this deal. You want the coyote trash who robbed you… you want them killed? Taken alive? Which is it?"

"It is no consequence to us. We only want the mummies back," I said.

"I can't guarantee their condition if we find them. How many are there again?"

"Six. We will take them back in whatever form they are found. And there is only one we must have returned, with his sarcophagus – his stone coffin box. That is not negotiable."

"I get the railroad money, plus four times that, for one corpse in its right box?"

"That is the offer as the lady presented it."

"Well, I like it better now after you said it. And you don't care who dies?"

"We would prefer not to die ourselves."

"You ain't going with me."

"We must. Not negotiable. We are the only ones who can identify the robbers and the remains of Amun Odji-Kek – the corpse in the box, as you call him. We go with you."

McTroy grumbled but nodded. "I'm not paying for daily expenses."

"We will pay," Evangeline said, happily.

McTroy screwed up his face as he was computing mental calculations. "Two quarter horses and saddles, bridles, blankets..."

Shirl had taken a pencil from her pocket and was writing down a list on a scrap of newsprint. McTroy shifted toward Evangeline. "Can you ride?"

"Of course, I can ride. Since I was a girl of seven."

"How about you, Doc?"

"I've ridden horses and camels."

"Shirl, you got any camels?"

"Nope."

"Then I guess the doc will settle for a horse like the rest of us. We'll need coffee, food, bedrolls, and such. I expect to be gone a week. Two at the most. Get the supplies from Abel's general store. Tell Abel to bill the lady. I said she's good for it. Can you find her some clothes that don't stand out like a Bolivian flag? The boy's not coming with us, is he?"

"Yes, he is," Evangeline said.

"Then he's your responsibility. He rides with one of you. I'll already be slowed and sweating it like a whore at church." He shook his head. "A dandy, a woman, and Jake Chinaman. These banditos better watch out. At least we'll have shock on our side."

Once we shook hands all around, even Yong Wu and Black Shirley joining us for this ceremony of harmonious accord, McTroy's mood peaked. He finished off the whisky and took Evangeline for a twirl around the kitchen while Shirl played a mouth harp and stomped her foot. She fashioned a fine tune, though none I could name off the top of my head, and they all tended to run together into one dancing opus. Evangeline was red-faced by the time they finished. She and her partner had worked up a lather.

This time when I excused Yong Wu and myself for bed, I meant it.

"You're right, Doc," McTroy said. "We got big business in the morning."

He bowed to the ladies and headed back to the barn.

Shirl went to the porch for a goodnight puff on her pipe. I ushered a sleepy-eyed Wu off to a much-needed night's rest. I pumped water for Evangeline and me to toast closing the deal.

"I'm no dandy," I said after the others left us.

"No, you aren't," Evangeline said. "He doesn't know you. And I doubt he's ever seen the flag of Bolivia. Don't judge him on minor matters. It will take time for us to learn about each other, the good and the bad. The important thing is we've done it. We're going to Mexico to beat those monsters and bring back our artifacts."

"We're going to Mexico. Let's wait and see about the rest."

"Hardy, I don't know you all that well either. Are you always so gloomy?"

"I didn't used to think so. But Odji-Kek might have turned me around since he wriggled his way into my brain aboard the *Derceto*."

"Don't say that." Her expression had fallen. She paled.

"I was being metaphorical," I said.

"It's not something to take lightly. From what I know about Amun Odji-Kek he might very well seize a person's mind and never give it back."

That bit of intelligence was most unwelcome. I had more than enough worries to burden me. The prospect of losing my personal psyche instilled a degree of crankiness.

"When I went on my expedition I knew almost nothing about this sorcerer. Not his name. Not his story, which is still sketchy. I didn't even know he was the one in the tomb. Your father did. You did."

"I'm sorry we didn't tell you more at the time. We thought you'd be scared off. You wouldn't have been the first to turn tail. In retrospect, it was a terrible mistake."

"Yet you're making the same mistake again. Withholding information from McTroy."

"Oh, we barely convinced him the way it is." Her spine straightened. I could sense the righteousness flooding back into her. "Thank you for getting him to join our search. You know as well as I do that would have been impossible if we had told him the truth."

"Perhaps…"

"Not perhaps, definitely not perhaps." She shook her head. "We have a big day ahead of us, and if I don't climb into bed I swear I will crumple to the floor." She placed her cup in the sink and walked around the table, heading to her bedroom.

I cut off her path.

"Why does your father want Odji-Kek?"

"Really I… I don't think it is appropriate… he may not want me…"

She was more flustered by my question than I expected. Words failed her.

"I can't tell you," she said, finally.

"Why not?"

"There are things I don't know about my father. That is one of them."

"I wish I could trust you more than I do."

"Hardy, I wish you could too."

How is it that I felt thwarted by her, and yet desired to embrace her equally?

I was about to touch her arm, as a preamble to what I could not exactly predict. But I had no chance to see where that contact might have led.

The door swung open, hinges screeching, and banged the wall. McTroy leaned forward. He was off-balance, grabbing me to keep from going sideways and sliding to the floor. I wondered how much whisky he drank in a day. He had his own bottle in the barn, I was certain. He smelled sweet and overheated. His clothes were glued to his skin.

"Sleep, you little hens," he said. "We ride at daybreak." He tottered out the way he'd come, not bothering to shut out the night. From the arch of his eyebrow and the gleam in his bloodshot eyes, I wondered if the devil had been listening outside the door the entire time.

22
LOBOS

I hadn't laid my head down on the pillow long enough to dent it before Wu was shaking me awake.

"What is it?"

"Time to go," he said. His face was puffy and his hair stood at odd angles.

Although I scarcely believed him, I opened my pocket watch near his lamp and found it was indeed the cusp of dawn. I groaned.

"Is Evangeline up?"

"Yes, everyone is. You are the last person sleeping."

"Would that I were still sleeping. Is that coffee I smell?" The door to our bedroom lay open, but all beyond it was murky.

"The tall lady says so, yet I am not sure. The paper package reads, 'Arbuckles' Ariosa Coffee.' But look." He held a red and white striped stick of peppermint candy in the light. "She said this came in the package and she gave it to me. Do you think it might be a trick?"

"You are too suspicious, my young friend. If Black Shirl meant us harm, we would be cold in the ground instead of cold on our feet in her boardinghouse." I slipped into my trousers. "I judge the aroma to be fine. Let's drink up. Save the candy for our ride."

I twisted my neck, feeling as if I had been beaten with iron rods. The soft bed called to me like a warm and pouting mistress. I finished dressing in the chill air. My toes detected cool drafts whispering up from the cracks between the floorboards. Soon I will be too hot and complaining of that, I told myself.

With cup in hand, I ambled to the front of the house and peeked through the curtains. Three horses, including Moonlight, were tied outside in the milky-blue semi-dark. They appeared loaded and ready to ride. I saw neither Evangeline nor McTroy.

I caught a whiff of pipe tobacco before Black Shirl strode up the steps.

I pulled back and let the curtain fall as if I had been discovered spying.

With the pipe stem of that giant calabash clamped between her teeth, she told me McTroy was wanting to leave, the sooner the better. Shirl had stirred Abel, the local storekeeper, out of bed to supply our journey, and though he wasn't happy to be disturbed, he did like the sizable bump in his business. When he found out we weren't paying directly, his mood soured again.

"Evangeline has a bag of gold coins in that purse of hers. We counted out a few and Abel saw the rest so he quieted down. He's not the only supplier in Yuma, you know," Shirl told me.

"No, I didn't know. About the choice of general stores or the lady's gold coins," I said.

"She paid me," Shirl said. "I do a bit of sewing and dressmaking. She looks real pretty in the one she picked today for your ride."

"Wait here, please," I said.

I went to my bedroom and searched inside my satchel. When I came back, McTroy was there. Blue shirtsleeves, gray vest, guns strapped. Black hat low on his head.

"Morning, Sunshine, how'd you sleep?" he asked.

"What little I had refreshed me."

"That's what the circus dwarf's wife said, ain't it?"

I ignored him. Black Shirl was smiling. I made her my offering.

"This is a unique sample of tobacco I purchased in New Orleans, and a fine cigar. I hope you enjoy them. You have been most hospitable in our time of need."

She accepted and showed her appreciation by clapping me vigorously on the shoulder.

"Come back anytime."

McTroy nudged her. "See there, Shirley, Doc isn't a puritan after all."

"Where is Miss Evangeline?" I asked.

"Why, she better be in her room. I've got one search on my plate already."

I had not noticed that Evangeline's door was shut, which is but a single reason I would not make a good lawman. I approached her room and knocked.

"Enter," she said.

I did as I was told and saw she had been writing, by candlelight, a note.

"I was wondering where you were. McTroy is in a hurry to go."

"Sending a telegram to Father to tell him I am alive, the mummies are stolen, we are Mexico bound, we've hired a professional to get them back, can he please talk to the railroad owner about rewards, and we need more money, et cetera."

"We have your bag of gold," I said.

"That won't get us far."

"Anything else hiding in your purse that I don't know about?"

"I suppose most of what's inside."

"Right, then. So much for building up trust between us."

"Do you really want to rifle through my purse, Hardy? It's there on the bed. Have your way with it." She gestured broadly toward the bed.

Heat rushed into my face. "I don't like secrets, is what I'm trying to say."

"All men like secrets, Hardy. If it weren't for secrets what a bore life would be."

"I'm not arguing philosophy with you. You know what I mean."

"I bought something at the store today. Would you like to see it?"

She thrust her hand under the desk. Playfulness marked her. Her knees bounced eagerly in their nook. The change in conversational direction threw me.

"What is it?"

"What is what?" She returned to her telegram, reading over the lines.

"What did you buy at the store?"

She slid her chair back, and from between her knees brought out a hat. Wide-brimmed and chocolate brown, of the slouch style favored by soldiers during the war; hers was edged in ribbon. She put it on. "What do you think? Does the color favor me?"

I could hardly think of a color that wouldn't favor her.

But I didn't say that.

"It looks... good on you. You will require a hat under the cruel sun."

"I'm glad you like it. There's no reason a thing cannot be both functional and attractive." She left the hat on, tilting her head at charming angles, checking the fit.

"I agree." What were we discussing here? I lost my place so often when we spoke.

She shooed me away. "I need to finish this telegram. You're not helping."

I closed her door.

"Is she in there, Doc?"

"She is writing a telegram to her father about your reward."

"Good deal," he said. "I like a woman who is organized."

"Do you really?"

"Damned straight." He grabbed up a bag of vittles from the table. "No time for breakfast. We eat on the hoof. You and the boy get acquainted with your horse. She's the browner of the two. Her name's Penny. She's a good animal. If there's a problem, you know it's you, not her. I saw riders gathering at the territorial prison. Word has likely gotten out that your train never arrived. Curious parties will go looking. That'll be our competition. But they'll be sleepy and stupid at the start. We've got an advantage or two. Saddle up. Don't forget to say goodbye to Shirl. You might not guess it, but she's sensitive when it comes to farewells."

Mid-morning: the sun was on us. Penny had proved to be a congenial beast. Wu, on the other hand, was not accustomed to traveling via horseback. He feared many outcomes, falling off being his topmost concern. He hugged my waist like an anaconda. An hour earlier I had fought for my breath and persuaded him to loosen his grip, but the slow pressure returned. I conjectured that the towering column of smoke accumulating like a thundercloud before us was no small factor in his hugging me close.

Something terrible had happened.

Evangeline extracted a spyglass from her purse of wonders and scanned the calamity. Her gelding, Neptune, remained steady underneath her as she swept her lens over the landscape. "The boiler must have exploded," she said. "Oily black smoke, and I see wreckage blown from the hole. Oh dear, I see bodies."

Here Wu's arms began tightening again. I could feel his forehead pressed against my spine. He clearly did not want to see anything at all concerning the dead. I did not blame him. The scene was beyond all description and impossible to ignore. If there were a Hell, this was it.

Evangeline put away her glass. She combed her fingers through Neptune's mane.

McTroy kept silent.

I guessed that any doubts he had about our story were gone.

We rode up to within a hundred yards of the inferno.

"Wait here," McTroy said.

He tied a scarf over his nose and mouth and galloped a swift circumference of that red region. When he rejoined us, his bare skin had turned smutty black. "This is a mighty sinkhole. I'll give you that," McTroy said. He lifted himself up in his stirrups and peered back toward the pit where the ruptured train combusted. The wind shifted. Smoke particles and unimaginable roasting smells overwhelmed us. Moonlight wagged her head in displeasure, and he steered her around in a half-circle away from the worst of it.

We followed him.

"We'll go around," he said. He motioned at a course westward and then south.

I knew then that even the slightest hope of tracking the worm's path into the tunnel was now impossible. So, I made no mention of it.

McTroy said, "I saw tracks on the Mexico side of the hole. Can't hardly believe they dug that beauty, the bastards. Must've taken fifty or a hundred men all night and still I don't see how they did it. But you say only a dozen robbed you?"

I nodded.

"Makes no sense." He shook his head. "There's nobody alive in that perdition. The corpses are pretty chewed on. Parts burned, parts scattered. Must be lobos and coyotes picking up the death scent. Moonlight doesn't like it."

"We should press on then," I said.

I didn't want him examining the improbable scenario too closely.

"Right, that posse will be here in no time. They'll ponder this for a good while."

Evangeline had taken out her spyglass, scouring the horizon in all directions.

"We are, as far as I can see, quite alone for the moment," she said.

"Let's make time, hens." McTroy snapped his reins and we navigated south.

The tracks were clear enough in the sand, though the wind would erase them as far as my inexpert eyes could tell. I was glad we rode hard for the better part of what was left of the morning. But as the noontime heat intensified, McTroy slowed the horses.

I rode up parallel.

"Have you given any thought to the mummies?"

"Like what?" he said.

"How will we bring them back? They are precious cargo. You can't sling them over your saddle like a dead horse thief."

"I can't track with a wagon either. How'd the banditos get that big coffin sprung anyway? No wagon in this group we're following. You said the bugger's heavy. Heavy leaves a mark."

He gave me a dubious stare.

"They used a tunnel in the bottom of the pit."

"Crashed the train then took the treasure out? Where'd the other end of that tunnel pop up, d'you suppose? In them hills back there? Where the caves are?"

"Maybe…"

"Don't matter. We got a trail right here and I know where they're headed."

"Where's that?" I asked.

"El Camino Del Diablo. You know what that means, Mr Jake Chinese?"

"His name is Yong Wu," I said.

"Know what that means, Yongwu?"

"No, sir," Wu said.

"The Devil's Highway." McTroy smiled. He rode relaxed, like the best camel drivers. "We'll stop soon. Water the horses. Sit in the shade. Get going again when the sun drops. There's usually water in those mountains. If there isn't, we won't need to worry about any coffin wagons but our own."

"You'll need to think about it sometime," I said.

I dropped my pace and slid back in line behind him.

"Find the mummies first," he called out. "Worry about cartage later."

Gila Desert, 10 miles NW of the Tinajas Atlas Mountains

We camped that night in a valley of mesquite and creosote bushes. The land lay dead flat and our position on it felt vulnerable as darkness fell. McTroy was unperturbed. He built a small fire and cooked coffee and beans. Evangeline, who had ridden the last miles in unusual silence, struck up a conversation, and McTroy, for his part, welcomed it.

She told him how she was trained as a librarian.

"I studied at the Boston Anthenaeum," she said. "And I have conversed privately with Melvil Dewey, chief librarian at Columbia College in New York, who was more interested with what was under my corset than inside my head. But, nonetheless, his ideas concerning cataloging are revolutionary."

"Never trust a Melvil." McTroy cut a piece of jerky with an elk horn-handled knife. He passed it to Wu.

"Want some, Doc?" he said.

I accepted a strip of chewy meat that came from an unknown animal. Evangeline declined his offer. It tasted gamey and of wood smoke and peppercorns. As soon as I ate my piece I wished I had another, but no more offers came my way this evening.

"Books are my life," Evangeline said.

"You and the doc liked school?"

We both agreed we did.

"How about you?" he asked Wu.

The boy shrugged. "I liked my parents teaching me things. But I don't remember school."

"You're lucky. I couldn't wait to leave. Bored stiff. Wish my arithmetic was better as I am sure I have been cheated by numbers men. Reading seems a poor substitute for doing."

"Reading is doing," I said.

McTroy laughed. "Good one, Doc. You're funnier when you're tired."

He broke out the blankets and loosened the horses' loads. I noticed him sipping occasionally from a flask, but he took his drink in private, in the shadows away from the fire, behind the horses.

As we bedded down, hand-sized black shapes flitted over the horses and our heads.

Bats.

That reminded me of something.

"Did you know they discovered bats deep inside the Great Pyramid?"

"Really?" Evangeline said, yawning.

She lay on her back under the stars. I could hear the exhaustion in her voice.

I bent toward the fire and tossed in a twig. "It's fascinating. The passages were full of guano. Just imagine climbing your way inside those tight, airless tunnels with only a torch to light your way, and then hordes of bats start flying out." I spread my fingers and wiggled them near the flames. "I'm no lover of small spaces. And frankly will admit to trembling a bit at the idea of sharing them with wild animals." Smiling, I glanced at Evangeline to see her reaction.

She had turned away from the firelight. Her blanket rose and fell steadily.

Reclining next to her, a fully awake Yong Wu shuddered and pulled his covers higher.

A scrimshaw moon rose above us.

The desert is a noisy place when the sun goes down. Nightjars called out their watery tremolo. A great horned owl hooted from a nearby saguaro. He pivoted his ample head and I saw him there, perched on a cactus arm. He blinked twice at me.

Then flew off.

McTroy tucked away his flask and banked the fire.

In the hills – a howling, not far away at all. Wu's eyes grew alert.

"You worried about the lobos?" McTroy said.

The boy hesitated for a moment and then nodded.

McTroy said, "The Mex she-wolf littered. The pack is out hunting on her behalf. It's a good way. They take care of theirs. Our fire will keep them cautious. They'll watch though, and that's what I like. You can see the lobos thinking right here." He pointed to his own glittering eyes. "Spooky critters – the desert has its fill. You get used to it."

He rolled on his side just outside the fire's glow.

Yong Wu pulled his blanket under his chin. He watched the sky.

My eyes were heavy but I didn't want to sleep. Not yet.

I looked at Wu who seemed highly vigilant, despite the late hour.

I knew this – he wasn't worried about any wolves.

23
TOUCH OF EVIL

Reader, let me assure you that what follows was no dream. I did not sleep that night, not after what I saw, so how could I have been dreaming? Was it a trance? A hypnotic state? Perhaps an example of long-distance mesmerism? Can such a feat be carried out by the dead upon the living? You may have your opinion on the subject. I certainly have mine.

What I can do is tell you this: I watched Yong Wu who was busy watching the skies. He did not seem to be searching the constellations, but looking more immediately in the mid-air above our camp, where the bats had been flitting. He cocked his head as one does when one is listening for a familiar call that is expected. I was about to ask him who exactly he was looking and listening for, but then I thought better of it. That line of questioning would yield nothing. He hadn't told me who his hopping friends were before and he wasn't going to tell me now – they had to be the ones he was expecting. So instead of asking, I waited to see if anyone entered our bubble of light in the dark desert.

I switched my gaze from Yong Wu's face to the

burning wood.

That is when I noticed two things simultaneously.

One: I was now transfixed on the fire. I could not look away, though my peripheral vision worked without hindrance. My eyes would not shift from the flames.

Two: someone had stepped into the firelight.

The shape was tall and wide and dragging behind it a trail of bandages.

Here was the vision I had mistaken for a sailor aboard the *Derceto* days ago when I happened upon him at the rail, staring forlornly into the waves. The mystery man who disappeared and yet who lingered, whose presence below decks caused odd vibrations in my legs. Here was a nightmare come alive, or coming alive, piece by piece.

Here, I knew as surely as I knew anything, was Amun Odji-Kek.

Sorcerer of Set.

He Who Disturbs the Balance.

Plague Bringer.

Corruptor of the Land.

Slayer from the South.

Lord of Demons.

The evil priest walked toward our fire. He put his hands out over the red coals.

As my eyes were fixed in place at the core of the conflagration, I saw the figure standing near it with clarity. He did not look like any man I ever knew in life. He moved like a man does, but more slowly, more deliberately, as if he were newly reacquainted with his body, a man waking from a long sickbed slumber, one who has been brought back from the brink of death. Or perhaps from beyond the brink of death, I thought.

I could, here and there, spottily, through the holes and tears in the bandages, see the fire dancing. What living man is perforated through like a moth-eaten blanket? No man.

It was an added shock to me then, when he spoke.

"I cannot feel it," he said. "The heat of this fire... does not reach me."

Knowing that I was suffering from some partial paralysis, I wondered if I was capable of speaking. I did not know what I would say to him. But I tried to test my voice and only heard a low moan escape my lips.

"Don't speak," he said. "Think and I will hear your words as you hear mine, though you and I never learned the same tongue."

"Who are you?" I thought, and it was like hearing my voice inside a barrel.

"You know who I am. Do not insult me."

"You are Amun Odji-Kek, Sorcerer of Set."

He turned.

I could not raise my eyes to his, though in the periphery I saw they glowed not with the firelight but crystal-hard and yellow. I was glad not to look into them directly.

"You should be glad. Men have died at the sight of me."

I will have to be careful here, I was thinking.

"No care you take will make any difference, dog."

Conversing with a resurrected demigod is not as easy as one might imagine.

Small, thudding steps brought him closer to where I reclined on one elbow in my blankets. For an entity that was a good bit hollow and in parts altogether missing, he appeared alarmingly massive. When he stopped advancing, his thighs were at my eye level.

"You are the one who found me in the sands."

"Yes, I am an Egyptologist. I study the ancient history of your people–"

"Silence, dog. You are nothing. Do you know where I have been? What I have seen in my years underground?"

"How could I?"

"They buried me alive. They sent me to the Land of the Dead lost, hungry, and thirsty, without provisions, without guides. I had nothing. I was ravaged by monsters."

Whatever his crimes, the punishment did appear extreme. Yet, he was surely not an innocent man. And perhaps he deserved all he got and more. I simply didn't know.

"Look, I am sorry if you suffered–"

"Silence! They wished me to be destroyed. But I am not destroyed!"

He shuffled one foot, then the other. He stretched out an impossibly long arm. His hand covered my whole face. The bandages smelled of wood smoke from the fire.

"Dog, do you know what the underworld smells like? It smells like shit. And do you know what wandering in the void of space smells like? Dead embers. For millennia Amun Odji-Kek, the greatest to ever live, greater than any pharaoh, was so deprived!"

He closed his grip over my skull. He shook with rage, and worms dropped from the folds of his windings into my lap. I could not move! He ground his palm hard into my eyes until they burned as if he had rubbed them with salt.

He took his hand away.

I gulped in fresh air.

"I am returned," he said, his words coming out almost in whispers.

He is not talking to me so much as to himself, I thought. But he did not react to my thinking words this time. He seemed not to see me any more. He wandered around the fire circle. When he reached Yong Wu, he stopped again.

"Like you, this boy is awake."

Kek altered his position so I could see Yong Wu's face; his eyes were open and locked on the sky. But I knew that he was as aware of what was happening as I was. The poor boy! As he did with me, Kek took Wu's head in his hand – his two hands, using both this time. "Shall I crush his head? Shall I squeeze out his brains like so much pulp?"

"No," I cried in my mind, and I heard Wu's voice join me.

"Do either of you know what it is like to smother in a box?"

"I do. I nearly suffocated in a trunk my grandmother kept for storage. It was the most terrible experience I ever had. I fear tight spaces. Let the boy alone!"

"So, you do know. But can you imagine that no one will ever come to rescue you? That your servants are screaming without air in boxes around you? That when you die you will enter an even more hostile underworld? Would you survive to return as I have?"

Above Kek the air grew dense, flickering with forms – with bats.

He ignored them at first. He was concentrating on smothering Wu with his hands. Bats dove at him. And their numbers multiplied until they enrobed his body in quivering black. He swatted at them with one arm, keeping his other hand tight over Wu's nose and mouth. The night fliers did not relent. They hissed and nipped at his wrappings until he released the boy. Kek roared, grabbing bats from the air, flinging them to the ground and into the fire, stomping on them if they did not recover quickly, crunching them into the sand.

Once Wu was in no eminent danger of being killed, the bats flew off.

I saw Kek's ivory bones exposed through the tatters of his shroud. His flesh was dried, wrinkled, and stiff like salted fish. Beetles skittered in his ribcage. Kek's eyes shined with strange light. As he had grown bored with me, he now ignored Yong Wu. For his lack of interest, I was grateful. He wandered back to the fire. His pupils shrank to snaky vertical slits.

"Soon I will be able to feel this heat. I will live."

"Where are you now?"

"I don't know. I am waiting for my servants. I need sacrifice. Magic and blood sacrifice."

He did not deceive me. I was too insignificant to lie to.

He crouched over the campfire. He poked at the embers until his fingers lit. He held them out like a candelabra, tipping his head, studying the jittery flames. Eventually he snuffed them, one by one, in his mouth.

"How can I find you?"

"You will serve me," Kek said. His voice was weak. Fighting off the bats had tired him.

"I may have discovered your tomb, but I will never serve you."

"You serve me already," he said.

I lifted my chin to argue, realizing in an instant – I could move and Kek was gone.

Immediately I went to Wu. His eyes were closed, but he was breathing normally. I could not decipher if he had fallen into a deep sleep or if he was only feigning because of his fright. I said his name several times and jostled him, yet nothing changed. I went then to Evangeline and McTroy and found them both to be so completely at rest that their condition bordered on stupor. My conclusion was that Kek's conjuring had done something to enchant them, though they seemed unharmed, even blissful in their states.

This discovery did not soothe me.

24
El Camino del Diablo

McTroy rose first and already had coffee boiling by the time I crawled from my blankets. The morning was windless and the sky still dark. From his saddlebag, our guide retrieved a knotted cheesecloth sack filled with Black Shirley's butter-and-guava jelly-filled biscuits. He bit into one as big as his fist and handed me the sack. Skewers of bacon spat over the fire. He inspected and moved them around. He looked eager to meet the day.

My stomach growled.

"Bacon's about done. I like mine burnt. You might not," McTroy said.

He drank his coffee, the steam rising past his hat.

I rubbed my cold hands together. McTroy wore buckskin gloves with lambs' wool sticking out at the cuffs. He had turned up his collar and slipped a gray falsa poncho over his head. I draped my bedroll over my shoulders and grabbed for a can of coffee.

He pushed me back with his boot.

"Cans are hot." He shucked one glove and tossed it to me.

The glove bounced off my chest.

"Bad dreams keep you up last night, Doc?"

"I slept roughly, that is to say – not at all."

With my gloved hand, I retrieved a coffee can and then a bacon stick.

"We'll get you back to your featherbed soon as we can. I, myself, slumbered like a drunkard in the arms of an angel."

I was sitting on the ground, and McTroy had procured a smooth curved rock for his seat. From this vantage point, I noticed a black stippling on the left side of his face, etched below the hairline. Previously I had taken it to be a smudge of dirt on a man who toiled and slept outdoors. The disfigurement was not at all new; it had the appearance of trying to heal and failing to do so. I wondered if it was the reason why he wore his hat so low, to cover the dark stain on his skin, a trace of vanity in this hunter of villains.

"If you don't mind my asking, how did you get that mark on your forehead?"

He touched the spot with his naked thumb.

"Feller by the name of Apache Zeb did that. You ever hear of him?"

I indicated I had not.

"Half-breed horse thief. Arsonist. Murderer, mostly of women. He was the first desperado I went after for the reward. I was a kid. Apache Zeb got the drop on me. Took my pop's Colt Walker and told me he'd see me in hell. Pulled the trigger before I could say anything back. Misfire. I socked him in the throat and ran. The powder burned me."

"That must've been a harrowing experience."

"Can't say I ever forgot it."

"Did you catch him?"

McTroy shook his head sourly then gave a light tug to his hat brim.

"He's still out there being a menace. Last I heard he went to Oklahoma."

A sniffing noise made me turn.

Moonlight: saddled and ready to ride. Her wet eyes stared.

"Say, Doc, you a sleepwalker?"

"Not to the best of my knowledge," I said.

"The best of your knowledge might need improvement. How else do we explain these draggy tracks all around our fire? You got big feet, son. I might've shot you."

"Thank you once again for not shooting me."

"Don't mention it."

"If, indeed, I was the somnambulist. You must sleep heavy for a hunter."

"Not hardly."

The fact he hadn't awakened bothered him. As it should have.

"Hey, Wu, these ain't your hoofprints dancing in the night like a warrior, are they?"

"No, sir," the boy said to McTroy.

His muffled answer came from deep under a pile of blankets.

"We got dead bats too. Some in the fire, others ground up in the dirt. Mighty odd business. I might be inclined to call it a bad omen. These your bats, Emperor Wu?"

This time Wu was slower to respond.

"I don't think so," he said.

"Ha. They're squashed pretty good. Whatever it was did the job, and then some."

I ate my bacon and biscuit. Drank my coffee.

Wu emerged. His pigtails were crooked, fraying. Despite my being unable to wake him from his trance in the night, he looked like he hadn't slept. I searched for some recognition in his eyes of our mutual firelight encounter with the mummy, a sign that he remembered what had happened. I got little more for my questioning gaze than yawns. He came over, and we three sat, facing east. Wu dropped twigs in the fire.

The sky stitched a pink ruffle across the black silk of the retreating night. Even as we watched, stripes of peaches and cream spilled out under the pink.

"Gorgeous morning," Evangeline said.

She'd come up quietly from a rock pile at some distance to the rear of us. Well, three stunned males looked back at her and then to her blankets which were bunched just so to lend the impression she was lying there. Maybe *she'd* been the first one awake.

"What were you doing?" McTroy asked, angry.

"Washing up," she said.

"How long you been back there?"

"Long enough to wash up. Is privacy forbidden on the trail?"

"No, but… you should say something before you go off."

"Next time I will wake you, McTroy. You have my word."

Nutmeg freckles sprinkled her clean, high-boned face. Our ride in the sun must have brought them out. She approached us slowly, taking languid, long-legged strides, both arms raised above her head, tying her hair back until a single torch of pale flames swung behind her. Those upturned agate eyes sparked in me both chills and fieriness at the dawn. I had never seen a woman look so beautiful in my life.

I gulped my coffee and scalded my throat.

"Ahhhhh."

"Are you all right, Hardy?" she asked, touching my convulsing back.

I nodded.

"Worried," I said, gasping. And I choked some more.

"I am surrounded by such concerned gentlemen!" Her dramatic statement teetered on the verge of laughter. She found McTroy and me ridiculous in differing ways.

"Breakfast is ready. Get some before it's gone." McTroy threw the dregs of his coffee on the fire and the smoke kicked up. "Saddle your horses. We're losing time with all this talking." He walked off and pissed on a cactus in plain sight.

I handed Evangeline the cheesecloth bag.

"The biscuits are good. But we have a problem. Kek was here."

"Here? When?" Inadvertently – and I could not fault her – she scanned the immediate grounds for signs of the sorcerer. If I had said there was a wolf in camp her reaction would have been the same.

"Last night. Wu and I saw him. Or we saw an image of him."

"An image? I don't understand."

"We saw him walk into our fire ring. He talked to us. He tried to smother Wu."

"You saw the mummy alive? What did he say?"

"He bragged about coming back from the dead. Only he's not all the way into this world yet. He fades out.

He needs... his exact words were 'magic and blood sacrifice.'"

Evangeline weighed this news. Her expression changed several times before she spoke again. I gathered she had so many questions she didn't know which to ask first.

"Odji-Kek tried to smother Wu. Was he trying to speed up his materialization?"

I tightened the cinches on our horses.

"Unlikely. He's very angry. Resurrection makes him moody, perhaps. I do know he wants to damage things, to hurt them, if that makes any sense."

"But he couldn't do it?"

"The bats stopped him. Biting. Thrashing. These nocturnals care a lot about our Chinese train boy. Kek killed a batch over by the fire. If I hadn't been paralyzed and in danger of having my own head crushed, it would have been remarkable to observe."

Evangeline watched Wu folding his blankets.

She said, "It makes sense that Odji-Kek can't sacrifice to himself. He'd need someone else to do that. A disciple to cut the offering's throat and worship him."

"The necrófagos? Might they bring His Awfulness back?"

"Perhaps they could do it. But... they don't have any blood inside them. Blood isn't the easiest thing to come by in the desert."

"Says who?" McTroy, astride Moonlight, broke between us. "This desert is soaked with blood. You're not hunting then you're hunted. Let's nail 'em 'fore they get too far."

He rode ahead.

We mounted our horses. I leaned over to give Wu a hand up.

"On the train, you told me the mummies couldn't hurt me," Wu said. "Was that true?"

One look told me he remembered last night and what Kek had done to him.

I'm sorry I failed to protect you.

I thought this but could not say the words aloud.

"I thought it was true at the time. I'm afraid I was wrong," I said.

"What if they try to hurt me again? What will you do?"

"We're not going to let that happen," Evangeline said. "Not ever."

At noon, we found the first coffin.

A little after noon we saw the sarcophagus. First, I thought it was another stone. Uncrated, sunken into the sand, the lid sliding off to one side and broken in half. There was no question the wood coffin we had passed earlier belonged to my mummies, to one of Kek's minions. I recognized the aged wood. To see it kicked apart (and empty)… I felt a loss. Here I had traveled and searched and dug it up and secured it overseas, only to have a thing I thought was precious stolen and thrown away like trash. But finding Kek's sarcophagus was even worse. It was damaged beyond repair. There was no wooden coffin inside. I didn't even know if Kek had an inner mummy case. He was not buried like other men had been buried. Nothing about him was typical. I had spent two years locating this sarcophagus, and many sacrifices had been made to bring it to America.

Yet, here it was, treated no differently than a common shipping crate.

There was no one around. This stretch of land spread out flat, bleached of color, devoid of movement. Sweat soaked my hatband and dripped down my cheeks, cutting the layer of dust that covered me like a mask. I would've paid a Half Eagle for a cool breeze. The mountains humped to the west, too far away to conceal any attempt at an ambush. Broiling heat. I could almost feel the temperature rising, daring anything to live in this wasteland. There were only rocks and scrub and cacti and Kek's burial box where it sat, plump as a Sonoran Desert toad.

I wanted to scream in frustration.

Oh, I would have screamed, if it weren't for the guitar music.

Sweet, melodious – the tune sounded Mexican. Like a love song.

"Where's it coming from?" Evangeline asked.

"It sounds close," Wu said as he hugged me tighter.

"Inside the damned casket is where it's coming from." McTroy drew a pistol and rode up alongside Kek's tomb. He looked in, pulled his head back, and then looked in again.

He started swearing to himself.

The music stopped.

"Who is it?" Evangeline asked.

"How the hell should I know? Get over here and you tell me."

McTroy leaned over the sarcophagus and said something, then spit on the ground.

Evangeline and I (and Wu) peered inside the sarcophagus.

Tucked in the southernmost corner, like a spider, was a necrófago, or half a necrófago. And a guitar. His gaunt body ended under the ribcage. Below that he was crumbly black. He had some whitish tailbone left. It was sooty too. He was looking up at us with black eyes. He had no weapon. His skin-from-a-corpse mask was gone. He held on to the guitar. It was a nice guitar. The index finger on his right hand was missing. I recognized him, or what remained of him. He was the red-handled axe-wielding train robber. The one whose finger Kittle shot off. The ghoul who killed Thomas the porter.

"You speak English?" Evangeline asked him.

"Sí, some I do."

"What happened to you?"

"Nothing good."

McTroy shot him in the chest. Twice.

"Why did you do that?" Evangeline asked, incredulous.

"It was unnatural," McTroy said.

"That was stupid of you," I said.

McTroy still had his gun in hand. It was not the smartest comment I ever made.

"What's done is done. That thing was an abomination. My mama read me the bible and I know an abomination when I see one."

"It was stupid because you didn't kill it," I said.

"What?" He glanced down at what he knew to be the freshest of corpses.

"Tell him," I said to the ghoul.

"It's true, señor. You no kill me."

The necrófago waved lazily at him in the hot sun.

"Why you goddamned sonofa–" McTroy pointed his gun.

"It won't do any good," I said.

"He's impervious to your bullets," Evangeline said.

McTroy shot him four more times. Each bullet made the half body jerk.

"Do you see?" I said. "You're wasting ammunition."

The necrófago began to play the song from before. A sad song, full of longing.

"We should talk to him," Evangeline said. "He may know something that can help us."

McTroy tugged at Moonlight's reins. He rode off a short distance, talking to himself, and finally he called back over his shoulder, "What's going on here? Who are you people?"

It would not have surprised me to see him ride away forever.

Evangeline answered him in a raised voice, "It's complicated. We'll explain it to you. Soon, I promise. But now we need to talk to this unsightly creature. Nothing has changed as far as my offer. You will be paid. Now come back here. We have work to do."

After a bit of reflection, and copious swearing and recrimination of the present company and of himself – McTroy rejoined us.

"I will be paid the bounty?" McTroy said, to confirm what he'd heard from Evangeline's well-formed lips. He rubbed his chin with the back of his pistol-waving hand.

"Yes, paid in full. When we achieve our goal."

She addressed the undead. "Now, ghoulish one. Do you have a name?"

"Nombre?"

"What do your dirty compadres call you?" McTroy said loudly. He spat again.

"Rojo," the necrófago said.

"How did this happen to you, Rojo?" Evangeline asked. "Did it have to do with the mummies you stole from the train?"

"Los mummies." He nodded. "Sí, sí, los mummies did this to me. I hate them."

"What did they do?" She avoided examining his vivid condition too directly.

"They burn me. El Gusano crawls up from his hole. We meet him. Aquí. El fantasmo del mummy gigante says to break out his amigos de las cajas. So we do. He then grabs me and burns me so he goes into his body muchisísimo más. I do nothing to him. I hate him."

"The big mummy is still a ghost?" I asked.

"He is like…" Rojo flopped around the sarcophagus bottom. "All of them the same… los mummies." He flopped awkwardly, rather fishlike. "They kill some conejos, but…?" He shrugged.

"Conejos?"

"He means jackrabbits," McTroy said. "The damned mummies were eating rabbits."

"They did not eat them. They sacrificed the rabbits to animate the other mummies," Evangeline said, nodding to herself. "Kek is powerful enough to force himself back into this world. He uses the animal blood to rejuvenate his servants. If what Rojo says is true, Kek is in his own body now."

Rojo picked up the guitar and began to strum it.

"Why did they leave you?" she asked.

"I can no ride. El mummy gigante – he took my horse. They're coming back."

"Ain't nobody coming back for you," McTroy said. He

had said this to other desperate men. I knew by how quickly the words came. Maybe he'd heard them himself.

The necrófago played. Slowly, then faster. The hot tomb could have baked bread. But the music rang out as beautifully as notes floating from the window of a concert hall.

"Where is El Gusano taking the mummies?" McTroy asked.

"I don't know. I am stuck in the box. I don't even see which way they ride."

"Good luck when the lobos come to pick your bones." He pointed at the exposed portions of the ghoul. "What's left of them."

"I think I no taste too good. They don't eat me."

"Something will. Eventually. Leave him." He acted as if he were finished with the truncated graverobber. "We'll keep following those horse tracks."

"You don't know where they go, do you?" Rojo said.

"You don't either." McTroy made his tone sound dull, like a man tired of trading.

"Maybe I do. If I think very hard, something maybe shakes loose."

"Look at yourself, Rojo. I think you know shit. And if the critters don't want you, you'll dry up like a lizard turd."

"It's not so bad. I am in shade part of the day. I have my music."

"Keep telling yourself that."

McTroy tilted his head, letting us know we should ride farther away. He took a coin from his pocket and flipped it into the shadeless coffin. It pinged on the quartzite.

The music stopped. I couldn't see him, but I pictured the ghoul stroking the coin.

"Say, where'd you learn to play guitar anyway?" McTroy backed Moonlight up, leaving Rojo with nothing but the white sun in his sight.

"I found one in a grave. Long time ago. But I lost it. Then I found this one on the train. It's better than my old one."

He plucked a few notes. A sharper sound. He was using the coin.

Moonlight walked to where we waited.

The sun burned my hands. I touched Penny's mane, combing through the hairs. Evangeline uncorked her canteen. McTroy put his finger against his lips. *Shush*.

"Hey, hey you still there?" Rojo asked. "I didn't hear you ride off so you must be here."

McTroy shook his head.

There came a quick rustling sound from inside the sarcophagus. The ghoul appeared to be trying to lift himself to the edge to peek out. But, being as he was, that is to say, half of his former self, he could not maintain his balance. He fell and landed on the guitar by the discordant sound of it. "I know where they're going! Lady! Tell the caballeros to come back here!"

"Where they headed?" McTroy shouted.

"You take me with you and I show you."

"Not good enough."

"They're going to a church. With monks."

"A monastery?" Evangeline whispered. "Do you know this place?"

"No," McTroy said, under his breath. "Could be a lot of places."

"Listen! Hey! They're not going to the church," Rojo said.

"Which is it?" I said. "Are they going to church or not?"

"They're going to the temple *underneath* the church. That's where they're going. You never gonna find it without me. That's where the necrófagos hide. Take me. C'mon."

That is how Rojo came to ride with us into Mexico.

Well, not exactly ride.

McTroy threw the end of the rope into the sarcophagus. "Tie it under your arms."

"You gonna drag me?"

"You smell, Rojo. Moonlight won't have it."

"What about the lady? Lady, you let me ride with you?"

Evangeline, Wu, and I declined to help Thomas' murderer.

"It's drag or dry up, devil. If you ain't tying, give me my rope." McTroy pulled and the rope pulled back. McTroy smiled. With McTroy's assistance Rojo hoisted himself to the rim of the vault. He had tied a solid knot against his bullet-riddled chest. He boosted himself up, using the guitar like a crutch. The ghoul looked my way.

"Señor, you do something for me?"

I had no desire to aid this loathsome thing. "What is it?"

"My body no feels pain. If I get to a graveyard I can feast and grow new legs. You know? But this is the best guitar I ever have. You take it for me? Please?"

I paused at first but then relented and took the

instrument from him and gave it to Wu.

Wu reluctantly slung the guitar across his back.

25

DEATH CASTLE IN THE GILA

The monastery was the ugliest building I'd ever seen. My first glimpse of it rising out of the desert gave me vertigo. It triggered a bilious wave in my gut. I burped, lurched in the saddle, and hung my head askew in case I lost my biscuits. Swampy gas-green acids bubbled up inside me. Awhirl, I felt slick and cold as a frosty window; my shirt suckered to my skin despite attempts to peel it away. Next the shivers commenced, my teeth chattering, my head vised so I was nearly struck blind with pain. I stopped Penny, climbed down, and knelt in the dirt before I keeled over.

"What's the matter?" McTroy said.

"Sick," I said. "Suddenly. Maybe the bacon was bad."

"Mine wasn't. We all ate it."

"Are you feeling dizzy?" Evangeline asked.

"Very."

"It might not be the cured pork."

At the words "cured pork" I heaved dryly. Evangeline dismounted and put her hand to my brow. She retrieved her purse from Neptune's saddlebag.

"You're feverish. I've seen this before. Your connection

with Odji-Kek is strong. I suspect he's close by and his power has grown vastly. This is a corporal stress reaction."

I said, "He's in the church... the sanctuary of that monastery. I sense him – enthroned."

McTroy screwed up his face. He looked down at me then at the church walls.

"That place is laid out like a fortress. If he don't want to come out, it'll be hell forcing him. Them friars might not be friendly if they're hiding undead scum."

McTroy reeled in his rope, wrapping it around his saddle horn. In the dust, Rojo bumped along, looking and smelling like a sack of dead mackerel. My sight returned – piecemeal, splotchy, and shifting in hue to nauseating effect. But I did not have to look for long at our fellow traveler to register that the day's ride had come at a high price – naked Rojo freshly skinned and leaking a panoply of gray liquids.

Two inky eyes squinted at us.

If I entertained any thoughts that the ghoul had somehow expired, they soon were dispelled. He blinked. He licked his scabby lips with a shriveled tongue. McTroy jerked the rope and Rojo popped into a sitting position. The necrófago braced up on his broomstick arms.

"How you doing back there, you ol' corpse chewer?" McTroy asked.

"I been better," the ghoul said.

"That's good to hear. Well, your directions were true. I'll give you credit. These monks at Our Lady of the Dirthole – what are they, slaves to Satan, something like that?"

Rojo nodded as if the slow action were pumping out the last of his juices.

"Sí, something like that," he said, grinning.

His teeth were in fine shape. He had too many of them, pointed like needles, curved like a snake's. Sand gathered in a moustache above his wide cannibal smile.

"How many are inside?"

Rojo closed his eyes while counting the evil monks in his head.

"Veinte... twenty?" he said. "Maybe less if El Mummy said to kill some for him."

"They're human then?" Evangeline asked.

I couldn't believe that I had arrived at a point in my life where this was a good question to start with. But it was. I had been thinking of asking the same thing.

"Human, but bad, bad men... they stop with the Jesus long time ago. Now they pray to other gods. If a traveler in the Gila has bad luck and he comes to them for food or a place to sleep... they get their necks cut in their beds. The brothers give us the bodies after they finish. The brothers never leave here, so we necrófagos tell them news about, you know, the world that we see on our rides. We send people to them too."

"Isn't that lovely?" Evangeline had been rummaging around in her purse. She found what she was searching for. A packet of what looked like hard candies. She gave one to me. "Suck on this. It might help you. Later I will make you tea if you're not better."

I popped the lozenge in my mouth.

"What is it?"

"Peppermint oil and some ginger."

It tasted not bad. Quite good, actually. I felt a little bit less horrible already. I sipped water from my canteen and sucked some more.

"Lay flat on your back. Here. Loosen your collar," she said.

I did as I was told.

Evangeline fanned me with her slouch hat.

Her thighs were wonderful pillows. If it weren't for the sickness I was experiencing, and the grave-robbing corpse defiler sitting a few feet away, and the fortress filled with devil-worshipping throat-slashing monks, and the other necrófagos, of course, and the mummies, and Odji-Kek himself whose mental link with me caused my acute distress – it would've been a most pleasant way to spend time in the desert.

"Are you feeling any relief?" she asked.

"A bit, starting just now. The very beginnings of not being unwell…"

"Give it a few minutes."

"I will."

McTroy said, "There must be a secret way in and out of that death castle. Don't tell me they swing the gates open every time you come home from gobbling in the graveyard. Where's the passage?" McTroy twitched the rope, and Rojo coughed.

"You squeeze me I can't tell you."

McTroy gave him some slack.

Rojo lost his balance then righted himself.

"There is no secret passage," he said.

The bounty hunter took up the slack he had given, and if there were a tree around, I'm certain he would have thrown the rope over a branch and let the ghoul dangle.

Rojo saw his irritation and added quickly, "But they always have one monk in the bell tower. Day and night he watches. Whenever we return from a raid, he climbs down and lets us inside. There's one up there now, I promise. He is watching, seeing what you are going to do."

We all looked at the bell tower.

It was too far away to make out details, too far to detect any cloaked figure spying out from the adobe arches surrounding the bell. But since Rojo had said what he said, I couldn't imagine the tower being unoccupied. It was like staring at a hole where you knew something nasty and crawly lived; itchy feelings raced over me. I narrowed my eyes, could perceive no change, no sign of habitation, yet in my mind a tower spy emerged: a hooded face, patient as a gargoyle, tracking us – an evil sentinel – that is who, or what, I felt ensconced up there.

I stood and dusted off my clothes. Vertigo subsiding.

"What *are* we going to do?"

"We ride past. After dark we backtrack," McTroy said. "Surprise them."

"How do we get the guard in the watchtower to open the gate?" Evangeline said. She had her spyglass out and braced along Neptune's rump. "I see someone standing there. Rojo isn't lying. What will he do to sound the alarm? Ring the bell, I suppose?"

Rojo nodded. "The monks have *el masa negro* at night. Rituals, you know? They sleep in the day when it is hot. Except for the watcher. You come back under the moon and they will all be awake. Busy, busy. Necrófagos too. I don't know if mummies sleep."

"Black mass? Where? In their chapel?" Evangeline collapsed her spyglass.

"Sí, they go to church at midnight."

"Then that's where we hit them. Block the doors and burn it," McTroy said.

"First, we need to get in," I said. "That's the tricky part. If they ring the bell, we'll be caught like ducks on a pond. And we can't even fly. They'll pick us off one by one."

"I can help with this."

It was Wu.

I had almost forgotten about him. He sat there on Penny's back. This was the first time I really recognized his talent for stillness and quiet. But it wouldn't be the last. Wu could be close to invisible when he wanted to be. And passing unnoticed is an asset in many circumstances.

He had more to contribute. He told us so.

"I could ask my parents to unlock the gate to the monastery," he said.

"Has the heat got to you, China?" McTroy asked. "You feelin' squirrelly like doc?"

Wu touched his face to check. "No. I feel like who I am. Like a boy."

"You say your parents will let us into that unholy fortress?"

"Yes, they will. I only need to ask them tonight."

"Are they with the devils inside there now?" McTroy's voice dropped to a whisper as he contemplated the disturbing idea that Wu's parents were within the monastic walls for reasons unknown. "Do they live there?"

"Absolutely not. Why would they go to a place like that?"

McTroy threw his hands up. "Where the hell are your parents?"

Yong Wu pointed north, in the opposite direction from the monastery.

"They have been following us," he said.

The horizon was empty. Nothing. Not even the floating speck of a bird.

McTroy sat tall on Moonlight and shook his head.

"I've got a pretty keen sense if and when I'm being followed. I haven't seen hide or hair of anybody on our trail. I think you're telling tall tales."

"Mr Hardy saw them. He saw them last night by the fire. They attacked the mummy when he stopped me from breathing…" Here Wu paused. My concurrence on the event seemed expected. All heads turned to me, even Rojo's.

"The bats?" I said. "Wu, you told me that your parents died."

"They did."

"Then how do you explain…?"

"Because they came back, Mr Hardy." Wu drew in a deep breath and spoke words that appeared to have been trapped inside him for a long time. "My father was the first to be bitten. Late one night in his tent the creature came to him. Some who saw it said it glowed green in the dark and it flew between the tent flaps. Others said it was a rotting man with wild hair smelling of mold. It picked him up and hopped off with him."

My shock at hearing of the supernatural was wearing off. There were happenings going on in the shadows of the ordinary world. They were real too. Once having seen them, I could not un-see them. In fact, I saw more, and more.

"Didn't anyone try to stop it?" I asked.

"No. They were too afraid. They pretended it was a bad dream they were all having. In the morning, his body was found outside the camp, near the railroad tracks where the men had been working. My father was dead. There were rocks nearby, and a small cave where a wolf had been seen the evening before. But no one would look for my father's killer. The men decided not to tell my mother about the cave. They buried my father there under the rocks, and told her he died from a terrible accident. Her job was to cook for the men. That night they said she did not have to cook. She stayed in her tent and cried. A week later my father came looking for her. My mother was screaming. The men recognized him, but he was not alive. He took my mother back to the rocks with him."

I was aghast. "Good Lord, Wu, how terrible. Where were you during this nightmare?"

"I was with my mother. I was in the tent when he came for her. My mother pushed me down under a blanket to hide me. I saw my father. He did not see us. I think he was blind, but he could smell things. He sniffed the air. That was how he found my mother. He knew her smell."

"You've seen your mother… afterward?" Evangeline asked.

"Yes, she is dead and then alive again too. They helped me to rescue you and Mr Hardy when you were staked to the ground. They will not hurt me. All they want to do is go home, but instead they are out here in the desert. They are lost together." Here his voice quivered.

"Forgive me, Wu, but am I to understand you're saying your parents are *vampires*?" I tried to sound gentle but shuddered at my own words.

"People call them that," Wu said. "The Chinese workers call them Jiangshi."

"Where do your parents stay?" Evangeline asked.

I noticed her scanning the horizon again.

"In caves, mostly. Sometimes they would ride the train with me."

"How on earth…?" I began. Evangeline halted me with her hand.

"They would hide under the coal in the coal-car, all the way at the bottom," Wu said. "At night, I would call them out of the tender when no one was around. They like to sit on top of the train when it is moving. To feel the air blowing. Smelling the desert smells. I'd sit too."

"Oh, I see," she said. Her expression had turned immeasurably sad. She pressed a finger to the corner of her eye. She did not want the boy to see her tears.

"Where'd they get their blood, son?" McTroy asked. His words had gone soft as spring rain, like they did when he talked to Moonlight.

"They never bit any passengers on the train. I forbid them to. I would bring them blood from the kitchen, from sides of beef and, when I could, slaughtered chickens. If they grew very hungry, they would fly into the desert. I don't know what they did out there. But they always came back to the train to be close to me. That is why they follow us now."

"I don't believe him," Rojo said. "I never met a vampire. They are only legends."

"They are not!" Wu threw the ghoul's guitar at him. Rojo caught it.

"I was out in the desert watching the trains and I never saw any vamp–"

McTroy jerked the rope and Rojo quieted.

"Wu, if you say your parents are following us, then I believe you." McTroy stretched his arm out to the boy. Wu hesitated. But the gunman held his hand out steady and he waited with a steady eye on the boy too. Something wordless passed between them. McTroy was a hard man, and he'd witnessed more than his share of tragedy and sorrow. I now know much of it was personal. I think that's what Wu sensed in him, knowing McTroy had suffered – he'd been alone and had to fix what couldn't be fixed all the way through to make things whole again. He'd survived. I guess they recognized each other's wounds and decided if they had pain in common, why not add trust?

Wu switched horses, climbing behind McTroy in the saddle.

"Me and Wu are going to ride out there a ways and see if we can stir up his folks so he can parley with them." McTroy uncoiled Rojo's rope and flipped it to me. "Keep an eye on the grave-robber."

I took the leash but not without cringing in repulsion.

Moonlight stepped gingerly over Rojo's half-body as he coughed and tried to crawl from under the horse's diving hooves.

It is an uneasy feeling – being watched by watchers you cannot see. The bell tower lay to the south with its scheming reclusive monks, and now to the north we had vampires, though they might be, if not exactly our friends, our allies. In the desert dwell mysteries and visions you will find nowhere else on the globe. To this I can verily attest.

"Here, ghoul," I said. "Here." I clucked my tongue. I

gave the leash little tugs.

I remounted my Penny.

"Is no reason to treat me like un perro," Rojo said.

"I wish you were a dog. You'd smell better."

"To each one goes his favorite smells. I will not judge you, doctor."

"Speaking of judging, how do you live with yourself?"

"What is this question? I live with me because I am Rojo."

"A ghoul's life is nothing but murder and eating the dead," I said.

"True," Rojo said. "But tell me if you never eat."

"All men eat," I said.

"You eat dead things? *Qué asco!* But that is muy repugnante." I think then he sneered.

"You're making fun of me."

"At least no one with a butcher cuchillo kills los animales for you to eat them…"

I grew frustrated with the ghoul's jibes and tugged his rope.

"I am no grave-robber," I said. "Let's leave it at that."

"Sorry, señor, but how did los mummies get to Mexico if you not dig them?"

I tugged the rope.

"Dig, dig, dig." He pantomimed shoveling as he said this. "Es divertido, no?"

A south wind began whipping sand clouds into the air. Soon Moonlight and her two riders disappeared from our sight. It was a hot, dry wind that scraped at my throat.

Evangeline tied a kerchief over her face and tugged her hat low.

"We need to find some shelter or we'll be skinned raw as your little pet," she said.

"Agreed," I said. "But we can't wander far, and our options are limited."

"Señor, there is a well not too close to the very bad church. She has a little roof over the top. It's not much but is something." I stared down into those sand-filled midnight eyes and wondered how much I could trust them. Not much at all, I decided.

"Hardy, what do we have to lose if we listen to him? The monks don't venture out of their fort and we can't remain here in the open."

Penny and Neptune were shaking their heads. The airborne grit pelted us without cease. It had a sound to it, this wind, an insectile buzz that added to the horses' anxiety and my own.

"Rojo, how far is the well?"

He shouted above the grinding whirring wind. "Is half way between here and the church, in the southeast corner, around the back. That's why you no see it."

I couldn't have seen it now if it stood ten feet ahead of me.

The sand blinded us, thick as a blizzard. "All right, then. Up with you." I yanked the malodorous creature onto Penny, in front of me. The guitar on his back kept a breathable space between us. "Tell me where to go."

"Is straight ahead, boss."

We walked our horses through the sandstorm in search of the hidden well.

26

PLAGUE BRINGER

"Where did you see this kind of fever before?"

"I'm sorry, Hardy, what? This cursed wind is driving me crazy. I can't hear you."

I mopped my brow and wiped the dust from my eyelids. The well was exactly where Rojo said it would be. It had a few thin slats built over it, hardly what I'd call a roof, and a beam with a rope and pulley, none of which did anything to stop the sideways wind attack, but the rim of the well was good blockage. I looped the horses' ropes over the biggest stone on the rim. Evangeline and I squatted inelegantly on the lee side of the well, our backs against the warm mosaic of stones. We had picked our way through an atmosphere increasingly composed more of earth than air. One cannot open one's eyes fully in a sandstorm. It is a hazy endeavor made of squinted glimpses revealing a hellishly dull and altogether obscure world. The lack of horizon in this smoky fog of sand exacerbated my vertigo, and despite the fact I could not see the church in the storm, I knew we were much closer to it.

"I said, 'Where did you see this kind of fever before?' Concerning my ill turn back there, you commented this was not your first experience along these peculiar lines."

"Oh, did I say that? I don't recall…" Evangeline had pulled her hat down to her nose, and her kerchief was tied just below. I could see her eyelashes twitching.

"You did without a doubt," I said. "Here, put this around you." I draped my blanket over Evangeline so we were like a pair of Esquimaux huddled in a squall.

"What an odd thing for me to say. Your condition flustered me quite a bit." She grabbed my knee and gave it a reassuring pat. However pleasant it was for me to receive this comforting touch, I wondered why I felt a signal to change the course of the conversation. I ignored the signal. I placed my hand on hers.

"Not so odd if it's based on personal history. When and where did you get yours?"

"My what?" she asked, as innocently as was possible for her.

"Your history with fevers and sorcery," I pressed.

"I can't imagine…" She waved off my question.

"Let's see – your father was struck almost fatally with a fever. Was that when he suffered his corporal stress reaction? His fever dream revealed the location of Kek's tomb. Being a dutiful daughter, you must've tended to your sick father. You even wrote the letter telling me how he projected his spirit to my tent in Egypt accompanied by a phantasm. Were Kek and the phantasm one and the same? I dare to assert they were."

Evangeline had emerged snail-like from under her chapeau. She untied her kerchief and attempted to remove the dust from her face, but a few dirty smears were all she got for her efforts. They did nothing of course to hide her striking appearance. In fact, the smudging accentuated her good looks! Perhaps my near proximity to her affected my judgment. I was still feeling kindly towards her for administering to my symptoms, this despite her deception and reluctance to admit to it.

"Well," I said. "Do you have an answer?"

"You seem full of answers already. I wouldn't want to overburden you," she said.

"Did Kek cause Monty Waterston's fever and mine? Was it Kek who led us to his tomb? Did you know Kek was pulling strings like a puppeteer from beyond the grave?"

"Yes! Yes! And yes!" She stared at me, furious. "Tell me, Hardy, does that change one thing? Does it?"

I fumbled for a clever reply, settling finally for a simple one.

"No."

She closed her eyes. Trying to calm herself, she straightened her spine and turned her head slightly away from me. Her chest rose and fell, rose and fell with deep breaths. I watched and waited. When she opened her eyes again, I could not deduce if she had succeeded in tamping down her anger, but she could stand the sight of me again. I even noticed the beginnings of a smile at the corner of her mouth; although it might have been of the variety a cat shows to a mouse before swallowing him whole. She said, "There you have it then. My father is old, Hardy. Although he has kept himself in excellent condition for a man of his years, his health has declined precipitously in the last year. That brain fever very nearly killed him. But he knew Kek was reaching out to him across time, space, and dimensions unknown. He told me so. Despite the risks, he welcomed it. Can you imagine making contact as my father had done? After decades of studying Egyptian occultism, he succeeded where others had failed miserably. If Kek wanted to show us the location of his tomb and his sarcophagus, why wouldn't we act on it? You read about the dream in my letter. And you followed the phantasm's map just as surely as we did."

"But I expected to find only artifacts."

"There is that difference," she admitted with a nod. "But artifacts do lead to other things."

I was about to argue about the value of field research versus the hazard of following evil spirit guides when we spotted something approaching the well through the sandstorm.

Tall and dark, moving slowly, deliberately – straight for us.

"If that is Amun Odji-Kek, what will we say to him?" I asked.

Evangeline peered ahead.

"We will remind him that if not for us he would be entombed."

"He doesn't care. We serve him. That's what he'll say."

"I serve no one."

"Maybe if you mentioned how he and your father go back years together…"

The figure stopped. It seemed to be orienting itself, fixing upon our location. The head was long and large, the chest wide, and it began moving again.

"Where is Rojo?" Evangeline asked.

The sand swept by us like curtains of rain in a downpour.

"Crawled off somewhere, never to die… What's

wrong with the legs?" I asked, pointing at the figure. "They're all funny, a jumble."

"What's wrong with the legs is there are four of them," Evangeline said with great relief. "McTroy! Here we are! McTroy! Moonlight, come this way, girl, come on!"

The amber veil parted. Moonlight emerged, following the sound of Evangeline's voice. McTroy rode low on the animal, leaning forward, and I could not see his eyes, only a slot like one in a suit of armor, between his poncho and his hat brim. He flung himself off the horse's back, and Moonlight joined Neptune and Penny beside the well structure, their noble, oblong faces turned away from the worst of the wind. McTroy hitched Moonlight to one of the splintery wood posts supporting the beam, pulley, and bucket. He made sure our horses were securely tethered there too. Then he joined us.

"Where's Wu?" Evangeline asked.

"Gone."

He picked up a handful of pebbles and let them slip through his fingers.

"Gone how?" Disbelief, fear, anger – these three emotions mixed in her brief query. I feared she might strike our guide if he gave an answer that she found lacking.

"I lost him," he said.

The last pebble dropped. He tugged the frayed collar of his poncho down past his chin and looked dartingly at us, then away again. I saw a man who would've welcomed a slap in the face because he hated his failure. Hated having to tell us he'd lost the boy.

Instead, Evangeline only showed him her shock. "What do you mean you 'lost him'?"

"We were on foot searching for his parents when this storm kicked up. One minute he was behind me, the next he wasn't. I called for him but got no reply. I was lucky to find you."

A steady stream of sand trickled off his hat as he spoke.

"You left him out there alone? That is unacceptable, Mr McTroy," Evangeline said.

The bounty man knew she was right.

"Perhaps, he found his parents," I said, grasping for any reason not to despair.

"I didn't see nobody." He gulped like a man with a sore throat. His face was red from the whipping sand. He had been out there, searching in the whirlwind. "Hell, there were some rocks, a big pile of them right where he went missing. Maybe he got himself in there for shelter. If he stays put, he'll be fine. I can spot those rocks again after this blows over. If he wanders, then he's in trouble. We may never find him."

"Don't you say that!" Evangeline slugged McTroy in the shoulder. I could tell that she surprised him.

"How close are we to the damned church?" he asked.

"It's right in front of us," I said, "a stone's throw, maybe a little farther, but not much. Rojo told us where to go. We needed protection from the storm."

"That's just dandy." McTroy peered over his shoulder down into the well. "I don't suppose you know where your friend is, do you?"

"I was telling Evangeline that he very likely just crawled away..."

"Just crawled away... huh? What do you think about that, Miss E?"

"It worries me some," she said, biting at her lip.

"As it should," he said. "'Cause if he's squirmed over to the castle and is talking to his devil-lovin' buddies, how's that gonna sort out for us? I don't like it, is how."

"He was a bit harder to keep track of than Yong Wu," I said, sharply.

"What are you saying? Spit it out, Doc." His right hand balled into a fist.

"I'm saying we each lost someone in this chaos, and I don't like to be blamed."

"Funny thing about blame is there's always – what in the Hell…?"

McTroy paused in his dissertation on blame at that moment as he had been struck lightly in the chest with something that stuck to his poncho. He plucked it from his chest and held it out for further study. It was long as my little finger, and just as plump, the color a bright, acid green. While he inspected it, another hit him. And another. Evangeline shrieked as a half dozen of the same creatures landed on her person. They pelted me as well. Did I mention they had wings? Fluttery transparent ones, two pair, the longer, thinner, and spotted set of blades being located nearer the head and the fatter hindwings resembled sails. Quite amazing. Their buzzing noise was louder than the sandstorm, which had died down substantially, not that our view of the world got any clearer. For the sand was replaced without interruption by these flying invaders.

"Crickets!" McTroy shouted.

"Grasshoppers, actually," I said. "These are desert locust. Right now, they're swarming as their kind is wont to do. Millions, even billions of them. They fly with the wind. You can eat them, did you know? Some cultures consider them a delicacy."

"Eat a cricket like hell." McTroy pinched one by its wings and flung it away. Before hitting the ground, the locust righted itself and joined its brethren in flight.

Evangeline was slapping the insects from her face, not quite quickly enough to keep them from landing, here and there, upon cheek and brow, ears and chin.

"They don't bite or sting or anything," I said, hoping to make her feel better.

"I cannot… take… much… more of… this…" she said, until an especially menacing-looking specimen fanned his merry way between her fine lips. Her eyes bulged and she spit the grasshopper out, looking as if she might shriek, but the prospect of allowing an entry for more bugs into her mouth made her hold back until the pressure grew and grew to such proportions that she was forced to act with her whole body at once, and decisively so. She stood, turned, grabbed the rope and bucket hanging above the well, and leapt over the wall.

I hesitated.

"Follow her, Doc. I think she's got the best idea."

McTroy took one last doleful look at the horses. But there was obviously no bringing them down into the well with us.

I know my phobia of tight spaces is as tiresome to others as it is cumbersome to me. But the thought of being down a dark well was not at all preferable to swarms of grasshoppers according to my sensibilities. Yet I am not one to hold up the group for selfishness. I took the rope, testing it for strength, and lowered myself into the water hole.

McTroy shimmied down the rope after me, and soon we three were out of the sand and insects and into water up to our ribs, or in Evangeline's case, slightly higher. The atmosphere of the well's bottom was not exactly cool, the water not particularly sweet. But I am not ashamed to say I sunk down to my neck bones and drank, and I did feel better for doing so. I felt almost clean too. It was dim down there, but we could see each other. Our voices were magnified so there was no need to shout as we had to in the storm. A quiet and sloshy place, the wetted stones were stained a displeasing brown. The grasshoppers grew thick topside, flying and buzzing, and the little well's roof added to my feeling of being forever closed in. I shut my eyes and dipped my face in the water and blew bubbles. Counting silently back from one hundred...

Ninety-nine, ninety-eight, ninety-seven.

Evangeline had recovered from her temporary panic. She splashed water onto her face. After dumping a hatful of well-water over her head, she wrung out her golden hair.

Ninety-one. Ninety.

Eighty-nine.

McTroy had an ear cocked upward.

Evangeline scooped water and drank.

I felt smooth gravelly rocks underfoot. I lay back. Floating with my legs out.

"Be quiet," he said.

I sat up. We waited as the ripples in the water stilled.

"What is it?" I asked.

"I thought I heard Moonlight squeal."

I listened and heard nothing. "What does that mean, if she squeals?"

"Means she's fixing to kick and bite some dumb sonofabitch that gets too close."

Evangeline snorted, and the sound was louder because of the stone walls.

"Sorry," she said. Her big eyes flashed upward. In the semidarkness, they were twin moons. "I hear something too. *Shush.*"

I heard it. Rasping. Steady, rhythmic.

A knife cutting into something soft–

We all heard Moonlight's high-pitched whinny then, something very close to a human scream. The other horses were squealing. One horse kicked at the posts. We saw the little planked roof shake over the well. Dust floated down. A dislodged slat dropped into the pool.

"Goddamn. I'm going back up there." McTroy drew his weapon. He tugged the rope with his other hand. He started to climb.

He had gotten ten feet above us when the rope snapped and he fell.

McTroy crashed into me, and at least I broke his fall. His weight plunged me underwater until I touched bottom and rebounded to the surface, gasping. McTroy, hatless, trod water beside me. Evangeline watched the circle of light above. Getting lighter by the minute it was, for the locust cloud had passed, and the sandstorm blew northward. We heard nothing from the horses.

Even after McTroy called and whistled for Moonlight, we got no reply.

"If those asswipes hurt my horse I will skin them and roast them."

I passed him his hat.

The frayed rope floated in the well water like a

headless snake.

McTroy snatched it up and inspected it.

"It's cut," he said.

I offered another possibility. "Maybe it's the end of the rope and the knot slipped. Maybe there's no one up there."

"Then why'd the horses get angry?"

"I don't know. The locusts were bothering them? I'm sure they're unused to that."

McTroy shook his head. "Your half-burned goblin friend, Rojo, should've been dragged until he was nothing but a skull full of sand. But you let him wander off."

"He's a ghoul not a goblin," I said.

McTroy shoved me across what little space we had. I hit the rounded wall.

I turned on him, and punched him squarely in the jaw.

He leaned back, and his hat was in the water again. I was glad to see blood on his lip. I realized he was smiling at me. It was not a friendly sort of smile.

"Doc has got some sand. I'll be damned. Don't think I'm not going to beat you, but damn, I didn't think you had it in you." He raised his fists.

"There's no cause for your foolishness." Evangeline looked at both of us with nothing short of total contempt. "We need to get out of here. Are you forgetting that Wu is possibly lost? He may even be injured in this storm. But he is most definitely terrified. Yet you two are the ones acting like children. It diminishes us all."

Her scolding achieved the desired effect. We dropped our hands and stared at the water.

"I have a plan," she added. "Care to hear it?"

"Yes, of course," I said.

McTroy located his floating hat, wrung it out, and put it on.

"Tell us what you got," he said.

A constellation of lights was still blinking before my eyes, the result of striking my head against the wall. Through this light show I did my best to show proper interest in Evangeline.

She continued, "All right then, gentlemen, these stones are laid tight and not good for climbing. But higher up, they are stacked less neatly and I believe I can manage enough of a toehold to pull myself to the rim. The question is how do I get that high?"

She waited.

We waited.

"The answer is: I stand on your shoulders." She was smiling broadly.

"Whose shoulders now?" McTroy asked.

"Yours and his. I think you, McTroy, are an on-the-bottom sort of man. Sturdy in the legs. Stout through the middle."

He considered this statement with much puzzlement evident.

"Hardy will stand on your shoulders. He seems more the balancing type, able to bridge the gap between me and you. I will stand on his shoulders. That will, if my estimate is correct, put my hands where I need them to be to grip that first ring of larger, looser-fitting stones. Then it's up and out. I'll take the rope." She took the rope from McTroy. "I'll drop it down to you when I reach the surface."

I was skeptical… and dizzy. But at the time, I did not want to fight McTroy, or disappoint Evangeline again. Also, I did want to escape this soggy pit. I was willing to give her suggestion a try. McTroy was not as willing.

"You won't be able to climb it," he said.

"I am an accomplished climber of trees. I think trees and rocks are not so very unlike each other. Now you stand here, braced against the wall with your hands out." She spun McTroy around, and she placed his hands on the stones as she wanted him. "Hardy, climb onto his shoulders. Here, I will boost you into place."

I don't know what was more surprising: the number of times we failed or that after each flubbing McTroy was willing to try again. I think it was the difficulty of the thing that drove him. He was a mulish man. Pig-headed – and every other beast that doesn't let his betters get their way. It was instinctual, bred in the bone – McTroy's desire to remain unconquered. He possessed other animalistic traits which over the years I came to see attracted women to his character and men too, for that matter. He wore his physicality easily and without pretense, a man of action, raw, uninhibited by civilization and its polite entrapments. He had little interest in self-examination but could be remarkably philosophical, especially if whisky was on hand. Alive in the world but almost unconsciously so – a wild man, an untamed one, or perhaps it is best to say: Rex McTroy was a man who did things his own way. He challenged those who sought to dissuade him from his private, in many cases dubious, ideas and prejudices, regardless of their merits. When challenged by others, if quarreling and boorish insults fizzled, he was prone to sulking. In the end, he was more than that, but what I mean to stress here is that he could be hard to be around. Exasperating. He tested the limits of one's patience. Impulsivity, rudeness, arrogance – he had those in spades. However, if he had questioned things too much, I wonder, would he have quit on us?

By any measure Evangeline knew best how to handle him. She made sure to keep the conversation flowing while we attempted our circus act.

"Didn't the cartouche mention plagues?" she asked me as her bare toes dug first into my hip, then into the meat of my shoulder, and made me realize I still had my boots (Staves' boots) on and how they must've been cutting deeply into McTroy's collarbones.

Evangeline's nimble form surmounted the scaffolding of our braced, male bodies.

"No, but it was one of Kek's titles. He Who Disturbs the Balance, Plague Bringer, Corruptor of the Land, Slayer from the South, Lord of Demons," I said. My knees buckled a bit, but I steadied them. I held on to the wall. My fingertips pried at every available cranny for some purchase. McTroy felt like an oak stump beneath me – inert, no doubt gnarled, and perhaps supporting a colony of mosses between his trunk and roots.

Evangeline was breathing heavily from her upward exertions, but that did not keep her from continuing our three-way chat. "There, you see? Just like the Plagues of Egypt, Mr McTroy. You know of them, the story of Moses in Exodus."

"Moses was fighting for the other side in that one," he said, as if he were leaning on a bar top and sipping a libation in casual idleness, and not anchoring a tower exceeding two hundred pounds of quivering (well, my legs were going wobbly) flesh.

"But magic is magic," Evangeline said. "First wind, then sand, now locusts – Kek is controlling this. Make no mistake. We must be on guard. Magic surrounds us. I am almost there, gentlemen. Wait, what–?"

"*What* what?" I asked. "I didn't… say… anything."

As it often happens when one is unable to scratch one's self, the skin along my untouchable cheek began to itch as if a colony of ants was exploring me. Evangeline shifted her weight. I grimaced and may have grunted softly as I embraced the wall and abraded my palms. Even the most petite woman seems less so when she is clenching you with feet like eagle talons.

"Can you push me a bit higher? I see strange markings on this stone here. Triangles. No, it's a pentagram. How odd to find such a sign in a place like this."

She moved again, stretching up to reach whatever it was she saw there – to get a better look. All her gravity transferred to a single, flexed leg. The ball of her foot stomped on an artery leading to my brain so that I felt suddenly hot on one side of my face; black waves were soon lapping at my vision. Inches from the tip of my nose, the stones began to ripple like draperies.

I clamped my boots to McTroy's neck.

Evangeline rebalanced. Cranial blood flow returned, my nerves prickling angrily.

McTroy decided to take that moment to school me on how we were going to do things once we climbed out of the well. It seemed to cheer him up.

"I notice you aren't armed, Hardy. But I'll give you one of my Armys as long as you promise you won't lose it. You'll cover me on the way to the chapel. I'll bar those bastards inside."

"I'm not going to use a gun."

"Sure, take it. Shoot whatever pops its head up, be it monk, mummy, or corpse-eater."

"No."

"Why the hell not?"

"I've never fired a gun before."

"Are you shittin' me? We ain't got time to argue, Doc. Point it at middles and pull the trigger. Use two hands. Keep shooting till the bastards go down. I've got bullets."

It was getting harder and harder for me to speak. My throat felt thin as a paper straw, with hardly any room for air, let alone words. How could I be expected to debate under these conditions? "Shooting them serves... no p- p- purpose," I stuttered.

"Like hell it doesn't."

I pinched my eyes closed. "When the time comes I'll find another way."

Evangeline said, "You can give me the pistol. I've hunted birds and foxes with my father. I proved quite accurate with moving targets."

"These are a mite bigger than pigeons. It'll be easy for you. See, Doc, even a lady can do it." My legs were trembling. I knew I could not keep upright for much longer.

"I *can* do it. I choose not to," I said. "There's a difference."

McTroy shook his head, and I almost lost my footing.

"Stop moving!" I shouted.

"Keep steady, please, the both of you. This pentagram rock is quite loose. If I can pry it out, the gap will offer an excellent foothold."

Bits of debris crumbled and dropped onto me. McTroy didn't seem to notice.

"Your daddy never taught you how to shoot? What side was he on in the war?"

I disengaged one hand from the wall, shook out the numbness, and replaced it as quickly as possible. "My father was a Quaker. He worked in a Union hospital. He never owned a gun. I've rejected my father's religious views but not all his ways. I don't believe in God, or guns."

"You're a queer fish, Hardy. Don't believe in guns? What's this here in my hand?" McTroy yanked his right arm away from supporting our improvised acrobatic column to draw his Army and brandish it, wildly.

"I'm not talking about the thing itself. Surely you know the difference. Put your arm back!"

"Surely I do not. If I didn't have my cannons, I'd be dead fifty times over. Maybe you never should've left the library. You can kill bookworms with your boot."

"I don't normally wear boots. These belonged to a dead Pinkerton agent."

"Damn, son! I swear I will beef you on principle alone."

Evangeline had partially removed the rock. The scraping of stone on stone was unmistakable. Her breathing was labored. I wondered if she *could* make the climb up and out.

"Those irons you so prize have tamed you about as well as they tamed this land," I told McTroy. "This is to say, negligibly."

"You should've seen it before men arrived with guns."

"Forgive me. I thought we were hiding in a hole."

"This is Mexico. It's always been lawless."

"I can't tell what side of the border we're on."

"That's because you're an idjit."

"Stop arguing!" Evangeline said. "You two are worse than my roommates at boarding school. And they were Scotch-Irish sisters!"

I looked down on McTroy as he looked up, grinning. "You mean they were a couple of nuns?" he asked.

"She means they were quarrelsome!" I could not suppress a smile.

"Be." Evangeline jerked at the stone with as much force as she had. "Still. I have it, I think." She did have it. The rock came away free from the wall, and a hidden doorway opened just above it. Evangeline gasped. I don't know how we stayed standing up. With a final push of her daintily arched foot off the top of my head, she wriggled into the passageway. "I feel air. Circulating air. This gallery must lead to the monastery."

She lowered the rope so we could join her.

It was then we heard the screams echoing from the tunnel.

27
A Baby's Rattle

"My God, the sounds those people are making," Evangeline said, her expression modulated from alarm to awe. She looked curiously up the passageway into the murk. It narrowed like a funnel, and the shape augmented distant sounds. "I've never heard anything like it before. Do you suppose the monks are killing them?"

"Probably wishing they *were* killed about now." McTroy opened the cylinders of his pistols, blowing out the sand and water and wiping the bullets with his shirttail.

"You still sure you don't want one of these?" he asked me.

"Yes, quite."

"Miss E?"

Evangeline accepted one of his Army revolvers, enormously gray and lethal in her pale hand, though she seemed accustomed to it and more than ready to move ahead toward the source of the tortured screams. We were huddled in the aperture of the pentagram-marked secret door that opened into a likewise secret gallery. The rock covering the door had pulled completely loose and fallen with a thumping splash into the depths of the well. The funnel-like gallery squeezed down to a uniform rectangular tunnel which ran, as best we could guess, perpendicular to the well and in the direction of the monastery. Our choice was this: would we prefer to exchange a dark vertical shaft for an even darker horizontal one? I hesitate to call the air blowing out this new hole freshened; it smelled of candles and blood. I was the last to climb in and therefore stationed closest to the well, and here in a moment of pausing, I experienced a heavy dose of déjà vu.

My mind traveled unbidden backward in time and across an ocean in mere seconds so I was once more crammed inside the horned skull rock, reliving my battle with the blind, pig-sized worm and the flood of gore that spilled forth in the aftermath. I choked for a good deep breath. To distract myself and bring my body into the present moment, I caressed the walls of the vestibule gallery, for they were strange and mesmerizing, though most of their wonders lay in obscurity. I am no geologist. But the walls were not the same as the brickwork or dull desert stone I was used to seeing. All four sides of the passage were studded with geodes, and the ends of the geodes facing inward to the gallery had been lopped off cleanly, and polished to a glossy shine. I lit a match and passed the flame near the rocks. The colors were stripy, vibrant, and multi-layered. Variants of chalcedony I supposed, or what may more commonly be known as agates. These flat shorn knobs varied in size, the smallest being about the size of a man's fist and the largest resembling an older child's blankly staring face. Many of the geodes showed oblong and irregular borders – those appearing face-like depicted features akin to ancient petroglyphs or ghostly visages best known for lurching out at you in a dream. Pockets of crystals lay trapped inside these faces. Too often they resembled ice-encrusted eyes or wild mouths crowded with sharp, translucent teeth.

"Evangeline, what do you make of these agates? I've never seen anything like them."

"They are protective. Put here to drive away fears. Whoever is in this gallery will find strength and courage, presumably to keep a cool head while secreted in the dark."

Hogwash, I thought, *or are my talismans not working properly?*

"What of these little lovelies?" I tapped a rock resembling a frozen scream.

"Why, they are watching us of course." She raised her eyebrows, giving a sly smile before she scrambled away from me, delving deeper into the hollow.

"You know the Egyptians, master builders that they are, installed plenty of creepy surprises in the skull rock. It's too bad you didn't come visit us. I will never forget what I saw."

"Don't you find most things you'll never forget are those you wished never happened?"

"Not always," I said. I was going to add something, but Evangeline had scooted off to converse with McTroy. Inching forward, I could not help but feel that I was crossing an invisible threshold from one realm to another, and the passage ahead seemed closer to something found than something manmade. What created it? I cannot say. Someone had clearly cut these agates and rubbed them smooth, but the corridor itself gave the impression of being formed by the earth – volcanic? – and not by human intelligence. This was no comfort.

Moving slowly, creeping, shaking my singed fingers now that my match had smoked out, I was seized by the sensation that I was being swallowed, alive and whole, down the gullet of a gigantic snake. Or a worm. I shivered at the thought. Never having seen El Gusano in his worm-state, I assessed him to be a much bigger specimen of maggot stock, and having witnessed his handiwork in digging out that tiger pit for the train and presuming he had lumbered for miles underground with a sarcophagus balanced on his gelatinous back, it was no leap to think he might fill both this tunnel passage and the recently vacated well with his bulk in a smothering instant. No lantern scorch would deter him and no volley of gunshots either. I reversed. I lingered with my face turned back toward the diminishing sight of the lighted well shaft. It looked better to me than it had minutes ago. The sky had cleared. Several planks shading the well mouth had ripped away in the storm. A golden drill bit of sunlight bore down. Wu was up there, and I hoped he was safe. I tried to keep that last vision of the sun inside me, soaking up the rays for my journey. I would have made a terrible mole.

"I'll go first. Doc, you take the rear," McTroy said. He vanished into the hole.

Evangeline followed him.

I took three deep breaths, closed my eyes, and crawled in – and when I opened my eyes it was to find Evangeline's bottom before me. I would follow it like a beacon. We went in on our knees, like supplicants do

when approaching a god. As I had that very thought, I
wondered if Odji-Kek planted it, if he were in my head
with me even as we crept closer to him. Did he watch
us through *me*? Was he mocking our feeble efforts?
This line of thinking was a short trip to madness, and I
wondered if inducing madness were the greatest talent
a sorcerer could hope for. I sought to block Kek's black
magic where and when I could, so I forced myself to
banish such theorizing on the spot. The gallery we had
entered was as straight as it was narrow, the blackness
becoming so complete that I observed hallucinatory
flashes of hues vibrant and otherworldly, from strings
of goblin greens that ran along the low ceiling to pink
puddles and dancing globular blue orbs. They appeared
solid, utterly real, and dimensional. I reached out to
touch them.

"Hardy!"

Evangeline kicked her foot back at me.

"Sorry, I can't make heads or tails of where I'm at–"

Evangeline covered my lips with a warm, damp hand.

"Something," she whispered.

"I see lights," McTroy said, his voice low. "Orangey,
flickering…"

"Do be careful," I said. "Perhaps we should wait until
the candles go out?"

Past Evangeline's shoulder, McTroy's head twisted
forth, crossed with shadow bars. "There's a grate." He
reached, grasping, and the shadow bars shivered. "It
moves."

"Can you see people?" I asked.

"This here's a room stacked up with bottles. Some
barrels. Might be they're filled with blood. The grate's

got a big sucker of a padlock I couldn't break with a hammer."

"Let me see," Evangeline said, too excited to keep whispering. She pressed in.

"Be my guest, miss."

She squirmed in one direction, and McTroy reversed to join me.

The lady's amusement was plain.

"It's a wine cellar. I dare say your 'blood' is claret." She lowered her chin, and began poking at the back of her head with her slender, nimble fingers.

"My blood's hellfire red, thank you. It ain't time for you to be fixing your tresses."

Her eyes opened wide to glare at McTroy, the disdain in them visible despite the irregular lighting. "I'm picking the lock. For that I need a hairpin. Quiet thoughts of encouragement would be desirable while I work the mechanism." Her request brought up an important fact: the screams had stopped. She leaned into the wall to concentrate, her hand fiddling at the pick and lock out of sight. McTroy nudged me.

"Where do you suppose she practiced a skill like that?"

"I learned it from my father. He learned from the Brothers Davenport who were more into ropes and knots, but they had other skills – here you go, boys."

She passed the sprung padlock to McTroy.

"You'd be popular in the jailhouse," he said.

"But not for long. Why bother with a key when I am one?"

Cautiously, we dropped from our hole in the wall into the monastery's wine cellar. The gate was hinged at the top and it lifted to a dangling hook. McTroy latched it.

"Maybe Rojo wasn't lying about a secret entrance," McTroy said. "This is an escape tunnel. Those cloaked devils could hide out in the well if lawmen or angels ever came a calling."

"Clever monks," I said. "We best remember that. Should we leave the gate so obviously open? If they see it, we are finished."

"I don't want to fuss with it when I'm looking for a way out."

"But it's not a way out, is it? Only a way back to another dead end."

"What's this here on the floor?" Evangeline interrupted.

A heap of personal items was piled against the far end of the long, narrow cellar, spilling outward into a kind of lost-and-found talus. I saw wiry spectacles, clothing fit for both sexes, an assortment of shoes, boots, and head-wear. All manner of jewelry and timepieces littered the miniature mountain. Evangeline picked through the under layers and came up with a stout, ebony walking stick topped with a silver grip in the shape of an ape's head, pitted, but not unattractively so, and coated with a lovely warm patina.

"I'll take that if you don't mind," I said.

She gave it to me without comment.

I swung the cane to and fro, testing the weight and battle effectiveness.

"This will do nicely in a tussle, I imagine."

McTroy had gone around the rows of wine racks, scouting our next move. Evangeline crouched at the edge of the pile and was holding up a small item for close inspection. She brought it nearer to one of the sconces set at eye level for further study.

"I know this," she said, more to herself than to me.

"What's that you have there?"

"I've seen it before. Recently. On the train. There can't be many like it, so the odds of coincidence are too great. It must be the same one I saw. But why is it here?"

I approached the candlelight and the object she cupped in her palm.

A mother of pearl ring with a bell pendant attached, the ring's circumference was far too large for a finger and yet too small to wear as a bracelet. The chestnut-sized bell was embossed with an image of the man in the moon. Smiling, jolly, winking.

"It's a baby's rattle," she said. "I remember the child. His mother sat…"

She cleared her throat. She did not say any more about the boy and his mother.

I wandered to the pile again, with new eyes. "These must be the things they've taken from their victims over the years. No use for them in the cloister."

Those screams we'd heard – the ones that fell silent – came from survivors of the train wreck, conveyed by monsters on horseback through the desert for hideous occult purposes, tumbled from one nightmare to the next, a descent into Hell. Their fate must have been incomprehensible. More than bad luck hounded them: cursed lives – lambs who'd simply boarded a train for Los Angeles never knowing hell-bound wolves waited for them in a church in the desert. It was as preposterous as it was sad.

"How unjust," Evangeline said. She laid the rattle back on top of the pile.

"We will put a stop to it."

She nodded. "People know right from wrong. But sometimes they don't know how wrong they are, the degree of their misdeeds. Selfishness blinds them. Horribly."

"The monks and necrófagos are beyond morality," I said.

"I'm not talking about them." Her voice rose. "I'm talking about my own–"

"Keep it down," McTroy slipped from between two columns of barrels. "There's a parade coming and we don't want to be a part of it. Snuff those candles."

I blew at the sconces, and we were back in the dark.

"Get under them clothes and boots. Do it," McTroy said.

We buried ourselves in the leavings of ghosts.

Between a silk top hat and a fiddle case I had enough of a gap to see the procession pass the archway where the cellar met the corridor. We heard the chanting first. Words I could not comprehend, though I know Greek and Latin and smatterings of dead languages from the ancient east. The closest match might be Akkadian or even Sumerian, though who can say what that tongue sounds like? What I heard I did not understand intellectually, but I knew it in my viscera, the words landing like punches into my gut, and my innards told me to remain still and hope I never heard such articulations again.

The monks were naked.

Initially, and improbably, I guessed they were peeled, fleshless, like Gaspar Becerra's famous etching of a flayed man holding his own skin, but in truth it was only the blood they wore on their skins that

made them shine so redly in the candle flickers. Their
bodily hairs, all of them head to toe, were painted and
matted down with clots of gore, a crimson mud, if you
will. Only the bottoms of their feet remained dry. The
ones who didn't carry elaborate and grotesquely wide
candlesticks bore knives and sickles and ceremonial
daggers that curved and recurved like metallic snakes.
A cloud floated over their heads. They burned some
stomach-churning mix of herbal shamanistic insanity
in their censors. My eyes watered, and I felt my brain
loosen in my skull and slosh like so much murky water
in a bucket. Dream-state inducement. They drugged
themselves into a borderland that I desperately wanted
to avoid, so I held my breath and hoped Evangeline
and McTroy were doing the same. The inhalant had
other physical effects I noticed, for each man walked
like Priapus in the garden. I conjectured that the drug
caused changes both neurological and circulatory – the
men's veins crawled over them like centipedes, and
the tautness of their sinews seemed utterly unnatural,
and yet they moved with salamandrine smoothness,
a glossy, silky coordination that spread from the
individuals to the group. They were as one entity, an
animated Blakeian vision, a dragon proceeding down
the corridor.

I saw no victims. No rattle-less baby boy, thankfully.

Whatever bloodletting they had been engaged in had
reached its intermission.

After the monks came the ghouls who wore their
stolen suits and dresses. Coffins were their closets,
mausoleums, their armoire, and it showed. I will say they
appeared bored with the ritual. I suspected they'd done

this before. The mummies were last in line. They did not
walk under their own power. Perhaps their legs were
still too stiff and their joints locked. They rode in high-
backed chairs. More naked monks carried them aloft.
These former corpses had served as Odji-Kek's acolytes,
and here now they presented themselves not delicate as
most mummies are, emptied of organs, hollowed out;
no, not these, because the monks shouldering them
strained with the effort. Apparently evil had returned
their bodies with leaden certainty, and extra weight.
The mummies stared ahead. Nobler in resurrection than
they had been before or after the tomb, their bandages
dripped from them like trimmings from the robes of
kings. But where was Kek?

I did not see Kek.

Anxiety, or maybe the hallucinatory smoke, seized
upon Evangeline. She found my hand in the pile and
squeezed it. I hoped she was not feeling what I was
feeling and doing my best to resist: a strong, persistent
desire to rise and follow the procession.

I squeezed back.

The chanting changed in volume and quality. The
voices diminished. They were mounting a staircase. Soon
they would be above ground, heading for the chapel.

My attention shifted abruptly from my ears to my
eyes.

Kek.

He stood in the wine cellar archway. He turned his
head.

This was not the Kek I saw in my dreams. He had
changed. He was without a doubt alive. Fully alive,
transformed. I tried to avoid his eyes. His mouth,

his lips – he smiled. He entered the cellar, and as he moved through the darkness toward us I knew that he knew exactly where I was hiding, where we all were. I believed he saw me – I was so convinced of this fact I could hardly hold my tongue. But I could bite it, and I did, grabbing the firm flesh between my teeth, clamping down tightly until I tasted the iron in my blood. After the jolt of pain came a swift clearing of my thoughts, like a scudding cloud passing from the brightest full moon, and in those seconds of clarity I speculated if Kek might be searching for me with his probing intellect, if he had called out, so to speak, to my inner ear with that big, vibrating voice of his, and if he had asked me to reveal myself, and my friends to him. *I will not answer you! I WILL NOT ANSWER!*

He stopped in front of the pile.

Inches away.

He breathed, in and out. His breath was sweet, wine-scented.

His long arm swept over the sad heap of belongings. It paused and dipped, and I feared for Evangeline. Had he discovered her? A lock of loose hair, a glimpse of her enflamed cheek?

I waited for the bark of McTroy's pistol. But it was suicide to attack now. Suicide!

Kek backed away and strolled from the room, joining the demonic cavalcade.

I heard it then as I hear it still, in my sleep, when I dream in the middle of the night here in twentieth century New York, where I live today, and everywhere I've ever been since that day.

I hear it.

The tinkling of a bell, the size of a chestnut…
The man in the moon bell.
And I knew how Amun Odji-Kek got his life back.

28
SMOKE AND FISSURES

I do not know how long we waited before emerging from our hiding spots underneath that small mountain of belongings, that mad, sad memorial to those unfortunate souls who had wandered into the upside-down world of evil monks and marauding robber-ghouls. When we did hatch ourselves and wiggle forth, it was McTroy who went first. The processioners had taken their candles with them and so half the illumination had gone too. But other candles guttered in sconces, and we were not left in a total gloom. McTroy scouted our way forward, slipping into the corridor. Footprints and a wide red smear marked the parade route. He returned winded but sounding excited.

"They went upstairs but not to the surface. There's a bridge that cuts over through an old cave. The chapel must be on the other side. Our boys headed that way."

"Kek would've been the last in line. Did you see him at the bridge?" Evangeline asked.

"The Rattle Man, that's him?"

Evangeline nodded.

"Then no, miss, I did not." He pointed with his

revolver. "It's a rabbit warren down here, he could've gone any which way. I would love to bag him and go. I count more monks and mummies than I have bullets for." He scratched at his jaw with the gun barrel.

"Yes, it is concerning," she agreed.

"I thought mummies were generally dead."

"That is correct," she said.

"He looked mighty robust for a dead man. I'll kill him if he needs killing. But, damn, I didn't expect this kind of job from the story you told me at Shirl's." He tipped his hat back on his head and leaned into a rack of wine bottles.

"I'm sorry. We… This is uncharted territory," I said, but I could not meet the man's gaze.

"No kidding. Hey, Hardy, did you know what you signed on for?"

I did not answer him. I was preoccupied with my own observations.

The ritual had done something to change the light, thickening it, adding fluidity and an unwholesome stain, making the air appear fleshy and corrupt. As I stepped from the wine cellar into the corridor, I felt as though I were gliding through a pudding gone bad, all my movements sluggish and my senses muffled; a cloying odor of putrefaction plugged my nose – me worrying if the obscene light were sticking to my body. I tried to shake it off, twisting like a dog wet from a pond. My thoughts growing fuzzy, confused, the speed of things happening all wrong. It might have been an effect of the hallucinatory incense. Probably it was. But that fact made no difference at the time. I was lost in it.

The horrible stagnancy.

Evangeline was talking to me, pulling at my sleeve.

"Hardy, Hardy, can you hear me?"

I listened as if from under a great volume of liquid. I grasped the ape head of my walking stick and banged the ferrule into the floor, over and over, checking the solidity of this wavy, murky, subterranean world, attempting to break through, to free my mind from its evil adhesiveness.

"Trap," I said. "Trap, trap…"

My voice sounded odd to me, thrown from across the room, like a magician's trick.

"What trap?" Evangeline asked.

McTroy looked me hard in the eyes, as if judging my sanity.

"I am not crazy," I said.

McTroy's smile gleamed. He had a gold tooth I hadn't noticed before. Back on the left.

Oh, yes you are, Doc, his grin seemed to say. *And I am too. Crazy as they come.*

McTroy put his arm around Evangeline's waist. He turned her and started to lead her away. Wantonness distorted and colored his visage. It would have been easier to accept him if he had suddenly, and without any logical explanation, transformed into a painted circus clown. He leered openly at Evangeline, and winked over his shoulder at me, as if we were in on the same dirty joke.

She looked shocked, at first, but attempted to conceal it. She was going with him.

I stopped them from leaving.

Evangeline gawked at my hand on her elbow. She covered it with her own and slid our entwined hands higher up her arm, and then she gave the gentlest, yet unmistakable pull toward her bosom. Her hand felt damp, heated. I almost let her guide me farther. McTroy watched us intently, silent, his mouth slightly open, transfixed.

I knew my mind was not entirely under my control at that point, and I worried about my companions. The drugged smoke lingered in the closed space, like the hazy cloud hovering above a saloon card game. But we were not playing cards.

I took my hand back.

Evangeline stuck out her lower lip, pouting, stamping her foot. She rolled her neck from side to side, as if she'd been on a long coach ride and the muscles had grown stiff. Her sleepy eyes, her swaying... that teasing, playful glare as McTroy gathered her in again. She was under some influence from the smoke.

"Best make our way to the bridge," I said. "These fumes are sickening me. I fear they may be clouding our judgment."

Color climbed Evangeline's cheeks. She appeared on the verge of laughter, unable to hold it in, ready to burst. Giddy. Her right hand conducted an unseen orchestra. Music only she heard. A lock of hair fell over her eyes, and she did not brush it aside. It was beguiling to see her like this, and part of me simply wanted to watch her continue.

McTroy rubbed his face. A string of saliva ran down his chin to his vest.

"I feel it," she said, sounding serious but also bewildered.

McTroy smacked his lips. "I could use a drink. Otherwise I'm good."

"I don't think so," I said. "Show us the way to the bridge."

I took Evangeline by the wrist.

"Why is there a bridge?" She pulled away from me. "Tell me, or I won't go."

She found her behavior quite funny and doubled over with the hilarity of it all.

"You'll go," McTroy said. "Follow me and Doc. Or we will carry you."

"I think I would enjoy that very, very much." She let her weight lean against us.

I pressed my handkerchief to my nose and mouth. "Bend low and try not to breathe the smoke." Like three drunkards making our way home from a night's reveries, we stumbled, arm-in-arm, up the staircase, and turned left until we reached a rope bridge over a sable black fissure cut into the earth. Like a knife slashed the hard rock, thin but not too thin, the span no more than crossing a street, but it felt farther because of what existed below: a void that contained, well, nothing – or nothing we could see. It gave off no sound, offered no scent; to reach out and touch it was to caress emptiness itself. The steep sides suggested they had been carved by waters, but the waters had receded ages ago, for no evidence of any flow was detectable. Only a current of air swirled up from the chasm and tousled our hair like a peculiar uncle at a Christmas gathering. I plucked a candle from a nearby sconce and released it over the bridge's guide rope.

It fell and fell and fell.

I never saw it bounce. The light shrunk to a pinprick and winked out.

Evangeline sat on the bridge, swaying a bit, with her head hanging over the edge.

"Be careful," I said. "It's a long way down."

She waved me off. Simultaneously she had loosened the collar of her dress and unlaced her bodice; she began scooping air to her face like it was water. For modesty and no other reason, I looked away. I found McTroy leaning his head into a wall – eyes closed, skin slack, looking altogether gray. I fanned him with my hat.

"You should feel better soon. I am clearing up now."

My companions did not answer me. I glanced from one to the other and then across the bridge to the now shut ornate door of what I presumed to be the Temple Underneath. In our quiet respite, the chanting had begun again. Very like the chanting of ordinary, non-Satanic monks until one noticed the jarring rhythms and virtually unpronounceable tongue. They had added drumming. Hypnotic, borne on the blood.

"I am almost myself," Evangeline said. She coughed once, but didn't raise herself up.

"Excellent, quite excellent. How about you, Mr McTroy?"

"A slug of whisky might wash this skunk spray from my mouth."

"In our saddlebags, I'm afraid. But keep breathing deeply."

He spit and then asked rather gravely, "Are we poisoned, Doc?"

"I believe the chemical compounds in the censors when burned and inhaled produce a trance-like state. You are drunk on devil smoke. But it does not last."

"Shamanistic practices often employ altered

consciousness." Evangeline pinched and slapped her cheeks as if she had been previously benumbed. "It is not that unusual."

Ah, the lady had returned. It was good to hear her speaking normally. Though I must admit that I did not dislike her in any state of consciousness I had so far observed.

I said, "Here is the chasm. This is the bridge over it, you see. And there is the door to the Temple Underneath. We are in a good fighting position, don't you agree, McTroy?"

McTroy nodded. He kept patting his vest, and I cannot help but think he habitually pocketed a liquor flask there. He grunted and grumbled and seemed in genuine physical pain. I saw him gaze backward to the staircase, and he took two shuffling half-steps in that direction before I read his thoughts.

"You can't do that," I said.

"Do what?"

"Go back to the cellar for a bottle of wine," I said.

He looked sideways, grimacing. "I'm only considering options. That's all."

"Considering going back for some claret?"

"No!" He stood tall and tilted his head back. "You ever been in a standoff?"

"Can't say that I have."

"Right. See, in a standoff there are considerations. And I am considering them."

Of course, I knew this was a lie, or at least a partial untruth. He was thinking foremost about drinking. Now that I am an old debauchee myself and more than occasional imbiber of demon liquor, I know categorically what McTroy wanted. I knew it then by intuition if not experience. He wanted a drink. I had to keep him on track.

"One way in, one way out." I pointed my stick at the door (I found I did fancy having a stick). "Take away the bridge, they can't cross the gap. Sever these ropes and wait for them. They will have to deal with us. They have no guns. We have guns," I said.

"I thought you disapproved of guns?"

"I disapprove of my using them. But you are a hired gunman. I hired you."

"Miss Evangeline hired me."

"That's true," she said, still sitting on the bridge, her legs dangling in nothingness.

"Nevertheless. What else is there to consider? We have them at a disadvantage."

McTroy crouched and scooped a handful of gravel. He threw it into the ravine.

"It is, for all intents and purposes, bottomless," I said.

"We don't know that," Evangeline said. "We don't know why it's here."

"It's here because thousands of years ago a river flowed through and dug it."

She said, "We don't know why the monks are here, then. Why did they choose this place to build their temple? Perhaps the chasm may serve a purpose other than guarding the chapel."

"Purpose? What purpose?"

She did not scream.

There was no time for a scream. Like a whip, the tail of the giant worm snapped around her right knee and pulled her down, and in her last second, she turned and

I saw her face, the fear alive in it, the sheer terror. There was nothing I could do to stop it.

Then nothing, nothing was all that was left of her. I faced the void where she had been.

The bridge swayed but not that much.

Evangeline was gone.

29
THE KA DOOR

For a long time afterward, I called her name in a stage whisper, my voice growing hoarse. I don't know what I hoped for. That she would crawl up, laughing, and say it was all a joke? That she might escape from the muscular embrace of that fleshy, prickly worm meat as it burrowed her down, down, down into the abyss? Nothing I wished for came back to me, of course, only more silence, and certainly not the woman herself. I shouted for her but once; a full-throated echo answered me, and a hand rested on my shoulder. *McTroy*.

"You can't do that," he said.

"But… but I, she… she isn't…"

"They'll hear you, Doc." He pointed with his chin to the heavy door behind which the monk's chanting never stopped. The drums were faster now, fast as my heartbeats.

"I want to climb in," I said. I gestured to the ravine.

"Let's look," he said.

I think he did it just to convince me of what he already knew.

McTroy seized a candle in each fist and, hooking his ankles around the rope bridge, lowered his upper half into the crevasse. He did not penetrate far into that oceanic gloom. His outstretched arms revealed twin vertical walls, smooth as bones and webbed with cracks though none much wider than a finger. This hell vent might have led straight to the center of the earth for all we could see: El Gusano's midnight lair.

"Useless," I said. "There's no way to follow."

Nimbly McTroy contorted himself and soon joined me sitting on the bridge to brood over our next move. I was not afraid of the worm. I was not thinking about him, yet all I was thinking about was him. What would he do with her? If we were going to hunt him, then so be it. The taste of blood was in my mouth. I sought a confrontation, but it was vain of me, immature and reckless, to think we might win any impromptu battle in this alien place where the crawler was perfectly at home. Remember, I was a young man when this happened and young men never figure on their own deaths. So into their graves they go too soon, and the soil makes room for them without judgment. Without McTroy at my side, I might've ended up in a hundred different graveyards. He kept me above the ground, and that is but one reason I need people to know about him.

"You want to go back?" he asked.

"What do you mean?"

"You said it before. We can cut this rope bridge. That'll slow the monk boys down. We take some rope for ourselves and head to the well. Climb out."

I thought about it. It would work. If our horses were alive, then we could ride home in a day or two. I doubt they would've pursued us. We were not that important.

I shook my head.

"I won't go. Not without knowing where Evangeline is. We don't even know if she's alive or dead."

"We may never know." He had found the pistol he had loaned to her stuck between the knots of the bridge. Evangeline must have lost it when she was stolen away. Little good it did her in her moment of peril. He spun the chambers and holstered it.

"I want the mummy. I want Kek," I said.

His cold eyes sparked.

"Revenge? Is that it, Doc?"

"No. I want to take him back to Montague Waterston, to Evangeline's father. I owe the man that much. He is my sponsor. She was… is his flesh and blood. I couldn't face Waterston empty-handed, could I? And with so many unanswered questions. No, no, no. It would be too dishonorable."

"I'm guessing he wouldn't be paying us either."

"Not that he should." I made a point I thought was obvious. McTroy frowned.

"Right, I see that." From McTroy's tone I was not sure he saw it very well.

"All this for nothing is a mite unsatisfying," he said.

"One other thing." I grabbed hold of the bridge rope strung before me and throttled it, while trying unsuccessfully not to grind my teeth. "I will not leave here without killing the worm."

"Now you're talking. Chasing after him isn't the way to do it. We make a big enough ruckus, he'll come a callin'. These are his compadres even if he ain't all human. He must cotton to them ghoulie Mexs for one reason or other. Why hell, they been robbing trains and

coaches together. That makes fast friends, doing a thing
like that."

"You were an outlaw then, once upon a time?"

"I did things I'm not proud of," he said. "But I wouldn't
take them back."

The first half of his answer sounded like a politician,
the second half like a scoundrel about to be hanged.
Putting them together somehow made them noble.

"Very well," I said.

"First thing we do is check that door."

"Agreed." Where would the doorway lead? To
answers? To more bloodshed? Perhaps to my own doom
and destruction? I did not care. I only wanted it opened.

We crossed the hammock-like bridge.

I put my hand on the door. Vibrations, the words of
the ritual taking place on the other side, carried through
to my touch. I waved my candle back and forth. The
door itself was quite extraordinary when viewed up
close. Extraordinary... and very Egyptian.

"This cannot be," I said.

"What?"

"This bas-relief carving, these figures are clearly
Egyptian. These here are called hieroglyphs. Writing.
Very old, so old I can't read it. Perhaps, even Old
Kingdom." I could not believe what I was seeing. I
knocked my knuckles against the wood.

"Maybe you shouldn't do that, Doc."

I knocked louder. The monks' chanting went on,
unabated.

McTroy grabbed my arm. "They'll hear you..."

"Get off me," I said. "They won't hear, not where they
are. It is too far."

McTroy could not have understood what I meant, but he trusted me and let go.

I tapped the wood as loudly as I pleased and moved from the middle of the doorway to the top as high as I could reach, then on my knees to the bottom, and standing, I tapped my way back to the middle again. "Yes, it makes sense. But why here? How did they get inside? Kek's magic must be powerful. I know what this is," I said.

"We both know what this is. It's a door to the chapel," McTroy said.

I could see that he was wondering if the drugged smoke was still in my head, if I had, after losing Evangeline, lost my mind as well. Indeed, I had not.

"This is a door, yes. But it is not the door to the chapel."

"Uh-huh." He sounded puzzled, looked cautious, but willing to go forward.

The wood was old and dry. It had been painted once, red and black. More red than black, in fact, made to look like rock, like granite. But this object was not what it seemed to be. I found a split in the grain and pried at it with my fingers.

"Do you have a knife?" I asked.

"Any hunter worth his salt has a knife."

"Well, for God's sake, do you have one I can use?"

McTroy slid a hand under his poncho and when it came out again there was a knife in it. He flipped the pointy end around so the staghorn handle faced me. I took it and stuck the blade into the crack in the door. I wiggled it deep in the wood. The split I had discovered was a separation between two panels of wood, cleverly blended to look natural, real craftsmanship on display, a treasure worthy of a museum.

I worked the heavy steel blade side to side, destroying the ancient artifact.

With a wrenching pop, a corner of the panel broke free, and a puff of yellow, powdery dust sprayed into my eyes. I wiped them. They watered and stung. I squinted and wiped them again. My hair fell over my brow but I did not pause to comb it back, instead I watched the sweat dripping steadily off the end of my nose as elsewhere it poured over my skin. The knife twisted wetly in my hands. I jimmied it upward.

Still the door would not budge.

I hooked my fingers under the panel and bent the board out as far as I could. My fingertips were bleeding, the skin raw, the nails ragged. I brushed blood and splinters on the lapels of my frock coat. I put the knife in my pocket and removed my coat.

The wood was very old, very dry. I was determined to beat it.

I grabbed my stout walking stick from the floor and worked the steel tip of the ferrule under the edge of the panel. I pried at it. My muscles tautened. My arms trembling as I forced the section – and finally broke it – SNAP! – from the frame.

McTroy stepped back, pistols raised.

Hammers cocked.

I took no rest.

The second, third, and fourth panels were easier to pull out. I tossed them, clattering, on the floor, not caring about all the noise I was making. No monks or mummies or giant worms were coming for us. They didn't care what we did. The chanting on the other side had never stopped. Never once had I interrupted its steady cadence. No one came to the door to confront me. They went on with their ceremony. One of my middle fingers was bleeding heavily, the nail torn to the quick. I sucked on it and spit the metal taste out of my mouth. The hole in the door was big enough to walk through. But I did not go forward.

"This is for the Ka, for the soul," I said.

"What the hell."

"The Egyptians built these in their tombs. It's a gateway, you see. Between this world and the Underworld, so gods and the dead could pass over. The door must always face the west. The Ka would go through this door." I pounded with my fist.

"I don't get it," McTroy said. He pushed at the unmovable thing I had revealed.

I sympathized with him. How could he understand? You see, behind the door was nothing. A wall of bedrock. The Ka door is always a false door. It leads nowhere. Or at least, it leads nowhere if you are human and alive and thus unable to cross its threshold.

30

LABYRINTH

New Year's Day, 1920, pre-dawn
Manhattan, New York City

The darkness engulfs.

My noticing it comes in a rush. Like a teacup over a spider it falls on me. The reminiscences of my horrible and historic western adventures are interrupted from their natural flow. I am a New Yorker again: alert, exhausted, sophisticated if a bit scruffy; an elder scientist sitting in his workplace cubbyhole where he does less and less each year, where he is no longer essential to the progress being made by the research team whom he dearly loves – wonderful colleagues and students who cannot be blamed for not being as thrilling as past companions. I am lodged in the grisly hours before a factual but heatless sunrise, precursor to bleak, sleety skies the color of sharks, a lonely time even for those who are not alone, and near desolation for those who are.

I've let my fire burn out.

I was preoccupied by my thoughts of days past, the

dead days, memories inhabited by ghosts. Memories *are* ghosts, I think, that live on in our heads, wandering the numberless rooms, occasionally treading out into the open where we can see them whether we'd like to or not. Hazy creatures most of them are, phantasmal fogs, made as much of imaginings as recorded details. But a few shine hard and bright as mirrors in the sun, don't they? These special ones sear themselves into the brain tissue. They glare and refuse to be ignored.

The laboratory is cold, drafty. Damnation! It smells like an icehouse. The air stings entering the nose and throat, and then settles in the lungs like seepage. I am chilled sitting here. I never seem to properly warm up any more. Cold and lumpen, huddled in my overcoat and fuzzy wool scarf, and my hair is but webs on a pumpkin. Where did my life go? Winter outside on the brittle January streets, but winter for me personally too. Oh, the morbid, self-pitying song of old men – is anything more tiresome? I am really not the kind of person who dwells on what is lost. Forever lost. But, understand that I am an archaeologist! I make my living digging up the past and sifting, sifting, seeing what I might've missed the last time I looked, staring at my artifacts, and using my special knowledge to breathe life into what appears lifeless. Fear not! I have more birch logs. However, the whisky is perilously low in the bottle. Let me tell you a secret: I have found another bottle behind the ushabti!

So, I will rake the embers until they glow like the eyes of the damned crying sparks in the pit. Here you go, Log. Burn for us. Make your sacrifice so we may have light and heat to tell our story to the end. It was pitchy then, too, in that cavernous space beneath the desert monastery where evil pooled like tainted water, slimy and rank.

Have you ever held a handful of squirming night-crawlers – those fat, juicy, liverish ones that are ideal for bass fishing – ever held them close up to your face and taken a deep sniff? No. Well, if you had, then you might understand the smell lingering in the air outside the Ka door. I can taste it now, if I shut my eyes and concentrate.

Wormstink. Candles fizzling down, smoking grayly, my clothes grown stale and stiff with desert grit and sweat, and McTroy ripe in his poncho… we were quite a pair. Caught in a bad spot. Up against the wall, literally. Where to go next? What to do? We were at a loss. Well, I was. McTroy didn't talk about himself much. My emotions were wet newspapers wadded up in a corner inside me, a pulpy mess no one cared to read.

There's no point sitting here, he said.

I was doing just that – leaning my back into the splintered Ka door, listening to the hypnotic chants and drumming on the other side, miles away, more than miles. My head felt hollow as a pumpkin and half as smart.

Let me edge closer to my fire and refill my glass.

I wish you were here with me, drinking. I wish they all were here. McTroy, Miss Evangeline, Yong Wu, so many others from my adventurous days… forever past. But we have our memories. The ghosts own us, and we shall let them take the stage again.

• • •

April 9th-10th???... I am unsure
The Gila, Mexico, underground

McTroy stood at the bridge, gazing over. "There's no point sitting here," he said.

"Suggestions?" I was sounding defeated. He had taken the last of the candles. I sat in shadows, reviewing what I knew of the Duat, or the Egyptian Land of the Dead.

Vibrating.

The drums. Voices chanting. The rocks were humming with a palpable energy. My body too shivered as if I had a nasty attack of ague. The earth itself simmered with rage about to boil over. Why would Kek travel to the Duat with his entourage? He had just succeeded in resurrecting himself, becoming very much alive. So why return?

McTroy beckoned. I joined him, distractedly, at the ropes and chasm.

"We backtrack to the wine cellar," he said. "Find another way to the Temple Underneath."

"They aren't there. They're..." I waved my hand. "Gone... over to the other side. Land of the Dead."

I gestured broadly at the wall behind us, the pointlessness of it.

"Rojo told us the monks go to the Temple Underneath for their black masses. They'll get to that bullshit before dawn. This mummy death thing can't go much longer."

"The Egyptians made a royal production out of death. You'd be surprised."

He ignored me.

"I'd like to ambush them in the Temple. We'll make ourselves a cute sniper's nest before they arrive. Set up in the choir loft or what-have-you. Catch them with their pants down, if they ever put any on. Maybe we'll get lucky and find a couple rifles on the way."

"I don't feel lucky," I said.

"Luck changes on a dime, Doc. Don't forget that. I don't give two licks about our odds. Let them come for us. We'll show those cutthroats how goddamned mean we are."

"What did you say?"

He cocked a speculative eye my way. "Luck changes–"

"No, the other part."

"We'll show them cutthroats just how mean we are–"

I snapped my fingers.

"That's it." I practically danced a jig. "That's what Kek is doing in the Land of the Dead. He's showing the gods how mean he is: how he defeated their priests and their curses, their violations of his burial, how he survived them. He's gone back to show them what a true bastard looks like. He wants them to see him alive. He's off bragging."

"How long you reckon that will take?"

"I have no earthly idea," I said.

"We best move on then."

I had no argument. In the moment I was basking in the satisfaction of knowing that Kek had done something predictable or at least decipherable, and in his arrogance, we might find a solution to his capture and eventual delivery to Los Angeles. He had human-like faults because he was human too. I had forgotten that fact. And another: he had been imprisoned once by men of law, and therefore he might be confined again. So with a renewed confidence I followed my guide as we backtracked to the wine cellar.

We never did find it.

It should have been a simple walk down a dozen steps and then a ninety-degree turn to the right where we expected to encounter the following: the bloody-foot-printed corridor, the monk's wine cellar, the passageway leading to the well – and our only known way back up to the surface. But none of these expectations were met. It was not so simple, you see, the opposite of straightforward. Yes, the lack of light played a role but not as much you might think. We had the stub of a candle, and before it snuffed out, McTroy did a clever job constructing a firebrand from a length of rope he sliced off the bridge rail and a piece of the shattered Ka door.

"Doc, lemme see your left hand."

I held my arm out, the palm turned upwards.

He took hold of my wrist.

With a quick swipe of his knife – I had returned the horn-handled blade to him – he slashed the shoulder of my only shirt and pulled the cotton sleeve completely off. He wrapped the cloth around the torch and poured the melting candle over it. When the wax was spent, he used the last of the glowing wick to light the torch. It burned with a steady, confident flame.

"That'll work," he said, his face smiling in the orangey shadows.

"My word! Why didn't you ask me first?"

"Would you have said, 'Yes'?"

"I might have." I rubbed my naked arm.

So we had light. Plenty of it.

We did not have any steps.

None whatsoever presented themselves. They had vanished. Where they should have been there was, instead, an unbroken, mineral smoothness that I found sinister despite the fact it was rock, only rock, I told myself.

"Where's the damn stairs?" McTroy said.

Before us lay a corridor much narrower and deeper channeled than the one where we had watched the monks and mummies parade and where we had followed them in secret. I might have walked in this new passageway almost brushing both walls with my shoulders. It reminded me of school dormitories or hospital hallways, that same sealed-off, smothered feeling which results from cramming too much into one place. It made my chest tingle. The subterranean darkness had done some good for my fear of enclosure. I could imagine space around me. And the many passages, even the worm's vertical crevice, suggested the possibility of escape.

In the torchlight I could see more.

I tried to focus on the puzzle before me.

No obvious doorways appeared along the corridor. Nor any steps up or down, nor any turns, except for a possible change of direction far off, like an enticement. The effect reminded me of my farm days and the slaughterhouse chute. I planted my feet. My neck hairs prickled.

"This is wrong," I said. "We haven't come this way before."

"I know it," McTroy said. "But it's the only path this side of the bridge. I can't figure it."

"It's as if the landscape changed behind us."

"We came up those steps before and could see the bridge. Now we've backtracked more than that and there's nothing familiar."

"It doesn't feel safe. Let's go back to the bridge. Perhaps we missed something." The suspicion crept over me that we were stepping into a cleverly laid snare.

"Start at the bridge?"

"That's my opinion," I confirmed.

McTroy's pride was hurt. He took the attempt to fool us personally. Yet I could see his senses as a hunter were engaged. "Doc, I know I didn't miss anything. Something weird is at work. Whether it's in our heads from that crazy medicine man smoke I can't say. You go first. Take the torch. I'll put my hand on your shoulder so we don't get going in different directions."

"That's a plan." I forged on. We would start over.

But I could not find the bridge.

We walked without seeing evidence of ropes or spans, no crevasse, and no Ka door. I counted fifty… sixty… seventy steps. I could still hear the chanting, but as we moved, it moved with us. Eventually, I came upon a turn neither of us recalled making. It was sharp to the left, and we took it. Another turn presented itself, also to the left. After which we encountered a split in the pathway shaped like a *Y*.

"Why, indeed!" I stamped my foot, staring at the entrances of two identical tunnels. "This is confounding. We've never come this way before this very moment."

McTroy crouched and passed his torch close to the floor.

"Circles. They got us walking in circles."

He touched the dust. He brought his fingers to his mouth and tasted them.

"Boot prints. Could be yours, or mine. Too shallow to tell," he said, and he spit.

"We've never passed here."

"Uh-huh. Glad you're so sure of yourself."

"I only express what I observe."

His eyes narrowed in the firelight. "See these other footprints crossing back and forth. Naked like an Apache's, moving on their toes, like they were in a hunt. Tracks go in one tunnel, then the other, back they come again. Lost, I'd say. Hard to get an Apache lost. The devil marchers we saw with the mummies had blood on them. I don't taste blood. Just dust."

"The monks were shoeless. Perhaps when they are not engaged in their ceremonies, they travel this route. It may lead to something."

"I'd like to know what 'fore I get there."

"Which tunnel?" I asked.

"Neither," he said. He cocked a pistol and poked the barrel back the way we had come. "I don't like the smell of them."

I tested the air for worm stink, for monkish incense, even for Evangeline's summer blossomy perfume. "I smell nothing of consequence."

"It's the feels, Doc. I got them and I don't like them."

He turned and waited for me to lead the way.

I edged past him; torch held high, chin up, and straining with all my acumen to solve our predicament. *Strange*, I thought, this dungeon lair was riddled through like a termite mound.

What did it mean?

That question was too abstract.

How did it function?

That was more scientific. I took slow steps, McTroy's hand grasping my shoulder. A Dante's *Inferno*, I thought, but that didn't seem the correct literary allusion. I fumbled for a better one. It would be lost on McTroy, of course. Lost. Damned, imprisoned, confused, and lost in a house of monsters. Dante and Virgil met the Minotaur when they trekked through Hell.

Who would we meet?

I placed one foot forward.

Down.

And I felt it.

Movement. Subtle. Greased. But I sensed it underfoot – a shifting, a change of horizontal plane, then a bump of resettlement – the gentle pressure of the floor dropping a few inches; followed by the barely perceptible motion of counterweights, levers, gears, and pulleys turning. I spun and watched the floor lowering behind us. The wall to the right swung on silent hinges until it fit snugly across the path, blocking the way we had come but offering a different course now, in a direction we had not traveled before, or perhaps we had, it was hard to judge. But I began to understand what I was seeing – a moving maze that altered as a person walked through it.

I was correct earlier.

The landscape had changed behind us.

"Don't move," I said.

"What the devil?" McTroy said, noticing the alleyway heading to the two tunnels was gone and replaced by a new lane.

"Not the devil. But perhaps the Minotaur."

I shifted my weight carefully and shoved at the wall. It was solid, unmovable.

"Wait," I said. "Do not stir until I say."

I stepped behind McTroy.

"Walk backward with me. Left foot, then right. Keep going. Nowww... Stop. Hold your position." We stood together. I counted in my head to one hundred.

"Are we going to stand here like a couple of–?"

"Give it time."

I counted to fifty. *That should do it*, I thought.

"Forward again, slowly."

As we approached the juncture where the wall had shifted, our flickery fire preceded us until– "There! Look!" The lane that had opened was no more. Again we had the *Y* and the two tunnels.

"How... how did you know?" McTroy asked.

I dodged around him for a closer look at the wall.

"It's ingenious. Devious is a better word. I've seen something like this before. In the tombs of Egypt. In Amun Odji-Kek's tomb under the skull rock. Traps engineered to preserve treasures, to keep people from stealing what's been buried. In Kek's case, his tomb was cursed. But it was also manually secured against those who would attempt to save his corpse and revive him. He had a defender in his mausoleum to protect him, a kind of guard dog – a guard worm to be precise, a baby one, apparently, and kin to El Gusano. It is no accident that the necrófagos robbed the mummy train and stole the sarcophagus. They brought the mummies here for a reason. This monastery and the skull rock are connected. I don't yet know how."

"What does that have to do with this witchery?"

"Not witchery. Unless you count mathematics as a warlock's domain."

I stamped my foot as I had the first time I approached the tunnels. "This solid seeming rock is not so solid. Slabs of stone weighing tons. We could not possibly lift them. But... they pivot and rock. You can't see it. Not now. Yet walking on them springs them into action. Yes, *yes*... ah-ha!"

I ran crazed from one end of the hall to the other. The floor moved visibly. Not by much. But we saw it creep. *I* saw it creep. McTroy wore a mask of skepticism.

"I presume the chanting hides the sound," I said. "But they're quiet machines, no squeaking whatsoever."

I pointed downward as I tripped along.

"You see, the mechanisms cause the floors and walls to make, let's call them adjustments. Open and close. Reveal and hide. You doubt me? How do stairways appear and then vanish? Stone blocks move, making new angles. The joints fit so perfectly it would take a magnifying lens to spot them. Gorgeous work, really, a marvel of ingenuity and geometry. I'd love to study the plan under more leisurely circumstances. I'll bet if I worked my way along this..."

I tapped my knuckles on the right wall and tried to push it. Nothing happened.

"I wonder if they use steam–" I said, before being cut off.

"Doc?"

"Yes?"

"What treasure are they guarding here?"

"Oh, if I'm right they're not guarding anything. Someone has decided to put these mechanisms to another use. Allow me to explain."

"That's what I thought you were doing."

I nodded.

"Can you imagine yourself thrust into these tunnels

in pure ignorance? Not knowing that you were entering a maze. In the dark? Perhaps with a candle, perhaps with nothing. No map. No sense of what was waiting for you around the next bend?"

"I can only wonder what that must feel like," he said.

"Yes, of course. Sorry." I realized it did not take much to envision mentally the very situation in which we found ourselves. Yet I indulged my illustration of our predicament as though it were something I was observing from outside, from a safe distance, in a controlled laboratory. "It does not take long. Panic sets in. Essentially blind, you walk on. Hunted. You suspect you are prey, perhaps for a worm or the bloodletting monks. Or both. Your heart pounds. In the darkness and the smoke, you hear the hypnotic chanting. Your senses are overtaxed. It is easy for you to make mistakes. Perception fails. Misdirection is the key to any magician's art. You look but you do not see."

McTroy looked around. "Where are they?" he asked, his voice a barely contained growl.

"I do not know. And that is the point." I clapped my hands together, glad as any teacher who has broken through to her thickest student.

"Doc, just tell me how to get to the Temple Underneath. I'll do the rest."

My laugh boomed in the tunnels. A madhouse bark, even to my own ears. It was an odd reaction, I admit, but I was jangly and on the brink of exhaustion.

"We have discovered the Temple Underneath," I said. "We are in it. There is no chapel *per se*. This whole place is their temple, their underground church. The Temple

Underneath is a labyrinth."

"Laby-what?"

"Laby*rinth*, like the one Daedalus designed to hold the Minotaur."

McTroy. Grim-lipped. A look of blankness, vaguely threatening.

"Never mind," I said. "That's not important. What is important is this. Judging by similarities to the tunnels I observed beneath the train wreck, and knowing that the worm himself is at this very moment squirming nearby, I might conclude that El Gusano dug all these confusing passages, but his contribution is only part of what we're seeing. The oldest spaces are natural caverns formed millennia ago. Still others were put here for mysterious reasons by whoever built under the monastery in the first place. They are too angular, too constructed, to be geological or worm-made. However, what we have found today, or tonight – for I feel night has fallen by now, though my watch has run down and I have forgotten to wind it – this is a system, adding layers over time to an elaborate maze whose purpose is to confound the uninitiated, to imprison them. Strangers are not supposed to get out of here alive. The church is a giant trap! We could spend hours, days, or... forever fumbling in the dark without any hope of escape. To enter the Temple Underneath is to be instantly, utterly, and hopelessly... lost."

"We're neck deep in the sumbitch," McTroy said. "That's what you're saying."

"Quite."

We both heard the sound.

A rapid thumping of heavy footsteps.

We would have no time. That much was certain.

Something was running toward us from inside one of the tunnels.

31
DEAD FOLKS

I never saw the first attacker coming out of the tunnel, and with good reason. He had disguised himself as a piece of the darkness. But he was capable of movement and wolfishly intent on killing. I would soon learn that along with his pack-mates he had been stalking us ever since the worm snatched Evangeline from the bridge. They watched us and let their excitement build. We passed them and they held their breath, biting their tongues and suppressing their evil giggles of delight, shutting their eyes so the whites wouldn't reveal their hiding spots. It must've brought perverse joy to their blackened little hearts – this ritualized sport of stalking people of various sizes and stripes: Apaches and American businessmen, railroaders, gold miners, mothers with their children in tow, stagecoach passengers, traveling Mexican farmers lost in storms, cowboys, bounty hunters, and even an Egyptologist from the northern shores of Illinois.

Everyone who entered the mysterious monastery unknowingly sealed their doom. Some had their throats sliced in bed. Blood sacrificed. Flesh fed to ghouls. Others were put in the maze. Set loose inside a clockwork labyrinth with its secret doors and ever-shifting maze walls.

The monks liked hunting humans.

We were game.

Our terror fed their bizarre appetites.

McTroy saw him – the first attacker. That's the important thing.

I don't know how he did it. His eyesight was a marvel both at long distances and in exceptionally low light conditions like we had in the Temple Underneath. All I saw were shadows bunched on shadows. Rich velvety black – like a fog of India ink enveloping us – I peered blindly into it.

McTroy said, "There's the bastard." And he fired one of his Armys.

The report deafened my right ear.

I hurled my body to the left until I hit a wall.

I slid down into a crouch with the torch in one hand and my stick in the other.

My fear and my reaction were equally primal. Man-as-prey has never strayed far from his jungle roots no matter what level of civilization he imagines he has cultivated.

I saw a spear.

Dual prongs, a long-handled shaft made of twisted iron.

The points aimed for my chest.

A second flash. A second roar. The sharp scent of gunpowder. A gray tendril of smoke escaped from McTroy's pistol.

A startled cry. The points lowering. Dropping.

The spear-fork clanged and fell, scraping along the

floor between McTroy and me. A mad monk stumbled out of the gloom and fell through my torchiere. Sparks burst! His face smacked the ground hard between my knees and I heard his nose break. Yet he did not curse in pain. A greater wound became obvious – his head was blasted open. I could've stood a candle inside the cavity. Another hole was visible where McTroy's first bullet exited between the man's lower ribs.

I flipped the body.

The last bullet had entered his forehead. His eyes were crossed stupidly. But there was no comedy in the moment, only my disgust at the violence and quick death.

"My God," I said.

"You'd have met Him if my shot pulled wide."

The body was oddly colored. I had trouble distinguishing it from the surroundings even under my firebrand.

"What's he got all over him?" I asked.

McTroy pinched at the dead monk's hair and sniffed. He poked his skin.

"That's tar gunk in his hair. His face has got charcoal smears, and it looks like he rubbed himself down in mud. All he's wearing is this black loincloth. And them burlap bags on his feet quieted his steps and mussed any tracks. I'd say he was night-hunting."

McTroy lifted the spear-fork. He touched one of the prongs and a bead of blood swelled up. He sucked his thumb. "Kept this sucker sharp as a rattler's tooth."

"Why did he charge at us, I wonder?"

"What do you mean, Doc?"

"It was not to his advantage." I indicated the monk's camouflage. "Concealment was clearly his strategy.

With that long fork he might've skewered us from far enough away. We would've had no idea where to direct a counterattack. Why didn't he simply knock the torch down and spear us at his leisure?"

McTroy thought about my question.

In the distance, we heard scuffling. Metal striking rock? Bodies in contact.

Something like pig grunts. Insistent. Hungry. Uncaring about the noise it made.

A shout of surprise. "No! Ayúdame!"

Then a regular tattoo of running feet. A scream pierced the dark. Cut off abruptly.

More footsteps. Another scream. Different.

This one sounded far away, or was it the echoes adding distortion, making it sound so? *No, definitely farther off.* I had time for analysis because the scream diminished like a wave flowing up a beach, thinner and thinner, until it was barely a hiss as the screamer ran out of air.

Silence. My heartbeat. McTroy's steady inhale and exhale at my side.

A third scream went up like a fast, wet rip, and very close by.

Coming from inside the second tunnel.

Clearly, footfalls… pounding out an increasing tempo – someone in a mad dash headed right for us. A person was moving in our direction with speed.

McTroy backed up.

"Maybe he wasn't charging," he said. "Maybe that boy was running for his life."

Another monk. This one was portly, built deep through the chest and swinging two arms a blacksmith would be

proud of. He also had exchanged his natural light skin
color for the night's cloak. In his right fist he gripped
a butcher's cleaver. Strangely, he had a long-stemmed
pipe he seemed to have forgotten in his left hand. His
stout legs pumped. Sweat slashed runnels through his
muddy layer of concealment, exposing flesh like raw
dough. He brandished his cleaver at us to clear a path.
As he passed, I tripped him with my stick. He flopped
and immediately attempted to crawl away on his knees.
The pipe crumbled. He chopped his cleaver at nothing
at all in front of him – but wait – after the last futile
chop he regained his legs to continue his race, and a
figure hopped out of the tunnel and secured itself to his
buffalo-sized back.

A slender thing in loose garments rode the monk to
the ground. The back rider reared its head and bit down
on the fat monk's throat. Red spurted through a screen
of snow-white hair.

I stood to one side, aghast.

McTroy held his fire, saving bullets.

Or was he as stunned as I?

Like a blood well, the dying man was pumped dry.

Ga-lump, ga-lump, pshhhhhh.

This proved to take less time than I expected. Soon
his limp head drooped, sagged dollishly forward as if
his bones had suddenly melted. And the creature on
his back maneuvered around him, pushing and pawing.
An overzealous lover, he drank until drinking turned to
suckling and suckling to licking and finally, lip-smacking.
And after, he threw the man aside.

McTroy fired one shot into the back of the parasite.

To little effect, I noted.

He did not fire another round because a second parasite, shorter, sprightlier – a female, judging from her contours – emerged from the tunnel, bounding and conveying yet a third mud-smeared monk wearing a scrap over his staff of life. This unfortunate had lost his weapon along the journey and most of the meat around his collar to boot.

The two vampires ignored us as they drained their kills.

It offered an opportunity for closer observation.

Inhuman faces, or formerly human. Noses shortened and upturned, their flared nostrils constantly twitching. Not very like a bat, but much, much worse. Skin the color of vegetables left to rot weeks in the garden. Smells of coal dust and damp decay. Their indigo-dyed shirts and trousers were covered in soot and hung unfilled on their bony frames. *Starving*, I thought. I recalled that Wu said his parents hid at the bottom of the coal car. The other smell reminded me of poking under logs in the forest. Wild hair ensnarled. Eyes insensate, bleached as stone. *So they are utterly blind*. Mouths and chins dripping bloody bits. Jaws expanded to display the unspeakable teeth. Lips working, chalky tongues darted. Sniff, sniff. Tasting the air. They put their hands up (long, filthy, gummy maroon fingernails). They reached out for me.

Grasping, clutching my bare arm. I had felt this hand before. When it had saved me from El Gusano's scorpion trap in the desert. I wondered if old times mattered now.

Cold.

The male's hands were strong.

I froze in place.

"My lead don't faze them one bit," McTroy said. But he fired two times.

Vampires – like necrófagos, and come to think of it, mummies – do not bleed.

Fingers still dancing in the air. The female. She wanted to touch my neck.

Slowly, I raised my walking stick.

From inside the second tunnel a stream of Cantonese orders shouted out.

The icy grip unclamped. His thin arms retracted. The dancing fingers quieted, lowered to her sides. Both male and female dropped their heads in shame and huddled together. Sadness emanated from them, stronger than the smells of compost and stale train smoke. But no tears spilled. Quietness settled. Trembling shook their loose rags.

Yong Wu stepped out of the tunnel to stand by his parents.

He put himself between us and them; whom he was protecting I could not tell.

He looked past us into the passageway.

"Where is the lady?" he asked. "Have you found Miss Evangeline?"

"No," I said. How did he know she was missing? Was their bond so strong he could simply sense her absence? I experienced again the acute physical ache of losing her, and the accompanying shame of not preventing it from happening.

McTroy slipped his weapons out of sight. "You made it through the sandstorm."

"Jiangshi can smell... people... even in a sandstorm. We scared the horses outside the well. But I knew you had been there and we followed you to help."

I bowed to them. I felt foolish. They could not see me. Wu bowed back to me, pleased that I had tried to acknowledge them even in this small way.

"You are alive! I'm very pleased to see you, Wu. We worried you were lost in the storm."

"My mother found me," he said.

"Are your parents... and I mean no insult by my question... are they capable of understanding what I'm saying?"

"No, they do not speak to or hear anyone who is not family. They cannot see either. But they follow with their noses. They helped me find you in the dark. There were others. Men with the hair on the top of their heads shaved. They were hiding. Even when the worm came, we were there. I wanted to talk to you... to warn you... but the men frightened me. Do you know the walls and floors move in this most unusual place?"

"We figured that out not long ago."

"They wanted to play a game with you, I think, but you would not like this game. These men scared me. They were moon men."

"Moon men?" McTroy asked.

"I think he means lunatics."

Yong Wu nodded. "Yes, lunatics. Like mad dogs who stare and snap, their mouths hanging open, leaking thick strings of bubbles." Yong Wu showed us what they looked like by using his own face as an example. Most disconcerting, we agreed.

"I think they might've been drugged," I said. "Visions enhanced their ritual."

"Goddamned Satan monks. Hang 'em all. Let the

crows peck at their parts."

Wu's parents had fallen into a state similar to sleep. Their trembling had subsided and their unnerving blank eyes were shut. They leaned heavily into one another. I noticed, with a start, that they did not breathe. I think their calmness came from Wu. Telepathically is my best guess in retrospect. Quite a boy he was, even then. Wu pointed with his chin, a habit he borrowed from McTroy, though I am not sure either one was conscious of it. "These *'goddamned Satan monks,'* as you say, were watching you. We were watching them! I told my father and my mother that they could take their blood. It would not be a bad thing."

Wu seemed less sanguine about it now with bodies stacked at our feet.

McTroy patted him on the back. "We thank you kindly for that, Wu. At least them shit devils were good for something. Hope your folks took a long drink."

"They did. But the thirst is always there."

"I reckon it is."

I remembered the whisky bottles in saddlebags and McTroy's desire to seek out the wine casks. I believe he and Wu were talking about the same sort of thing.

A brilliant idea lit up my mind (if I may be immodest).

"Wu, how did you know we were looking for Evangeline?"

"As I said, we were there at the bridge when the worm–"

"You saw the Ka door? The one with the hieroglyphs painted on it that I broke apart?"

"Sir, I did."

"Do you think your father and mother can lead us

back to the door?"

"Oh, yes. That would be no problem."

"Excellent. Can your parents tell you if they smell Evangeline's perfume, and if so where she is? And if she is still alive?"

I saw the twinkle in Wu's eyes brightened by the brimming of tears.

"Oh, yes, sir, they can!"

McTroy caught hold of the same idea that had turned my mood. "Hey!" He clapped both our shoulders and shook us. "His dead folks might help us out."

"Help you again," Wu said, more accurately.

"That's right. You're right."

I shone the torch on the cursed loved ones of our young companion.

"I will have two favors to ask of them. And, if I am correct, for once we will have the upper hand on Amun Odji-Kek and his monstrous crew."

The pair of Chinese vampires slumbered blindly in the firelight.

32
THE VAPORS OF TIME

I had never followed hopping vampires before, but it was not as difficult as one might imagine. McTroy passed our torch to them. Wu asked his parents to proceed – hop, as it were, for hopping was their preferred mode of terrestrial ambulation – in a deliberate manner so that we might follow their beacon proximately, allowing neither walls nor slipsliding passages to come between us. If there were any smudgy, death-obsessed monks left to be had in the maze, they soon fled upwards to the moonlit desert floor that hunched over our heads with all the subtlety afforded several million pounds of rock and brick red soil.

We reached the Ka door in less time than it takes a fat man to eat a slice of pie.

That is: sooner than expected.

The Ka door lay in pieces on the floor, and the place where it had been framed on the wall remained as it was when we left it – stony, impregnable, and the definition of a dead end. *Dead end, indeed*, I thought. I knew that Kek and his entourage had traversed the chasm from our time to out-of-time. After all, the chants had never faltered. They were our background music. Their unwholesome notes and rhythms offered a constant thrum, flowing, energetic, and ceaseless as the rivers that carved Paleozoic limestone into miles of wandering canyons. Kek still taunted the timeless gods.

As I had told Wu, I had two favors to ask of his parents.

The first concerned the whereabouts and safety of our kidnapped lady.

I lifted the torch from Wu's father's cool fingers. He had no need for light, of course, and he seemed ready enough to give up the brand. I do not think he liked fire, as an element, for he shied from its source. I wondered if the heat reminded him of his own bodily coldness and what he had lost after being bitten in the night by a cursed thing.

"Thank you," I said.

His face was a pale study in impassivity.

Then I remembered he could not hear me.

"My friend Wu, will you ask your parents to turn their unique senses in the direction of locating our missing Evangeline?"

Wu nodded and translated my request. I could not help but notice the deep redness of his mother's lips as she answered him. The color came from blood, not her own, and my observation arrived with a dose of queasiness and a tingle of fear that until that moment I had kept at bay.

She and her helpmate moved along the edge of the chasm in a manner most inhuman. Their noses twitched. The mouths slightly opened, like a cat's.

When they had finished tasting the air, they conferred with their son.

"Miss Evangeline is down there," Wu said, indicating the abysmal crack. "In a side cave."

"And her condition is..."

"Alive."

"Thank goodness," I said, filling with relief.

"I am afraid they smell the worm too. He is with her."

"What is he doing? Can vampires deduce that from the... smell?"

"I will ask."

This next conversation took longer than I anticipated. I listened to many exchanges back and forth. When I inclined my head for clarifications, I received none. Patience frayed. I had time to wish more than once that I had studied Chinese dialects instead of ancient Egyptian. Wu appeared determined to get his information straight before relaying any content to me. The effort I appreciated, the suspense – not nearly so much.

"The two are drinking piña juice with oranges and salted chili peppers."

"Good." I sighed. I had thought her dead. "Very good news, I'd say!"

Confusion on my part – seeded, rooted, flowered in seconds. The burring of alarms began in my head, or in my chest. *Oranges and salted chili peppers?*

"Wait... what is piña?"

"I don't know, sir. My parents tell me it's something the traqueros drink."

"McTroy, help me. Do you know of this concoction?"

"Traqueros are Mex railroaders. Piña? That's maguey mash. Shee-it. The worm is drinking the mescal! I wish I had some. It'll warm you all the way down to the holes in your socks." McTroy pantomimed taking healthy swigs from an invisible bottle.

I am no prude. My puzzlement may have obscured this fact.

"Why would they be drinking spirits?"

"He's wooing her, pard. Probably got a piano stashed in that den of his. Fancy lace curtains hanging every which way. The gal's smart, though. She'll hold off the ol' wiggler long as she can. Don't you worry, Doc. He was sinful ugly. Or his tail was."

El Gusano had brought her to a grotto and changed himself into human form.

I was not pleased. But I preferred the idea of a wormly courting to other more forceful, even digestive alternatives.

"She is safe for the moment. We have no time to lose, then." I strode to where I had pulled the Ka door loose from the wall. I ran the flickering torch over the surface. I knocked the ape's head of my walking stick – once, twice, thrice – against the cold stone. "Wu, here is where I ask your parents to do us a second favor."

Wu approached. His palms spread to touch the smooth hardness. He was shaken. Without moving his head, his eyes rolled sideways to regard me with something more than skepticism and less than the pity commonly offered to town fools. "My father and mother have strength beyond humans. But they cannot bite through rock."

"Of course they can't." I laughed. "I don't want them to eat the rock, merely to pass through it to the other side."

Now I knew how town fools felt. Wu turned to McTroy for assurance.

McTroy did his best to endorse me. "He sounds loco.

But you're hearing him right. I've seen things in these burrows that I wouldn't have believed in the daylight. This here's mummy rules. Let Doc tell it."

I nodded my thanks for his... support.

I continued, "Amun-Kek has opened the Ka door and passed over its threshold to the Duat with his procession of monks and mummies. They dwell in the underworld at this very moment. A living being without occult charms cannot follow them. Forgive me, Wu, for saying this so bluntly – but your parents are not strictly alive, are they?"

Wu watched me so intently I feared he might cry. He did not. But he steeled himself.

"They are between," he said.

Brave boy. I was counting on him.

"Between is often not a good place to be. However, it is just what we require. I am asking you to ask your parents to use the Ka door. I cannot tell you what will happen to them if they should go through. What I know comes from the *Book of the Dead*. For reasons that are obvious I have no firsthand knowledge of whom or what they will encounter once they have crossed over. The gods control it. Yet, make no mistake, the Duat is highly dangerous. Kek and the monks are there. My hope is that your parents might drive them back to this side."

"Flush 'em out," McTroy added. He made a motion that was intended to convey pursued creatures bursting forth from cover. Birds perhaps? Foxes? I could not discern which. He had a way with theatrical flourishes though, and the boy was thusly engaged.

"To act like hunting dogs?" Wu asked. His expression verged on sourness.

I was ready to object to the comparison.

McTroy interceded, taking a different tack.

"That's right," he said. "Like good ol' scent hounds they'll chase them monks and mummies back here. I'm gonna kill the monks, and we'll grab the mummies for Doc."

Wu was quiet for a moment. He drew nearer his parents who stood slackly like two automatons who had run their mechanisms down. Skeletal bodies, flesh like puddled wax. They did not stir, or breathe, or blink, or acknowledge in any demonstrative way that their only son, still a young child, paused before them filled with emotions far greater than his age could possibly accommodate without suffering great pain and inner turmoil. He touched their denim sleeves, caressing the rough, dirty material, for even that was preferable to their corpselike skins. The cobwebbed silver nimbuses of their hair trembled as he sighed.

"Father and mother have done awful things. They do not mean to, but they do." His voice thickened with grief. "If they help people, maybe they will find peace with our ancestors. Maybe they will leave hell. Maybe they will stop being hungry ghosts."

Evangeline would have known the best words to say to the boy. McTroy remained silent.

I tried to imagine what she might say.

"I'm certain they love you, and they know you love them too."

"I miss the way they used to be." Wu wiped tears from his cheeks.

He spoke gently to his parents in their dialect. They woke slowly as one does to the morning songs of birds outside a familiar window.

• • •

They went through the door together, Mr and Mrs Wu, in one hop. The wall became like a thick mist. I might have imagined the smells, but I think not. It was frosty at first, a whiff of iron rust lingering about like the old farm equipment in the corner of my father's barn, a trace of burnt matchsticks too, not one but a whole pile collected together, heaping, sulfurous. Out from under it all – as Kek himself had told me it was in the Void of the Underworld – arose a scent of shit that forced me to stop my breathing, and then it disappeared again with abruptness like the banging of an outhouse door on a black, winter morning. My parents dead and gone these many years... why did I think of them? I knew why. *Book of the Dead. Duat. The Land of the Dead.* Were they there?

I covered my nose and kept staring. Vapors swirled. Nebulous. No colors.

The vapors of time, I thought, *reveal nothing to us*.

Wherever the vampire couple landed, it was in silence. The vapors slickened.

I tapped my stick and heard a rocky report. The Ka door was closed again.

Wu had turned from the scene before his parents jumped. He waited at the rope bridge with his back to me. McTroy and he were talking. I raised the torch. I was too far away to make sense of their words. Wu straightened his shoulders and nodded. Sleek as a crow, McTroy perched on the rim of my light, one hand on his Army pistol, the other steering Wu away from the chasm's edge. The dead would be here soon.

Are we ready?

33
Gunfight at the Temple Underneath

This then was our task: to wait for the vampires to drive the mad monks, mummies, and ghouls from the Duat through the Ka door and back to our "side" of things so that we might sort them out, dispatching the monkish and ghoulish accordingly, capturing the resurrected Egyptian sorcerer and his acolytes, helping, or at least not harming, the Nosferatu-infected parents of our youngest companion, all without rousing the ire of the worm who in his side-cave lair plied with his liquor and charms the young though quite resourceful and canny Miss Waterston before presumably, ultimately, he would swallow her body, perhaps whole, perhaps piece by piece. I reviewed this plan with my partners.

"That's about the size of it," McTroy said.

Wu nodded in accord with the bounty man.

"It seems a size, or two, too large to me," I admitted. "For just us three, I mean."

"We'll do it. Maybe not as neatly as you said but done just as well."

For the sake of clarity I must mention that we were not sitting idly by the by, like three schoolboys fishing from a bridge in the sun on an endless summer afternoon. I squatted, holding what remained of a still excellent torch. Wu knelt on the bridge, his nose pressed to the slats. McTroy hung underneath us like a ship's monkey, sawing at ropes with his stag knife. This positioning did not affect our ability to converse, though I could not see McTroy's face and was prevented from reading any trace of irony thereupon. Hand over hand he pulled himself back to relative safety beside the boy.

"That ought to work," he said. "I might've cut too deep on the left cable."

The left was where I squatted. I shifted toward the middle. "Will it hold?"

"I'd like it to hold some, but not too sturdy. We'll find out." McTroy raised his knee high and stomped his boot. The ropes creaked. A brief interval of quiet followed, and then my ears detected a noise like the breaking of banjo strings.

"Get your asses off the bridge, boys!" McTroy shouted.

Wu and I were quick to comply.

A laughing McTroy stayed behind. The bridge swayed under him, cockeyed, as he straightened up to his full height, ignoring the threat of death that yawned below. The gold tooth shined in the corner of his grin. *He looks like a pirate on the deck of his schooner*, I thought. *A mad pirate*. He freed his Army irons from their leathers and let his arms hang down. "My bullets are low. I've loaded the last from my belt. Got twelve left for the job at hand."

"There are more devils than that," Wu said. He had opportunities to count as he shadowed us through the Temple labyrinth.

"I know it." McTroy winced as if in pain. "I need to think."

He aimed his right-hand barrel at the Ka door.

"Speed your thinking, McTroy," I warned. "They may flood through that portal at any second."

Wu and I stationed ourselves judiciously away from the edge of the crevasse, on the opposite side from the Ka door. McTroy turned in a slow circle at the center of the bridge, looking it up and down. He had the habit of disparaging higher learning, schoolroom education of every kind, books in general (except for the holy bible), and scholarly works in particular. I knew him to be more intelligent than he pretended. His "thinking" had much to do with angles and what we bookish, chalk-covered types might label *geometry*. Probabilities entered into his calculations as well. He was studying how best to deliver his twelve remaining shots. His balletic pacing on the span halted. He'd formulated a strategy. Those glittering gray eyes made me glad I was not a hell monk.

"I'm sticking to this side," he said. "I'll tuck up in that notch." Here he gestured to the shadows where I spied no indentation a man might use for cover, but I suppose that was what made it a good place to hide. "Them friars are gonna be running. We need them bunched on the bridge. But we can't let 'em cross over."

I guffawed. "How do you propose to do that?"

"You have to stop them."

"Me? By what means?"

McTroy shrugged, paying little attention to my degree of shock. He walked off to his hiding place adjacent to the door, crabbing his way along a narrow, brittle-looking ledge hardly suitable for pigeons, eventually slipping into a patch of total stygian gloom. Like a phantom he was gone. Also like a phantom, he had a leftover thought he wished to express.

"Use your walking stick, Doc. Swing it. Dent a few heads."

"I cannot hold back a horde!"

The Phantom McTroy made no further comment.

Wu said, "Twenty-five is not a horde, I think. With the ghouls and mummies added in it is still less than fifty. Fifty might be a horde. But you want to capture the mummies, yes?" He tugged at my surviving sleeve when I did not answer. "You want to bring them back to Los Angeles?" he asked. "The Egyptian corpses go to California?"

"Yes, to Mr Waterston, Evangeline's father. He funded my expedition..."

"Then you had better not let the mummies fall into the chasm."

"I had better not... I agree." *Keep the monks back with a stick?* Was the man a lunatic? I was more likely to be trampled. Or speared. I didn't want a gun. But I was no willing human sacrifice either. The ghouls did have guns. Deadly arms were their métier. If I blocked their way, what was to say they wouldn't simply shoot me *tout de suite*? Was I expected to block bullets with my stick as well? I could not conceive of a more ludicrous, outlandish, and absolutely reckless assignment–

"Dr Hardy?"

I went on mumbling to myself. "McTroy would have me killed outright so he might save Evangeline. The noble gray knight, oh how charming. The lady, seeing him, is overcome with gratitude. Won't that be dandy? If only I were around to witness it–"

"Dr Hardy! Dr Hardy! *Dr Hardy*, sir…?"

"Damnation! What?"

"The chanting has stopped. Does that mean something?"

I listened until my ears rang with the silence. I heard my own blood coursing.

No drumbeats, nary a voice.

I had thought the chants were maddening, but this negative switch was far worse.

We had wanted them to stop. They had stopped. But what were the chanters doing? Were vampires killing them, or were the chanters in this moment too busy piking our vampires through the chest? Lopping off moldy bat heads with glinting blades? Would pikes and blades be our destiny?

"Get behind me. Here, Wu, take this torch. Hold it high. The monks are going to run toward the light. I will dispatch them as they arrive. If they pass me, you must halt their progress. Burn them. Kick them. Punch them. Do not allow them off the bridge. Understood?"

He was only a boy. It was too much to ask of him. But he would be a dead boy if he failed. Boys have gone into battle for millennia. They do not know better, or as in this case, they have no choice. Survival does not question your age. Neither does death.

"It is like a game," Wu said. Squaring his shoulders, he brandished the torch.

"A game we cannot afford to lose, Master Wu. I'm glad we're on the same team."

"I am also happy that McTroy and Miss Evangeline are with us."

I nodded solemnly. "We will get her back, Wu. You have to believe that."

He swatted invisible monks with his firebrand. He jumped onto the bridge and back again. The idea of a game was preferable to trepidation. The boy was adaptive.

"Be careful now. Stay off the bridge." I hauled him in by his collar. He weighed little more than a cat, or that was how he felt – all bouncy, twisty, and acting frolicsome.

Wu glanced at the chasm, drawing fiery circles in the air. "My parents said they smelled a man in the cave with Evangeline and the worm. But I think they're wrong."

I startled upon hearing this new information.

"A man? What sort of man?"

"A gentleman. Probably they smelled you or McTroy, or maybe someone the worm ate but had not fully digested. When El Gusano turns himself into a man-shape, mustn't he wear clothes from a man he killed? I guessed so. The scent of this man's old suit is what they smelled. But it was confusing. Mother insisted it was a gentleman–"

"What exactly did she say?"

"Let me think… Mother said, '*In the cave are a woman, a worm, and a gentleman drinking piña juice, oranges, and salted chili peppers.*' But she meant only two people in the cave, not three."

Did she?

A third in the cave with Evangeline and El Gusano? A mystery mescal sipper?

Wu parried with his imaginary monsters. Too soon they would be real.

I leaned into the crevasse.

I saw nothing but emptiness. The dark worked its trickery on my vision. Then I found something real in all that barren blackness – a glowing – subtle, maybe a mile or so down, that is how far off it seemed, too distant at any measure. Unreachable, but steady.

I marked it. Looked away.

Marked it again upon a second viewing.

Like Venus afloat in the night sky, only the sky was under me instead of above me and more than half of it was rock. That hazy dot of straw-colored light – Evangeline would be there... with the worm... and was there an obscure, imbibing gentleman in their company? The thought unsettled me. My, oh my, but how the unknown is always worse even if the known is adequately dreadful. I stuck my face into the dark. Chills ran over me as I half-expected faces other than my own to pop out and mock me. None did. If I extended myself into the abyss too hastily, too eagerly, I'd lose my balance. Gravity would snatch me to my death. I'd fall right past Evangeline, my body tumbling, my arms wheeling uselessly in the air, until I burst like a bone-and-blood-filled balloon at the bottom of this bottomless pit.

I struck my fist against the bridge.

Cool yourself, Hardy. Wait for an advantage. Be ready.

I pulled back, coiled up, resolved and watchful. She would live through this. Worm or no worm, I would make certain of it. I could not bear to think otherwise.

"The door, Dr Hardy... Look at the door..."

The Ka door began to fluoresce with a greenish alien color. Very like foxfire one finds deep in the woods. Eerie to observe, even more troubling when the observer knows what lay on the other side – and that this lambency before us was no patch of mushrooms growing along a damp log, but an emerald-shaded hell filled with demons.

Still, we waited.

Time is not the same in the Underworld. It must move slower, or not at all. What came through the door came at a choppy pace, stuttering like a flipbook animation.

I gawked.

What was it?

A jet of blood so copious that I mistook its shape for the improbable head of a red horse – its wild, scarlet mane flowing, the horse screaming... but it was a monk who was screaming... he followed his leaping blood from one world to another as he stumbled over the threshold with his legs shaking, wobbly as a newborn colt's. But here was as far as he would ever go. The time lag mended. At full speed his two hands clasped a ruined throat. He gurgled. Bug-eyed, bewildered, damned. Collapsing dead.

Bedlam cries followed upon his heels. His brother monks were running.

They rushed out of the Ka like guests from a burning hotel.

Pushing one another, squeezing against the doorjambs, clawing at the air. Fear released from their collected mass like musk and compounded to the odor of pure animal panic, which soon clouded the underground hall. I covered my nose. It might've been an amusement to watch bad men struggle, if not for the bite marks. Such ragged lacerations. Scores of them. The result of a frenzied attack. The salty metal stink of blood unsprang a memory in me of farm butchery at the time of harvest. Our vampires had hunted quickly. Slashing monk skin to tattered, pink ribbons. I once saw a beggar ravaged by dogs in Cairo. He was less unstitched than these friars when he died.

"Here they come, Wu. Be brave."

I braced my legs on the rocky ledge.

Wu's hand gripped my shirttail.

"Hold. Hold them here for McTroy!" I shouted.

Wu said nothing. From the corner of my eye I saw his fire. The torch rose and waved for the monks to take notice. The horde responded. To say they flooded onto the rope bridge is no exaggeration, for they did not move so much like a group of men but rather as a single thing: a snaky, foaming (at the mouth), and unstoppable tide of wounded, terrorized flesh. When they reached the midpoint of the bridge, the ropes sagged into a great curvaceous belly. Still they kept loading onto the span. Some toppled over the sides. Or jumped. They did not scream as the pit ate them. This detail led me to conclude they were suicides. The survivors were close enough now that they could see me silhouetted beside the open flame. They did not slow but dropped their heads (the first few did) and charged for us.

I met them with determination.

Swinging my ape-headed stick like a baseballer's bat. The sound of ebony striking flesh-covered bone is both hard and soft. I did not, could not, look at any individual gore-painted monk as I beat them back. There was no time. I simply repeated my swings as often and as ferociously as I could. What answered me were grunts, sighs, and occasionally a sound like cracking dice which I later realized were liberated teeth. These sensations only came to me in retrospect. For in the moment I lost sound, felt as though I were plunged under thick syrup, and despite my trying, I could not swing a very fast bat and was sure that I would be overrun. Wu, for his part, acquitted himself admirably. He yelled like a boy possessed, and his yell disquieted even me. His small flying fists and furious low kicks struck blows that stole the air from drug-saturated monk lungs and brought the brothers down with looks of surprise and, yes, fear. They feared a boy! And well they should have. What Wu lacked in training he more than made up for in passion. He singed the men who darted beyond my reach. Tonsured hair still burns. The monks' blood-smeared skin smelled like pork roast. He batted them roundly and sparks flew each time he hammered away.

A pair of actions saved us: one a surprise, the other a well-planned tactic.

The surprise was that the stampeding monks, after we batted the first dozen or so to their knees, clogged their own passage over the bridge. They piled up. They tripped themselves and acted as a barrier to their brethren at the rear of the pack. Violence broke out among them, and this fortunate outcome lessened the burden on Wu and me.

As the last monk fleeing the Duat launched himself onto the bridge, McTroy, whose patience was that of a seasoned hunter of wild game and wilder wanted men, fired a bullet into the nether regions of the bridge and, striking rope that he had already partially severed, pushed the structure past its limits. The rope failed. The entire bridgework tilted dramatically, pitched to one side, and spilled better than half the monks into the crevasse. While the earlier death-seeking monks had fallen silently, submissively, chasm-bound, these monks screamed until their breath ran out, and so, for the record, the unfathomable depth of the pit was proven once and for all.

Wu and I stepped away from the edge.

Two categories of monks were left on the remains of the bridge: clingers and climbers. Climbers were the more immediate threat. McTroy picked off a half-dozen before they could clamber to our far shore. His shooting turned the remaining climbers into clingers, and gravity began to peel them away at a rate of approximately one every ten seconds. The agitation on the bridge caused a second rope to snap. Ten of the most vicious devil-worshippers adhered to the bridge. There was no question they would die if they stayed where they were, and so they began to scurry in the most spidery manner toward Wu and me. I readied my stick. Wu's firebrand was but a smoldering stump, yet he was game for action. I do not know if any of the monks gained demoniac powers in their travels to the Duat. But I do know that the ones creeping along the web of ropes had eyes of pulsating, clotted red and an abundance of muscle growth I have never observed before or since. I was seriously in doubt whether or not we could fight one let alone ten of them. Before I could tell Wu to make a run for the escape tunnel and the well's mouth, McTroy fired another shot.

His aim was true.

The bridge fell away completely from our side of the chasm. Its last connection to the Ka door side only served to dash those final ten monks against the stone wall. They dangled helplessly from a single rope into the pit. The bridge was no longer a bridge.

I gasped in relief.

Short-lived relief as it so happened.

Some facts from the world of the supernatural and occult are more important than others. These particular facts were greatly significant to us that night in the Temple Underneath: Mummies are slow. Ghouls are leery. Neither is much afraid of vampires.

Not one of them had ventured onto the bridge.

They stood at the edge of the other side of the crevasse. They had fat, red candles sputtering in their grubby hands. They were watching us. Waiting for something. A few moved off to one side in the direction of McTroy's notch. But there appeared to be no rush on their part. McTroy held his fire. I couldn't see him, but then again, I never had throughout the battle on the bridge. The mummies and ghouls did not talk to us or to each other. Looking bored, they played with their weapons in the candlelight.

I did not spot Amun Odji-Kek anywhere among them.

It took me a minute.

My mind was fatigued and jittery from fighting. Every nerve in me twitched from an electrical storm blowing along the ridge of my spine.

But when my brain gears finally meshed, I quickly covered Yong Wu's eyes.

Wu did not see. And I did not tell him.

His parents occupied the Ka doorway.

They were not alone.

Odji-Kek wrapped his knuckles in their long white

hair and bashed them together like a pair of marionettes. Then he dragged their limp bodies back into the Duat. The sorcerer stepped through into our world again and quickly sealed the Ka door behind him. Wu's parents were trapped in the Duat. Kek turned away from the stone wall calmly, a banker locking his vault, and showed the interdimensional door his wide and bandaged back. He smiled at me.

It was then I felt the earth vibrate and I knew the worm was crawling again.

34

DEALING WITH THE WORM

"Do you feel him?" Kek called out across the crevasse. "The Grub of the Desert rises. As he rises, your chance for escape falls. Did you think dropping a few idiots down a hole made you heroes?"

I hated to admit that I *was* feeling rather heroic in the moment. With a few jaggy words he was able to take that away. My teeth gritted so I feared they might crack. It required all my strength not to turn and run. During my life I have discovered that many powerful men seize upon what little spark of gumption they find in those they deem beneath them – to grind it out like a cheap cigar, toss it in the gutter, and then piss on it for spite. This even proved true for a two thousand year-old magician who had brought himself back from the dead. He wanted us to know we were dog shit stuck to his heel. Call it domination or old-fashioned schoolyard bullying – I'm ashamed to say it worked on me as a drop of sulfuric acid would, eating down, eroding. I began to doubt myself.

I should say here that being in close proximity to either Odji-Kek's magic or the door to the Duat (perhaps both in combination?) had a profound effect upon my five senses – they were intensified. I saw things larger, more vividly, this despite the parsimonious light. Sounds gained depth and sharpness. Smells, touches – each were more acute than they had been. My attention twisted in and out of focus. A torrent of stimuli threatened to drown my logical and orderly brain. I verged on tears, on laughter, on spouting snippets of pure nonsense. This giddy augmentation deepened my reality and paradoxically made my experience of it feel unreal, akin to a waking dream. While this breaking free of the ordinary came with a rush of exhilaration, I also tasted a dash of sorrow, because the ordinary does have its comforts.

How these sensory changes altered young Yong Wu's still developing mind is a subject upon which I might only speculate. Add to the mix his raw emotions involving the uncertain fate of his parents, and however one classifies it, the Temple Underneath amounted to a hallucinatory assault upon the child, the boundaries of which I still cannot draw.

Wu pried my fingers from his eyes, wanting to see the mummy.

Odji-Kek walked to the edge of the chasm. "Tsk, tsk," he said. "What do you know about bravery? It is more than killing ants."

Using his bare hands, he tore the root of the bridge from its moorings. A knot in the rope the size of a very decent cabbage dissolved to particles as he twisted it between his fists. All it took was a sudden worm-induced updraft to scatter these fibers like the filamentous seeds blown from a dandelion clock. He clutched the rope end. I wondered what he was intending to do with it and knew only that it would be bad.

Knocked-about and bleeding, the final ten monks clung to the netting of the bridge as they cheered on their rescuer. With one arm he supported them over the pit. They trusted him. They were fools.

He opened his hand.

The monks fell, screaming.

"I care nothing for ants," he said, dusting his palms.

El Gusano's dank odor filled the chamber. His slithering made the rocks drone.

"Worship me," Kek said. "Get on your knees and beg for your lives."

"I will not," I said.

"It is your only choice. You have dug a god up from the sand. Honor me or die."

"We will not!" Wu shouted. He threw what was left of his firebrand. It fell short.

Kek leaned over to watch the flame plummet.

I had almost forgotten McTroy hidden in his dark crag along the ledge. As Kek straightened to his full, towering height, McTroy fired one of his Army pistols. The bullet struck the Egyptian sorcerer-priest in the back of the head. I fully expected him to tumble into the abyss, and so I cried out a premature "Hurrah!"

Amun Odji-Kek remained upright.

But the bullet had hit its target. Kek's head jolted and a tuft of hair lifted out of place, curving upward like a broken, shiny black wing. There it stayed.

He glared in surprise.

A trace of smoke showed me where McTroy secreted himself in the rocks. The ghouls turned in unison, training their weapons on him.

"Good shot," Kek said. He regained his composure. Smoothed his hair. With an elegant finger he explored his right eye. Deeply. Producing a succulent sound from inside the socket. The prodding turned my stomach until he finally called, "A-ha!" and, making a hook with his forefinger, he fished out the still-smoking lead slug. It was a bloodless operation. But it left me dry-mouthed. He flicked the ammunition in the pit.

"I hope you have learned something," he said.

Kek's unharmed eyes shined rich, lemony amber, as if they had been freshly shellacked. Their pupils were slit vertically, a notable feature of jungle cats, but not what one expects to find in the faces of people. Remarkable though they were, it would have been a stretch to call them supernatural. On the surface, Kek appeared like a man. Of course we knew him to be other. For one, he would not die. Two, he did not bleed. And three, perhaps also four, his physical strength and mental powers exceeded the limits of humanity. If Kek were my teacher, I trusted he would be proud of how quickly his lessons impressed me. I had always been a good student.

"Tell the ghouls not to fire upon Mr McTroy," I said.

"Why would I do that, doctor?"

"Because we are *prepared to go now*. To *leave here*. Please, understand me."

I kneeled on the stone floor. I laid my stick down and bowed. I groveled.

Wu dragged on my shirttails. "Stop, sir. You mustn't do that. Stop it!"

"Get down, Wu. Our fate lies ahead of us. Embrace it."

"No, no... we must not listen... this is evil–"

I grabbed the boy and pressed him flat next to me. I held him there. I spoke firmly and loudly. "Who are we to stand against gods? We must *jump* at the chance he is offering. It is our best option. The worm will soon be *upon* us. I see his *mighty back*."

Kek kept the ghouls at bay with a raised finger.

"Let the cowboy live," he said. "Bring him to me. Do it now."

Red candles and guns shifted onto the ledge. I hoped McTroy had deciphered me.

The chasm filled with maggot. Like a waxen, lumpen whale he floated up and filled the gorge with himself. I had not yet seen El Gusano in his worm-form. He was much different than his younger relative, the worm-sister's offspring whom I had battled in the bowels of the skull rock. Here a question popped into my head for which I never found an adequate answer: *Are not most worms hermaphroditic?* Never mind this. His size was gargantuan. Days earlier he had tunneled under the train tracks, and I now could see how that engineering feat was possible, for had he lazed on a set of rails, one might easily have mistaken him for an idle engine (if viewed at a distance). His body spilled out in a boneless, uniformly cylindrical pattern, tapering at both extremities such that the head and tail were indistinguishable. When at rest he would mash the ground mercilessly without space for a draft of air. This grandeur of size only multiplied his repugnancy: bald, segmented horror the color of raw pork sausage links and very like them in shape and plumpness. But how he moved!

Part liquidity, part animal sentience, and a third part gross obscenity.

He would be our ticket. To death or freedom, I knew not which.

I hoisted Wu by his collar, clamped him round the waist, and yelled.

"Jump, Wu! Jump as far as you can!"

We leaped onto plush maggot-back. The touch was – *ugh* – moist, the texture doughy, without scales, cave-cool. An oil-like lubricant sweated out of the beast in heavy globules, painting our clothes with residue that promised to stain everything permanently. *The smell*– I wanted an immediate, scalding hot bath and a bar of soap.

Instead, I hugged the mammoth crawler and coached Wu to do the same.

"Grab him! We mustn't be thrown off. Hold on!"

The worm felt our presence upon him. He reared the way a horse would rear if it were a limbless, grossly fat, dirt-borer by nature. That is – he proved incapable of bucking us off in the narrow (for him) confines of the abyssal channel; so he opted instead for a robust side-to-side thrashing. The cliffs of the chasm cracked into webs and star patterns; plates of loosened wall fell like melting ice sheets. I lost my grip for a moment and flew over the top of Wu. His clawing fingers unsuccessfully sought a rib or wrinkle in the slick skin as he skidded back into me. We refastened ourselves together and clutched the invertebrate leader of the banditos. Worms, thank God, are not noisome creatures. In the skull rock the nephew worm's mouth had emitted only an eerie pip-pip-pipping. El Gusano did him better. He vented *basso profundo* grunts, growls, and a cannon-like BOOM that rattled the monastic ritual chambers.

The ghouls assembled above us. Transfixed by the worm rodeo, no doubt.

I dared to turn my head, glimpsing their omnipresent weaponry. Stickmen sporting a hodgepodge of Sunday outfits they'd pilfered from graves. Those leathery, false faces they always wore – sliced from the same bodies. They weren't fooling anyone into thinking they were alive. They could not hide their defiling nature. I almost pitied them. Having passed on shooting McTroy, they were eager to shoot something.

Us, most likely, I thought as we bounced.

The shots began.

Being correct was little solace.

A steady *pock-pock-pock* of slugs punched El Gusano's humpback and burped out gouts of tepid worm-slime. His bellowing picked up a screechy quality. We felt him tremble like a feverish baby. Tiny, nervous wavelets rippled front to back. *Pock. Pock.* I am no worm mind-reader, but I think he wished he had his human form so he might talk to his compañeros. *Pock.* They did not seem to understand they were hurting him. Or they didn't care. *Pockety-pock.* A thrown knife whizzed by and stuck with a *thwaptt!* Next a war hammer went spinning past my jaw and lodged in his jelly blubber. Blood pumped up gray around the handle. The leakage made holding him more difficult. The ghoul's shots were getting better, though the worm shimmied and rocked in an attempt to avoid them. Dust from the pulverized walls helped to hide us. But it would not last.

"We must move, Wu."

"Where?"

Pockpockpock.

An excellent question. The head seemed a wrong choice. Tail, then.

"Backward, towards his tail."

I pulled my knees under me. Moving into an unsteady crouch, I made myself less of a target. I tried to stand on the trampoline of semi-taut, soft flesh. But it was like standing on the skin of a chocolate pudding. I used my stick for balance. With my other hand, I hauled Wu up on his tiptoes. When I took my first step, the flesh beneath my boot yielded and swallowed my foot and ankle. I hesitated before taking another.

What if I sink into him, I thought. *Like a nail driven into a tub of cold butter.*

The decision to step or not step ultimately was not mine to make, for through the rock dust came a figure hurtling and landing on my back whereupon I sunk to my thighs in worm. But the clasping demon yanked me out again, and seizing me with vise-like arms and legs as tough as crab claws, likewise pinching me from neck to knees in an embrace I could not shake off, we both sledded along the spineless worm to the tail. I was the whole time dragging Wu by the wrist in a death-grip that would sooner have torn his arm off than let him go.

"Haw!" the figure yelled in my ear.

"Release me, fiend!"

"No can do, Doc."

McTroy dug his spurs into El Gusano's rump and plowed a pair of deep furrows which brought our three-man slide to a messy halt. "This bugger's juicy!"

If worms can be said to scream, then El Gusano did just that.

The sound so shocked the ghouls they ceased firing.

El Gusano squirmed backward into the abyss with alarming speed. His mouth boomed at them. The great, grooved, heaving segments of the worm's body made the barest of kissing contact with the walls as he descended taking us along for the plunge. Short of freefalling but not by much. Soon the dark enveloped us.

"Side cave," McTroy shouted. He still had me wrapped up. I could hardly breathe.

"What–?" I gasped.

"Find the dang side cave where Evangeline is. Get in there 'fore he does."

"Immobile... ssssshhh... crushing my..." McTroy rode upon my back, pinning me against the worm meat like a rodeo calf he was trying to tie down.

"You're squeezing him too tight," Wu said.

"Sorry," he said. His bandy legs unlocked.

I had the capacity for taking air once more and began coughing. "That's where the cave will be." I shook a finger at shadows where even in the pitch black there was a hint of solid wall rushing past. "Starboard. Look for a light in the opening." I cleared my throat. I did not see any light or the cave. What I felt was a sense of falling slower. Without light I lost my spatial sense. I do not know if it was the change of speed or the rubbery quality of the worm beneath me, but I found myself slipping again, not toward the tail end but starboard, in the direction where I had been staring so intently for a sign, a flicker of candles, or a lantern's warm glow. This time I could not stop. I had my stick in one hand and Wu in the other. McTroy had only just unclasped himself from me. I searched for him with my stick hand as Wu and I rolled off the roundness of the worm into nothing but empty air.

Something like a breeze blew across my cheeks. I realized it was McTroy, sweeping his arms out and trying to catch me. Alas, I was too far over the edge. His fingers snagged my one intact sleeve but it was slathered in worm-slime, and the material snaked through his grip.

Bottomless, I thought. We will fall forever. I have failed the boy and Evangeline.

In anger and futility I struck out with my stick.

And the ferrule punctured the side of the worm.

I was hanging there like an Ourang-Outang on a branch with Wu like an infant version of myself clinging to my leg. This was stalling death and that was all. A pause. The stick was too slippery. My hands were sweating. The worm still moved with stout, barely contained fury and bashed his hugeness into the rocks. I could not climb up. Down was endless murk *ad infinitum*. McTroy remained undetectable to me. Perhaps he was dead already. Darkness hooded the entire ordeal. I looked down at Wu grappling my leg and I searched my brain for some consoling word. He was only a boy.

A boy I could see in silhouette.

How was that possible?

"A lantern, Dr Hardy! I see the entrance to the cave," he cried out.

"Excellent. How far is it?"

"Right below me."

My palm slipped along the frictionless ebony stick. "Do you think you might–?"

His weight was no longer attached to my leg. I looked down. Saw only my boot dripping worm-slime, and a faint, orangey glow that started somewhere under my heel.

"Yong Wu!"

El Gusano twitched at the pain of my stick-thorn in his side. He shivered like a horse. He contorted himself, flexing into the far wall, bending like a giant "U" with me deep in the letter's well. I knew then that he was planning to bulge out and catch me like a gnat with the hard knuckle of his belly and smear my guts across the stone. When he tightened and I heard the explosion of stink leave his mouth as he exerted himself, then I withdrew my stick from his gooey hide and let his momentum throw me in the vicinity of the orange light. I spread my arms to fly – to fly! – and landed not unlike a clumsy duck on a frozen pond.

The pond was the floor of the side cave. Wu was there, waiting for me. He was holding a bull's-eye lantern which he pointed at the back of the cave.

I scanned the well-lit space, no bigger than a wealthy family's parlor.

Evangeline was not here. We were alone.

Wu was studying something: a tableau in need of interpretation.

A round table. Around the table three wooden stools. All the pieces scarred but functional. One of the stools was tipped over. On the table: a half-empty bottle. I picked it up. Pulled the cork. The clear liquid sloshing inside smelled smoky sweet, herbal, floral – I concluded this concoction was mescal (I had never tasted it before and wasn't planning to try some now). Beside the bottle, a pair of overturned glasses. Remains of a third glass lay shattered in the corner. Papers were tacked to the wall. Railroad maps. Timetables. Coach schedules between cities and towns on both sides of the border. Also on the tabletop, the skins of oranges whose fruit was sucked dry and the pulp chewed. Touching the wood, I felt graininess on my fingertips and put them to my tongue – salt.

Wu's mother had a good nose. She had been correct on all points.

"What happened? Where is Miss Evangeline?" Wu asked.

"I have the same questions," I said.

The worm knocked against the edges of the cave's entrance. His hot breath filled the cave. He grunted and pushed hard enough into the rock that fine dust rained down.

"Give me that lantern," I said, "quickly."

I turned the bull's-eye glare on the chomping mouth of El Gusano. The hole of his maw was wide enough to swallow a barrel as if it were a pill. I saw boots in his mouth. I swung the lantern closer. "Those aren't McTroy's or Evangeline's," I told Wu. "He must have snatched one of the ghouls off the ledge and ate him to show his displeasure at being shot."

"I do not want to be eaten," Wu said.

"Nor do I, friend, nor do I." I picked up one of the stools and tossed it in the worm's trap. He cracked the legs and gulped the splintered wood. I fed him the other stools, one at a time.

"Wu, help me with the table. It will at least slow him down."

We were about to heave-ho the table into his jaws when the distinct pop of a gunshot rang out, nearly deafening us. El Gusano's chewing stopped. A stool leg poked from its lips like a toothpick. He sagged at the rim of the cave. A river of gray poured from his mouth, running all the way to the back of the cave where it pooled.

"Oh, it stinks." Wu stuck out his tongue. "I never smelled anything so bad."

Just before the last of the worm's tensile strength failed, a hand appeared above his deflated-looking head. Then another hand and the top of a hat. Finally, McTroy hopped off the worm. He turned and kicked El Gusano under the chin, and the mighty bandito, leader of the necrófagos, and fearsome, giant, shapeshifting annelid-man went over the threshold and silently began his fall to the bottom of the bottomless abyss.

"Last bullet," McTroy said. "I figured brains are pretty near mouths. So I took a chance and plugged him."

"You waited long enough," I said.

"I had to take a measure," he said, poking around the floor, uncorking the bottle, sniffing and upending it for what appeared to be the longest swallow in history. He blew out a long breath. He wiped the mouth of the bottle and offered it around. "Wanna slug?" When no one drank he took it upon himself to finish the final, smoky sweet drops.

35

MYSTERIOUS THIRD

McTroy's boot pushed through shards twinkling in the lantern light. The pieces added up to one glass. Smashed to smithereens. The scintillating bits lay directly under a yellowed, finger-begrimed, oft-folded and unfolded map tacked askew on the wall. A railroad map. Desert, mountains, and mines. Not much else. Rails moved people and money in and out of the Arizona Territory. That's why the necrófagos cared. Why El Gusano studied maps. Rails meant treasure. For filling the purse and the ghoulish belly. A stain showed where the glass exploded. Drips wept down the page, leaving a wiggy shadow face that covered Yuma, Opa, Pinal, Pima, and part of Cochise County.

McTroy pressed his nose to the map. He went cross-eyed as a Siamese cat. For an anxious second I feared he might actually lick the paper.

"Some people don't like mescal," he said, backing away. His voice sounded sad, baffled. He took the wasted dram of Mexican agave spirit as a personal affront.

"I dare conjecture it was our Evangeline," I said.

McTroy frowned. "Seems like a woman of varied

tastes to me. But you may be right, Doc." He'd stuck his finger into the empty mescal bottle, carrying it that way as he searched the cave for further signs. All while tapping the bottle against his leg.

I continued. "She refused something they proposed to her. Vigorously refused."

"They?"

"El Gusano and, as Mrs Wu told us, a mysterious third. A gentleman."

"You think worm-o and this polished man were acting indecent?"

"That had not entered my mind," I said (though briefly it had). "No. This is not a den of that particular shade of sin. The evil they discussed here was of an esoteric nature." I knocked the ape head of my stick on the center of the table. "See this carving?"

McTroy cocked his head. "Looks like an eye."

"An eye with sunbeams radiating out in every direction. I believe this to be the Eye of Horus. The All-Seeing Eye is a powerful occult symbol in many ancient cultures."

"Deviltry?" He popped the bottle off his finger and tossed it to the abyss.

"Black magical business, to be sure." I loomed over the round table. "What I see here is a meeting between three people. An attempt at cordiality is made. The two men are talking to her." I pushed the table back exactly where it had been when Wu and I arrived, amid the now absent, worm-devoured stools. "They sat triangularly around the circle. The eye is within both the circle *and* their human pyramid. This is no coincidence. Extra-dimensional gods are being summoned. Evangeline would know more about this than I do. I am treading to the farthest limits of my knowledge."

McTroy stood at my side, his hands on his hips. Imagining.

"What do these gents want?" he asked.

"I don't know. But they can't force the matter. There is an element of persuasion involved. Requiring, at least, a private chat. They ask for something only she can give."

The bounty hunter rubbed his flinty chin whiskers. Maybe he hoped to spark an intelligent theory. "I never reckoned the maggot as a strong persuader of females. Too full of himself. Kind of fella who bulls a lady into a corner with his belly. Demands attention but doesn't give any. Sloppy hands at the saloon, you know what I mean?"

I nodded, indicating I thought I did.

"He was amply lacking in social charms." I concurred with the essence of what McTroy said even if I lacked any firsthand tavern experience. "So he is a bystander. Used, likely, as a silent threat. The stick rather than the carrot. It is the other gentleman who inveigles her. Or he tries to. He is the key to this parley. He calls the meeting."

"And our little miss whips a glass at his head. Whew." McTroy smirked and slapped his hands together. "Guess he didn't know what he was steppin' into."

I reserved my judgment.

"Or he knew and made the effort nonetheless—"

"Excuse me, sirs," Wu said. "But may we please get Miss Evangeline back now?"

"There's an idea I can hitch my wagon to." McTroy tipped his hat. The twinkle had returned to his gaze. I was certain the mescal in his blood was no small reason.

"Excellent request," I said, nodding. "You keep us on the right track, young man, as always. First, calm yourself. We see no evidence the lady is dead. Everything speaks to the contrary." I exaggerated for his sake. "Second, we have clues that she was kept alive for a reason." I paced the hollow bandshell of El Gusano's cave. Careful to step over the stream of gray-toned spew – those heavy juices the worm had disgorged in his final death throes. The smell was most vile even among the disgusting array of odors associated with the worm. I tucked my face into my elbow, preferring my own stink.

"Thur. Hah di he con and gaw fra heer innis numa four?"

"Say again, pard." McTroy screwed up his face in bewilderment.

I lifted my mouth above the bend in my arm. "Third, how did he come and go from here in his human form? Surely, this was a cozy enough notch to snug into when he changed to the crawler state, wanting to put some distance between himself and the ghouls, steal a bit of quiet, reflective time alone, but he has his clothes to consider, the liquor, the furniture and maps… see, he idled here as a man too. How did he get in?"

The last question sprung from my lips as I made a quick re-crossing of the vomit trail. A small step. Smaller than before. The initial sludgy river of gray had reduced to a stream at my previous pass but now, here, underfoot, it was but a webby mucus trickle.

The great volume of liquid – where did it disappear to?

I followed the meandering spillage to the point where the wall and floor intersected. Rock to rock, tan on tan. A thin shadow was etched between them. There I crouched. I aimed the lantern. Squinting.

A separation. At the base of the wall.

Fairly uniform, approximately horizontal. Was it natural?

I jabbed my stick at it.

The gap ran as wide as a man's shoulders. I placed my wetted fingers there and felt an air current– "A secret passage," I said. I cannot recall ever using the phrase in daily life before this adventure, but it had become part of my regular lexicon. "Behind this portion of wall is a space that vents outside. The worm vomit seeps underneath and does not return. Gravity is showing us the way out. The question is: Where is the catch?"

"What catch, sir?" Wu had moved in to peer at the neat sliver of darkness.

"There is a release hidden somewhere in the room. It will be accessible but not obvious. When we find it, we find our escape… and Evangeline. It's as simple as that."

My comment sent Wu and McTroy into a flurry of wall slapping, floor tapping, and general pushing and pulling at every suspect cranny and square inch of the side cave. Funny, the cave was small for a giant worm, adequate for a man, but positively huge for hiding a secret button or lever that might unlock the door we needed to open.

Wu began taking down the maps and coach timetables. He stuffed them inside his shirt. Behind the last coach timetable – a protuberance of rock – a speleothem, common to caves – this example appeared to be calcite, root beer brown with a smudge of olive and a band of rhubarb crystals – earthy, but aren't all rocks earthy?, and yet this peculiar specimen seemed quite out of place sticking straight from the wall at ninety degrees, shaped like a pig's nose, twitchy really, how inquisitive it was. Wu's eyes lit up.

"Do you think this is the catch?"

"It is quite catchy looking, isn't it?"

Wu's hand hovered over the rock. "When I see it, I'm thinking I want to touch it. Maybe that's why it is hidden behind the poster."

McTroy stopped searching and joined us.

"Push it and find out," he said.

Wu pushed the pig's nose in.

The door made a *click!* and swung open.

A staircase.

I shined the lantern at the steps. Going up. I could smell fresh air pouring down like a waterfall. Should I tell you we ran like boys? (Well, Yong Wu was a boy), but we did. Wu went first, ducking under my arm, bumping the lantern, outrunning the beam.

"We don't know what's up there," I said.

"She is up there." Wu took the chiseled stairs two at a time. I was on his heels. McTroy over my shoulder, breathing mescaline breath. *He has no bullets*, I thought. The scarred wooden door at the top stood open. Outside. Night sky. Stars like pinholes in a black blanket. We were in a courtyard. Monastery walls surrounded us. Evangeline was in the middle of the courtyard. Standing still, under the moonlight. Wu ran. We all did.

36
MYSTERIOUS THIRD, CONT'D:
THE BLOODY SCRATCHES

Evangeline was waiting beside a fountain. Sand clogged the tiers of the fountain; dry stones filled its lower pool. Water had not bubbled here in years. I shined my light ahead as Wu ran to her. She did not react to the light or to us. The sand in the fountain sparkled like freshly fallen snow. As I stepped closer, I saw the stones in the pool were smooth, sun-bleached, and all about the same size. Their sides were oddly eaten away with small holes. Acidic waters? I wondered.

No. Not holes, and not stones either.

Skulls.

Human skulls. The monks had built a monument to death at the center of their compound, making a mockery of life-giving water in the desert, and they had decorated the bottom of their font with the picked-clean heads of their victims. Ghastly bastards.

Evangeline remained motionless.

Did this charnel house bone pile transfix the lady and freeze her in place?

It did not appear so. Her head was turned away, toward the gate.

I shifted the bull's-eye lantern.

A coach. Painted black. It seemed to absorb my light, to suck it inward, leaving little detail for me to descry but merely contours of the wood and a team of six black stallions, impossibly huge and muscular and snorting what I can only describe as blue flames. They stomped their skillet hooves. Manes like black, black smoke. Their eyes glowed hot cherry-red, and on the nighttime desert floor I felt the heat pouring off them, tightening the skin on my cheeks, as if they were a living, breathing, fiery furnace.

I swung my beam higher and cried out in surprise.

In the driver's box a coachman rose up. Whip in one hand, reins gathered in the other. My light flooded over him. Unlike the coach itself, he appeared of this world. In fact, I knew him. It was Hakim, my old friend and the foreman of my Egyptian dig in the Valley of the Kings. A man whose death I had mourned. Yet here he was, in Mexico. I was stunned. There was no mistaking him. I had presumed him to be executed, a meal left for the jackals in the shadow of the skull rock. Obviously, he had not only survived that day at the tomb, but he played some part in this macabre Mexican affair as well.

"Hakim!"

He did not answer me. He settled back into his seat and whipped the horses. The coach jerked, and the team of six pulled it swiftly through the gate. On the ground where the coach had been lay a coil of dirty linen bandages. It reminded me of the skin a snake sheds; only this skin was man-sized. The evidence left no doubt

that the mummies were riding inside the coach. Kek
finally had attained his freedom from any ancient curses
imposed upon him as punishment for his sorcery. He had
broken the shackles of death.

Before the coach disappeared, a fish-white face
emerged from behind one of the coach's leather curtains.
The skin was stretched over high, noble cheeks. Big eye
sockets full of milky wrinkles and a pair of weed green
eyes. Lips slanted: opening wordlessly, closing. A hand of
thin bones appeared. Was it waving? It held a bloodied
handkerchief to its cheek. Whose face? Not Kek's. More
like something hooked from the ocean floor. It stared.
Not at me, but at Evangeline.

Then the face was gone. The coach sped off.

A dust cloud enwrapped us like fog.

Wu had stopped short of Evangeline. As the dust
settled I understood the reason for his hesitancy.
Evangeline was not our old Evangeline. She was she.
But altered. I noticed less trauma evidenced in her
countenance than anger. Her chin pushed forward,
her neck held stiffly at an odd position, almost formal,
as if she were being forced to endure an unpleasant
conversation; a strong pulse drummed in a vein above
the notch of her collarbone. She breathed through
her nose. Her eyes fixed wide and wet and unfocused.
Something black stained four fingertips of her right
hand as if she had dipped them in a shallow bowl.
I turned the bull's-eye on her and they changed to
red: blood. She looked at us without any sign of
recognition. The light bothered her. Wincing, she
raised her bloodied hand. I redirected the beam at the
ground. Her braid had come unraveled, flared into a

white nimbus around her face, witchy-colored by the moonlight.

"Miss Evangeline?" It was Wu speaking. I was glad he went first.

"You're not dead?" Her voice was hoarse like a person unaccustomed to conversation.

Was she a madwoman? Had the encounter below driven her insane?

Perhaps she sounded worse than she was.

A simple case of rawness in the throat...?

I was suddenly aware of my own thirst. Don't judge her too quickly, I told myself. We've been through an ordeal here – massive, bizarre, and freakishly violent – except for the death of one maggot and a score of devil monks, it remained wholly unresolved. I knew the gist of my night underground. I was missing a large part of Evangeline's. What had passed between her and the worm? Who was the Mysterious Third? What did he say to her over mescal and broken glass?

She studied each of us in turn clinically. Never have I felt more like a preserved frog pinned belly-up on a table. She kept her emotions checked.

"You seem alive and well," she said, and said it rather neutrally, I thought.

"For the most part we are." I slapped the dust from my shirt.

Her eyes narrowed. "But how can you be? Answer me that."

Wu spoke in a rush. "Mr McTroy killed the worm. He shot it right in the brain. Dr Hardy and I jumped from the worm's back into the cave and... and then we looked for the hidden catch. I found it behind a map!

When I pressed the catch it released the secret door and we discovered the steps and we climbed straight up here and we saw you." Wu gestured to the passage. He bowed and smiled. But he did not go nearer to her. Even he was taken aback by her strangeness. Absent was her usual warmth. She felt dangerous to be around, like a cool but fierce beast that might eat any one of us at any time.

"We tried to save you," I said. "When we got to the cave you were gone."

"I am lucky to have so many men wanting to save me."

What did that mean? We had not in fact saved her, true. But was she angry with us? No, no, it was not just anger I detected now but a whirlwind of attitudes and strong emotions that frankly left me uneasy. I was more in the dark than when I fell into the abyss. I did not know what to say to Evangeline, but I had absolute confidence that whatever words I might choose, and however artfully I might arrange them, they would still be wrong.

Therefore, I chose silence.

McTroy was more direct. "What the hell happened to you?"

The dust cloud settled, but another form of obscurity replaced it. My eyes stung and I wiped them, but it did no good. A reluctance to breathe gripped my chest. Smoke drifted over the courtyard. Thickening. I interrupted my silence to cough into my fist.

"The monastery burns," Evangeline said, with no more care than if she had been mentioning a passing cloud at a summer picnic.

Fire danced on the roof. It kicked and stretched. Red legs and orange arms. A lot of them, poking through, reaching up and touching new places. It grew and grew.

She said, "The ghouls torched the chapel. Soon this will be an inferno. The wood has been baking in the desert for who knows how many years... no one can stop it. A ruin. That's what's left when everything is over. The world ends in fire."

McTroy grabbed her elbow. "Have you seen our horses?"

Evangeline shook her head.

I tied a bandana around my nose and mouth. I told Wu to do the same. "The smoke is what kills you. Stay low. Crawl if you need to."

Evangeline covered her face with the hem of her skirt. She took my hand.

"We have to get outside the gate," McTroy said.

The fire snapped. It growled. Savage, crazed, hungry. Devour, it said. Devour.

"The stone well. Back where we started. It's far enough away that we should be safe for a while," I said. "Let's go there."

"We'll need water," McTroy said. "A walk without it, we're good as dead."

He led us through the smoke. Embers fell like crimson snowflakes. Sparks, like floating matchheads. Fire raced along the charred brick walls in zigzag patterns, and the wooden gate lit up bright – a wavy, raging curtain hanging before us and threatening a fatal delay to our escape. I smelled lamp oil. Spilled – here, on the sand, a shattered jug – I kicked it. The ghouls had set a fire trap to snuff us out. Evangeline was right. The monastery would be a smoldering ruin by morning. But we wouldn't be inside. I bent half over and took a firm hold of McTroy's gun belt at the small of his back. I was good as blind. Gasping for air. Smoke wrapped like a poisonous hot towel around my head. Evangeline squeezed my hand. Wu had hers, and she encouraged him to stay calm and keep going. We cleared the gate just as a dragon's roar erupted behind us. The chapel exploded. Chunks of splintered wood and adobe and yes, more human bones rained down. Debris covered the desert like a battlefield. A blazing crucifix ten feet tall dropped from the heavens and stabbed, inverted, into the sand. It was a scene from Dante: the Circle of the Heretics – an infernal sepulchral plain outside Satan's city – a hell on earth forged by men with nothing better to do than to add chaos to Creation.

"They must've had a storehouse of gunpowder," McTroy said.

"There's the well." Evangeline let go of my hand, and pointed. "The horses!"

Moonlight, Neptune, and Penny were tied to the post where McTroy had left them. The conflagration terrified the animals, but they were glad to see us. McTroy got a rope from his saddle and skilfully fished the bucket from the well. Wu and I hoisted water for the horses and for us. We drank. We filled the canteens and sheepskins. We cleaned our sooty faces. All while the monastery pumped smoke into a predawn sky, but the wind was blowing in our favor and it carried the foul pollution away from us, to the south.

The air was cool. Wetness from the splashed well water brought a chill to Evangeline. Her body shivered. I placed my hand on her shoulder. She was small, really.

Her constant motion, her energy, augmented her. But that fact was easy to forget.

"We are out of it," I said. I meant, of course, the inferno.

She made a snorting sound, a mirthless laugh. "Hardy, we are in deeper than ever." She scrubbed the blood from her fingers, rinsing them again, and again.

A shiver ran through me.

McTroy checked his rifle, slid it back into its scabbard on Moonlight's saddle. He unbuckled his saddlebag and was about to turn up the flap when a voice spoke from the other side of a nearby cholla thicket.

"I don't think you want to do that," the voice said. "If you want to live…"

McTroy had his Marlin repeater out of the scabbard and levered before I could lower the canteen from my lips.

"Who is it?" he said. Then to me, "Shine the light, Doc."

I shined it.

"It's your old amigo, señor," the voice said. "How soon we forget."

"Show yourself or die."

"I don't think so, but I will come out and talk."

From behind the cholla came a dragging sound, then a dragging figure, low to the ground, in the dirt, pulling itself along by its arms, balanced on the palms of its hands. It had a guitar strapped to its back.

"Corpse muncher!" McTroy shouted. "What'er you doin' hiding in the bushes?"

The necrófago did his best to shrug. "Nada. I am enjoying la hoguera – the bonfire." Rojo smiled a needle-toothy smile. "You make it out of the Temple Underneath alive, huh? I think you leave something cooking in the oven. Maybe monk meat? I never see that before."

McTroy waved. "Weren't nothing. Like eating pie. We hardly broke a sweat." He screwed up one eye and said, "Is it me, or ain't you looking better since last we parted?"

Indeed it was true. The ghoul looked – this is a relative term I employ given the circumstances – healthier. Certainly, he'd grown more robust from the waist up. His face was in one piece. He was blessedly clothed in what seemed a ragged brown animal pelt. He appeared to be sprouting two fresh legs, though at the moment the limbs were little more than a forked, greenish-gray, almost tentacular nub of flesh; the nubby protrusion jutted from under the fur sash he wore and followed after him like a budding iguana tail. Ghouls, who are neither alive nor deceased, regenerate by eating dead things. I wasn't sure if I wanted to see behind the cholla. Rojo must've sensed doubt in the twist of my brow.

"I ate a coyote, doctor," he said. "An old one – he had a bullet in his neck. He died in that bush. Dying alone is sad, you know?" He shook his head. "I think maybe he was sick because he tasted funny. I make a poncho of him." Rojo squared his shoulders.

"Ro, you complaining about the menu?" McTroy asked.

"I no complain. Everything is on a necrófago's menu."

McTroy chuckled. I think he was actually beginning to like the ghoul. "Rotten coyote sounds like a meal made for ghoul kings."

"A little stringy. Not bad, if you have teeth." He snapped his. The horses stirred.

"Probably had rabies," I whispered to Evangeline and Wu.

Wu wrinkled his nose.

"Did you see the mummy coach pass by?" Evangeline asked Rojo.

"Oh, yes. She was rápido, señorita. Never have I seen one like her before."

"Where did it go?"

"El Norte." Rojo pointed with his chin. "She'll be over the border before too long."

"What makes you think she's heading to the US?" I asked.

"Where else she gonna go?"

I had no retort.

"Hey, Crazy Red, I need to reload. Why'd you keep me from my bullets?" Despite the friendly conversation, McTroy had not let down his rifle. Out of politeness he aimed the barrel to the left of Rojo, slightly.

"Señor McTroy, I am sorry to inform you that your saddlebag is full of snakes."

"Bullcrap, if you'll pardon me. Moonlight wouldn't let a snake get close to her."

"The mummy hypnotized your horse. She no moved. She no made a sound."

"No bandaged bastard can hypno-whatever my mare." McTroy reached for the unbuckled flap and turned it up. "See!"

"Don't–" Evangeline tried to warn him but it was too late.

The asp lunged from the saddlebag. If McTroy did not possess a gunfighter's reflexes I dare say he would've been bitten on the nose. As it were, he batted the viper with the stock of his Marlin rifle, knocked it to the sand and shot it twice. A second asp slithered from the bag, and as McTroy had his back turned in the execution of the first reptile, I carefully removed this inquisitive serpent with my walking stick.

"Where should I put this?"

"Christ Almighty! Fling it toward the ghoulie!"

I jettisoned the Egyptian cobra. McTroy dispatched it with a single shot to the head. He used the muzzle of his rifle to close the saddlebag flap. The bag bulged and subsided; a heavy squirming was also noticeable inside the opposite leather pouch.

"I don't recognize those snakes. Big ole heads, flat as the bottom of my boot."

"They're asps from Egypt. Hooded vipers. The story goes that Queen Cleopatra killed herself with an asp," I said. "The rearing cobra is a symbol of royalty and divinity."

"Asps! What son of a bitch puts asps in a man's saddlebag?"

Rojo scurried over to the dead snake and stripped off its skin with his teeth. He sucked down the small bones and flesh. "I saw Odji-Kek do it," he said, around a mouthful of asp.

"I know who it was, dammit. And, Doc, I don't need any symbolical lecture."

Rojo was confused. "Then why did you ask what son of a–?"

"It's an expression, Ro." McTroy loosened the saddlebags from Moonlight and gingerly carried the parcel of certain death over to a rock pile as I lighted his way.

"If I dump these fellers out, they gonna bite me?"

"I venture they will slip away seeking greener pastures."

"Good luck finding any, you belly-crawling sons of Satan." He emptied both bags into an inky wedge betwixt two boulders, mindful not to drop his ammunition boxes into the crack with the cobras. "I'd shoot 'em all, but I'm short on bullets as it is."

"They are only following their nature," I said.

"So am I."

We rode through what was left of the night, past the dawn, straight into a fine morning. The sky turned hard enamel blue. The heat was tolerable. Our horses were hungry and McTroy led us to a wash where they munched saltgrass and desert marigolds. Sensing their first decent food in days, the horses fussed nervously; their hooves stirred up moths sipping at the salty mud in the wash. I pressed my lips together to keep the paper-winged creatures from flying into my mouth. No one talked. Evangeline and Wu shared Neptune's saddle. Rojo accompanied me. We had decided he acquitted himself nicely concerning the asps and should no longer be presumed an enemy. Though I can't say he smelled any better.

"Riding is better than the dragging," he said.

"I would think so."

"But sitting with nothing to do is the best."

"You display unforeseen depths, Rojo."

"It is not on purpose I do this."

I put Rojo down on a rock so he could play his guitar. Despite being a brigand and a disgusting graveyard scavenger, he strummed a pleasant tune. We all dismounted. McTroy borrowed Evangeline's telescope, climbing to higher ground to take a survey. Wu finally started to feel the disappearance of his parents into the Duat. He had a long, hiccupping cry and fell asleep afterward. Evangeline and I were alone.

"Before we go any farther, there is matter we need to discuss," I said.

"Speak plainly, Hardy."

"I know of no other way."

She smiled and turned to study a moth that had alighted on her wrist.

"Who was the third individual with you in the cave?"

She continued to examine the lepidopteran. "I did not know him."

"Was it your father?"

That greenish-gold flash – her stare locked onto me. I felt like a rabbit that has spotted the lioness and realized his chances for escape are few. Thumping heart. A cold block in the belly, melting away. Events slowed yet rushed by far too quickly for the mind to sort them out properly. It would only start to fit together later. In retrospect.

"Do you think I don't know my own father?" she said.

"My father was a farmer and we barely spoke–"

"Well, my father is more than a farmer. In our home we converse daily, deeply."

I carried my stick in case we might run across a rattler or two. I was crushing the ape's head. My knuckles whitened under the pressure of my grip.

"Insulting my family is out of order," I said.

"An order you fail to follow."

"I have reasons. But let's forget the question of 'who' for the moment. What did this mysterious third person want from you?"

She had begun to walk away. Now she spun on me and charged so we stood inches apart. She pushed up on her toes. "If you'd like to know – he asked me to kill him."

"What? That's preposterous."

"I thought so too. He appeared to be well on his way to dying already. I threw a glass at his head. But he had a second even more perverse request conjoined to the first."

"Which was?"

"After I killed him, he wanted me to take responsibility for his burial."

I had sought clarifications, but here was only muddying. I poked the tip of my cane into the dark sand, digging at the bottom of the wash. "A stranger wouldn't ask that," I said, half to myself, half to her. I exposed a smooth stone and covered it again.

She shrugged. "Murder and bury him... That's the sum." She twisted her hands.

"And you told him 'no'?"

"I never thought you were thick-headed, Hardy, but..."

I stopped digging. "How right you are. I am thick-headed. I saw him watching you from the coach. I couldn't place exactly what I saw. Not then. Now I know. His face in the window... stricken, gaunt, yet an unmistakable resemblance in the bones of the face..."

"I scratched him. Nothing felt real. He never thought I would do such a thing." She showed me her claws. The same ones she had washed and washed as though they'd never come clean.

The temperature of the desert was rising with the sun. But I felt none of it.

"Despite his obvious grave illness, the man I saw in the carriage bore a striking similarity to you, Evangeline. I have never met Montague Pythagoras Waterston, but I know he is a sick man. He'd suffered through a brain fever. He couldn't write. That's why you took over penning the letters. It's why he sent you to escort the mummies to Los Angeles."

"That's correct." Evangeline had a sad, hopeful look. I guess it is the same with every drowning person who is thrown a life ring. I was about to pull that life ring away.

"Except your father didn't send you, did he? He had no idea you came to New York. No clue you were on that train. He knew the train would be hijacked. He'd planned it. The mummies were never supposed to arrive in Los Angeles. Were they?"

Silence. Dull as her eyes. A cloud over the sun. No longer the huntress.

"You knew your father was lying to me about the dig. You knew he needed to steal the mummies because what he wanted to do with them was something that had to be kept a secret, hidden away in the desert. That's why you hired the Pinkertons, Staves and Kittle. You tried to stop the robbery. Only you didn't stop it."

"How could I?" she shouted. "I never expected any of this. Robber ghouls and mummies coming alive... worms... I am a librarian! I read books. I didn't think the legends were true. I knew my father had his... his unusual beliefs, but he is an unusual man, a special man. It wasn't until after his fever dream that he changed. He went from being a dreamer to a blind follower. In that dream he met Kek and talked to him. My father and I were friends, Hardy. We were partners in our passion for oddities and esoterica. We even talked about opening our own museum. But after the dream he became a man of secrets. He lied to me. I knew he was lying and he could see that I knew. But that didn't stop him. I had some money of my own. I went to New York and hired the detectives. I bought a train ticket. I suspected... but I was never sure what my father wanted to do with the mummies."

I snapped my fingers. "When you employed McTroy, the bank wired you money. That's when your father discovered you were interfering with his scheme." She nodded.

I was close but I was still missing one piece.

"What is his scheme?"

"Power. Forbidden knowledge. When we get back to the US, you should walk away. Go back to Chicago. We Waterstons are bad news. I like you, Hardy. I don't want you to get hurt. But it's going to happen. My father is used to getting his way. He is a bully. What he can't force, he will buy. What he can't buy, he will destroy."

"But how does he think he can control Kek?"

"I don't know. He's... my father will die soon. His judgment is impaired. It must be."

"A desperate man can convince himself of anything," I said.

Evangeline rushed into my arms. I drew back in surprise but she held onto me.

Her cheek pressed against my chest. "You don't realize what he is capable of. No one does. I thought I did, but now... it's too much to comprehend. He's too much. Do you understand? What he can do, what he will do to get what he wants is limitless, without bounds, moral or otherwise. Nothing is going to stop him. Not even his only child."

I smoothed her hair.

"And what does he want?"

"Everything – he wants everything."

37
RESURRECCIÓN MINE

April 12th, 1888
South of the US–Mexican border, Sonora, Mexico

An avalanche of pebbles slid down the face of the outcrop. McTroy stepped off the tail end and adroitly handed the telescope back to Evangeline. His face was desert brown and his beard had not been touched by a razor in almost a week. A fine layer of chalky alkali dust covered him from boots to hat brim. It was hotter at the top of the outcrop and rivulets of sweat sluiced his neck. The last shade in the arroyo had disappeared. Once we passed through these low hills, the heat in the playa would only grow worse. He squinted at Evangeline and me, detecting a shift in mood. For all his slit-eyed, lizard-skinned toughness, the outlaw tracker could read people as well as the desert pavement. From beneath his rifle scabbard he retrieved a secreted hip flask of whisky. He unscrewed the cap and tipped it between his teeth. He swallowed, exhaled. I was surprised his breath didn't spontaneously combust.

"Who died?" he said.

"It is not a question of 'who died' but rather who is afraid to die," I said.

"Any man says he isn't afraid of the Reaper is a liar. Take the hardest hombre and after he gets a taste of the scythe, he'll be calling for his momma and lookin' for angels."

"Or devils," Evangeline said.

"You best explain, Miss. I'm too hot for guessing games."

We told McTroy about Monty Waterston – everything from his fevered liaison with Odji-Kek on the astral plane, to his unexpected appearance in El Gusano's cave, to his pale-faced, forlorn, parting wave from the window of the Stygian coach. Evangeline revealed his role in the train robbery and her failed, yet nonetheless brave, attempt to thwart her father from the path of his mounting occult ambitions.

"Who's going to pay me?" McTroy asked when we were through.

I grumbled. "How can you talk about money?" I was awestruck at the baring of his self-interest under these dire circumstances. His insensitivity astounded me.

"I'm out here on a job, Doctor Egypt. I'd like to know what for."

"You wouldn't consider helping out of a sense of moral duty?"

He mopped the sweat from his brow. Tossed the empty flask at a saguaro.

"No. I would not."

"You are a disagreeable, uncouth reprobate–"

"I am going to pay you," Evangeline interrupted. Not that McTroy was listening to me. "I can sell my rare books. My mother left me a chest of jewelry when she died. It will more than cover your fee and whatever expenses we incur from here until the end."

McTroy nodded, apparently assuaged – although he needed a further clarification. "Which end is that? What is it you want out of this mess, Miss E?"

"I want the same thing my father wants. I want Amun Odji-Kek. But I want him destroyed. If he cannot be killed, then put him away. Imprison him the way he was when Dr Hardy found him."

"That's right. It was you who let him out, Doc, and escorted him to our shores."

I scoffed. "What I brought over were artifacts. A sarcophagus and five coffins. Six mummies – I meant to study and display them to the public for the sake of learning."

"We learned plenty. I bet folks would love to meet your arty facts."

McTroy liked arguing. He enjoyed fighting and all the things most educated men hate. He would trade barbs with me until the stars fell. I would not oblige him. "Miss Waterston is right as usual. We have drifted into your area of expertise. Bring the mummies back the way you bring all the scum to Yuma. Dead or alive, shall we say?"

"You think you're clever, don't you?"

"Cleverness is no fault. Proud ignorance however is a different story–"

"Gentlemen!" Evangeline stepped between us. "Each of you in your own unique way is vital to this mission. And special to me." McTroy and I were caught not knowing whether to blush or exchange punches. Why did I feel like a schoolboy? Our ears had perked up.

And our fists were slowly unclenching. I tucked in my shirttail.

"We must work together," she continued. "Our foes are formidable. Do I need to remind you of this?"

"No, ma'am," McTroy said.

I scuffed my toe in the dirt and shook my head.

"Very well." She crossed her arms, held a finger to her heart-shaped lips, and then said, "I have been thinking about those snakes."

"Asps in my saddlebag. A goddamn sacrilege," McTroy said.

"But why would he put them there unless he knew we would escape the monastery? Amun Kek is nothing if not confident. He must regard us with a certain amount of respect."

"Strange way of showing respect," I said.

Her eyes crinkled in a most enchanting way. "Strange, but not so strange. I think he relishes this battle we've been having. He enjoys the challenge after all those years imprisoned in the earth. It is a game to him. And that makes it more dangerous for us, because he is anticipating our next move. We must be on our highest guard."

"I'm always on guard," McTroy said.

"We must match you then, Rex."

Hearing her use McTroy's first name was not enjoyable. Familiarity between employers and their hired hands leads to the most unpleasant conundrums down the line. If I hadn't suspected that she was flattering McTroy to get him to perform more professionally, then I might have even been offended. As it was, I was merely annoyed.

"Assuming we have raised our level of play, the question then becomes: where did your father and Kek go? Your father must have a plan. Was there anything he told you during your conversation in the cave that might indicate his direction?" I asked.

Evangeline pondered.

"They're headed over the border. Arizona Territory. Even the putrid little half-Mex, half-carcass knows that," McTroy said gruffly.

The strain of a lovely corrido – so subtle that I hadn't even noticed it playing in the background – paused. Rojo uttered a polite "Muchas gracias, Señor" and returned to strumming his guitar. I may have noticed the slightest trace of sarcasm in his thanks.

"My father," Evangeline began, "wants to live forever. He knows he is dying. His time is short. The state of his health is fragile. He will not be traveling far. The journey from Los Angeles to the monastery has been hard on him. I smelled death on his breath. His awful, chalk white face… But he will have thought of everything beforehand. Wherever they are going was set long ago. Probably before the sarcophagus left Egypt. My father wanted a test. To see if Kek had the power to bring the dead back to life."

"Hakim!" Now my dead friend's rebirth as the night coachman made some sense.

"Yes. I believe that when Kek came back from the Duat – from his taunting of the gods – he used the Temple Underneath's Ka door to bring your murdered foreman back with him. To prove he could. Hakim was the test. The final proof my father needed."

"Proof of what?" McTroy asked.

"Life everlasting," Evangeline answered. "Kek's ability to master it."

McTroy grunted.

She grew exasperated. "Immortality – that is the treasure. Never dying. Can you perceive what it would be like to live knowing you will never die, that life is endless?"

"Miss E, that don't impress me. I am ready, when my time comes, to leave this vale of tears. Heaven waits. Or hell. The bible tells me so. I can't see why anyone would want to stick around here forever."

I glanced at the sweltering arroyo. "That is because you are not a rich man, McTroy. When a rich man has everything, he doesn't stop. He fights to keep his treasure for as long as possible. He is like a dragon sitting on his gold and jewels. A monster."

I looked up into Evangeline's face.

"Well put," she said.

She was a daughter of privilege. I did not condemn her, did not intend to indict her for her father's crimes. All rich men were not the same. Were they? The greed that transfigured her father, it didn't taint her. She was good. But she had said her father was good once too. There was no time for talking about this. The temptation of gold. The temptation of time. But I had studied the pharaohs. I knew the extremes to which men would go if they believed themselves to be gods. What is the possibility of eternal life if not the chance at being a god? What person can resist? What humanity can survive?

"I agree with McTroy. To live without death is a curse." Wu climbed up on a large, speckled stone, like an enormous fossilized egg. It was about the size that he might've hatched from it. He sat quietly. The heat did not seem to bother him in his black suit. He had tightened his pigtails. What terrible storms raged inside this boy? He knew his parents had been doubly damned in the Duat. That alone would have sunk most minds in despair.

"Will these maps help?" Wu unbuttoned his tunic and slid out the sheaf of maps he had torn down from the side cave's wall, when we had been looking for the secret catch to release the door.

Evangeline accepted the maps from him.

"Wu, you are as resourceful as you are brave."

She flattened the papers out on the ground and crouched over them. The pink tip of her tongue curled upward as she concentrated.

I walked over to Wu, feeling as though we could have done more for the boy. He had witnessed the murder of Mr Thomas, his guardian, and had lost his job on the railroad. He'd been forced to reveal his parents' vampirism, only to have them subsequently locked in the Duat where they suffered hunger and unknown tortures. The extreme physical perils of our southern excursion only added to the growing list of traumas. We were all adding emotional scars along the way which would haunt us long into the future, but Wu's cut the deepest. They would shape the man he would become.

"How are you holding up, son?"

He stared at me. Shrugged.

I shot a look at the shady rocks. Was Rojo playing the saddest folk songs in the entire Spanish catalogue? Despite the cauldron heat my eyes filled beyond dampness.

"Before we deal with Kek, we will ask him about freeing your parents," I said.

"And if we get them back, then what?"

"They can leave. I suppose they might return to the desert." I made a kind of flying motion in the air with my arms and regretted doing so almost immediately. My arms dropped to my sides. I smiled feebly. "They will be free to…" I trailed off.

"Go back to their unfortunate feedings?"

"No… well, yes… I don't know what else."

"I don't either," he said. His small hand patted mine where it rested on the warm, oval stone that had likely sat in the dry streambed for millions of years. "Thank you for not leaving me on the train, Dr Hardy."

"Of course," I said. "No one is leaving anyone. We protect each other."

He looked at me, knowing that I could not promise such things.

Evangeline jabbed the map. "My father owns this!" she shouted. "He has marked it. I know his mark anywhere. Look, see for yourself. Hardy will recognize this."

McTroy craned over her shoulder. Wu and I gathered on either side of the lady. Even in the ceaseless grime and sweat of the Gila, she maintained a fresh aura. I won't go so far as to call it the scent of roses, no. But I did not mind being very near her in any way. I welcomed the occasion. Our heads were close to touching. Four shadows merged, looming over the map.

"Here, Hardy." She twisted her finger into the paper. "Can you see it?"

I studied the topography of the Arizona Territory and borderland.

Bold, fairly straight lines meant railways. Town names mixed Indian, Spanish, and colonial English. Mountain ranges resembled microscopic amoeboids squashed on the page. Little evidence of water. Much blankness.

There off the edge of Evangeline's fingernail – a simple, penciled-in symbol.

Black star. Five-pointed, aimed down.

A pentangle.

I had seen it before. It was the same as the one Waterston had used to label the map that led my expedition to the skull rock. Anyone might have drawn it. But, like Evangeline, I was certain her father had done this. I read the tiny print below the star.

"La Mina Resurrección."

"The Resurrección Mine is Waterston property. It belongs to us. I've seen the deed in Father's office safe." Evangeline grabbed my arm and squeezed. "It's a goldmine. Gold and silver. Derelict now. But the vein was productive a few years ago. Officers in my father's company were surprised when he ordered it shut down. He never sold the claim."

"Figure that's where he is?" McTroy asked.

"I do, Rex, I really do."

"Why?" He was skeptical but ready to believe her if she supplied him with facts.

"First, it is already a tomb. The digging is done. Second, the gold is there. He could've had the mining continue secretly, off the books. My father would want a golden sarcophagus for himself, nothing else would suffice. Third, this place is abandoned. Private. Isolated. Not a town or any people for miles. He has everything he needs there."

"Have you ever visited this Resurrección?" McTroy asked. "Seen any gold?"

She shook her head. "No. But we have a map."

"All right, Miss. We'll sleep now under that canopy over yonder. There's enough shelter for the horses, too. Give us all a rest. Let them eat more of this grass and flowers. I've got hardtack. We ride out at sunset. Get to the mine by first light. Take a survey."

"And if we determine they're inside the goldmine?" I asked.

"We seal the sumbitch. Go home early."

"Sooner said than done," I said.

"Ain't it always though?" His gold tooth shined. He folded and pocketed the map.

38
DOS MUMMIES

I woke with a start. Night had fallen. Stars salted the heavenly dome. I left my blanket and stood stretching and yawning by the horses. Penny and Neptune were hobbled. I untied their ropes and saddled them. They nickered softly. I checked the immediate vicinity outside the rocky overhang. Moonlight was not there. I rushed back to the campsite. My heart was thudding in my chest. Evangeline and Wu were still asleep, side-by-side where I left them. I lit the bull's eye lantern and checked over our provisions.

I shook Evangeline's shoulder.

"Wake up," I said. "McTroy is gone. He's taken his horse, all of his gear. At least he's left us food and water."

Evangeline's eyes were puffy. She twisted at the waist to inspect the empty sweep of cool, hard-packed dirt where hours earlier McTroy had lain with his bedroll.

"This must be a mistake," she said groggily. But the panic was creeping in.

"It's no mistake, Evangeline. He took the map. I should have said something. Damn it! It's the gold he's after. He has a fever for it. Remember how worried he was about being paid for his services? Well, you won't need to sell your mother's jewelry. He's off to steal all the gold from Resurrección."

"One man alone against the mummies?"

"Oh, but you forget. He's the great McTroy. He'll probably get himself killed. But he's not the one I'm concerned about. We have food and some water, but I don't know the way out of the Gila. We go north, obviously. Try to find El Camino del Diablo. But without a guide, without a map, it may very well be hopeless…"

Wu had risen and was standing silently behind me. I turned to look over the provisions again and I saw him.

"McTroy would not leave us," he said.

"I am sorry, Wu. You have learned many tough lessons on this trip. I'm afraid this is yet another. Never trust a drunkard."

Evangeline rolled her blanket. I passed her the lantern.

"Make sure we don't leave anything," I said.

Wu had not moved.

"McTroy is a good man," he said.

"Wu, pack your things. We must ride out now. If we're lucky, we'll come across some vaqueros or maybe a prospector or two. If we make the Tinajas Atlas Mountains, we'll have a chance at a waterhole."

"Maybe Rojo knows the way?" Evangeline asked.

"I wouldn't want to trust my life to a corpse-eater. He could likely make himself whole again if he fed off the three of us."

Wu said, "But he is our friend. He helped us."

"He's a parasite. If it is advantageous to him, he keeps his host alive. And if it is more advantageous, he kills his host. Law of the jungle and the desert as well. *Survival.*"

Evangeline had finished with her things and was helping Wu.

"We will talk to Rojo," she told the boy. "I think it is worth talking to him. He went to sleep in those rocks right there." She lifted the light to show him the spot. "See if he's awake."

"Hand me that lantern," I said. "I'm going to make sure the horses are ready." I started walking away but looked over my shoulder to add a point. "Rojo is only following his nature. McTroy is the one you should be angry at. He is our Judas."

I turned, raised the lantern, and walked away from the shelter.

As I emerged from under the stone awning, I saw movement at the edge of my field of vision. An oscillation like a flag stirring against its flagpole in the gentlest of breezes – but there was no breeze. Behind the swaying motion, a column of smoke rose off the gully floor in a low, thick V shape. But we had built our fire elsewhere, and I could smell nothing burning. These vague, gauzy images appeared at the same rocks where Rojo had bedded down. I switched my direction, needing to investigate, wondering if the ghoul had seen our guide vacate the campsite, if he knew more of this sunset desertion than the rest of us. My anger at McTroy filled me. I was arguing with him in my head. Telling him he had no right to abandon us, cursing his name, accusing him of being no less than a murderer for leaving a woman and child behind in the desert. Because I was preoccupied with making these charges, I failed to register fully what I was seeing coalesce before me. The flag – not a flag at all – but more like a large, grease-stained, untidy puppet, suspended by what means I knew not, dangling in space a few feet above the rocks. I marched toward it, wanting satisfaction for my curiosity.

I slowed.

El Rojo faced me, afloat in midair, as if attached to invisible wires. The smoke behind him revealed its solidity and my mistake: a man-shape, but not any normal man.

A giant stood partly concealed behind the graverobber.

My steps faltered. The lantern shine trembled like a golden pool of poison. The handle *creak*-creaked shrilly in the steep-sided gulch, but despite my efforts I could not steady my arm. Rojo had a claw digging into his sinewy shoulder, clasping him. The claw was the giant's knotty, fuzzy-knuckled hand. He twisted Rojo's limp body this way and that, as one would a string over a kitten; toying, luring me out here, alone.

"Stop," a voice I knew said. "That's far enough."

He moved Rojo to one side so I could see the two of them. Kek, grinning in the lamp shadows, his jaw muscle clenched like a rubber egg. His skin glistened, new-looking, and clean. I smelled black licorice, recognized it as myrrh, coming from him. It was as if he had risen from a perfumed bath into our dirty little desert camp.

"What are you doing?" I asked.

"Enjoying the night and all it offers. I stepped on your dog." He shook Rojo.

"Where's McTroy?"

"Dead. I ate his heart." Kek delivered the words with frosty flatness.

McTroy dead? Cannibalized? Was that how Odji-Kek

gained his newfound strength? I saw no body anywhere on the ground, no Moonlight either, and surely she would be wherever McTroy was. Yet where had they gone? Fled into the night, I feared.

"I expected him to taste like a lion but his flavor was more like duck," Kek said.

"He's lying to you, amigo," El Rojo said. "He has no eaten McTroy—"

Kek's hand dashed like a spider from Rojo's shoulder to the crown of his head, where it paused. He squeezed Rojo's skull until it gave a pop. Under the skin, sharp pieces were scraping. The hand curled tighter. Gurgling, a modicum of liquid escaped.

"Bark, bark, little dog," Kek said.

Rojo blinked but stopped talking. His eyes rolled up ivory in their sockets then came down too far, trying to find me, rotating in different orbits, eyelids fluttering, widening, only to repeat the cycle. His mouth worked as if he were choking on a bone.

I tried to swallow. All my spit had dried. I wanted to run, run, run…

"What do you want?" I asked Kek. It seemed a strange, rather weak query, an effort to buy myself time to think of a way out of this situation, but the sorcerer's eyes lit up with clear excitement. It was as if I had finally discovered the right question. Like a teacher waiting for his not-too-bright pupil to learn the lesson, Kek's approval shined through anticipating my once-and-for-all following the assignment.

"Go kill the woman and the boy. Join me. You will live forever in my service."

"Why don't you kill them yourself?"

My question met with a sour, rebuking stare. "Perhaps, in time… I ask for obedience first. Good servants are hard to find. Blood is easy. Bring me some." He flicked his long fingers at me to speed me along in my task.

"Is Waterston here? Is that why you won't kill his daughter?"

Kek lowered both arms. Rojo's truncated extremities brushed in the dirt. Kek seemed to have forgotten about him, although he not had released him. He took several paces away from the rocks. He lifted his hand – the ghoul-free one – and gestured past me, over and beyond the steep edges of the arroyo. "Waterston is ahead on the trail traveling fast with the black horses. I am with him, asleep. I am also here with you. I sense the carriage is rocking. Moonlight drops pearls on the sand." Kek rolled his neck from side to side, slitting his eyes, seeing things I could not. I could tell that he was speaking the truth. He was present in two places at once – as he had been on the ship crossing the deep, frigid Atlantic, at our first campfire, and now again in this dark arroyo. Paying me these visits of his – social calls conducted on the underside of the day. Our little talks.

"Is this magic?" I asked, marveling despite his evilness, awestruck by his talents.

"I died thousands of years ago and I'm here with you. Everything I do is magic."

I fell to my knees. I felt him pressing me down, not physically, but the contact was just as strong. There was no room for the two of us in this arroyo. His size dwarfed me.

"Will you kill them for me now?" He had grown impatient with my questions.

"I will not." It was a struggle to utter these words when their opposite would have been much simpler. I might have submitted, acquiesced to his power. Yet I fought like a drowning man yoked in chains and with more chains piling on. I sunk down farther than my knees, sinking inside myself. He hated me for resisting. My last chances to give in to him vanished like breaking bubbles. Then the pressure around me stopped.

"Others will pay for your refusal. In the end, you all will die," he said.

"Afterward there is nothing," I said. "I make my peace with that."

"But this never ends, fool. Time and pain are forever, I promise you. Like this dog you will be ripped apart for eternity." He spoke calmly, as one might to an idiot.

With both hands he stretched El Rojo out. Air wheezed from the flattened sack of Rojo's skinny, birdcage chest, and the clicking of billiard balls I detected was his spinal column, wrenched and overtaxed.

"Migo, my guitar, please–"

Red, off-kilter eyes pleaded with me. For what? To play a last request? To save him from this fate? Maybe to pass along his cherished, dead man's guitar?

I don't know.

He had no time to finish before Odji-Kek tore him to pieces. The sorcerer beat the shredded ghoul flesh against the rocks and scattered it into the crags that ran between.

Kek wiped his palms.

Unsteadily, I climbed to my feet. My gaze strayed over the rubble strewn with bits of El Rojo. Even an eater of the dead did not deserve such a fate. Rojo had been more than his nature. I experienced a hollowness that felt like being carved out, having all my organs and juices sucked from me in a single gulp. Like an automaton I moved stiffly, surveying the rocks, keeping my light over them. Did I think he would climb back out?

Kek spotted something lodged against a wedge of sandstone.

He bent and picked it up.

El Rojo's guitar. The lacquered wood was curved, milky blonde glass under the bull's-eye. Kek ran his thumb lightly over the strings. The tuning pegs winked at me as he rotated the instrument in his grip, bringing it high over his head...

"No!" I shouted.

He smashed the body against the stone. Splinters flew. He tossed the neck away.

I did not want him to see me at that moment so I found the moon to stare at.

When I looked again I was alone.

"I take it you didn't find McTroy?" Evangeline asked upon my return to the shelter.

I had debated with myself about what to tell her and Wu concerning Kek's intrusion into our camp and Rojo's destruction. I was having trouble finding words that would do the least amount of damage. We were in dire circumstances. Our attitude going forward might very well determine whether or not we survived and returned to civilization. A report of Kek's visit would only scare them. Knowledge that he had tempted me to murder them would do worse. I would be receiving wary sidelong glances for the rest of the journey. Our morale was low enough. It did not occur to me that Evangeline's first question would be about McTroy. She was doing her best to put on a good face, but I could tell his forsaking of us had struck her at her core. She appeared close to panic, which was something I did not like to witness. Her smile was forced and fragile, as if she were holding a razor in her mouth. Her manner turned awkward and self-conscious. She's acting, I told myself. And she knows it's not very believable. I touched her elbow, feeling tremors flowing through her like electricity.

"I saw no sign of him," I said.

"Who're you going after, Doc?" McTroy walked into our circle of light.

I jumped at his voice. Evangeline did too. I cocked the lantern back against my shoulder defensively, prepared to strike him with it if necessary. That glittery, chilled gaze settled on me. I knew then the fear that outlaws with money on their heads had felt when they saw them. Looking at the last man they would ever see. I had no gun. My walking stick was stuck in Penny's saddle. But even if I had a proper weapon, I was no match for an experienced, coldblooded mankiller like Rex McTroy.

"I was searching for El Rojo. He seems to have… left us."

"You all look like you seen a ghost," he said, cheerfully.

"Where were you?" I asked.

"I was scratching up a fire to put some coffee on. Spied something stalking out there in the rocks. Moonlight and I rode out to take a look-see. Lobos. Probably the same pack we heard from before. They was curious is all. Run off when they saw me. You say the sawed-off cemetery defiler has parted ways with our cozy posse?"

I looked at Evangeline who was staring at me with quizzical eyes. I nodded confidently as I answered. "I am sure he wishes us nothing but the best. I noted before turning in this afternoon that his legs were longer. He did not want to slow us down. Mexico is his home. Plenty of things die around here. Other ghouls will come along soon. Scavengers always reunite. I, for one, will remember him fondly, and his guitar."

I wondered if my lies were working. McTroy seemed to grow more skeptical in his expression as I talked, while the reverse was true for Evangeline. She gave her attention over to our bounty hunter. Her panic had subsided, what replaced it was cautious relief.

"You have the map?" Evangeline asked.

"Right here." McTroy patted his breast pocket. "I never been up that way. You're paying for a guide. You oughta get where you're going."

Wu ran to McTroy and hugged him. The boy had remained out of sight until that moment. No doubt he was sizing up the shifting moods that had my own head spinning. My assortment of half-truths made me queasy. McTroy was surprised at the tightness of the boy's embrace but clearly not bothered by the display of affection. Hugging back would have been asking too much. He looked upon the boy with genuine tenderness, as he did in quiet pauses with Moonlight, which is no insult to Yong Wu, for McTroy valued four-legged creatures, particularly of the equine variety, more than people.

"You ready for action, Wu?" he asked. "It's a good night for a ride."

Evangeline and I left them and went to load our

horses. "Here, you take the lantern," I said. "It's dark out there. You don't want to run Neptune into a saguaro."

"Is Rojo really gone as you said?" she asked.

"Oh, don't worry. He's an old scrounger. He can look after himself. He'll gobble a few deceased snakes and lizards and be playing his guitar under a desert willow in a fortnight. Good and whole again. It wouldn't surprise me to meet him in the future."

"I suppose you're right," she said.

"I know I am." I looked off in the direction of the rocks, though it was too dark to make out anything. I was glad for it.

Wu brought us coffee from McTroy's newly kindled fire.

Together we drank. I was a damned heel and I felt every inch of it.

McTroy was right about the night though. It was beautiful and clean. Not blacks and whites, but a wash of lunar grays. It served no purpose to dwell on what might happen when we ran into Kek and his servants again: an ultimate confrontation in every sense. We might end up dismembered in the rocks like poor Rojo or a prisoner of some occult, other-dimensional torture chamber, if Kek's threats proved to be real.

Tonight we were alive. Tomorrow, together, we still had a chance.

I left the ugly thoughts of treachery and betrayal behind me in the dust. None of us was alone. Four rode out against los mummies.

We rode through the desert to la Mina Resurrección.

• • •

Friday April 13th, 1888
Resurrección Mine, Arizona Territory

At sunup we reached the outskirts of the former mining camp. Warm sunlight poured pastels over the rugged, rock-strewn landscape. The wind mixed the colors. Pinks and mauves flowed snakily on the ground, crisscrossing like streams of watered-down pigment spilled by beautiful accident from a painter's cup. Lilacs, roses bloomed above us. Fat peaches hung in the cloudy sky. It was as peaceful a vista as I had ever beheld. I could hardly imagine the evil men and death's head tombstones that lay hidden within.

But I knew better, didn't I?

So, as we rode in silence, I pretended the bloody violence didn't exist, that this wind-lashed land contained only raw, wild power and nothing else – no gold barons or monsters – simply a museum of natural wonders, geological and timeless. I was but a small creature in a big universe. My heart ached. I tasted the ashy bitterness of one who knows he may die in the coming day.

I put these feelings away.

Instead I watched the stones around me catch fire and glow like gems thrown up from the very center of the earth just for me to marvel at their sparkling. Realizing my insignificance made me brave; perhaps it made me a fool too. I was ready for the day. I felt lightheaded, almost giddy. My melancholy young man's heart bobbed in my chest like a cork at sea.

McTroy pulled the reins on Moonlight and put up his hand.

Evangeline and I stopped our horses. The animals lined up, almost touching.

The bounty hunter's squinty gaze filtered everything in sight, searching out danger the way a prospector pans for gold. He cut a plug of tobacco and thumbed it behind his lower lip. He spit on the sand: a sound like slicing. The sun inched higher.

"It's awful quiet," he said, finally.

"That's good," I said.

McTroy stared at me as if I had sat in horse flop and praised its warmth.

Evangeline put her head down and smiled. Wu had a wide grin.

"Resurrección is beyond that plateau." McTroy tilted his chin. He checked the map. "See that purple notch? Looks like a lopsided V? That's where we go in."

"What do we do now?" Evangeline asked.

"We go in," he repeated.

McTroy tucked the map under his poncho.

"Doc, you ride first. Miss, you give him a little space. Follow behind. If they shoot him, high tail it for them red pointy rocks on the left."

"If they shoot me?"

"Calm yourself. I ain't seen one mummy could handle a rifle worth a damn."

"These are the best odds we've faced since we started," Evangeline said, sunnily. Her eyes were like polished jades. "My father has no familiarity with firearms. Kek and his five minions are likewise ill-equipped for modern warfare. It is four against seven. And we have Rex."

Rex. I urged Penny forward.

"There is the small matter of the mummies' immortality. Kek's supernatural omnipotence and Monty Waterston's masterful planning are trivial in the face of Mighty McTroy, eh?" Penny seemed as hesitant as I did to take the lead. I offered her words of friendly encouragement. The wind whipped up fine grit and seemed as though it wished no less than to peel away our skins, layer by layer, molecule by molecule. I felt rough – a collection of saddle sores, leg cramps, a stiffened, twinging back, and sunburnt cheeks. I was in dire need of a hot bath and a bar of soap. My hands resting on the pommel had mysteriously shrunken over the journey to look like chicken feet: dusty, scaled, and gnarly. I flexed them to make certain they were still mine. I glanced over my shoulder. Evangeline and Wu rode together in the saddle. They were falling in place behind me. McTroy, stationary, pinned his attention to the horizon. "Have we given any thought to how we are going to kill the unkillables?" I asked.

"Crush 'em. Burn 'em. Cut the bastards apart with lead or steel," McTroy called.

My mind flashed on Rojo, on what Kek did to annihilate him.

"I believe there is historical precedent for beheading and de-limbing as a method of neutralization, if not actual execution," Evangeline said.

"If we had a fish pond we might drown them," I said bitterly.

"You jest, but they might well disintegrate in large quantities of water."

"If only you had told me sooner, I would have buried them in the blue Atlantic."

Penny had slowed again. Her hooves struggled as if we were mired in swamp mud. She pulled her head back. I bent over her neck to study the terrain underfoot.

"Sand is soft here. And rather deep," I called back. "What is it, girl? Do you smell something you don't like?" Snakes? I didn't see anything but a miniature dune. Penny was standing in a drift of sand as high as her knees. Directly before us, the quality of the sand changed. It flattened into ribboning waves, like the ripples a stone makes when tossed into water. The sand appeared raked in a large circle. A continuous, widening groove, a spiral curve. A gyre.

"There's something on the ground here. It looks manmade. Like a pictogram drawn in the sand."

The hand came up from underneath Penny.

I didn't see it. Not at first. And she didn't see it either. She felt it. Not the hand itself, but what it held.

A spear.

The chiseled flint tip stabbed at her belly. Penny reared up and threw me. I landed hard on my back. My head smacked the gravel, and a shower of golden sparks flew like embers kicked into my eyes. I shook my head. A mummy was sitting up in the dune. His dingy ivory bandages leaked sand. Grains spilled off him, following the creases, like rainwater. He swiped at the horse with a long, wooden spear. His bandaged hands gripped the shaft. Penny was bleeding. He hadn't managed to impale her as he wanted to, but he'd given her a deep scratch along her ribs; her brown abdomen was awash in crimson, and she was kicking her forelimbs. Her big, yellow teeth protruded, her eyes bulged out in fear.

I scrambled to my feet.

The mummy was on his feet too. An unraveled strip of bandage looped under his chin, swaying back and forth as he shifted his weight. I saw his mouth grimacing, a few skinny, ochre teeth, and a wedge of khaki bone that was his jaw.

He lunged at Penny. His spear cut horse flesh. Penny shrieked. She backed up and nearly trampled me. I darted aside and slipped my walking stick deftly from the saddle. I raised it like a cricketer's bat, readying myself to take a swing, but the horse kept herself between me and the sorcerer's desiccated servant.

"Hardy, look out!" Evangeline shouted.

I had the mummy squarely in front of me. What exactly was I to look out for?

I shot a questioning look to Evangeline.

Out of the corner of my eye I spotted the second assailant and the reason for her alarm. This mummy had unburied himself like a trapdoor spider. His hidey hole gaped behind him. His head was a mass of dirt and camouflaging creosote-bush twigs. He brandished a rather alarming weapon in his right hand. My background in Egyptology allowed me to identify it quickly as a khopesh: a sickle sword. The khopesh has more in common with hook or bludgeon than sword, actually. I'd compare its function to that of a battle axe rather than a cavalryman's sword. Nonetheless, it is a proper killing tool.

He swung the khopesh. I deflected the blow with my stick. But the flat, unsharpened edge of the khopesh caught me above the hip, rather painfully, in the region of my kidney, knocking the wind from my lungs. I did not fall, but I staggered.

To give myself a chance at regaining a degree of composure, I retreated two steps and found I was standing at the center of the sand spiral. The khopesh-wielding mummy lost interest in me and joined his soulless partner in the harassment of poor Penny. The first mummy wrapped his spearhead in Penny's reins. She tried to bite him. He batted her nose with a closed fist. She nipped again. He let go of his spear and took hold of the cheek piece of her bridle. He was trying to drag her toward me.

No, toward the spiral.

She would not budge. She tried her best to toss him.

Then she was up on two legs and the mummy was dangling in the air with his hands locked on her muzzle. The second mummy maneuvered behind her and smacked her flank with his khopesh. Driving her forward.

She lurched in my direction. The mummy fell off.

Penny and I were both inside the spiral now.

The mummies gathered at its edge.

Dust exploded from their chests as McTroy filled them with hot lead.

The gunshots did not faze them. But I was no longer focused on the mummies, because the sand under me had begun to shift. Rotating. Like the gyre it resembled, the spiral turned, and like ships caught in a whirlpool, Penny and I were being sucked down.

"Run! Get away from the center!" Evangeline yelled to me.

Riding on Neptune's back, she positioned herself and Wu along the opposite rim of the whirlpool from the mummified attackers. I saw anguish in her face.

Knowing then how critical my situation was.

The vortex picked up speed.

It moved as if powered by an enormous underground engine, the sand spinning counter-clockwise, grains tumbling over and under other grains. Sifting, sifting, everything going down into a giant funnel. I was up to my thighs already, and it was impossible to walk through, heavier than water, paralyzing, or so was its effect once a body part was submerged. I tried swimming, as one is supposed to do in quicksand. But this wasn't quicksand. The gyre hauled me in, gravitationally, it seemed. I could not escape its force. The more I strove to leave, the faster I lost myself in the warm, granular grind. I struck out with my stick, hoping to grab a bit of purchase on more solid footing.

But my effort failed. I was sliding the wrong way. The entire terrible wheel tilted inward towards its devouring core. Shushing like surf on rocks, spitting granules like bits of salty seawater. Hypnotic, really. If one were not caught in its clutches.

"Oh, Hardy," Evangeline said. She shut her eyes.

McTroy had put his guns away. He roped one of the mummies by the neck – it was the one who had employed the spear – and he wrenched the ancient Egyptian off his feet. Moonlight stomped her hooves into the mummy's bread basket until it was like a man crushed by the wheels of a coach.

The khopesh mummy noticed the extreme damage, and ran.

"The rope!" Wu shouted to McTroy. "Throw Dr Hardy the rope."

Now despite his raging hatred for anyone who might

harm a horse and his loathing of cowards who ran from fights they started, McTroy paused in delivering punishment long enough to keep me from dying an unspeakable death.

He dismounted. Cutting his lariat (he left a noose attached to the trampled mummy), he tied a honda knot, and on his very first toss, roped me around one arm and shoulder.

"Slip that over your head. Get your other arm in the hole," he said.

The spiral hugged my upper chest. As I breathed in, the sand squeezed me tighter. I expected my ribcage to cave in and fill with loose earth. I could not expand my chest. Breathless, I raced with clumsy, thick-seeming fingers to get the rope around me.

I succeeded.

In three long pulls McTroy towed me to stable ground, outside the deadly funnel.

There was no time for my horse.

Penny screamed a terrible scream.

I tipped on my side to witness her last moments.

Her head jerked as if she were crossing a deep, cold river full of undercurrent. She was choking, blowing and coughing sand. Struggling to keep her nose up. She corkscrewed. Hundreds of pounds of sand crushing in on her. The long, brown face went under. Then no sound. The spiral slowed. Stopped. A thin, dirty amber cloud lingered.

I lay panting. "No," I said. I climbed to my knees. "No…"

"Nothing you could do," McTroy replied.

He spit into the killing circle.

In the distance, the slashing mummy was running. Loose-limbed. A shamble here, a stutter-step there. Never quite straightening out and never managing to fall down either. His top half shimmied while his bottom danced across the Sonoran floor. It was a crazy thing to watch. Funny if it weren't so damned weird. In my gut, I knew it shouldn't be. This undead thing was perverse. Abomination is the biblical word. But I am not a biblical man. *Unnatural* would be mine. McTroy pumped two rifle shots into the ghastly thing on principle alone. He hit it between the shoulder blades. But it kept on going. Until it disappeared into the V notch.

"Least we were right about their location," he said. "Now where's that other shit sack?"

Moonlight stood guard over the demolished mummy, one hoof anchoring its rags in place.

"Ease up, 'light," McTroy said.

When the horse withdrew, McTroy straddled the mummy. He reached down and seized its head. He grunted with effort. Cords popped out in his neck and his face turned red as a rooster's comb. A sound like a broomstick snapping – he pulled the mummy's head off. He left it there on the ground. Without a word he rolled the headless body into the spiral. The sand churned, sucked the body down.

It grew still again. Quiet.

"Bring me the lamp oil," he said.

I went to Evangeline's saddle and unhooked the bull's eye lantern. I unscrewed the oil reservoir. "Here," I said, passing it to McTroy.

We four watched the undead thing's head. Its mouth was moving. Chewing air like bread. Utterly mindless.

The crusty eyes blinked. Did they see like we see? Were thoughts being registered in its brain? It reminded me of a dying insect. Once, though, it had been a man. Like me. I swallowed.

McTroy splashed lamp oil on the head. He sparked a match on his thumbnail and flicked it at the mummy's forehead.

A great *whoosh*.

A sudden burst of heat.

The head quickly changed to black. Smoke poured upward as if from a censor. A smell of frankincense released bluely into the morning air. The head crackled like a pile of kindling pine needles. McTroy crushed the charred remains flat, grinding the bones under his boot heel.

Something shined at the outer limit of the spiral: the ape's head of my walking stick. I leaned over and snatched it. I joined McTroy on Moonlight. Evangeline and Wu rode beside us. We followed the coach's wheel tracks into the notch cut into the plateau.

The shadows felt like home.

39

PRELUDE TO A DESERT DEATH RITUAL

The notch led us into a twisty canyon. Red rocks lined both walls. The sides were too steep to climb, and the winding trail pinched too narrow for the horses to turn around. It was one way in, no way out. Saguaro and organ pipe cactuses grew from the upper ledges along with flowery yellow splashes of brittlebush and spiky soaptree yucca whose stalks of droopy, white blooms leaned inquisitively over our heads like faces of concern.

Neptune paused. Wu jumped down to retrieve something from the path in front of the horse: the khopesh. The mummy must have dropped it in his shambolic retreat.

Wu handed the sickle sword to Evangeline and climbed into the saddle.

Evangeline turned the weapon back and forth, studying it.

"This comes from my father's private collection," she said. "I'm sure of it."

"Can we assume the same about the flint spear?" I asked.

"Father owns several spears of bronze and flint. It might have been one of his."

"What other weapons may he be supplying to the mummies?"

"Oh dear, an arsenal, I dare say. Bows and arrows, of course – those were the preferred arms of the ancients, and they would be tipped in iron, bronze, or flint." She counted on her fingers. "Throwing sticks. Battle axes. Slingshots and maces – Father possesses fine examples of both. He collects daggers by the dozen. We keep an entire hall devoted to displaying edged weapons. Who doesn't love a beautiful old dagger?"

"My mother often said the same to me when I was a boy," I agreed.

Evangeline rolled her eyes. "He doesn't have a chariot, thank goodness."

That reminded me of a question I had concerning the map.

"McTroy, is this the only access to the Resurrección Mine? How did the company transport their equipment and loads of ore? Not through this ravine, that is for certain."

He swiveled toward me. Eyebrow cocked and cheek bulging with tobacco.

"We're coming in the backdoor. There's a road to the north. Five miles 'round the plateau. I reckon it's gated. Might be a guardhouse. This way's quicker."

"Hakim didn't drive that coach and stallions through here," I said.

McTroy uncapped and drew on his flask. He offered me a sip of whisky.

I took a swallow and it spread warmly from my belly. However, when I attempted to breathe again, I began a fit of uncontrollable coughing. My eyes watered. McTroy politely passed the bottle to Evangeline while he slapped me thunderously on the back. This did me no good, but McTroy seemed pleased in his attempts. I hiccupped. He walloped my spine. As we were engaged in returning me to equilibrium, Evangeline finished the remains of the liquor. This allowance was more generous than McTroy intended it to be. He received his flask with an instant realization that it had become dangerously weightless.

He said nothing but sucked in his cheeks and uttered a chesty growl.

Evangeline nodded cordially.

"Who knows where the black magic broncos mightn't go," he said. "Those wheel tracks stopped at the notch. They didn't circle." He tipped the flask and worked his lower jaw like a landed fish. But not a single drop fell. He spied into the bottle. "Don't matter. We know where they are." He chucked the glass into the pink-red rocks where it clinked twice but failed to shatter.

After the ambush at the spiral, McTroy had given one of his Army pistols back to Evangeline for protection. Now she resettled it in the belt of her dress. She moved her braid off to her shoulder. Her neck was the color of spring peonies. She spoke to Neptune using words of gentle, yet firm encouragement.

We resumed our slow ride.

The canyon narrowed. We approached a stone arch, like the gateway to a forbidden city. It bridged the ravine. A myriad of thin, meandering cracks branched throughout the span from stem to stern. The arch had probably been there for a thousand generations. A sign bolted to the rock read: Resurrection Mine – Peligroso.

Some objector had blasted away the lower half of the sign with a shotgun. A group of ravens perched along the upper edge; their feathers gleamed shiny and black as an undertaker's shoes. They were silently watchful.

"An unkindness," Evangeline said.

"What's an unkindness?" I asked, puzzled.

She lifted her chin. Her hips rocked in perfect synch with Neptune's equine forward motion. Shading her eyes with the flat of her hand, she said, "That's what you call a group of ravens. An *unkindness*. When you write a book about our adventure, you'll need to remember that."

"Why do you think I'm going to write about this?"

"The way you study things. Tucking them into your memory, like an old scribe brushing away on his papyrus scroll. Making certain you jot everything down correctly."

"I'm not old," I said, testily. "I estimate us to be about the same age."

"You're old inside, Hardy. You've probably always been old."

Whatever did that mean? It was true my boyhood had been truncated, bookish, and to a large degree solitary. I was an only child who grew up on a farm. I could hardly be blamed for that. After quick self-review, my school days were less occupied with acts of immaturity and impish pranks than with diligent library work and preparation for a life in academia. Other boys simply bored me; I antagonized them. I was better off alone. Romantically speaking, I had never been inspired to be one of those starry-eyed, amateur poets who follow debutantes around scribbling sonnets, odes, and whatnot, but… but… oh, I feared Evangeline was right again. My view of the world was cast in sepia tones. Very like the pages of a book on a shelf in the dimmest-lit corner of the library.

That did not mean that I never intended anyone to read me!

Or read of me, for that matter. *Perhaps I will write a book*, I thought. *Gothic romance because no one will believe this is history.* If I claimed it were true, they would lock me in an asylum. I would lay under a pile of blankets all year round, and mumble to myself as I watched the sunlight bleed across the wall. Mice would befriend me. But if I said: *Here's a novel to terrorize and titillate your senses.* Well then, perhaps…

We proceeded through the archway, and a prickling gnawed at my skin as if I had passed under an icy cataract. Moonlight's skin quivered. At the corners of my vision blue undulations swam like vertical eels. Once we left the arch's shade, the visual disturbances and the chill subsided completely. It was hot desert again. I did not have to ask my companions if they felt these sensations, for McTroy had gone temporarily rigid in the saddle, and Evangeline and Wu were shuddering like a pair of newborn puppies. No lasting damage appeared on our bodies, so my assumption was that we had tripped an alarm set by a spell, and something like sleigh bells were ringing in Odji-Kek's ear.

McTroy pointed at the sky.

Half a dozen wobbly check marks revolved beyond the arch.

"Vultures," Wu said. "They smell the dead. I've seen them follow my parents."

"Who else do we know might smell like Mr Reaper?" McTroy clucked his tongue. "Here comes the end of the line, boys and girls." He pulled up and dismounted. Freeing his rifle from its leather scabbard, he never took his eyes off the notch's exit. "I don't like us flushing out of this split with no cover. Damn hairy. They know we're due to arrive."

"What is your plan?" I asked.

"I'm gonna take a scramble." He pointed the barrel of his rifle at an ugly collection of boulders, stacked high and off to the right. "From there I can see the whole mining camp."

"What should we do? I'm not waiting here," Evangeline said.

"Miss, could you make your way discreetly over to that ledge – the one stabbing out like a crooked witch's finger?" McTroy asked.

"I could," she said, swinging off her saddle.

"I could too," Wu said.

"Then we'll go together," Evangeline said before I raised any objection.

"Am I to stay with the horses?" I asked, trying not to sound dejected.

"Doc, if the mummies kill these two horses it won't matter what we do. There's no walking out of here. The birds will eat us for dinner. That's about the sum of it."

I nodded and, climbing down, took hold of Moonlight's and Neptune's reins.

McTroy started his ascent.

Likewise, Evangeline and Wu crept along the reverse side of the ravine.

Hardy, old inside, forever old, remained with the horses. He was a bookman first, a scholar second. He swore he would never fire a gun, even in the face of his enemy. Did you know he was afraid of tight spaces? How odd for him to seek the profession of tomb raider. Odd, indeed. But isn't "odd" the perfect word for the man? He lived mostly in his head. The one expedition he supervised brought back unspeakable foreign monsters that had been imprisoned in the earth for millennia…

Internal thoughts go better with a pipe full of tobacco. I had lost mine in the train wreck. The horses eyed me with suspicion. I was talking to myself. Aloud. Too long in the sun, too little sleep… too much thinking and too little doing… my gaze ventured back toward the arch…

Amun Odji-Kek stood at the apex of the span.

He looked straight at me.

He wore a yellow skullcap. His amber eyes shined, their outlines had been rimmed in black, and the black smudges extended far into the corners. The eyes appeared to float in darkness. They stared at me from within pits dug into his skull. Dressed in a long, golden robe – he was motionless. The robe's hem brushed the ground. His arms hung at his sides. I could not see his hands. His sleeves flowed into the robe so he seemed like a carved block of yellow flashing stone come to life, his smooth head glowering from atop a tower of great height. His lips closed together in a cruel line.

"Kek, you are here," I said, my mouth turning as dry as if I had been eating sand.

He nodded.

"We knew you would come here," I said. My words seemed to float away from me, and my mind felt loose and not altogether under my own power.

I put my hand over my mouth to stop myself from talking.

"I have been in darkness for ages," he said. "Yet I tire of the desert. I want to go to somewhere green. I want to see water. I saw water on that ship. Do you remember?"

I had first met Kek's apparition at night on the deck of the tramp steamer *Derceto*. We had watched the waves together. It felt like years ago, lifetimes.

"Yes, I remember."

"I would like to see water again. To visit a place that is green." He looked out across the Sonoran landscape. "Is there water in Los Angeles, California?"

"Yes… some… there is the Pacific Ocean," I muttered through my fingers.

"Are there tall palm trees?"

I nodded. My body trembled uncontrollably.

"I will live by the Pacific Ocean," he said. "I will have many sons born to me."

The sun flared above us. Separate tendrils of fire whipped out across the sky, uncurling, reaching earthward across the solar system; millions of pulsating suction cups covered each tendril. Upon further inspection, the cups were mouths. Mouths filled with pin-sharp teeth. What was I seeing? The heavens in revolt of their natural order – an unholy god unleashed. This was a glimpse of Kek's vision for the future. His paradise.

Gazing at the sorcerer injured my eyes, but I could not look away.

Kek's shadow fell into the ravine, where it multiplied, stretching out of proportion to its source, and although he remained quite still (only his eyes and lips moved), his shadow-self twisted and writhed over the rocks. The hot rocks hissed as if a liquid had spilled onto them. I smelled burning cedar wood. Myrrh. Water lilies.

And rot. He might have left the tomb, but it would never leave him.

He looked down at me again, smiling a ridiculous, jackal-toothed smile that spread his face as if it were about to tear apart. Anger dwelt there. Pain too.

"I will be the King of Los Angeles," he said.

Where was McTroy? Could he not hear Kek? And Evangeline and Yong Wu? Did no one but me hear his voice booming all around?

"Soon you'll know what it is to be dead." He laughed. "But that *woman* intrigues me. Tell me, good doctor, has she ever been with a king?"

Wild, canid giggles. *Tee-hee. Tee-hee. Tee-hee.*

Growing louder, echoing in the ravine. His head went tipping back, the wide mouth opening, eyes hooded as they pinched and glittered. His laughing face: sharp teeth and hard, pink gums, the wavy folds of lips like salt water taffy pulled and pulled; his sloping tongue creased down the middle, lolled fatly, then obscenely flexed as if it had a life of its own – the rough shrieks poured out from canyons deep within him–

TEE-HEE-HEE-HEE-HEEHEEHEEEEEEeeeeee

The sun exploded.

I threw my arms around my head. I knelt, shielding myself. However, I did not die as I expected I would – in a scorching blast of flesh-melting, bone-blackening wind.

Instead, spotty bits of vision swam about as if they were trapped in a fishbowl around me, and shaking my head only made them spin more furiously than

they had before. Slowly they returned to me –
little, broken bits of landscape, irregular chunks
of sandstone and sketchy palo verde scrub – like a
swirling jigsaw puzzle. I struggled to assemble things
in three dimensions, not knowing what final picture
they would make. The desert phosphoresced white. I
kicked at stones in frustration and, losing my balance,
barked a shin and cried out, swearing. Blurs darted
around me – ranging from jackrabbit in size to a full-
on shaggy buffalo – unfocused, ocular phantoms
hindered me from drawing any conclusion until they
settled. Blinking, I blotted tears. I looked and looked.
But there could be no doubt.

The arch was empty.

40
ARRASTRA

I had to find my party. To warn Evangeline, McTroy, and Wu. It was a mistake to have come to La Mina Resurrección. Odji-Kek was more powerful and unpredictable than we had thought. Waterston didn't control him. No one controlled him. In fact, we knew next to nothing about his powers. We were walking into a slaughter, or worse. If we left now we might be able to contact someone in the US government and get an army to Mexico. It seemed absurd. But even an army might not be enough to stop Kek. We needed scholars, experts on the occult. We needed Egyptians! Ancient Egyptians!

Moonlight and Neptune appeared asleep. I stumbled past them, pausing only long enough to slip my walking stick from Moonlight's saddle. I used the stick to steady myself. *Pik pik pik* – the stick's ferrule dug shallow craters in the sand as I proceeded.

My head was still ringing with the sorcerer's laughter. The sound penetrated my bones. It was as if a part of him lingered inside me. Feeling soiled, I tried to throttle my racing mind, because Kek lurked in me like a spy. How could we combat such a creature! I looked left and right, seeking my companions amid the high rocks. I saw no trace of McTroy among the lumpen boulders, or Evangeline and Wu – the ledge where they were to climb lay barren, and as McTroy had noted, it pointed like a witch's gnarled finger toward the goldmine.

"McTroy! Evangeline!"

My shouts brought no replies.

Without thinking, I walked straight out of the notch and into the mining camp. My limbs felt heavy, my whole body did, as if I had fishing sinkers sewn into my clothes. I was flapping my arms, waving my stick, trying desperately to get them to see me.

"Hello, search party!" I called out. "Yong Wu, are you there?"

A dark shape zipped overhead.

A buzzard? Did one of those high-circling scavengers decide to swoop down for a closer look? I scanned the air, squinting. I saw nothing but washed-out sky. The golden orb of the sun stole away the colors. My eyes were left temporarily damaged by the vision I'd had of Kek and the hallucinatory solar explosion. The world around me was rendered in pencil sketches and smudges of charcoal – a grayness that for some unnamed reason caused my level of panic to rise steadily like steam rattling inside a tea kettle. If colors were now bled away, all but vanished, could death be far behind? It was irrational. But my rational mind had been sorely tested.

The mining camp was smaller than I expected. Two buildings constructed of flat, stacked stones, mortared together with mud, and topped off by rust-eaten tin roofs that curled at the edges. The smaller of the two was closer to me. I went there first.

A door of rough planks that had been hammered hastily together hung askew. When I pushed it inward, it dropped from its hinges and clattered to the ground, sending up a dust cloud that choked me. After the dust cleared, I stepped inside. It was a good thing the door had fallen off, because the building's only window was boarded over, and the airless room was hot as a furnace. A solid block of shadows was packed inside. I used my pocket watch to reflect the sunlight, probing the corners of the room.

Mining equipment.

Shovels and picks. Hammers, chisels. A battered ore bucket with a huge dent kicked into it. I moved my light around shakily. A huge snake lay sleeping in the farthest corner, and catching sight of the reptile made me jump inside, my heart pounding, until I realized it was only a pile of chains. A torn burro harness hung from a nail. A wooden ladder missing two steps leaned against the wall like a tired, skinny, brown man.

That was all I found in the first building.

When I walked outside I saw another flicker in the air, moving toward the high rocks on the left side of the notch. It was too fast to be a bird. I rubbed my eyes. I stood there for a full minute, watching. I saw no movement in the rocks or above them.

I turned to the second building.

As I went closer I noticed, between the buildings, a circle of stones like the wall of a well. But it was no well. A thick post in the center attached to a longer horizontal arm, and a chain ran through the wooden arm and hung down; the other end of the chain hooked to a decently-sized boulder with a hole drilled through the top. Flat stones lined the bottom of the circular pit. Bits of broken quartz lay scattered inside. This was an *arrastra* – a Spanish grinding mill used for thousands of years, dating back to the ancient Mediterranean. Mexican miners introduced them to the American southwest. The end of the arm extended outside the pit, and miners would harness a burro to the arm to drag the boulder over the flat stones, crushing any rocks they dumped into the pit. They would sift through the crushed remains looking for signs of gold. That explained the chain in the storehouse and the torn harness I'd found. But arrastras had been replaced by stamp mills, which crushed rocks more quickly and in greater quantity. Why was there an arrastra at Mina Resurrección? Two reasons. One: the mine was old – old enough to have been discovered by Mexicans long before any Americans explored this desert, thus the arrastra might have been here for a hundred years, or more. Two: a stamp mill required water to power it – a great deal of water. This place was far too dry for a stamp mill. Waterston's mine managers must have taken their ore elsewhere to pulverize it. Yet the bits of quartz in the arrastra's pit sparkled. No dust covered them. Dust, in the Gila, covered everything in no time at all. Someone had been looking for gold… recently. They didn't want any curious minds at the stamp mill knowing what they were doing. Well, I knew who ordered the search for gold to continue. I only wondered why he had kept it a secret. It made no sense. Well, whatever surreptitious mining had been taking place at Resurrección was over now. This place was deserted.

And haunted. Or so it began to feel to me. Spirit-laden, and oppressive.

I left the arrastra and walked to the second building.

This had been the miners' living quarters. The front door was missing. The unkindness of ravens from the stone archway had relocated to the roof. They followed me with their oil-drop eyes, their feathers like charred wood. Inside, I surprised a turkey vulture. His red, bald head bobbed. And his red feet hopped until he reached an open window, and flew out. Skeletal frames of bunks were built along both long walls of the rectangular house. Sand heaped on the floor. Tiny, sculpted dunes like a miniature desert spread from one end of the bunkhouse to the other. Several windows gaped free of boarding. Even now a stray breeze carried grit over the sills into every crevice of the former lodging. I approached a rear window. Gazed out. Here I found a small graveyard. *Dead miners.* Their bodies were buried in unmarked graves; each grave bordered by loose stones gathered from the edge of the plateau. I was willing to bet that the humble adornments were the doing of the other miners and not Waterston's company overseers. The miners would have been largely illiterate and unable to write names on tombstones other than their own. These tombs had plain, unpainted crosses. Waterston probably saw the deaths as a nuisance, the cost of doing business; a broken chain, a dented bucket, a dead man killed in the mine – they all amounted to the same thing: replaceable parts in the Waterston machine. Like the other Egyptologists who came before me – Ned Krazwell and the rest – I too was an interchangeable piece in Waterston's quest to locate the skull rock and the tomb of Amun Odji-Kek. We were only means to an end – his end.

Gold and mummies. Treasure.

I could not bear to look at the graves any more.

I returned my attention to the bunkhouse. Its interior was surprisingly barren. There was no indication of any previous human occupation. Nothing left behind. Not a book or a cracked bottle, not so much as a candle stub or soup pot... no chair to sit in, or even an ill-fitting, odd boot. As an archaeologist I found this strange. People leave things behind. We always do. But not here. In this place humanity had been utterly erased. The storehouse had its old tools. This was an empty shell. And that was all.

But there was a bad odor to the bunkhouse.

I hadn't noticed it before. Probably because of the breeze. Or my senses being overtaxed. The odor came from the far end of the room, where I'd seen the vulture.

There was a door there. Shut. No doorknob, only a round hole where it should have been. I went to the door and pushed.

The odor was overpowering. This is what brought the vulture indoors, what attracted the ravens to the rooftop: a half dozen dead Mexican miners. Their bodies piled atop one another. All of them shot once or twice. At close range. They had been dead a few weeks by my estimate. Flies had come and gone and done what flies do. Rodents obviously had access to the office. That's what this room had been in times gone by. A table stood against the wall. Away from the dead men.

Well, away from all but one dead man.

This corpse was fresher than the others, although technically he had been dead the longest. His neck was broken. His head twisted the wrong way around, so despite the fact his body was lying on its stomach, he

was facing up. I knew the face. I'd seen him only a day
ago, driving the midnight coach and a team of jet-black
stallions. It was Hakim, my Egyptian friend and foreman.
I knelt beside his body. His eyes were cloudy, as if fog
had crept inside, and finding no way out, gathered at the
windows. His jaw stuck open in a last gasp of surprise.
I flipped the body over. His head moved loosely, like
a doll's. Most of us will die but once. Hakim had died
twice, and it didn't look like it got any easier the second
time. I hoped everything was finally over for him. He
was a good man, and whatever perversity Kek's magic
had made of him, he bore no more responsibility for that
post-mortem change than he did for lying here with his
neck screwed in a helix. As I turned him, I noticed a
lump under his jacket. In the pocket I found something
about the size and shape of a large cigar, wrapped in
clay-colored paper. I held it under my nose. The tube
gave off a strong, burnt fruit smell that nauseated me. I
rose to my feet and stepped nearer the table.

On the table was a crate filled with tubes like the
one in Hakim's pocket. The print on the side of the box
read: GIANT POWDER COMPANY. Beneath that was an
address in San Francisco.

Dynamite sticks.

Hakim had stolen one. This final act proved to me that
he was driven by forces beyond himself to do unspeakable
deeds, but the real Hakim had not completely evaporated
in death. He'd rebelled. From the looks of things, he had
planned an honorable, if catastrophic, act of resistance.
Interrupted – he'd paid for his rebellion. But I can't
imagine death is any worse than being the puppet of
a mad sorcerer. I took two more sticks from the box,

making a bundle of three, and I added a length of fuse. Put the sticks and fuse into my coat. I bent down and closed Hakim's eyes. He had deserved better than what he got in the end.

A lot of people do.

"Hardy! Look out in the bunkhouse!"

I ran to the door in time to spy McTroy kneeling in the high rocks. I waved. Glad to see he was alive. He was pointing off to my left. I turned and saw the mine portal. Heavy beams framed it. Twin rails led into darkness. But my attention quickly diverted.

Two missiles (like the ones I'd witnessed earlier) zipped through the air.

I heard a dull clatter hitting the rocks. Then I saw the second projectile come to an abrupt stop right at McTroy. From this vantage point I could make out what they were – not birds, but arrows. McTroy rolled over. An arrow stuck out of his upper body. He dropped his rifle and grabbed at the arrow's shaft. His rifle slid off the slick rocks, down into the ravine, disappearing between boulders with a dreadful clack. He ran for better cover. A barrage of arrows followed him, coming from two directions.

An arrow hit his leg. He fell, tumbling head over heels into the canyon.

"McTroy!"

No reply.

Then a cry came.

"Hardy!"

But it wasn't McTroy's voice. It was Evangeline's, shouting from the opposite side of the notch. Two mummies scurried up the steepness like gray spiders.

Evangeline moved out onto the narrow ledge. There was nowhere she could go to get away from them. It was only a matter of time. Another mummy, this one with a broad-bladed and brutal short sword, picked his path carefully, but speedily, to the spot where McTroy had terminated his fall.

I gripped my ape-headed stick. I was prepared to attack as a wild beast would if his family group were threatened. However, a terrible decision faced me. *Where to go first?* McTroy appeared incapacitated and his assassin stalked on, yards away from finishing him with a throat slashing or beheading. Sweet Evangeline crawled out to the tip of her ledge. She had her Army pistol in hand, true, but I knew what little effect bullets had on the mummies. She could at best delay but never defeat her assailants. Yong Wu was either hidden or…

I dared not think we had lost him. It would be too devastating…

Indecision had been my undoing in the past, but I was determined not to let that happen here. The stakes were too great. I made my call. Yes, I would go where my heart ordered me. I had not taken but a single step when Evangeline shouted again.

"Hardy, be on your guard!"

Her tone seemed less panicky than a warning. As it happened, indecision did not undo me, but striding into open terrain without proper caution or heeding the repeated shouts of warning from my companions was another matter entirely. I cleared the doorway. Over my left shoulder, the fourth servant of Odji-Kek had sidled his insidious way along the bunkhouse, pressing his back to the outer wall. His gray bindings blended with the bunkhouse stones, and my temporary color blindness made matters worse.

It was too late.

I turned. He punched me squarely between the eyes.

The bandages felt hot. Dry. The hand inside was very cold. Like a frozen club it hammered upon my head. Again. And again. He bashed my face. *Crack*! One of my teeth popped out onto my tongue. I tried raising my arms, but my brain had disconnected from the rest of me. I was untethered. Another hard blow, another enamel crack. Did *my* neck just break? I thought it might have. But it was darkness for me either way; that was certain. Darkness and an instant sleep.

Was this a dream?

For an unconscious moment I entertained the possibility that I had simply drifted off into a slumber, napping on my desk, my heavy tome-filled head tucked into a pair of folded, tweedy arms, snug in my cubby carrel in Chicago. Safe in the musty, old library. No Egypt for Hardy, no sir. The Sahara so studded with puzzles and curses, the Gila, here in the Americas, equally chockful of dangers… mummies, banditos, Chinese vampires… a smart, cat-eyed, occultist librarian whom I fancied – how preposterous was that! – and a steely bounty hunter with a name like Rex McTroy. Please…

This was dream stuff, surely.

Pure fancy. I mean… it had to be. Didn't it?

Bloated, slickened worms the size of toppled silos… asps… killer train wrecks and horseback-riding grave eaters – one who played flamenco guitar! – these materials lived in dreamland, not the borderland. There was peace in knowing it was all a dream.

I smiled and my smile hurt.

I awoke. Jarringly. My mouth filled with penny-flavored froth.

I spit blood. I tried to open my eyes.

Managed the right eye, just a crack. Dizzy-making. Desert scene. Sparsely illuminated or was that me dipping into blackness again…

Waking–

All the colors were bone.

There were two mummies with me now. Servants of Kek, neither one the Slayer from the South, Lord of Demons, et cetera. Two minions dragging me, arm in arm. Three jolly stumbling drunkards were we. My legs had gone the way of boiled noodles (limp). My feet raked sand. They bumped along crossties set between twin rails. We were headed into the mineshaft. Where smoky lanterns were spiked to chiseled walls–

Smother me now – oh, I hate being closed in. Shadow-trove. An eggy smell gassing up from somewhere below. Stinkdamp? Damned dust everywhere in here too. Coolness emanated. I was blind in my left eye. I had to swing my head around to see what was what. *So the neck's not broken*, I thought. But it turned stiffly with an audible grind. My face swelled lumpy as a fruit pie. Couldn't feel it much and was glad for that. I spit out a tooth and tried to snatch it as it dropped in the dirt in the dark.

"Aaarggaahhh," I said.

I'd bitten the inside of my mouth. Bloody specks flew out with my attempt at speech. I'd only wanted to swear at my captors.

We climbed into a mine cart.

They high-stepped; I was shoved and dumped. They

mashed me in between them, undead fore and aft. Their bodies: pokey as tree limbs bound by burlap. Jabby knobs of elbows and sharp, crooked fingers prodded my ribs. At least they let go of my arms. I was tingling. I touched my blind eye, hoping not to find a gooey hole. Tender and bulging – my eye was still there. I pried the thick lids apart. It bothered me to look out, but I could see things – a sliver of passing, glowing streaks (the lanterns), and the back of the mummy who sat in front of me, his dull gray head like a bulbous hornet's nest, papery, whorled, pointed at the top, and drilled straight through with a hole. One of McTroy's bullets did that, I was sure. I felt happy about it. He didn't seem to care.

The cart went down. Down. Could the mine be this deep? Fast, jostling us side to side. My jaw throbbed. I knew where the missing tooth had come from, below the battered eye. I tongued the gap and an electric pain jolted into the center of my head. I yowled. The motion of the cart was too much. We kept going, and going… the wheels shrieked madly. My head was a spinning top. The view tilted, warped, and suddenly I was sick, bent over, emptying my stomach along the rail margins. The tunnel above us carved low and tight, but the air caressed and felt as clean as cool spring water on my skin. I rested my chin on the edge of the cart, breathing through my nose, until the mummy behind me grabbed a handful of my hair and hauled me into my seat.

"Bassstaarrr," I growled, as I pawed at my lips to wipe the slime away.

The cart braked with a jerk – slowed – jerked again. Stopped.

We had arrived.

41
A Sarcophagus for Pythagoras

"Doctor Hardy, I am so very pleased you are here with us."

Montague Pythagoras Waterston finally stood before me. He was not as I had imagined him when I first received his letter. No, the Monty speaking to me was a man of matchstick arms and broomstick legs. He teetered on his feet. His shock of white hair must have been a source of great pride... once. But a tinge of unhealthy tarnish had seeped in. Limp strands fell over his eyes. He combed them back with a jaunty flip of his fingers, but they would not stay in place. His hands were nervous yellow crabs. He'd made a mess of his last shave, leaving bits of beard and cuts on his face where he'd nicked himself. Dried blood and soap stained his collar.

The mummies shoved me toward the wall and chained me to a beam overhead.

"This is a most special day," Waterston said to me. "You are privileged. People would pay a fortune to see what you're going to see. I will be made immortal. This is an historic moment in American magic... by way of Egypt, of course." His smile was ghastly; the teeth grossly prominent as if the skin around his mouth had shrunk away. I might have believed he was the resurrected corpse among us and not Kek. It seemed only fitting to meet him underground.

"You're insane. Kek's going to kill you and take your money," I said.

"Tut, *tut*... Show respect for your superiors, young man."

"I thought you were smarter than this, Waterston. You don't know what I brought back. He Who Disturbs the Balance. Plague Bringer. Corrupter of the Land. Do you think the ancients gave out those titles lightly?"

Waterston looked at me the way one looks at a dog that has eaten the Christmas goose. "Gag him," he told the mummies. But they remained still, as if they hadn't heard.

A low chuckle from an obscure corner – Kek emerged. His standing next to Waterston exaggerated the differences between the two men. Waterston, white, thin, and fragile as a fishbone: a fossil of earlier life. The sorcerer grew larger every time I met him. He was like a bonfire that raged out of control and consumed the town. The air around him popped and crackled with combustion. "Silence the doctor. When his friends join us, we can talk. Their sounds will be a song to my ears. The tomb is a quiet place, Monty."

"I shan't be there for long," Waterston said.

"Don't be too sure–" I started to say.

One of the mummies tore a bandage from his leg and stuffed it into my mouth. Pain throbbed from the holes where I had lost my teeth. Saliva ran copiously down my chin. The burial cloth tasted of salt and onions. I felt my gorge rise. Acid bathed my inner throat. I breathed through my nose, and swallowed my own blood in a rush of panic and revulsion. *Calm yourself, Hardy. Don't end up choking to death on your vomit.* It was my voice in my head, not Kek's.

They were leaving me alone, busying themselves with the ritual at hand. I had an opportunity to look around, as I concentrated on slowing my breathing and calming my nerves. I have learned that coldly observing facts can sometimes steady me and keep my mind from galloping off the first available cliff. The mine cart I'd ridden in with the two mummies lay off to my right, and to my left was a dome of unbroken rock. The vein of gold within the rock had crusted over scabby red like an old, dark wound. My chemical background taught me gold and iron ores often mixed; blood red and yellow gold accompanying each other in geology, as in life. This specimen stood out boldly in the lamplight, as wide as my hand in most places; it forked across the expanse of the dome like lightning during a hellish thunderstorm. But gold imprisoned in the raw earth isn't nearly as impressive as gold extracted, molded, and polished to please the human eye. Here before me I had examples of both, and there was no comparison.

Monty Waterston, Odji-Kek, and the duo of mummy-guards gathered around a pair of newly-made, but historically accurate, golden sarcophagi; the sarcophagi were open, and their lids waited, propped against the far wall. My attempt at slow breathing failed miserably. Bookended between the lids stood a Ka door like the one from the Temple Underneath. The profile of the first lid resembled a much younger, healthier, and robust Montague P Waterston.

The second lid was a dead ringer for his daughter, Evangeline.

I must have made a noise showing my alarm, because Waterston lifted his head from inspecting the confines of his soon-to-be coffin to grin at me.

"It's a beautiful Ka door, is it not?"

I shook my head.

"No doubt, Dr Hardy, you have noticed the sarcophagi. Fine craftsmanship. We mined the gold for them right here. Off the books, mind you. I don't need any record of my private digging on the company ledgers. I employed men like the pharaohs did. They will be buried in the mine with me and Evangeline. We're very old-fashioned that way."

I struggled and pulled at my chains. Dust showered me. The beam held solid.

"You disapprove? Even after you've seen the abundance of evidence? Amun Odji-Kek, May He Live Forever in the Endless Night, will bring us back good as new. Better than new. Bodies die. I have outlasted mine. That must be obvious. Some people are born to live and die. Others are destined to be eternal... like me. The Sorcerer Kek has defeated the gods who sit in judgment. I am not so fond of judgment. Better to make your own luck. What would be the point of all my wealth if someday I had to walk away from it?"

I kicked gravel at him.

"If you like having legs, I would suggest you stop doing that," he said. "Now, where was I? Ah, yes. You have likely noticed I only have the innermost coffins. No outer boxes of wood and stone. Why hide such luxury? You see, I have no fear of grave robbers. We will seal the mine, of course. That's only prudent. The Sorcerer Kek will apply a nasty curse to the portal. I own Resurrección Mine and will continue to do so *ad infinitum*. There will be no more mining. I can post guards if I so choose. The sarcophagi are quite safe, believe me. And no one will be looking for my tomb, because as far as the world will know, I will be alive and healthy. As will my lovely daughter, once she sees this is her best path going forward. She is impetuous. Being young, she does not think things through. She will have her time. We both will. All the time in the world..."

There was a rumbling in the mine – a burring vibration I felt through my feet.

"Speak of the devil and she doth appear," her father said.

Another cart was riding along the rails. McTroy had dispatched one of Kek's servant mummies at the sand whirlpool, leaving four to contend with; two of those remaining had guarded me, and were presently preparing for the death-entombment ritual, meaning that the other two mummies remained on the surface. Before being knocked unconscious, I had witnessed a bandaged automaton, armed with a short sword, lumbering in the direction of McTroy's inert form lying on the rocks.

I swiveled around as far as my bonds allowed. I wanted to see who was in the cart when it arrived, but nearly every combination of passengers that I could imagine made my heart sink. I sawed my chain back and forth over the beam. It would take me hours, even days, to cut through the equivalent of a tree trunk from which I hung suspended.

The cart wheels screeched. They were getting closer.

Kek gestured to his servants, and they, in turn, lurched their brainless way to the empty cart we had used previously on our downhill journey. I wondered for the first time if Kek spoke to them mainly in their thoughts the way he did to me. I had not heard any of them talk to Kek or to each other. Were they thoughtless creatures? A quartet of detached torsos and limbs that merely acted out Kek's commands, according to coded transmissions they received like electromagnetic telegraph machines? The second cart was braking now. Shrieks rang from the tunnel. Then it appeared: a boxy blur of shaking, rattling rust. It slowed. The horrid grinding made my (remaining) teeth ache.

A hairless, gray form sat stiffly with its hand clutching the brake lever. The bandages that once wrapped around its head were missing, stripped away, and a tattered scarf of formerly intact bindings dragged behind the cart. The mummy was male. They all were, I had assumed, but Kek was the only one I had seen uncovered. This fellow was far less handsome. He had been in a close struggle – that was apparent – and he had paid a price. His exposed skull looked like a tree after children peel the bark away and weather and insects have had a go at it. Two bulging, inflamed eyes were the only parts that seemed the least bit vital. They rolled in flaky, tobacco-brown sockets. He had no nose. It was a juiceless affair, all told.

He released the brake. As he rose in the cart, puffs of dust wheezed from his armpits and leg joints.

Evangeline was with him.

I hadn't seen her before, but now I could. The mummy had his arm clamped under her chin. She was tight in the crook of his elbow. Her skin had changed from peaches and cream to maroon. Her eyes were shut. I dreaded the worst: that she was dead, or near death. Her father wouldn't care, would he? He'd simply ask Kek to summon her from the Duat, and in whatever state she might be. *Would she be herself? Or would she, like Hakim, find annihilation preferable to infinite undead limbo?*

The mummy hauled her around, swinging her body up and out of the cart.

As she came over the edge, she planted a foot on solid ground and kicked out her other leg into the side of the mummy's knee. His leg snapped with a loud *crack*! Like dry kindling it sounded, before one throws the little pieces in the fire. Standing on one leg and holding onto Evangeline proved impossible.

The mummy teetered. The mummy fell in a jumble.

She put a heel to him as if he had crawled out of her cupboard.

"Oh, my dear girl, please do stop," Monty Waterston said, warmly chiding her. He hung his head in mock shame. "Such high spirits! You are your father's daughter. Come to me, Evie."

Evangeline reached under her skirts and retrieved her Army pistol. She pointed the gun at Waterston. His expression registered a mixture of shock and social outrage. Then she lowered the barrel to aim at the mummy on the ground, who was inching himself away from her. She pulled the trigger. But the hammer fell on empty chambers. Still she kept pulling it until Kek walked over and took the weapon away. He tossed it into a corner where it broke into pieces.

"Please join us," he said. The sorcerer offered her his hand.

She did not take it, but she walked with him. She saw me hanging from the beam, the tips of my boots scraping the dirt, but she did not react. Monty went to her. He grasped her forearm, the way the elderly often do, and he guided her to the pair of gold sarcophagi. She did not resist. He was talking to her quietly. Encouraging, chastising, correcting her in the manner fathers have employed for centuries. He led her to sit on the lip of the open sarcophagus he had ordered for her. He brushed back her hair from her face. He kissed her lightly on the forehead. She looked into his eyes and smiled, but tears ran down her cheeks and her mouth trembled, as Monty went on talking, pointing at the coffins, the Ka door, and Kek.

The sorcerer approached me. On his way, he stepped on the head of the mummy still crawling in the dirt. The head burst like a dry husk. Kek never glanced down. He stood in front of me. His ribcage was at my eye level. His deep voice thrummed strings in my nerves, bristled my hairs. Honey-smooth. I knew why men followed him.

"She is bold," he said.

I nodded. He removed the rags from my mouth.

"She'll never have you," I said.

He gave my cheek a gentle, playful slap. His fingers slid along my jaw.

Monty called out, "Let's begin now. I don't want to wait any longer."

"I am ready. Put your wrists together." He turned and gestured to his pair of servants. "They will bind you."

"Bind me?" Waterston's voice climbed. "Is that necessary? I'm not running away."

"The ritual is not a matter of choice. Do you want it to work?"

"Absolutely," Waterston said.

"They bind you. Wrists and ankles. You will lie on your back."

"I see."

"Do you have my dagger?"

"It is my most treasured artifact. The dagger led me to you. I bought it on the black market in London. The seller had no idea whose it was. He lacked knowledge."

"Present the dagger to me."

Waterston reached into his coat and withdrew the dagger. He turned the handle so it faced the evil priest. The flint blade was wide and very, very old. I did not recognize the monster carved into the ivory handle. It bore no writing of any kind.

Kek took the blade from him.

Waterston raised his arms. Purple veins creeped like centipedes over his bulging, arthritic knuckles. The mummies bound him. He winced when they tied his feet together. They lifted him and put him carefully in his coffin.

"Father, don't do this," Evangeline said.

His features softened. "My precious girl, have no fear. This business is only a formality. Join me. We can journey together to the Land of the Dead and back again. We will see wonders."

She looked at him tied up in the gold box. She shook her head.

Waterston nodded. "Let's talk again when I return." He pointed with his bound hands. "I'm coming through that door in a matter of minutes. You can decide then what you really want." He turned from his daughter to Odji-Kek. "I am ready for the rite to continue."

Kek moved the dagger from hand to hand.

"You are prepared to leave this realm?" he asked.

"I am."

"Kek's lying to you!" I shouted. "You aren't going anywhere."

"You ought to listen to Hardy, Monty. He is smarter than you are."

"What?" Waterston attempted to sit up in his sarcophagus. But Kek easily pinned him in place with one hand. He held the dagger up.

"Is this part of the ritual? But I read all the books. You strike quickly at my heart. I shall die instantly. Then... then I travel to the Duat to meet the gods. But you will intervene! The Lord of Demons will deny the gods and return me to this world."

He quaked. The flesh of his face rippled in disbelief, incredulous.

"Why would I?" Kek asked. "What is my interest in you?"

"I saved your damned soul from the skull rock. You owe me."

Kek sneered. Pride and haughtiness dropped over him like an ugly, gaudy mask. But looking again, it was not a change overcoming him, but his true self, the inner Kek surfacing. "I owe you nothing. It was I who made you search for me. From realms distant and beyond your imagination, I directed you to find me. Hardy dug me up. You, Monty, were but a blind servant. Like these two." He pointed at the silent mummies.

"You will never have my money," Waterston said. "The banks won't give it to you. Not one penny. My lawyers will see to that." He talked like a petulant child on the verge of crying, clasping his favorite, shiniest toy to his bosom.

"Your heir will give it to me."

Waterston stared with pleading eyes at Evangeline. She, in turn, appeared as a statue of marble, immune from comprehending what was happening right before her eyes.

Waterston looked back at Kek.

"Why can't you grant me this favor? It costs you nothing. Let me live as I once did."

"Enjoy the shit smell of the underworld."

The veins in the old man's neck swelled as he struggled to free himself.

"Do something, Evie! You must help me. He will kill us both."

"I think she is going to stay with me. Every god needs his goddess, or at least a good concubine." Kek lowered the dagger. "I'm not going to kill you, Monty. Time will."

Kek stepped back. His mummies lowered the sarcophagus lid over the screaming body of Montague P. Waterston. The muffled cries grew increasingly hysterical. Then they stopped completely. I honestly believed that Waterston had shouted himself to death; that his fear of dying had torn the channels of his heart or perhaps drowned his brain in blood.

The sorcerer ignored the sounds from the coffin, turning his attention elsewhere.

He summoned Evangeline. Without breaking eye contact, she drifted to him.

He inclined his head to her perfectly-shaped seashell ear and whispered in it. She drew a deep breath. Her face flushed. Both of them were smiling. Evangeline's eyes were glazed and wet as if they'd been painted with a clear, syrupy varnish. Her fists clenched.

I was the only one who heard something coming from inside Waterston's coffin.

Barely discernable, rhythmic. Like singing, but not exactly.

I did not understand a word of it.

Chanting.

The mad, decrepit millionaire had begun chanting.

42

GODS OF GOLD, LORDS OF LEAD

A rumbling soon covered up the monotonous intonations of Monty Waterston. Another cart was riding the rails into the depths of the mine. Kek straightened from his conversation with Evangeline, his spell temporarily interrupted. My suspicion that he held hypnotic sway over her consciousness was confirmed by her expression of befuddlement – like a sleepwalker who has awakened mid-stroll at the edge of a precipice. The two mummies' alertness peaked simultaneously with Kek's shifting focus, and they watched with an intense interest directed at the mouth of the tunnel, as floury dust sprinkled down, triggered by the vibrations of the speeding cart.

The blood had drained from my shackled arms. They were as numb as if they had been made of ice. I used the tip of my boot to scoop together a small pile of rubble. I had to swing out like a pendulum and, with my feet acting as a pair of pincers, I collected a few of the larger, rounder lumps of hard rock scattered around. But I quickly succeeded in building a sizable mound under me. I stepped up onto it and thrusted my hanging limbs toward the ceiling. I expected relief, and relief did eventually come, but what I got first was pain, as my circulation returned and my tender nerves signaled to my brain that all was not right with the corpus Hardy. I would have sworn an invisible devil was plunging red-hot pins into my shoulders. My hands, I was quite certain, were squeezing live bees.

The imminent arrival of the third cart distracted us all. My pain diminished, or I got better at ignoring it. I was actively attempting to test my ten digits and keep them moving in hopes that, whatever fate awaited me, I would at a future point be unchained.

The braking cart shrieked to a stop. The last mummy of Kek's crew was driving the cart, but he was not my concern. Yong Wu slumped across the mummy's lap. He appeared unconscious. A lurid smear of blood painted his cheeks. The mummy exited the cart and tossed Wu's limp body over his shoulder like a feed sack. The boy never cried out, never fluttered his eyes. Now I knew this mummy was the one who had been hunting McTroy in the rocks, because I saw the same brutal short sword tucked between the loops of soiled bandages knotted around his waist.

The blade was thoroughly encrimsoned.

In fact, he had gotten McTroy's blood splashed all over him. To think that McTroy had been cut down by this inarticulate henchman made my blood boil with rage. He lumbered just like his raggedy companions – they were a slow-marching band of clods, I decided, hardly worthy of matching up with the likes of Rex McTroy. But this one swordsman mummy in particular raised my ire. He possessed a physical cockiness that the others lacked.

Where they were interchangeable and oafish, he exuded
the brash attitude that I associated with gunfighters and
duelists. Despite his stiff gait, he carried himself as a man
with a reputation would. I wondered who he had been
in his previous life. Surely, I'd have been as displeased to
make his acquaintance then as now.

He halted a few feet away from Kek and Evangeline.

He dumped poor Wu on the ground.

Evangeline went to the boy. She listened for his
breathing and nodded to me that she had, indeed, heard
something. His chest did rise and fall. Then, licking the
corner of her skirts, she began to clean the blood and
grime from his face. But his eyes stayed closed. His lips
parted, but not to talk, only to breathe. His color was
much improved.

In the meantime, Kek scrutinized his mummified
lackey. Again, this caused me to wonder if he
communicated with his servants through mental
telepathy. After a prolonged interval of staring, during
which neither of them blinked, Kek finally pointed to
me. "Are you ready to come down, Doctor Hardy?"

"Yes, I am."

Kek frowned. "You have made a mountain to stand
on. How is the view?"

"I have seen better things at the bottom of a hog pen."

"We will make you comfortable." He switched his
gaze to the swordsman, who gawked dumbly ahead,
unmoving. "Sever his bonds. Bring him to me." Kek
clapped his hands, loudly, once.

The swordsman responded by slouching towards me
at a quickened pace.

I readied myself to give him a double-heeled kick in

the middle. He drew his sword and flicked the stained blade back and forth. I changed my mind.

Kek said, "How do you feel about little boxes?" He tapped the coffin that Waterston had intended for Evangeline. "The air grows scarce. Monty would tell you that. I laid in my box for thousands of years. You think you will go crazy. And you do. But that does not make it stop. You are still trapped. You have no choice. It is the end."

"Please kill me another way." I did not want to beg him, but I did. I was awash in ammonia-tinged, icy sweat as if I were a snowman drowning in a self-made puddle.

Waterston's chanting returned – so he was still alive – his eerie, rhythmic verses rising in volume like nightmare cries coming from under a thick, down-filled pillow.

The swordsman mummy reached up and began chopping at my chain, but the chain was thick and would not break. I feared he might miss and lop off my hand and almost shifted to make it so. Then I would bleed and die from exsanguination. But even in the direst of circumstances it is against our nature to offer ourselves up to the blade or the noose or the volley of bullets. I pulled my hands aside and let him strike at the chain.

Kek grew impatient. Soon another mummy was there with a key. A quick turn and I fell from my shackles to my knees. The swordsman hauled me up. He grunted. I watched as the wet, bloody patch on his shoulder spread its petals like a flower. *Good*, I thought, *I hope it hurts*. He stuck his face close to mine.

I saw his gray eyes.

Mummies don't bleed! He grabbed a handful of my shirt front.

"Hey, Doc," he whispered.

"In my coat pocket," I said. "Don't let them see."

Mummy McTroy held the sword's blade under my nose. He touched my pocket, then turned me around and shoved me forward. He hadn't taken the dynamite. I walked to Kek, and to Evangeline's yawning coffin.

As I passed, I let my fingers graze Waterston's sarcophagus. The low hum of his voice was still there, chanting away. *Perhaps he is praying*, I thought.

But praying to what?

I looked at the Ka door. The ancient hieroglyphs stood out boldly, as if they were slowly being extruded through the wall. Had the paint always been so vivid? Was there a bright greenish piping around the door? Did it radiate ever-so-subtly?

The two real mummies grabbed me roughly and bound my wrists and ankles as they had done for Waterston. They lifted me and deposited me into the narrow confines of the second sarcophagus. Despite McTroy's presence, my heartbeat pounded and my breathing shallowed. A cold sweat broke from my pores. I fidgeted with my feet. A clammy coolness swept over me as if an oceanic fog blew across seaweed-strewn boulders and icy little pools of brackish water. I tasted salt and a bit of that sea tang.

"You are unwell?" Kek asked. He draped his flipper-sized palm over my eyes. "Imagine the dark. The lid of the coffin is above your face. If you lift your neck, you may knock your forehead against the gold. When it closes, you will never see light again."

I waited for McTroy to make his move. I followed him out of the corner of my eye. Well, not followed him exactly because he was not moving, had not moved.

He stood slackly away from the sarcophagi, arms at his sides, staring off into space as blankly as if he were an actual mummy. Trust can be difficult even under the best of circumstances. When one is about to be entombed it is exponentially more challenging to master.

"I am ready," I said. "Right now, in this very moment, I am ready."

I was not talking to Kek. But he did not know that.

He uncovered my face.

"I want the woman to watch as the lid goes down," he said.

"Her name is Evangeline," I said.

"Evangeline," he said, his voice rising. "Come. Join us."

When she did not respond, he twisted away from me, looking for her where she had been kneeling on the ground, tending to Wu.

They were both gone.

"Where is she? Find her. Kill the boy." His commands set all three mummies in motion. "Wait." He raised his hand, the one that still held the flint dagger. He slipped the dagger into his belt and waved to hurry the mummies along. "First seal the coffin."

I bolted up. McTroy rushed forward and held me down. He nearly slashed me.

"What are you doing?" I was losing control of my fear. My world felt rushed, plunging over a border from which there would be no return. My heart flopped like a dying fish in my chest. I- c- c- could not breathe.

The other two mummies lifted the lid. They aligned it overhead. A shadow fell across me. Logic fled. I was a boy again. A boy trapped in an attic inside a trunk. I felt the sarcophagus shrinking against my sides. The lid dropped down with a thud. *No, no, no… this cannot be! What is he doing? My heart will explode. I cannot stand this. The darkness. The absolute, incontrovertible darkness… was not entirely absolute.*

A crack of lantern light seeped along an edge of the coffin lid, which lay crookedly over me. I attempted to push it off, but it was too heavy, at least several hundred pounds, and I had no leverage. As I pushed, I noticed with a start that my wrists were no longer bound. McTroy had sliced through the leather thong during our struggle. I sought my pocket and found the dynamite still there. My claustrophobic panic had not subsided, but the wave of terror crested, and I was riding high on a strong current of nervous energy.

I investigated the opening where the light entered. I fit my hand through the slot, but what good did it do me? I ran my fingers as far as I could reach along the crack. There, right below my hip, I grasped some cold object very like a carved doorknob: the ape's head! Surely enough, a few inches of my walking stick blocked the lid from closing, but better still, the stick gave me the leverage I needed to tilt the heavy top askew. I pried it up, and over, creating a space for my knee, and then I worked my body into the breach.

Quite a commotion had erupted between the two sarcophagi. When my head fully emerged, I perceived the cause: McTroy was busy fighting off the two mummy servants. They were confused by this sudden betrayal of their partner in eternal mindless servitude; too addled were they to comprehend his disguise. He took advantage of their surprise and with his short sword managed to disarm one opponent (and by *disarm* I mean he removed

the creature's arms, hacking through the shoulder
joints). I bent myself up like an accordion and untied
my ankles. The armless mummy butted McTroy with his
head. McTroy's noggin proved the more substantial of
the two, and the disoriented mummy staggered sideways
before tripping. Tripping over Yong Wu! The boy was not
only alive but apparently unharmed. He had been a full
participant in McTroy's dramatic rescue charade – and,
no doubt, the hidden supplier of my stick.

No time for fancy reunions. Wu said, "The Ka door,
doctor. It is like before."

So it was.

Sickly green fluorescence emanated from the
doorway. It was Waterston's doing, I realized. From his
tomb he had chanted the ritual phrases needed to unlock
the Duat portal. I touched his coffin and felt no signs he
was alive inside, nothing.

"Help me remove this," I said to Wu.

The occult industrialist had paid dearly for his
sarcophagus, and the ornate cover luxuriously designed
to portray the man inside in his everlasting glory was
sealed too tightly; the fitting matched with precision,
and once closed the seam all but vanished. We could
find no finger holds. It was impossible to lift without
additional help.

McTroy's bandaged feet slipped in a puddle of his
own blood. The arrow wounds, while not instantly
fatal, were nonetheless grievous and depleting him
of a dizzying volume of blood. His mummy assailant
toppled him backward. McTroy lost his sword. The
mummy grabbed his throat in a two-fisted vise. McTroy
battered him to no effect.

Evangeline stepped from the gloom at the far end of the mine.

With a pickaxe.

She drove the pickaxe into the mummy's skull with such force that the skull crumpled into itself and disintegrated in a puff of dusty smoke. McTroy threw the mummy's carcass off. The headless body twitched and curled up as if it had been singed.

McTroy retrieved his sword and used it to dispatch the armless mummy.

"Armless or headless, take your pick, so to speak. I'd go headless myself." McTroy stripped the wrappings from his face. "I never knew how these suckers could keep their bandages on. Damn. Hotter than a Texas bed nymph with a bad case of–"

"There is a child here," Evangeline said.

"Hotter than hell," McTroy said, by way of apology.

"What do you know of hell's heat?"

The sound of Odji-Kek came from behind me and I turned in time to duck as he hurled the lid of Evangeline's coffin. It brushed back the hair on top of my head. Wu, who had been standing beside me, was too short to be in danger, yet he shivered involuntarily in pure mammalian fear as the golden weight passed above us, flying.

McTroy was not so lucky.

The lid sent him into the wall. It caught him squarely and took him off his feet. There was an awful concussive boom. His chin lay against his chest and blood poured from his nose and mouth. The lid pinned him in place.

Evangeline, who had barely escaped the projectile, gaped in shock.

"I will make more servants," Kek said. "I will make *you* my servants."

I smelled a horrible smell – excrement and stagnant waters, old filth and death, and burnt things that refuse to be consumed. Kek was not paying attention to the smells.

"I will take the boy first," he said. "Then the woman. Hardy, I will take you last."

"No, you will not," I said.

He reached for me, and I swung my walking stick at him.

He grabbed the stick. It was easy for him as I knew it would be. I never intended to hit him with the stick, I only wanted him to fill his hand so I could take the flint dagger from his belt. As I said before, it was a very, very old dagger. Older than Kek. That monster carved into the ivory handle? Well, I suspected that the creature was what Amun Odji-Kek looked like when he roamed the Duat. His spirit doppelganger, if you will. Monty Waterston had been wrong. This dagger didn't belong to Kek. It had never been his at all. But he knew it. He knew it because he'd been killed with it a long, long time ago.

I slipped the dagger from his belt.

I stuck it in his heart.

He roared.

He jumped back from me and slammed into Waterston's coffin, knocking the top loose. He pulled at the dagger, but the dagger would not budge.

The Ka door opened. Out from the portal hopped a white-haired woman with tusk-like fangs. She carried with her the odor of mushrooms, damp earth, and coal dust. Mrs Wu sniffed the air. Her blind eyes floated up like moons. She had detected the warm boy-scent of her son. She spoke to the doorway. Green smoke. Thumping feet. Her husband bounded through and went to her side. They swayed like a pair of snowy wildflowers on a windy hillside. Their finger and toe nails were more claws than nails. Mr Wu lashed out in the direction of Kek. Both vampires hissed and sprayed silvery strands of saliva as long as eels that hit the ground, making loud splats. Yong Wu spoke in a voice cracked with pain but also with joy at seeing his parents when he had believed them to be forever lost. In three hops the family was together again. The older Wus put their boy behind them for protection. They faced toward the other one they smelled, the one who had beaten and locked them away. Lord of Demons. Plague Bringer.

Kek did not bother to look at them. He pawed at the blade in his chest. His muscles swelled as he struggled to free the dagger. He quaked. He screamed. The handle won out. He slumped against a wall to regain his strength for another attempt. Panting.

The Wus talked. Mr Wu hopped away from his family, jumping into the green smoke from the Ka door. The smoke thinned. I glimpsed a ruby glow behind the green.

Kek had been some combination of dead and undead for so long it really was improbable to think we would kill him off for good. Not by any ordinary means. Annihilation seemed overly optimistic. One could hope. But I feared he was only injured. "We should think about leaving. Up the tunnel," I said to Evangeline. "When Mr Wu comes back," I added.

"What about McTroy?"

"I'm afraid he's—"

"No! We are not leaving." She strode away from me, to the beam where I had been shackled. She picked up the chains. Before Kek realized what she was doing, she had locked his wrist, turned the key, and tossed the key into the Duat.

He raised his proud head.

"Fool." The word rasped. The effort to keep his head upright grew too great. He chuckled and tore away his skullcap. His bald head glistened. A delta of veins spread over the bone. I watched it pulse. What might he have been without the lure of sorcery?

I grabbed the end of the chain. Together we tried to drag him toward the Ka door.

"Spirited fools," he said. "Stop."

But he came away from the wall. He resisted. Yet we were making progress.

"I will NEVER GO BACK!"

We edged him closer to the door. Where the green smoke had vanished was a reddened gateway now. Kek noticed the change. He dug his heels in, wrapped the chain around his fist and wrenched it from our grips. "Never going back," he said quietly to himself.

Mr Wu leaped through the doorway. He sniffed and pointed a long finger at Kek.

He had not returned alone.

A procession of dark-eyed men followed him into the mine.

"No." Odji-Kek fell on his back and, flipping over, began to crawl.

The men were judges. They carried... instruments. And rolls of bandages.

• • •

I will not offer much detail about what happened next, partly because some stories are too gruesome to tell, and more so because I did not, could not, watch. For the historical record, in an effort to give simple facts, I will go as far as to say this: the judges seized Kek, they bandaged him in linen, but they did not embalm him. They cut out his tongue. They removed the dagger from his chest and out of the hole they plucked a living scarab beetle the size and color of a human heart. The judges put the beetle in a jar. Rods of heated iron were inserted into Kek's ears and a steaming liquid followed (here is where my curiosity ended; I looked away). The judges did not want Odji-Kek communicating with anyone as he had with Monty Waterston. This time they took precautions.

But the judges were not the only ones to cross over from the Duat that day.

It is said that if a human views a god, death is the result. I refute this claim. It may be that there are no gods at all, or it may be that we, each one of us, are godlike. Either way, I witnessed a being who I cannot classify as... typical. Mythological might ring correct. I do not ask you to believe me, but really, if you have come this far in my tale, is a god going to stop you?

"Don't look, Rom," Evangeline said as she squeezed my hand.

But I am the One Who Remembers – a scribe, a brusher of facts. I peeked.

So help me I did.

It was as though I viewed her through a different medium – water or smoke – but my vision was not clear. It wavered. I can tell you this: the judges opened the jar and fed Kek's scarab heart to a female beast. The beast was demonic. Part crocodile, part lion, and the hindquarters of a hippo. I know the mythological name for this beast is Ammut. Devourer of the Dead. She is real. She ate his heart in one gulp. When the judges took Kek back into the Duat she went with them.

Before the Ka door closed, I saw a lake in the distance. A lake of fire.

Then the door shut.

43
STRANGE FUTURES

The Wus lifted the gold coffin lid off McTroy. He was not dead, not yet, but I had no question as to whether or not he would be dying soon. His breathing shallowed. He did not rouse when we said his name. Internal damages plus the arrowheads still lodged in his shoulder and upper thigh were more than sufficient to kill a man. Even the bleeding from his mouth and nose slowed to a trickle, as if to say, "Enough." His skin turned as ashen as the bandages he had stolen from the mummy assassin who attempted to finish him in the rocks. Yong Wu told us how McTroy foiled his attacker, sent him headfirst into the ravine bottom, and rolled a boulder on his head for good measure. Evangeline was gone from the ledge by that time. Captured, carted off into the mine. It only was Wu and McTroy. The bounty hunter evaluated his wounds, and broke the arrow shafts. Together they unraveled the mummy and dressed McTroy in the bindings. He smeared his bloody hands on Wu's face to give the appearance of grave injury. The blood was warm. Yong Wu clutched McTroy's limp, rough hand as he talked to us.

"Is he dying?" Tears dripped down his cheeks. He hiccupped.

"Yes," I said. "He needs a hospital, and a real doctor, not like me. But I don't think he feels anything. It's like he's sleeping right now, and that sleep will get deeper and deeper. Then he will drift off."

"People shouldn't drift off," Wu said. "They… they just shouldn't."

Wu's parents stood away at a polite distance. Their noses twitched. The scent of blood, which filled the air with a smell like rain falling on old iron machinery, must have been overpowering. In the Duat, they had nothing to drink.

Wu's mother asked him something in Cantonese.

I feared the worst. I understood the why of it, but an anger rose in me.

And revulsion. While I had a strong sympathy for Wu's parents, I did not relish the thought of them feeding on a half-dead McTroy. As it turned out, I was wrong in my prejudiced assumptions. Ashamedly so.

"My mother knows a way to help McTroy," Wu said. "She has good medicine."

"What curative could she possibly have?" Evangeline asked.

"She will show you. But, please, do not interfere with her."

"McTroy is doomed," I said. "We have no better options." I waved my arm in invitation for Mrs Wu to make contact with our fallen guide and friend.

She couldn't see me, but she hopped to McTroy's side. With a rapier fingernail she pierced his shoulder wound. A deft swirl of her wrist, and the arrowhead emerged.

She extracted it. Crouching, sniffing, she repeated the operation on his upper thigh. For his part, McTroy did not stir. Then Mrs Wu did the strangest thing: she extended her left arm on a downward angle so the crook of her elbow rested on McTroy's chin. With the index fingernail of her right, she sliced open her vein. Her blood defied gravity; rather than flowing toward the ground, it traveled up, and followed a channel between the taut muscles of her forearm. It behaved like no liquid I know. The stream seemed, well, intelligently controlled, as if a string pulled it from the incision in the vampiric arm to the slack parting of McTroy's lips. It had the hue of an aged tawny port. As soon as the blood touched McTroy's lips, Mrs Wu massaged his throat. And he drank. Very eagerly, like a suckling infant.

After he had a few good swallows, Mrs Wu broke their connection – though McTroy's mouth continued to pucker and root, his tongue sweeping the last drops. She lowered her sleeve and hopped back to her husband.

In a hush, we waited.

McTroy's eyelids fluttered. He yawned. Stretched. He scratched his whiskers.

"Why are you all sitting there smiling? Is it my birthday?"

"In a manner of speaking, yes, I believe it is," I said.

"Well, I hope somebody baked a pie."

We had a good laugh at that.

McTroy did not transform into a vampire because he had never been bitten. Wu informed me, and Evangeline concurred, that it takes more than a thirsty drink of vampire blood to achieve the full metamorphosis. As a subsequent note, McTroy had no memories of his near-death, or of the sarcophagus lid that had crushed him, and especially no recall of sipping Mrs Wu's blood; though in the years after, he developed an increased fondness for the night, which he remarked upon often, claiming to be able to see farther in the dark than in daylight.

"I can almost smell the moon," he told me once.

"Is it cheese?"

He ignored my jest.

"A man just lighted a campfire. He's cooking beans with smoked hog jowl. Five miles. Thataway." He pointed in a direction of absolute onyx obscurity.

I never shared the source of his heightened senses. But it pleased me to know something about McTroy that he obviously did not know about himself. Another result of the transfusion gave me more than amusement. I was overjoyed to recognize the close bond that instantly deepened between McTroy and Wu. He became a mentor to the boy. No substitute for his true father, of course, but about as caring a replacement as any father could ever want for his son. You see, the Wus knew that they could no longer stay together as a family. We covered Mr and Mrs Wu with tarps so the sun wouldn't burn them, and they hopped out to the stonewall equipment shed. The boy remained with them and they talked. For the first time, I heard Wu sobbing loudly and uncontrollably, and I attempted to enter the shed, but Evangeline stopped me. When Yong Wu emerged, he had regained composure. At nightfall, he said, his parents would head for the mountains. He tells me they still live there.

Monty Waterston was another matter altogether. He never died in his sarcophagus. The lack of oxygen caused him to faint. But when Kek, in his throes of agony, knocked the top off his coffin… Monty slowly revived. He had helped us in his own way, though I was never sure helping us was his intention. I think he wanted revenge. Pure, simple revenge. While we were reviving McTroy, Monty slipped out of his tomb and creeped back to the surface. Evangeline was the one who noticed he was missing but decided not to look for him. That solution didn't satisfy McTroy. He and I climbed to the high rocks. We spotted Monty leaving the notch, his weak and stumbling steps kicking up dust. McTroy had his rifle back from the crack between the boulders. The stock was broken, but he assured me it would still fire. He aimed for Monty's cowardly, fleeing back.

I lowered the barrel.

"Let him go. He's more dead than alive. The desert will finish him. Perhaps he will think about the magnitude of what he's done before it's all over. I don't want to see Evangeline standing over her father's coffin again. Do you?"

When Evangeline came out of the tunnel we told her Monty got away.

She tried to hide it. But what I saw was relief.

"He wasn't always this way," she said.

"He loves you," I said. "Despite his… faults."

I informed them about Hakim and the dead miners. We carted all the bodies back down into the mine. We took nothing. McTroy and Wu set the box of dynamite between the sarcophagi.

At dusk we finished.

"You ready, Doc?"

I nodded.

McTroy struck a match off his boot heel.

"Wait!" I said, pinching the flame. "I've forgotten something." I ran back down into the mine and came up a minute or two later.

"Now you can blow it," I said.

McTroy lit another match and touched fire to the fuse.

I watched the sparks flying from the bundle of dynamite sticks in my hand.

I tossed it into the mine.

The four of us ran like hell.

Late April, 1888
Arizona Territory, riding on a train to Yuma

"Going through life is like riding a train backwards," McTroy said.

"Really? How is that?" I asked, amused.

Evangeline raised her eyebrows. Wu readied himself to receive wisdom.

"Time's the train. Movin' one way." He jerked his thumb toward the engine, "Forward." His finger shot out. "But we look at life backward. It's like we're sitting on a train, facing the caboose. We look out the windows trying to figure what's coming round the next bend, but all we see is pieces of what we already passed up. Not much to go on, if you ask me."

"Interesting metaphor," I said.

"Call it what you will, Dr Mummy. The next bend is always a mystery."

"Given certain facts, I think we can make reasonable–"

"Horseshit," he interrupted. "Nobody knows what's coming."

McTroy tipped his hat, hiding his eyes. He put his boots up on the seat beside me and crossed his ankles. Our conversation was over. Within a minute, he was snoring softly, hands folded on his chest, as content as a cat in his bright wedge of sunlight.

Wu, in true apprentice fashion, followed his mentor into napping.

Trains will do that.

I, for one, was wide awake.

I tilted my head toward Evangeline. "What will you do now?"

"Sleeping looks like a pleasant choice for today," she said.

"I don't mean now on the train. I mean once we get to Yuma."

I could tell she knew what I meant, but she was having her fun. Her expression turned serious. "I will return to Los Angeles. The Waterston Company requires new leadership. I plan to be that leader. Someone needs to put the house in order."

"A-ha. And your interest in occultism?"

"I have my father's library – now, my library. I will further my studies."

"At your leisure?"

She smiled. "At my leisure." She nodded. "I like the sound of that." She stretched out like a cat. Her cats' eyes sparkling green as jewels. A little sleepy, still alert. Her breath was warm on my cheek when she asked in a whisper, "Where will you go, Romulus?" To hear her pronounce my Christian name – a name only my mother ever used – was oddly stimulating. I wanted her to say it again. I was sure I would never grow tired of finding

ways to make her call to me just so I might listen. But
would she?

"I don't know," I said, answering honestly. I could take
no credit for my only archaeological dig. I had no sponsor.
No prospects. "Back to school? I miss the stuffy library."

"Nonsense," she said. "If you go back anywhere, it
will be to Egypt."

"On whose dollar?"

"Monty Waterston's. I am funding an Institute for
Singular Antiquities in memory of my father. Based in
New York City. For the study of ancient cultures and
their most uncommon artifacts. Something like that,
oh, I haven't worked out the details yet, but we will
probably be able to scrape up some coins for Rom Hardy
to get back into the grave-robber business."

Return to Egypt? On my own terms this time, without
the burden of another man's agenda and ethics? I was
nearly speechless at the prospect. The ancient world
opened up to me once more: renewed, mysterious,
deeper than it had been the first time, and overflowing
with treasures even before I stuck another shovel into the
sand. The chance to remain in contact with Evangeline
enticed me more. It was as if my world had doubled,
then quadrupled in size. I felt dizzy watching it grow in
all directions.

"Are you serious?" I asked.

"Always," she said, her voice growing husky.

She wrapped her arm around mine, and leaned
against my chest. But a second later she pulled her head
back and said, "What is this awful lump in your jacket?"

I fished into my pocket. "Oh, I had nearly forgotten
about this."

I showed her the ancient flint dagger that I had returned to salvage from the mine.

She traced the shape of the unnamed monster carved into it. The edge of her thumb played along the exquisitely sharp blade.

"The judges from the Duat left it behind," I said.

"This will be the first artifact in our Institute for Singular Antiquities."

She handed me the dagger, resumed her napping position, and soon entered dreamland.

In Yuma, we went our separate ways. McTroy and Wu returned to Black Shirl's with our horses, Moonlight and Neptune. Evangeline bought a train ticket to California.

Parting was sad business as it always is when we separate from those of whom we have grown fond. There is a taste of death, a pinch sprinkled into the mix of goodbyes and promises to write letters that we all can taste. I hated most to leave her. Her sudden offer to sponsor my work, to sponsor me – felt like more than pure scholarly interest or a mere investment in a potentially lucrative exotic venture. But what if that was all it was?

She was bolder than I. If she wanted something beyond a decent Egyptologist for her Institute, then she would leave me some clues. It would be my job to decipher them.

I went to New York, and waited to hear more.

New Year's Day, 1920
Manhattan, New York City

> *Dear Rom,*
> *I regret to be the one who must tell you the great man*

is among us no more. He has gone to the stars. That was his wish, he confided, as I sat him up on his horse only two evenings ago, and we walked around the corral. Our world is more desolate for his having left it. I remind myself the bottomless grief I feel at this moment too shall pass. At least he did not suffer. I happily took away his pain during these final twilit days. My medical training proved worthy of the years I spent in study if only to accomplish this task. The opium tinctures made him sleepy yet inclined to conversation. We talked about old times! About Mexico, and the "bandaged bastards" as he still called them. To the end he slept with loaded pistols hanging from the bedpost, saying he saw the raggedy, gauze-bound corpses lurching forward in his dreams.

Going through his night chest, I discovered a newspaper cutting of Miss Evangeline I had never seen before. Does a public recital in San Francisco ring any bells? It was sweet of him to keep it for so long. Would you not agree? I hope this subject is not too tender to broach. I am aware your last parting was not on the best of terms, and in recent years no communication passed between you, the great rift only widening. Yet history – beginning with our dangerous ride south and the ill-fated Mexico expedition! – will always bind you together.

So I was wondering if we three survivors – you, Evangeline, and me – might we not get together for dinner in Manhattan? I will be attending a New Year's party in the City. Are you interested in a social call on New Year's Day? Please say, "Yes!"

Truly, one of your oldest friends,
Dr Yong Wu, MD

December, 1919
San Francisco, California

My windows were frozen. I scraped ice from the inside of the glass and looked down on the streets. They were, for the most part, empty. My whisky bottle was empty too. Hail McTroy! My head: achy. These bones creaked when I moved. Can everyone hear?

I put away the ushabti. When I stood, the blood rushed to my head and I had to steady myself. Where was my ape's-head cane? Ah, by the door. I grabbed it. What a comfort, better than a dog. I never had to take my walking stick out for a walk. Ha! Ha!

I closed the cabinet, located water, poured it down my parched throat.

Dry as a desert...

Once I knew a dangerous young woman and we shared some adventures you never would believe. Old men get to dreaming in the idle hours... what never was... what might have been... I can't go back. You never go back. But in your mind, you do. You can't help it. You pick at your past and dust it for clues. Your heart beats faster, but you're lucky that it beats at all. Old man, you've enjoyed a good, full life. It's never enough. The thrills return to me. The perils, too. We are side by side. Evil gathers like a thundercloud, but oh, I wish to live it all again...

The old knees were knocking.

No, it was a door. Three floors below. Someone was pounding on the front door.

I went to the window and scraped.

There *was* a man. Not too tall. Well-dressed, in a top

hat. And a woman was with him.

I didn't need a clear view to know who she was. Her shape was enough.

I was down the stairs in no time. The walking stick hit each step like a drumbeat. When I reached the ground floor and opened the inner door leading to the vestibule, I heard her talking to him, to Yong Wu.

"Perhaps, he isn't here," he said.

"He always comes to the Institute. Trust me, I know." She sounded the same as she did years before. But since I had been caught up in memories, I heard something fresh in her voice.

I touched the cold, cold doorknob and I paused. What if opening this door is a mistake. The past should stay in the past. Odji-Kek and the mummy brethren. McTroy with his guns and horses. His rough charm. Why ruin old memories? Things had settled. Like layers in a dig, my life had settled. Why go back and re-live what can't possibly happen again. But do I know what is over? Or what is merely paused? Does anything vanish as long as we still remember?

You think too much, Rom.

Snow had blown under the door sill. White as sugar, soft as sand. For someone who has spent the better part of the last four decades digging, burrowing like a scarab, day and night it seemed, into mountains of dry, golden trickling, windswept tombs, I have never gotten comfortable with the stuff. The electric winds of memories were standing my hairs on end. How did I get here? Egypt. Egypt and Evangeline made me who I am.

I opened the door.

ACKNOWLEDGMENTS

It is a true pleasure working with everyone on the Angry Robot team. I especially want to thank Phil Jourdan, Marc Gascoigne, and Penny Reeve for bringing my words up from the tomb and into the light of day. Thanks to Gary Heinz, Bob Tuszynski, and Shari Wright for being my early readers. Special thanks to fellow writer and damn fine novelist Steve Hockensmith for reactions and advice on craft. My extraordinary agent, Ann Collette, told me to write this book, and without her there would be no cowboys and mummies. Lastly, I would not make it through the day without the support and inspiration of my wife and children. Lisa, Emma, and Quinn – you're the best.

THE FALL OF THE GAS-LIT EMPIRE

NOMINATED FOR THE
PHILIP K DICK AWARD

ENGLAND IS
DIVIDED, AND THE
MUCH-FEARED PATENT
OFFICE IS IN
TOTAL CONTROL

THE MAP OF UNKNOWN THING.

OF ALL

THE QUEEN

CROWS

THE
MAP
OF
UNKNOWN
THINGS

ROD DUNCAN

SET FORTH FOR ASTONISHING NEW ADVENTURE

MOONSHINE

JASMINE GOWER

It's a kind of magic...

"Refreshing... intriguing...gloriously wild." – PUBLISHERS WEEKLY